SAVING GRACE

SAVING GRACE

STATE OF GRACE 5

COLETTE RHODES

COVER DESIGN BY: COLETTE

ISBN: 978-1-99-117327-0

CONTENT WARNING

**Violence, Drug References,
Sexual Content, Grief**

"EVEN THE DARKEST
NIGHT WILL END
AND THE SUN
WILL RISE."

-VICTOR HUGO

DEDICATION

To my editing team, for putting up with me.

THE STORY SO FAR

Our angelic agathos, Grace, met bad boy daimon, Riot, outside a club in Milton—a daimon town she'd moved to in a bid to escape her overbearing parents and community. At age 25, Grace had expected to feel a pull towards her four agathos soul bonds by now, but it never came. Instead, she felt pulled to Riot, even though a connection between agathos, worshippers of Anesidora and servants of humanity, and daimons, worshippers of La Nuit and designed to lead humans astray, shouldn't be possible.

Grace's parents found out about Riot, and had Grace taken from her job at a shelter and dragged to the basement temple in Auburn for a cleansing ritual to break the connection. Riot was given instructions by the psychic daimon, Bullet, on where to find Grace. With assistance from one of her fathers, Riot rescues her from the agathos attempting to do a cleansing ritual and praying to bond her to recently widowed agathos men. They drive to Bullet's place, where Grace encounters her second soul bond for the first time.

While Riot is stuck working for the daimon, Viper, as part of a deal to keep Grace hidden, Grace gets to know Bullet. Bullet, as an Oneiroi, has known Grace her whole life. He has visited her dreams every night, and had thousands of "first meetings" with her that Grace doesn't remember. He teaches her about the true origins of the gods La Nuit (Nyx) and Anesidora (Gaia), and their feud. Grace is given a prophecy and tasked with bringing 'forth the Second Age of Heroes.'

An attempted meeting with Grace's cousin, Mercy, goes awry, and Bullet is injured. They are rescued by the silent and mysterious Wild, who reluctantly allows them to stay at his nightclub complex, avoiding Grace even though he is her third soul bond.

Grace seals her bonds with Bullet and Riot, and hunts down Wild to find out why he's avoiding her. It turns out, Wild has encountered the gods before. In a moment of arrogance where he claimed to be stronger than Death himself, the God of Death snatched him up and spirited him away to the underworld, kicking his ass in front of the deities who reside there. Thanatos stole Wild's voice and has haunted him ever since. Worried that he'll pass this curse to Grace, Wild runs.

Meanwhile, Bullet is in increasingly bad shape, and is warned by Nyx to make the most of the time he has left. Riot's deal with Viper is dissolved after Viper discloses information about Grace to Mercy when he helped her escape town, breaking the terms of the original agreement. Riot, Bullet, and Grace drive to a sacred waterfall, hoping to have a productive conversation with Gaia. Gaia learns of the prophecy, and nearly buries them all in a landslide. Wild has followed them from a distance, and is led to them by a divine voice, freeing them all from the dirt and taking an unconscious Grace back to a motel and calling a daimon doctor to attend to her.

Bullet learns the full extent of Wild's history with the gods in the dreamscape, telling the others when they wake up. Thanatos appears, bedecked in sequins, and takes them to the underworld to meet Hades and Persephone. They wish to see the Olympians restored to power, and offer their support. Grace is introduced to the soul of a daimon who recently passed into the underworld, who she later discovers is Dare's mom. She was murdered in her home by agathos, and Dare struggles with the aftermath in the upperworld, enraged at Bullet for not telling him, at Riot for abandoning him, and at all agathos for the violence and suffering. He throws himself into the street wars between agathos and daimons back in Milton and eventually picks a fight he can't win. He's found by Mercy's abandoned soul bond, Dice, who takes Dare back to his sister's house where Dare recuperates, helping Rogue out with baby Quinn until Onyx can convince him to get his act together.

Persephone gives Grace a mysterious pouch as a parting gift, as well as removing the block on her memories of the dreamscape with Bullet. They all come rushing in at once—Grace remembers everything. The four of them make their way out of the underworld through a cave, finding themselves in a remote corner of Greece. They eventually stumble upon a community of agathos and daimons living together, alongside Kakodaimonistai—humans who drink a hallucinogenic and can know about the other kinds of mortals who inhabit their world. Vasileios, the daimon leader of this ragtag group, invites them to stay, and once they hear Grace's story, they are all eager to help in the hopes of improving the lives of agathos and daimons. They make offerings and prayers to the Olympians to strengthen them through belief, hosting an orgy in Dionysus' honor.

Wild and Grace seal their bond, while the tentative feelings between Wild and Bullet grow. At the same time, tension comes to a head between Bullet and Riot, when Riot grows frustrated with Bullet's decision to keep Dare away. A plane crashes off the coast of Greece, which they later find out was carrying Dare, and the relationships grow more fraught, but there's no time to reflect on it because Gaia has set a plague of giant scorpions on Athens. Gaia possesses a local Basilinna, speaking through her body on live television, telling the humans that they enraged Gaia with their disrespect. Exposing agathos and daimons to the wider world, promising it will be made wonderful again when the daimons and their influence are eliminated.

Their group of allies rallies around Grace, and they all head into Athens together by bus. The scorpions won't attack the agathos, so Grace and the other agathos run off on their own, heading for the Temple of Zeus. Some enemy agathos have lined up in front of the temple, and Grace's side livestream what they're about to do. Grace steps forward alone, pulling out the pouch Persephone gave her and dropping the sharp seeds into the earth, little scratches on her hands mixing her own blood in with them. From the "seeds" grew a hundred Ancient Greek soldiers—the Spartoi—armed with spears and shields, who quickly dispatched the scorpions.

The temple's magic drives the agathos away, and the mysterious voice of guidance tells Grace to offer her blood and her service, her devotion to a world of gods and mortals, to the ideal. The others follow, lighting the temple up gold as the marble knitted back together. Grace makes a peace offering to Gaia, but promises that she will see the prophecy through. The group, including the confused Spartoi, travel to a nearby villa used for agathos retreats. After some thought, Grace reveals herself to the world with a video explaining who she is and what she has been tasked with. Recovering in a nearby daimon's home, Dare sees the video and rushes to Grace's side.

Dare and Grace attempt to seal the bond right away, but Dare is in too much pain from his multitude of injuries and collapses. Hygeia, the original agathos of good health, appears to heal him, having pooled all the power the agathos have to get her there. Hygeia suggests that Grace and her soul bonds travel to the agathos temple in Ephesus. There must be a sacrifice for healing him, so Dare's injuries transfer to Mercy, who has found sanctuary at a campsite in Maine run by single agathos men who were sent away having never discovered their soul bonds. Here she encounters Harbor, Felix Lyon's younger brother. He is not her soul bond, but she develops feelings for him anyway.

Grace and Dare get to know one another, and Dare and Bullet resolve the tension between them that Bullet hadn't called Dare to Grace's side earlier. They're interrupted when Grace's mother appears on TV in an interview with humans, talking openly about the agathos and about how Grace is a traitor. Faith hints that Grace struggles to comprehend reality, undermining Grace's words. Wild comforts Grace, and Dare uses the portable tattoo kit he was given to tattoo the images the Fates used to represent each of them in Bullet's visions.

The human authorities declare that Grace must be apprehended because she is inciting violence, but in the process announce that Nyx and Gaia are unequivocally not real. Offended by this, Gaia dissolves all the wires and pipes that run through her earth, and Nyx pulls a veil of darkness over the sky, plunging the word into night.

Grace and her soul bonds decide to take up Hygeia's offer, traveling to the coast under the cover of darkness where riots are already breaking out, and traveling by boat with Vasileios' daimon friend to the coast of Turkey. Grace and Dare grow closer, sharing their first kiss. After Grace, Wild, and Bullet fall asleep together in the cabin of the boat, Bullet fails to wake up, giving everyone a scare. At Wild's suggestion, Grace follows the bond to find Bullet's soul at the banks of the Styx, and uses her tether to the others to drag them both back to the world of the living, tying her and Bullet even closer together. Bullet tells Wild that next time, he needs to let him go.

Dare and Grace seal the bond, and they all disembark on a beach, traveling by foot on most deserted roads to Ephesus. They meet Sophia, the agathos of wisdom, who invites both Nyx and Gaia to a meeting to try and come to a resolution. While sleeping, Grace is pulled into Nyx's dreamscape in Bullet's place, she has accidentally taken on his power in saving him, and tied his life to their bond.

Eirene, the keeper of the temple, appears with her dog, Milos, and invites them back to her home to rest and recuperate after their journey. The five of them have one final moment of passion, before Nyx comes to Grace in the dreamscape and says that it's time to meet. They all return to the ruins, stepping through the columns and into the Realm of the Gods.

The confrontation between the goddesses is contentious. Nyx agrees to lift the darkness which is steadily killing off the earth if Gaia will provide a path to Tartarus for Grace so she can fulfill the prophecy. Out of spite, Gaia destroys all of the bonds on her way out. The bond that was keeping Bullet alive is broken, and he says his goodbyes to those he loves on the steps of the temple. Thanatos appears to collect them, assuring them that he is not entirely gone yet, but his body will be safest on the Isles of the Blessed while his soul is in the balance. Losing Bullet tips Wild into bloodlust, and Riot volunteers to fight him while encouraging Dare to get Grace away from the ruins as the sun finally rises again. As they leave the ruins, they stumble across an enormous pit—Gaia's pathway.

A day passes while Grace grieves, and Riot and Wild don't return. They return to the pit and encounter Vasileios, Foster, Estrella and some of their other friends who decided to follow them to Ephesus. They search the ruins, and only find Riot's bloodstained sweater. Grace doesn't know that Thanatos has taken Wild, sick with guilt at hurting Riot, to do a mysterious job. Riot is missing. A giant monster emerges from the depths of Tartarus, spewing a stream of fire into the sky.

And that is where our story picks up...

RIOT

CHAPTER 1

"Come on, Moros."

No, fuck off, I replied in my head, my thoughts hazy. I'd just had the shit kicked out of me, didn't I deserve a little lie-down? What did a guy have to do to get thirty seconds to relax after being beaten up by one of his friends?

Speaking of...

"Wild," I groaned, forcing the words out even though my tongue felt three sizes too big for my mouth. "Next time, punch a wall or something, yeah? Sparring is one thing, but I don't think I'm up for that kind of fight. You've got a mean right hook."

I was pretty sure said right hook had dislocated my eyeball.

"The Keres isn't here."

"What? Why?" I tried to force my eyes open, but they were swollen shut and weighed a hundred pounds each. Where was Wild? Yeah, he'd lost his temper and the bloodlust had taken over, but we'd just lost Bullet and I didn't blame him for losing control. But surely he'd worked through the worst of the rage now, and I couldn't imagine him just *leaving* me here.

We were friends. He wouldn't.

"You have a job to do, Moros," the voice said, ignoring my question.

"Here's an idea, mystery voice. You do the job. I'm having a real fucking day here, you know? I'm pretty sure my nose is broken, and Wild is missing. And my friend is dead. Or a little bit dead? I don't even fucking know. The bond to my girl is gone, and I don't know where she is either, I'm just hoping Dare is keeping her safe. I have shit to do."

What felt like cold stone pressed down on my face, sliding down either side of my nose.

"Hey, what—"

Crunch.

I gasped as pain ricocheted up from my nose, spreading to every other part of my body. Forcing my eyes open, I found some kind of immortal being directly in my face, staring impassively down at me.

She was wearing a toga-looking dress made of heavy dark blue fabric, pulled half over her head like a veil so only the front of her dark brown curls were visible, framing her face. She wasn't beautiful necessarily, but she was ethereal looking, with porcelain skin and wide golden eyes.

"Your nose is fixed. Will you stop your incessant whining now? You have a job to do."

"Who *are* you?" I cradled the poor aching bridge of my nose with my fingertips, silently cursing every deity to ever exist. Interfering motherfuckers. She hadn't fixed anything else either, I still felt like I'd been repeatedly run over by an 18-wheeler.

"I am Arete, of course."

Arete. That rang a bell, though my brain was taking its sweet time

1

in figuring out why.

"Well, good for you," I muttered, my head spinning. "Where am I?"

Now that the world was coming into focus, it was clear that I wasn't in Kansas—aka, the ruins at Ephesus—anymore. Great. Just fucking great.

Had I died?

No, this didn't look like the underworld. The underworld had a purple sky, I'd seen it for myself. The sky here was a pinkish gold, and it looked more like the heavenly realm place we'd met Nyx and Gaia at, but there was no looming mountain of palaces above us. It was just a garden.

A surreal, definitely not human garden, with flowers the size of boulders in shades of gold and peach, glinting in the light like jewels. It looked like some kind of angelic fever dream painting, and I half expected to see a fat little cherub float past above me, mini bow and arrow in hand.

"Where am I?" I asked again, unsuccessfully keeping the hard edge of panic out of my voice.

"Back in the Realm of the Gods, of course." Arete sounded impatient, peering down at me like I was a peculiar insect and she wasn't sure whether to squash me or not. "As I keep saying, you have a job to do. Travel is more expedient this way, and you have given me enough of a blood sacrifice to stay at your side for the time being."

"How generous of me," I muttered. "My blood doesn't even do that. Gracie's does. I'm just a regular daimon."

"There is nothing regular about any of you." Arete tutted. "You chose to keep your agathos. Chose your soul bond."

"Well, yeah. Obviously. Grace is *my* soul bond—even without the bond." My throat tightened painfully. As much as my muscles screamed in protest, I forced myself to sit upright, catching my breath for a moment before climbing to my feet, narrowly avoiding hitting my head on a mysterious giant flower. "I'm a daimon. Daimons are possessive. It's the most *regular* thing about me."

"You clearly don't know what a soul bond actually is," Arete said mildly, apparently content to watch me struggle. *Fucking immortals.*

"I know just fine. I have a soul bond." *Had* a soul bond. The pain I felt in the rest of my body was nothing compared to the gaping emptiness in my chest where the bond had been. I had to get back to Grace; not knowing where she was, how she was feeling, was making me lose my mind. "Why am I here? I can't do whatever this job is you have for me, I have to get back to Grace. Where is Wild? Is he in this realm too?"

"The Keres has his own job to do." She paused, looking somehow thoughtful and disinterested all at once. "With the pit to Tartarus open, the possibility of the prophecy being fulfilled is real, in a way it never has been in the past. We all must do our parts. Immortals who have watched and waited for an opportunity to challenge the Great Mother's authority finally have the chance to do so."

Pit?

"I don't know what you're talking about." I looked around, trying to see through the thick shimmering bushes and pearlescent flowers, seeking out an exit. "What pit? What is Wild doing? Is he okay? He shouldn't be alone right now."

Arete took a step forward, her hand snapping out to grab my forearm with surprising speed. She brushed her icy thumb over a patch of grazed skin, filled with rocky debris from where I'd scraped it on the ground avoiding Wild's next hit.

"Do you really care to know? The Keres injured you. Why should you care about where he is or what he's doing?"

3

"You immortals are really something else," I mumbled, taking a healthy step back the moment she released me. "Wild is my friend. It's not his fault that he's a Keres. It's not his fault that the man he loved di—" I choked on the word, not quite able to get it out. No, Bullet wasn't dead. I couldn't accept that.

I didn't know where exactly he was, or how to get him back, but he wasn't dead. I couldn't accept that the Fates would heap that much suffering on us. Hadn't we been through enough?

"Just tell me how to get home, okay? I'm sure you think you have some super important task to assign me, but the most important thing right now is that I'm there for Grace. She needs me. I can't let her down."

"I'm not going to tell you how to get home. I'm going to tell you about how soul bonds work."

By the fucking gods, it was like talking to a wall.

"I don't—"

"You have a job to do," Arete insisted, crossing her arms and glaring at me imperiously. "Do you know who I am?"

"Arete. Yes. You already told me. You're an agathos."

"An agathos of?" she prompted.

Shit, I knew this one. What was it...

Arete sighed. "Many things, in truth. I am a broad, abstract, hard-to-define idea of excellence and bravery and virtue. Ultimately, what I can be defined by is potential." She gave me a long, searching look. "Of your group—your soul bond, her soul bonds—you are the one who has come into my care because of your potential."

"My potential," I repeated slowly. My potential for what?

"Indeed, your potential. The way you squander it, mostly. Such a waste. It's difficult to witness."

"Are you going to actually tell me what you want from me or just insult me?" I asked, throwing my hands up in exasperation. My failure to live up to my potential was something I'd been aware of my entire life. Even my useless father had seen it, though what he wanted to use my potential for was a little more nefarious.

"I want to tell you how soul bonds work."

"What does that have to do with my potential? Does it even matter anymore? The bonds are gone. Gaia ripped them all away."

"Indeed. So, are you going to live up to your full potential and restore them, or not?"

GRACE

CHAPTER 2

"Who are you?" I repeated. "Why are you here? What do you want?"

I was staring into the flaming eyes of a monster, a dark shadow of black and red scales with enormous wings and snakes for legs. The sky behind the beast was lit up a brilliant orange, sparks of tiny flames raining down over our heads from the stream of fire it had spewed out into the air.

It was terrifying and mesmerizing all at once.

Maybe I was losing my mind, but for a moment, all I wanted to do was stand there and watch. To make sense of what I was seeing, of this new world of myths and monsters.

"Time to go," Dare rasped, wrapping a hand around my forearm and dragging me backward. I was dimly aware of everyone else already moving, running as far from the pit as possible, but my limbs were slow to cooperate despite Dare's insistence.

"Wait, what if it isn't bad? What if it's on our side?"

Dare didn't answer, half dragging me along behind him as we ran in the general direction of Eirene's house, Milos barking frantically at my side.

"Follow us!" Dare yelled, gesturing frantically at Vasileios and the others without slowing down.

The monster stayed at the mouth of the pit, hovering in the air and spewing fire. An actual, honest-to-goddess *monster*.

Was it guarding the entrance to Tartarus? Was this Tartarus' version of Cerberus? Bullet would have known the answer. He'd have known exactly what the beast was, and whose side it was on, and how to communicate with it. I was lost without his guidance.

"*Run*, Grace," Dare urged. *Right*. My grief would have to wait.

We stumbled over the uneven ground, each taking turns at catching the other, Vasileios and hopefully all of the others hot on our heels. The sky still resembled lava, but we weren't being followed.

We'd only *just* gotten a reprieve. The sun had only been shining again for a day after nearly a week of darkness. And now the sky was on fire. It was relentless.

"It's not chasing us," I gasped, struggling for air and slowing my steps slightly.

"I'm not taking any chances," Dare replied, sounding just as out of breath as I was. Milos was all but herding us toward Eirene's house, running circles around us and barking in encouragement. "It has giant bat wings, Grace. It could just be letting us run for entertainment before swooping down and eating us in two seconds flat."

Logically, I knew that he was right, but there was something about the creature that made me want to reach out and check that it was okay.

Less than a mile from Eirene's house, Milos skidded to a stop, falling completely silent. After her constant chorus of warning barks, the quiet was eerie.

"What is it, girl?" Dare asked in a low, placating voice, stumbling to a stop. He reached for Milos carefully, running his fingers through her thick fur.

I was no expert in canine body language, but if I had to guess, Milos looked kind of... sad? She tipped her head up to the sky after a moment, letting out a mournful howl that I felt all the way down to my bones.

"Eirene," I whispered, taking off at a sprint. Suddenly, the fiery sky overhead didn't seem like the most pressing issue.

The others were catching up, and I took the lead this time, shoving my shoulder against the gate to knock it open and running for the house.

"Grace!" Dare yelled, snagging the back of my coat and hauling me against his body before I could get to the front door. "Stop, stop, you need to stop. Let me go in first, okay?"

He moved fast enough that I didn't bother arguing with him, silently pushing open the door and stepping into the dimly lit living room. Milos rushed past, heading straight for Eirene.

She was sitting in the armchair, looking as she did the first night when she'd fallen asleep there next to the fire. The tension in her face was relaxed in rest, even if the sadness and exhaustion from the recent loss of all her bonded were still present in her features. Just like last time.

Except this time, she wasn't breathing.

Milos' claws clicked on the hard floor as she crossed the room, curling up at Eirene's feet and letting out a series of soft whines that broke my heart.

"This is your friend?" Vasileios asked quietly, stepping through the door behind us. Dare wrapped his arms around my shoulders, hugging me tightly.

"Yes," I rasped. "Her name is Eirene. She's the custodian of the

8

agathos temple. She... she took us in." I couldn't bring myself to use past tense. In the back of my mind, I'd suspected this was coming. Suspected that the Fates could not be so cruel as to keep Eirene here in the upperworld for years after all of her bonded had been called to the afterlife. But there was no real preparing for death, was there? Even if she'd been sick, laying in a hospital bed with a clock running down until the final moment, *this* moment would have still been agony, filled with what if's and all the things I wished I could have said.

"Eirene was kind to us," Dare murmured. "Her bonded are all in the underworld, she'll see them all again now."

Yes. Yes, that was a nice thought. Eirene would be happier there than here, alone, in a world that grew more confusing by the day. It was hard for us to say goodbye, but Eirene was leaving the fear and uncertainty and grief she'd experienced in this life behind.

Dare looked over his shoulder through the open door, the worry clear on his face. I could see Ovie and Fox, two of the daimons who'd traveled here with Vasileios, standing guard in the doorway, keeping a watch out for the beast we'd just run from, but there was no sign of it. The fiery orange sky had faded back to blue, and the world was quiet and still again, as if the monster had never appeared. As if, just a few miles away, there wasn't an enormous hole in the ground that led directly to the deepest, darkest, most treacherous realm in existence.

Was this split second of peace what it felt like to be in the eye of a hurricane?

"We have to give her a proper burial," I said forcefully, giving Dare's forearms a light squeeze.

"I know," Dare sighed, resigned. "And we will. It's the least we can do. But there's a literal monster on the loose; I don't think we should hang around here for any longer than we have to."

"I'm not leaving." I knew I sounded stubborn, but I couldn't help myself. "Dare, I can't. Aside from the fact that the pit is the only way to Tartarus, we need to be close by in case Riot and Wild come looking for us."

"Wherever Wild and Riot are, they wouldn't want you at risk, Grace. Keeping you safe is everyone's top priority."

There was a sense of *something* simmering in my chest, ready to bubble over. Something I was struggling to identify.

Maybe it was *helplessness*. My entire life, I'd been stuck dancing to someone else's tune, trying to find ways to cope within the confines that had been set for me as best I could. That feeling was magnified by a thousand now. I'd had all these titles, all these responsibilities, foisted upon me and yet I felt entirely helpless to protect any of the people I cared about.

"Can you give us a minute?" I asked Vasileios with a tight smile, disentangling myself from Dare's embrace and pulling him toward the kitchen by the hand.

"I'm not trying to upset you, Grace—"

"I know." I dropped his hand, turning to face him. "But you are coddling me, and you can't. You've all always taken such good care of me, but we don't have that luxury anymore."

Dare snorted. "Good luck trying to get us to stop, Grace."

I smiled before I could stop myself because I knew he was right. They couldn't turn off their instinct to keep me safe any more than I could do the same for them. I was just going to have to show them that I didn't need to be wrapped in cotton wool because I didn't know how I was going to get into that pit otherwise.

And it had to be me.

"There has to be a middle ground," Dare said quietly, stepping forward. He reached for me, more hesitantly than usual, and I practically threw myself into his arms, wrapping myself around him and hugging him tight. As much as I didn't want to be treated like spun glass, I couldn't stand the idea of upsetting Dare either. Not when everything was already so uncertain and the others weren't here. What if he disappeared too? I didn't want to waste any of the moments we had being upset with each other. "We'll leave Wild and Riot a note or something. A code only they understand."

"I don't want to stray too far from the pit," I reiterated, voice muffled against his chest. "As much as you don't *want* to accept it—and trust me, I understand why—that is where I'm going. It's what all this suffering and death and destruction is *for*, Dare."

He made a strangled sound, holding me a little tighter as Vasileios appeared in the doorway, clearing his throat awkwardly.

"We're going to take turns on watch duty. We already have a schedule from when we were on the road traveling here."

"Well, let's hope the pit monster gives us plenty of warning before flying here faster than we can blink," Dare sighed.

Vasileios hummed in agreement but politely said nothing if he was questioning my sanity.

I swallowed thickly. "Let's begin the burial rites. Worrying about the monster can wait until we've said our goodbyes."

There was a pyre at the bottom of the garden.

Or the remnants of one at least.

While agathos—and daimons, apparently—were traditionally cremated with a gold coin, it was mostly done at cremation facilities these days, not on the ritual pyre. Was the pyre always here? Or had Eirene built this as her bonded had started dying one by one?

Estrella and Rue, one of the other daimons, helped me lay out Eirene's body in the house on a makeshift stretcher and I went through the motions of lighting the cast-iron fire in the living room with shaky hands and setting a pot of water to heat. Once it was warm, I washed her face, gently pushing her jaw shut, her eyes already closed as the rites dictated. I'd learned them—years ago in my agathos classes—but I'd never carried them out myself. It wasn't my place really. Eirene's daughters or sisters should be doing this part, but they weren't here, and I wasn't going to disrespect Eirene by not following tradition.

Instead, I pretended in my head that she was family. A beloved grandmother being laid to rest after living a long and happy life, surrounded by loved ones. That was the ending Eirene's life *would* have had if the world hadn't fallen apart, if the goddesses hadn't gone to war. Her children were scattered because of all of this, denied their final moments with their mother. There was such an abundance of unfairness that I'd borne witness to recently that I sometimes worried I'd become desensitized to it, but I was feeling that injustice acutely now.

Estrella appeared with a small glass bottle—the oil used for anointment—and a gold coin.

"It was all already sitting there on the shelf," she rasped, setting them down next to me.

I nodded, drying my trembling hands. "She would have used them recently. And perhaps she… knew."

"Thank you for your kindness," I whispered to Eirene, unstopping the bottle of olive oil and brushing the golden liquid over her brow, down the bridge of her nose, and over her cheekbones with my thumb. "For taking us in when we had nowhere to go, and showing us that agathos of any generation can embrace change if they choose to. You gave me hope—more than I even realized at the time—and I wish I'd told you that."

I pushed the coin, Charon's payment, between her lips before slipping into the bathroom for a moment to wash my hands and collect myself. There were logistics to consider, things I hadn't even had a chance to think of yet. Eirene had children, all scattered around different sacred agathos sites. How were we going to tell them? A note seemed so impersonal, but there was a good chance we'd have to leave before they returned home.

One thing at a time.

I returned to the living room and together, Estrella, Rue, and I shrouded Eirene's body in the largest white sheet we could find, and Ovie and Dare quietly met us at the door to carry the stretcher down the length of the garden, Milos at my side each step of the way.

Night had fallen, and the moonlight shone down on us, stars glittering in the distance. I thought I'd hate the darkness after Nyx had veiled the world, but strangely, it was like seeing an old friend again. Comforting and familiar.

Vasileios handed me a heavy, wrought iron torch, already burning. My arm ached under the weight of it as I held it out in front of me, leading the way to the pyre. It was a silent procession except for the crunch of dead plant life beneath our feet. What had this garden been like before the darkness? I imagined lush green leaves and brightly colored flowers, fat bees buzzing around on a hot summer's day, maybe a light breeze floating through the walled-in garden, rustling the plants.

That world was gone, and we *had* to get it back. We couldn't live in this desolate, lifeless place. I wasn't liberating those gods unless they *promised* to fix what had been broken.

I stood aside with the others as Dare and Vasileios laid the stretcher on top of the pyre. Dare had already stacked branches beneath it in preparation, and the torch felt even heavier in my hand at the thought of lighting the tinder.

"It's so unfair," I whispered to Dare as he came to stand at my side. "Eirene deserves to be farewelled by loved ones, not strangers."

"We may not be standing on a battlefield, but we are in the middle of war, Grace," Dare murmured. "And we're honoring the fallen. The others may not have known her, but she was still their ally. And she was our friend."

"You're right," I whispered, my throat tight. "Perhaps she won't be farewelled by loved ones, but she'll be welcomed by them in the underworld. I think that's better."

And with that, I stepped forward and kneeled on the ground to set the branches alight, praying quietly under my breath that Eirene would have a peaceful journey to the underworld, that the gods in the land of the dead would be kind, that her bonded were waiting to welcome her with open arms. I promised to tell her children about how wonderful she'd been to us, and to assure them that their mother had been given full burial rites so she could pass to the underworld. One day, when peace reigned again, I'd visit them and make sure that their lives were good and happy like she would have wanted.

Milos let out a mournful howl, laying on her belly with her head resting on her front paws. I was going to take care of her too, somehow. Vasileios took the torch from me as I stood, pulling me into a rough hug before leading the others away to give me and Dare a moment.

We sat on the ground next to Milos, Dare close enough that his side pressed against mine. I glanced at him out of the corner of my eye, the flickering golden flames highlighting the dark circles under his eyes. He was tired. We both were. But the idea of sleeping was... absurd. How could we sleep right now?

The burial rites had given me something else to focus on for a moment, but now all my problems were catching up with me again. Bullet was in some kind of in-between state in the Isles of the Blessed—somewhere in the Atlantic, according to Thanatos, though his soul might slip into the underworld at any moment. Riot and Wild were still missing. The path to Tartarus was open, and a monster had emerged from its depths. The bonds had been broken, and my soul was irreparably fractured. That was just the beginning of my list.

There was too much to do, to worry about, to contemplate something as mundane as sleep.

"The Fates did you a disservice, leaving me as your only companion," Dare said, staring at the pyre. "I was already struggling to comprehend what exactly you'd all gone through, and I have no idea what to do now. What the next step is."

"I have to enter the pit." Was that my voice? It was so thin and reedy. Milos shuffled closer, and I absently scratched between her ears.

Dare made a strangled noise of protest. "It's a trap, Grace. Did you see any kind of pathway? The walls were smooth. If you *jump* in there, which was the only way down, you'll die. You may be marked by the gods, but as far as I know, you're still mortal."

"Maybe that's a requirement," I whispered, vocalizing the terrible thought that I'd done my best to repress. "Maybe I have to die to get down there."

"Grace, no—"

"But Bullet always talked about me living a long, happy life," I pushed on, needing Dare to understand. "He talked about my future, our future. So if I have to die in some way... Well, it can't be a permanent death. There are stories of mortals leaving the underworld. I've left there myself."

"Not after dying, you haven't. Do you really think Gaia would give you a safe, easy path to fulfill the prophecy she hates? She's literally the villain, Grace."

Villain.

The word triggered the memory of a chilly fall morning in Devil's Den, next to a calm, sparkling pond. I could almost feel the coffee cup between my hands, warming my fingers, as Bullet told me stories of gods and goddesses, his pale blonde hair glowing gold in the orange light. Grief sliced through my chest like a knife, and I desperately held onto the memory of his amethyst eyes, filled with mischief, and the slight twist of his lips when he was planning something.

What if I never saw him again? What if I forgot what he looked like someday? I had no photos of him, nothing to remind me.

"Grace?" Dare said softly, pulling me back to the present. "Where'd you go?"

I shook my head, shoving the wave of grief away. Not now. I'd bawled my eyes out until I was catatonic the day the sun had reappeared. I didn't have the luxury of repeating that experience.

"Bullet told me once that there are no heroes and villains among gods." Dare twisted to face me, waiting patiently for me to gather my thoughts. "They don't think like we do. They don't experience fear the way we do, they never feel the crush of time running out. I'm not sure any of them are good or bad, so much as selfish."

"That doesn't make me feel better about the whole pit thing, you know."

I managed a feeble laugh, resting my head on Dare's shoulder. "Me neither. But Bullet always said to do what scares me, and I can't imagine anything more frightening than this."

DARE

CHAPTER 3

Today had felt like a week.

Foster had heated water for us, and Grace and I had taken turns bathing, while the others scrounged up food and set up places to sleep. Despite being packed in here like sardines, they'd insisted Grace and I keep the upstairs room where we'd been staying. Perks of being the Prophêtis, undoubtedly. If she'd been more clearheaded, Grace would have probably objected, but she had plenty of other things on her mind.

I sat on the edge of the bed, a towel wrapped around my waist, and dropped my head into my hands.

We'd been so fixated on lifting the darkness, maybe even getting some semblance of the technology Gaia had wiped out back, that we hadn't entirely thought about what would come after. What the effects of days of darkness would be, how *severe* they'd be. Without light and in freezing temperatures, the plant life had mostly died. No food meant the animals must be dying off in droves too, though, in the darkness, I hadn't seen it for myself.

How were we supposed to recover from this? Not just those I knew personally, but the planet as a whole?

How had we—our little group—gotten to this point? It was a question I asked myself regularly, and every time the tone of it grew more desperate in my head. There had been five of us, a whole team, and now it was just Grace and me.

As much as I hated the idea of staying here, so close to where the giant weird monster thing guarding the pit was, I'd been quietly hopeful that Wild and Riot would track us here at some point. But it had been forty-eight hours, and there was still no sign of them.

They had to be alive, didn't they? The memory of Riot's blood-stained sweater haunted me.

The bonds were broken and Grace couldn't feel us the way she could before, but surely she'd know if they'd died on some kind of spiritual level. The fact that she was still semi-able to function made me think that that wasn't the case.

Grace knocked softly on the door frame before letting herself in, huddled up in a thick robe Eirene had given her to use days ago, damp hair hanging straight down her back.

"Hey," she said quietly, closing the door behind her and leaning back against it.

"Hey." I braced my elbows on my thighs, looking up at her. Even exhausted and crippled with grief, Grace was so fucking beautiful that it hurt to look at her sometimes. Before, it was because I thought it was a trap. Now, it was because I knew I'd been wrong.

No matter what else we had going on, I was still frustrated with myself for not trusting the connection between me and Grace right away. For wasting even a millisecond of the time we could have spent bonded. The time we'd never get back.

For a long moment, Grace and I stared at each other, an unspoken conversation passing between us. There was a stirring in my chest that was rapidly moving lower, and even though the circumstances were awful, we were both alone, each covered in flimsy bits of material with nothing underneath.

"Is it wrong?" Grace whispered.

She didn't need to elaborate. I knew exactly what she was talking about.

I extended my hand, encouraging her to come closer. She took a step into the room, slipping her palm into mine slowly, as though she was savoring the very act of touching me.

"We're all pretty different, your soul bonds," I murmured. "Different from other daimons, but different from each other too. I'd rather sell my soul to the gods of the underworld than go to a Broadway show like Bullet." Grace's lips twitched. "The only thing I'd enjoy less would be jumping in the ring at Wild's underground fight club." At that, I got a full-bodied smile, and I committed it to memory. *One every day, just like I'd promised Bullet.* "Riot and I are probably the most similar, though he's more antisocial than I am. But one thing I've learned is that nothing is more important to all of us than making you happy, Grace. Making you smile, making you feel safe and comforted and *loved*."

Tears welled in Grace's eyes, and without the bond, I had no idea if they were the lovey-dovey kind or if I was traumatizing her.

"So, no. I don't think it's wrong for us to make love to one another right now. For us to hold each other close and cherish each other while we can. It doesn't mean you've forgotten the others—we both know you haven't, that you never could."

"Never," Grace agreed weakly, as she clambered onto me. She didn't so much climb onto my lap as *melt* onto it, draping her arms over my shoulders and resting her forehead against mine.

"Just so long as we both remember that this might not... fix things."

"I know." Grace closed her eyes for a long moment before opening them again. "I know the bond is gone."

I nodded once before wrapping a hand around the back of her head and dragging her mouth to mine for a long, slow kiss. Her hands slid down to my chest, nails digging into my flesh slightly as she held onto me like I'd disappear if she didn't.

My fingers flexed against the back of her neck, pinning her in place as my other hand slipped between our bodies to unbelt the robe, pushing it out of the way. There was no self-consciousness this time as I stroked Grace's skin, softly kneading one breast before taking a nipple between my fingers and teasing it to a hardened bud.

"Dare," Grace whispered, rocking her hips slowly, trying to get closer. "I need..."

"I know."

I traced her curves, running my fingers over the soft skin of her stomach before slipping my hand between her legs. Grace was waiting for me, angling her hips and grinding down on my palm without any guidance from me. I slid my middle finger in her pussy, pumping lightly before dragging her wetness up to stimulate her clit.

Grace let out a keening gasp, tipping her head back and circling her hips, bearing down for more pressure. The firelight danced across her golden brown skin, long wet hair swaying side-to-side with each movement.

I could watch Grace come all day.

I kept going, prolonging her pleasure as long as I could. On a different day, in a peaceful time when we were both filled with joy and not worry, I'd lean back right now. I'd drag Grace down with me and encourage her to crawl up my body and sit on my face so I could lick her pussy until she begged for a break. But today was not that day, and while there was pleasure in what we were doing, it wasn't *for* pleasure.

This was about connection. Love. Holding each other tightly when it felt like everyone and everything was conspiring to rip us apart.

"Towel," Grace mumbled, fumbling between us to undo the fabric at my waist. I shifted my hips, helping her out until there were no barriers between us before guiding her forward, gripping my shaft and notching it at her entrance.

"I know not to hope for it," Grace whispered, slowly sliding down, feeling like fucking *perfection* around me. "I know the bond has been destroyed."

I wrapped an arm around her waist, gently guiding her movements while I thrust into her from below. "We're mortal, Grace. We hope."

She braced her hands on my shoulders as we found our rhythm, pulling each other so close that we shared each breath. It wasn't frantic, it wasn't fast, it wasn't loud. It was just us. It was quiet gasps for air, grasping hands, and *desperate* movements, illuminated by the flickering firelight.

It was beautiful and perfect. And my chest was as hollow as ever, the bond so thoroughly gone it was as though it had never been.

"It's okay," I rasped, wrapping a hand around the back of Grace's head and pulling her face into the crook of my neck. She nodded, a muffled sound of disappointment escaping her as she continued to roll her hips, sliding her hands down to dig her nails into my chest. "It doesn't change anything. I loved you then, and I love you now, and I'll love you when we're in the underworld someday, reminiscing about the life we lived. You hear me, Grace? Bond or no bond, I'll love you until the end of time."

"I love you," Grace whispered, lips moving desperately against my skin, kissing me and marking me in equal measure. "I love you, I love you."

Never stop.

THE SPIRIT OF DREAMS

CHAPTER 4

The baby was laughing again.

Whatever I was, whatever this place was, it was paradise, and I didn't want to leave. Sometimes there was silence, in a sort of floaty, tranquil way and that was nice. Other times, I'd hear a baby—mostly happy, sometimes shrieking—or birds singing and insects chirping. The air always smelled of flowers and the ocean, and it was always warm.

I knew what these things were and I knew that they were good and peaceful, but I didn't know *how*. How did I know that?

Had I existed once? Laughed like that child laughed?

Was I dead? Or was I yet to be born?

No, that didn't seem right. How would I *know* things if I hadn't been born?

Maybe this was the entirety of my existence. Maybe I just was. Whatever I *was*.

Light flickered just beyond me, blistering heat giving way to a more temperate warmth and a refreshing breeze. The world was nothing and everything all at once, and I existed.

I just existed.

Occasionally, I tried to move, to feel, to see if I had some kind of physical form. Not because I wanted to leave the paradise place, but there was a niggling sense of unfulfillment at the back of my mind that I couldn't quite shake. That while I was happy and comfortable here, I wasn't being very productive. That I was *meant* to be doing something else.

"Of course you are meant to be doing something else. You are the Spirit of Dreams," a soft voice whispered, feminine and gentle. Comforting and sweet.

Huh. I knew that I was partially connected to some kind of other world—the laughing baby didn't exist in this black void where I was—but I'd thought I was alone here.

"Who are you? What is the Spirit of Dreams?" I thought, with no mouth to ask.

"The Spirit of Dreams," the voice began, ignoring my first question. *"Carries dreams of prophecy and malevolence on their wings through the dreamscape. You see what you're shown, deliver what you choose to deliver. Your mind was once a vast repository of the presents and futures of everyone you'd ever met. Too vast. Too much for any mortal mind to bear."*

Wow. That sounded important, like I'd been someone who mattered once. It was sad too, though. Wasn't it? I'd once had a mind full of knowledge, and now I had none. Or rather I had some abstract understanding of how things worked, but I couldn't remember people. Other beings.

Was that my baby laughing? It had never occurred to me before, but now I was horrified that perhaps that was my child and I'd forgotten them.

"The child is not of your blood," the voice said gently. *"Unusually,*
24

you have an infant as one of your phylakes. *Your guardians. The child and her mother are caring for your physical body while your soul resides here.*"

Oh. Well, that was nice of them. "Do I still have wings?"

There was a long pause before a tinkle of delicate laughter. *"The wings are metaphorical, Spirit of Dreams."*

Hm, no flying out here—wherever here was—then. There was a strange feeling suddenly weighing on me that I hadn't experienced since I'd realized I was in paradise. Disappointment? Yes, that word felt right. I didn't know how or why, though.

"Am I alive?"

"You exist between the world of the living—the upperworld—and the world of the dead—the underworld—with one foot in either. Which way you go is dependent on you."

I wanted to be alive, didn't I? That seemed like a logical thing to want. And I had to thank the kind people who were caring for me. My *phylakes.* It would be rude of me to go ahead and die while they'd been going through all that effort of looking after me.

Then again, there was a sadness that accompanied that thought too. No—an apprehensiveness. I couldn't *remember* them. Had I once known all about their presents and futures too? And now I knew nothing, not even their names?

Would that make them feel sad?

"For what you are, you are unusually compassionate. Then again, your thread of fate wouldn't have wound the way it had if you weren't. You were very loved, you know. And you loved fiercely in return."

Wow. Whatever this emotion was, I didn't like it. Despair, perhaps? It was an acute kind of agony, crushing and overwhelming, too big to escape from. I was going to drown in this terrible feeling. There was no way out.

"Come to the underworld with me, Spirit of Dreams."

"And die? What about the people I loved? Are they in the underworld?"

"Not yet. One of them might be, soon. You could stop it. You are between worlds, you can do what no one else can."

It sounded like a trap, yet I was struggling to fully conceptualize what a trap was. If I existed in between living and dead, surely going to the underworld meant choosing death. Or did it? I wanted to *know*, to understand what it was we were talking about, what I was potentially getting myself into, but it felt like there was a hole in my mind, and no matter how much I reached into it, nothing was coming out.

"Not so long ago, you sat in a room in your home with the woman you love—her name is Grace—communing with the gods."

Grace. That was a pretty name.

"What is she like? Does she remember me? What was the message?"

Did she miss me? How long had I been in this place? Maybe she'd forgotten me. That was a sad thought. Then again, the idea of someone loving me and missing me while I was... wherever I was, was also a sad thought. What if she was lonely? No, I didn't like that idea at all.

I didn't want anyone to suffer for loving me. I was a floating glob of missing memories in a void, I wasn't worth suffering over.

"What is she like?" the voice mused. *"I don't perceive mortals the way you do, I don't think I can truly say. However you always called her your Amazing Grace, so I suppose that is how you see her."*

Grace. Amazing Grace.

"There's a man you love too, a Keres daimon named Wild. Grace loves

you both, and they have been torn apart. She is increasingly alone in the world, facing trial after trial with no reprieve. She has been given an inordinately large burden to bear."

"What can I do?" I asked immediately, my own feelings of suffocating despair easing in the face of this mysterious woman's suffering. If I'd loved her once, I couldn't not help her. That would make me a monster. "Where is Wild? I want to help them both. You still haven't told me who you are," I added, realizing that perhaps taking advice from a mysterious disembodied voice wasn't the best course of action. Or was it?

"I am Persephone, Queen of the Underworld. And you are the last Spirit of Dreams. You are beloved of Grace the Agathos, and she needs you. We all do."

Beloved of Grace.

"If I go with you, can I help her?"

"Yes. Only you can."

The baby laughed again, the warm sun beating down on me from wherever it was, even though I felt floaty and disconnected from my body. This in-between was bliss, a perfect state of peace.

But someone I loved was in danger. I didn't know who Grace was, couldn't picture her face, couldn't recall a single thing about her, but I'd loved her once. Before. Back when my mind was whole, filled with dreams.

I couldn't abandon her now.

"Why were we communing with the gods?"

"They had a message for you: Liberate the treasure held in the deep,

Where no sweet-smelling smoke or prayer can reach,

Bring forth the Second Age of Heroes."

"I don't know what that means." That gaping hole in my mind felt larger than ever.

"*I know,*" she replied sympathetically. "*But you will. This message, this prophecy, was delivered only to the two of you. Will you risk the life of a loved one to see it come true? Or will you accompany me to the underworld and take her burden as your own, knowing that you might never return here?*"

Fear. That was what this emotion was, and it was impossible to ignore. But I couldn't let it stop me from doing the right thing. In fact, there was a sort of reassuring sense of rightness at the idea of intentionally doing what scared me.

"I'll go with you to the underworld."

MERCY

CHAPTER 5

"Anyone need batteries?" I called, wandering through the tent city that had been rapidly forming over the past few days. The sun had returned, the agathos bonds had broken, and somehow, the world seemed to be more unstable than ever. "Water treatment tablets? Matches?"

I stopped at one of the tents, unloading some essential supplies from the crate I was carting around. We didn't have a lot, but we shared it all. Those who'd ended up here were in the most dire situations, many of whom were city people who'd thought they could drive out to the middle of nowhere and "live off the land" without any real concept of what that entailed.

Shouting broke out at the end of the row, and I stiffened, finishing up with the family I was with and backing toward The Lodge. I steered clear of the fights. Brio was an agathos of *Harmonia*, he was best equipped to defuse those situations.

"Mercy," Harbor called, beckoning me over as I got to the porch steps from his spot a few feet away. I quickly ditched the crate inside the door before jogging over to join him. He was exhausted, we all were, and yet he looked more handsome than ever.

Perhaps tonight, I'd be able to sneak in a few stolen kisses in the corridor when the rest of the house was asleep. It wasn't much, but it was all we could manage right now, and even then, it was clear he felt conflicted about it.

"Hi," I said breathlessly, staring up at him. "What is it? Did you need me?"

There was a flash of something unidentifiable in his eyes. I hoped it was lust. "Your uncles are at the gate."

My happiness at getting a moment with Harbor morphed into confusion. "What uncles?"

"Grace's fathers. Well, two of them, at least. Chance and Creed. And the two boys—I forget their names."

"Leon? And Tobin?"

"Right, those are the ones. They're here seeking sanctuary."

I shook my head slowly. "No, that can't be right. Without Aunt Faith? They'd never leave her."

Then again, the bonds were broken, and that changed everything. Leaving had never been an option before, and now it was. What did that mean for the agathos community? How many bonded would choose to stay together, if they were given real, meaningful choice?

"Can I see them?" I asked hesitantly. "I don't... I'm not sure it'll be good. I didn't exactly part on great terms with my family."

They'd used me as a spy while secretly planning to kill Dice and Grace's soul bonds the moment they separated us. Most of my rage about the incident was directed inward at the stupid, trusting little girl I'd once been. When I thought about my family, it was mostly with bitterness.

Harbor nodded once, placing a supportive hand on the small of my back as he walked me to the gate. "I'll be right by your side the whole time. If you don't feel comfortable having them here, we'll send them away."

I shot him a withering look. "We both know that's not true. Maybe if my uncles had come alone, but you'd never send two kids out into that madness."

Harbor's lips twitched, his hand bunching up the back of my sweater briefly before releasing it. It was a simple, chaste gesture that sent a small army of butterflies stampeding through my stomach.

It was selfish, given the desperate state of things, but all I dreamed about each night was getting some alone time with him. Imagining the campgrounds with no one else around, just the two of us in The Lodge without all the other single agathos who we shared a room with, making out under the covers on the big bed.

I never told him about those dreams, because they always ended up veering wildly off-course. Dice would appear, a harbinger of doom, followed by doom himself, who I *really* wasn't supposed to be thinking about. At least with Dice, I had an excuse.

The bonds may have been broken, but it didn't change the fact that Dice and I had been made for one another. Our souls were mirrors, and that was a difficult truth to forget. I really hoped he was okay, wherever he was. Probably hunkered down in Milton with his sister, Rogue, and her daughter, Quinn.

It had never been harder to *not* complete the bond between us than it was when Dice was looking after Quinn. He'd been so good with her, and it had given me visions of what he'd be like as a dad one day, and *ugh! Don't think about it!*

The era of agathos soul bonds was over. I had no idea what my future entailed, but I struggled to envision romance in it. I couldn't even conceptualize how a serious relationship would work *without* a bond, because that was all I'd ever seen and aspired to.

Sterling opened the gate with a small nod of reassurance directed at me. I managed a tremulous smile in return, stepping out of the safety of the camp and into the wild, unpredictable world.

"Mercy!" Little Tobin launched himself at me with such ferocity that I nearly fell on my ass.

"Hey bud," I said cautiously, steadying myself before lifting him up under his armpits and snuggling him tight. "It's been awhile, huh?"

Tobin buried his head in my shoulder, sniffling quietly, and I squeezed him a little tighter. Had he always been this light? No, I didn't think so. Leon stood close by, watching us, and I was struck by both how much weight he'd lost, and how much older his eyes looked. As though he'd seen things that no eight-year-old should see.

"Mercy," Chance rasped. His gaze dropped to my cheek for half a second, to the scar that wouldn't heal from the bullet that had grazed me that day at the community center. The last time I'd seen Grace. "It's so good to see you."

It... was?

Chance was definitely not the kind of agathos who could lie, and yet I struggled to believe he was telling the truth. He and Creed hadn't been directly involved in the conspiracy to use me as a double agent to capture Grace—in fact, Aunt Faith had derisively said they refused to participate, if I recalled correctly—but the distrust was still there. They may not have fed me to the wolves, but they'd certainly stood on the sidelines and watched the wolves devour me.

"You're looking well," Creed added with a tired smile. "Freedom suits you."

"Thank you," I murmured, not entirely sure how to respond to that. They definitely did *not* look well. Chance had always worn his dark red hair in a more shaggy, undone style than Aunt Faith preferred, but now it was almost down to his chin and so matted that it looked painful. Creed's wrinkles had formed wrinkles, and there were deep cracks in his lips and all over his hands. The boys looked far healthier by comparison, like their dads had been sheltering them from the worst of the elements, but all of them had the zombie-like complexion of those who'd come here seeking refuge. It was from a combination of no sun, little food, and not enough water, and it took time to get them back to some semblance of health.

"How are you here? *Why* are you here?" I shook my head at myself. "No, never mind. You need food and water and rest. We can talk later."

"Mercy." Chance stepped forward, resting a dust-covered hand on my sleeve. Harbor moved closer to my back, silently reassuring me with his presence. "We can never apologize enough, never make up for the suffering you went through at the hands of our family. But I can promise you that we mean you and your people no harm. That we have left the others behind for good."

Tobin trembled silently, and I held onto him a little tighter, though my own limbs were feeling shaky. They'd *left* Aunt Faith behind? And Earnest and Valor? *How?* Leaving Dice behind had been agony, and we hadn't sealed the bond or spent decades together, had *children* together.

"You'd better come in," Harbor murmured, gesturing for Sterling to open the gate. "It sounds like you have a lot to tell us about."

We showed the remnants of the Bellamy family to the bathroom, heating water for the tub so they could wash off the grime from traveling. There wasn't a single inch of space in the house or cabins, so Harbor disappeared onto the grounds to set up a tent for them while I heated up some soup and bread. It wasn't much, we had to be sensible with our rations.

The four of them came down to meet me in the kitchen, freshly washed and in different clothes, though equally as in need of laundering as their last outfits. When had they last stopped anywhere? It was five hundred miles from Auburn to here, and gas was almost impossible to come by right now.

"How did you even find this place?" I asked, frowning to myself. "Did you know I was here?"

"Felix," Creed offered. "Felix Lyon, Harbor's older brother. When things were getting bad between the agathos and daimons, Harbor sent him the address and told him to bring his family here."

Had he? Harbor had never mentioned it.

"There were rumors you'd headed in this direction." Chance squirmed uncomfortably. "Some daimons were, er, harassed for information about you. A woman who traveled with you out of town eventually told us what she knew."

I closed my eyes for a moment, letting out a shaky breath. What had her name been? Stacy? Stephanie? I'd tuned out her stream of chatter at the time, when she'd dressed up as Grace so Viper could smuggle me out of town and fulfill his bargain to Riot at the same time. Oh gods, I hoped she was okay and that she hadn't suffered because of me.

"They let her go afterward," Creed said weakly.

"Right. Sit, please." I gestured at the table. "I guess that means Aunt Faith knows about this place too?"

"It's likely." Chance grimaced. "We're not expecting her to follow. I certainly hope we haven't brought trouble to your door."

I nodded silently, filling up bowls and setting them down in front of them. Chance grabbed Tobin's wrist, physically restraining him from shoveling the piping hot soup into his mouth.

"Thank you," Creed murmured, watching the exchange. "It's been a while since we've had a hot meal. We're very grateful."

I nodded, sitting down at the head of the table. It wasn't a position I would have ever taken back when I lived with them, but they were on my turf now and I didn't entirely trust them. Maybe it was petty, but I wanted them to know that I was in charge.

Chance and Creed fussed getting the boys' food ready, both turning to me when Leon and Tobin were settled eating.

"We're in love," Chance said quietly. I blinked at him, my brain taking a moment to catch up.

"The two of you?"

"Yes." Chance swallowed quickly. "Always have been, actually. We met through Aunt Faith—Creed was already bonded to her; I was last. We hit it off right away, finding an ease in our interactions with each other that we never found with our soul bond."

"Right," I replied slowly, glancing nervously at the boys. This was quite the conversation to be having about their mother right in front of them.

"They've heard worse," Creed muttered, massaging his eyes with his thumb and forefinger. "*Seen* worse. It was not an easy journey here. I'll carry the guilt over what they've endured for the rest of my life. Over what all of our children have endured."

"Grace?" I asked softly, feeling that familiar stab of pain whenever I thought of my cousin. I missed her more than anything, and I knew that we'd probably never see one another again. Before the world had fallen apart, she was already becoming some kind of mystical, goddess-like figure. Even if she found it in her heart to forgive me, I doubted she'd have time for me now.

"Faith was not an easy partner to live with," Chance said, staring down at his bowl of soup. "And we deferred to her in all ways, because that was what we had always been told to do for our soul bond. When the closeness of the friendship between Creed and I had bothered her, we pulled back completely. When she wanted to take the lead on raising Grace despite her obvious disappointment at having a daughter, we let her."

Creed was shaking his head, knuckles turning white where he gripped his spoon. "Only the gods know how much Grace has suffered because we were too cowardly to defend her."

That he referenced *the gods* rather than Anesidora surprised me. I'd believed every word Grace had said about the Olympians, but even here at the camp, not all the agathos had been so ready to accept the idea of *other* gods.

"Mom was mean to Grace," Tobin said solemnly, setting his spoon down in the bowl with a clink and looking at me with far too much seriousness for a five-year-old. "She even went on TV and said mean stuff about Grace."

I grimaced along with my uncles at the memory of that interview. "I'm guessing you didn't know she was going to say all that."

"You're being too generous in your assessment of us," Chance replied wryly. "The bond... Well, it made it difficult to keep secrets. We knew enough. Enough to have done more. It was the biggest fight we'd had in twenty-seven years."

"We left the moment the interview was done. Took the boys and ran, consequences be damned. We couldn't let them grow up that way. It had gone on long enough. The things she said—" Chance's voice cracked, and he cleared his throat, glancing at the boys. "And then the world went dark."

"The endless night," Creed agreed gruffly, finally spooning some now-lukewarm soup into his mouth.

"We started off with a vehicle, but we were carjacked just outside of Littleton. We've mostly made our way on foot since then."

"I saw a lady die," Tobin said, far too casually.

"Shh!" Leon hissed, elbowing his brother. "Everyone gets sad when you talk about that!"

Both Chance and Creed looked slightly nauseous, and while I was basically one step beyond being a kid myself and knew nothing about parenting, *this* I kind of understood.

"You can talk about it, even if it makes you sad, or other people sad," I told Tobin lightly, giving Leon a small smile so he knew I wasn't mad at him. "Sometimes we need to talk about the sad things to find our way back to the happy things. Do you want to tell me about what you saw?"

Tobin glanced around the table, as though he was waiting for someone to tell him no before he eventually decided to speak. "Some people were fighting over bread, and a man cut a lady with a *knife*. And then there was blood everywhere, all over the ground and the people. Why would he cut someone with a knife over bread?"

"We haven't done the best job at talking about this," Creed murmured. "I'm an agathos of wisdom, and yet I'm struggling to find any wisdom now, when everything feels so bleak."

Perhaps that was the case, but I guessed Creed had still bestowed plenty of wisdom to humans on his travels, and Chance would have done the same with his gift of self-restraint. To be an agathos was to feel called to help, no matter the personal risk.

I nodded slowly, still watching Tobin. "Sometimes, people do terrible things when they're afraid. Terrible things to *survive*." My throat tightened, and I waited a moment for the feeling to pass before I could carry on. "I did something bad when I was afraid, and I think about it every single day. One day, when the world isn't so hectic, I'll find the people I wronged and apologize for what I did, and do whatever I can to make it right again."

Was that a lie? It used to feel icky and hard to tell them, but it had gotten easier with practice. I liked to think I'd be brave enough to face Dice again someday, but I wasn't confident.

"Did you cut someone with a knife?" Tobin asked solemnly.

"No! Oh my goodness, no. That is, like, *super* bad. Don't ever do that, okay?"

"I won't," he agreed, nodding his head.

"The tent is ready," Harbor announced, his voice carrying from down the hall.

"I'm sorry we don't have a proper room for you—"

"Please don't apologize," Chance cut in. "We're more than grateful for anything you can provide for us. And once we've got the boys settled in, I hope you'll put us to work. The sanctuary you've created here is amazing, and we want to help in any way we can."

CHAPTER 6

I didn't care that Thanatos was the God of Death, I was going to find a way to kill that bastard myself.

And then I was going to burn his silver Elvis-style jumpsuit with the jangling bells around the waist and sleeves, that I swore he was wearing just to piss me off.

This living room was particularly grim. I'd traveled all over the globe over the past two days with Thanatos, and it was clear the damage that both Gaia and Nyx's games had wrought extended over every inch of it. Based on the scorching heat, I guessed that wherever we were now was close to the equator, and the elderly woman here had been dependent on electricity to keep the suffocating temperature down. Gaia's disintegration of what appeared to be every pipe or wire that had been buried in the earth meant there was no power, no water, no working sewerage.

There was no evidence of anyone else in the house; I doubted it had taken long for the elderly woman who lived here to succumb to these awful conditions. Based on the smell alone...

It had been a while.

"Nearly there," Thanatos said cheerfully, gently extracting her soul from her body, seemingly out of midair. The soul appeared—a carbon copy of the body it had just been removed from except more lifelike, albeit slightly gray—looking at Thanatos with a mixture of confusion and relief. "I'm running very behind schedule, you know. All these deaths make so much work for me. I bet Nyx and Gaia weren't thinking about all the additional admin for the underworld when they were whacking off mortals, left and right. No one ever does, you know—been like that all through history. Ares and Athena would have their wars, prance around the battlefield in all their glory, and I'd be stuck on clean-up duty, scraping the souls out of half-decapitated soldiers for weeks."

If souls could piss themselves, the poor old woman would have made a mess of her hardwood floors.

Thanatos sighed dreamily. "I can't wait until those days are upon us again. Soon. The prophecy will be fulfilled, the warrior gods will return, and life will be exciting again. Anyway, let's pop you down to the Styx, hm?" he said, finally turning his attention to the trembling soul. "Unfortunately, you'll be killing some time with the Restless Dead since you weren't given a proper burial, but it's really the place to be right now. Very bustling, since almost no one is given a coin for Charon these days. You'll probably see a familiar face or two. You know the drill, Keres."

I rolled my eyes, having given up on my attempts at respectfulness about twenty reaped souls ago. Instead, I wandered out onto the patio for some fresh air while Thanatos blinked out of sight, taking the confused soul with him.

Wherever we were, it was tropical. Or rather, it *should* have been tropical. Dead tree trunks were the only remnants of what had probably once been lush palms. This house was high on the hill, and I had a good view of sparkling aqua water, bright blue skies, and dead, dry land. Why hadn't Gaia fixed this yet? Was she choosing not to? Or was this some power play to prove how much mortals needed her?

Or was fixing the damage Nyx had done with her days of darkness more work than Gaia could handle?

I let out a long breath, wondering what sky Grace was looking at right now. Was she missing me, or glad I was gone? Where was she? Was she safe? Was she with Riot, and was Riot okay?

He had to be okay. But I couldn't think about it, because I had an unknown job from Thanatos to do, and I knew him well enough to understand that I wasn't getting back to Grace until I'd done it.

Much like he wouldn't let me leave the underworld until I'd fought him, he wouldn't let me get back to Grace until I'd completed whatever quest he'd sent me on. Unlike when I'd fought him, this time I was confident I'd come out on top because nothing in this world or any other could keep me away from Grace.

I'd already lost one of my loves, I wasn't about to lose the other.

"What a grim sight," Thanatos observed, startling me with his sudden appearance. He was doing it on purpose, the wanker. "Don't you worry, earth dweller." He clapped me hard enough on the shoulder that I stumbled forward a step. "Demeter will fix this right up. She's got a real green thumb, that one. Anyway, I think it's time for you to get to work."

Fucking. Finally.

"I *have* been busy—running errands, as you've seen—but I was also doing you a favor. Waiting until your company was at a more reasonable distance for you to walk. I hear it's quite tiring for mortals to walk for days."

There was no chance to absorb that information, I was already blinking through time and space to wherever Thanatos wanted to take me,

41

completely at his mercy. *Please don't deposit me on the other side of the world.* I needed to get back to Grace, it had been too long already.

"Here we are." I stumbled out of Thanatos' grip, finding myself standing on one side of the longest suspension bridge I'd ever seen—I couldn't even see to the other side of it. There was a body of water below it, the surface calm, and the landscape was just as dry and dead as everywhere else I'd seen. I didn't recognize it at all.

"This is the Çanakkale Bridge," Thanatos explained, already heading for the dead body of a young man slumped against the side of the bridge. "Oh, look. This nice young fellow has a bag full of supplies you can raid while you wait, very polite of him."

I snatched the bag out of the air as Thanatos carelessly threw it toward me before focusing on disentangling the man's soul from his body.

"Just wait here. You'll know what you're meant to do when you see it."

That's it? Those were the laziest instructions ever. Did Thanatos not have underlings he had to manage in his role as God of Death? I hoped not. He had no management skills. I was a far more effective manager of the many daimons I'd employed in Milton, and I couldn't even speak to them. Fucking lazy deities.

He vanished a moment later, soul in tow, leaving me alone on the bridge. Well, not quite alone. There was still the corpse I was standing next to, and I said a silent apology to the young man as I stole the large shawl he had wrapped around his shoulders. Was this what it had come to? Robbing the dead? Things were truly dire.

Not wanting to sit too close to the decaying corpse, I wandered further along the bridge before sitting up on the metal barrier where I could survey my surroundings. As much as I missed modern technology—and I missed it a lot—there was definitely a peacefulness that came with the absence of cars. While the bridge was quiet, it wasn't entirely unpopulated. Small groups and occasional stragglers walked the length of it, carefully giving each other a wide berth, hugging whatever supplies they had close to their chest.

No matter how hard I looked, I couldn't tell where exactly I was from my surroundings. There was a landmass at the end of the bridge, but no identifying markers to indicate what it was. The best clue I had to go on was the body of water beneath me.

The coastline had been pitch black when we'd first approached on Arsène's boat, but we'd definitely disembarked on a beach before walking to Ephesus, and it had seemed like a prettier residential area, if not a tourist spot. In contrast, the area directly below the bridge looked to be concrete and industrial, though most of the structures were burned-out husks now. The bridge itself crossed some kind of inlet, and I couldn't see past the two land masses on either side of the sea.

For fuck's sake, I could be anywhere. All I knew was that I was near the coast, and provided Grace hadn't gone anywhere, then she was near the coast too. If I had to swim back to her, I would. Whatever it took. I'd find a way.

For a moment, I let my eyes fall closed. I shouldn't—I wasn't even a little bit safe here—but I hadn't slept in days, and I was barely holding it together. I'd never been so fucking tired in my life. Tired and lonely and wracked with grief.

Was I allowed to grieve someone who hadn't officially died? I couldn't even think his name or I'd be overcome by bloodlust all over again, and I didn't have Riot here to handle my shit for me this time. Not that I planned on finding myself in that situation again if—when—I saw Riot. I was going to keep perfect fucking control over my temper and not endanger the people I cared about.

There was a rumbling noise coming along the bridge that had me breaking out of my melancholy mood and paying closer attention to the road.

I noticed the feathers first. A red plume rose into the air, atop a shining bronze helmet. Followed by a hundred more.

The Spartoi were on the march.

My bones creaked as I stood, shrugging on the satchel and walking slowly into the middle of the road. Theras held up a hand the moment he spotted me, and the men behind him came to a perfectly well-timed stop, staring directly ahead. The ultimate soldiers. I knew we needed them—Queen Persephone wouldn't have given them to us if we didn't, but I didn't know how or why exactly.

"*Stratēgós*," Theras said respectfully, inclining his head when I came to a stop a foot in front of him. "Hello. Wild."

I raised my eyebrows in surprise, though I shouldn't have been shocked really. English had been the most commonly spoken language when we were staying at the villa, and it made sense that they'd picked up some.

'Where are you going?' I signed, hoping he remembered the sign language I'd taught him. Without one of the others here to translate, suddenly the task ahead of me felt impossible. Theras looked at me for a moment before gesturing for one of the others to step forward—Ariston, from memory.

'You.' Ariston signed. *'Look for you.'*

'You found me. We need to get back to Grace.'

He nodded, translating the instruction to Theras and the others. I fell easily into the front ranks, and they didn't hesitate for a moment to accommodate me.

44

The industrial area directly around the bridge slowly changed into farmland as we moved further inland. As much as I tried to hide how exhausted I was, Theras made the call to set up camp at an abandoned barn we found not too far from the road.

The Spartoi were used to roughing it, and they didn't hesitate to split into halves—one resting, one standing guard. And it was strange to realize that I felt safe enough to rest too. To lie down in the dirt, close my eyes for a moment, and to actually find myself falling into a much-needed sleep.

There was no food. The Spartoi had been scavenging as they went—walking all the way from the fucking villa we'd left them in near Athens—but there just wasn't enough. Not when everyone was hoarding what was available, when nothing was growing, when the animals had all been killed for food before they'd died of starvation. Perhaps there were still fish, though from our experience in sailing across the sea, it had grown so cold that I wouldn't be surprised if much of the ocean life had frozen to death.

The Spartoi shared their limited rations with me, but I hadn't truly realized how desperate the situation was until now.

Not just for us. For *everyone*. Lifting the darkness had only been the beginning.

My muscles burned from walking over the rocky, dry, uneven ground, and my head spun from hunger, but I didn't give myself a second to pause or think about the pain. Instead, I walked between Ariston and Theras, giving them a crash course in ASL while they translated back down the ranks. I had no idea how accurate the information those at the very back were getting, but I wasn't about to sit everyone down and give them a silent lecture so they all got the same information either.

We had to keep moving.

The road looked like it had once been lined by grass and trees, but was now an arid wasteland. There was no reprieve from the sun beating down on us overhead, and as much as I tried to be grateful for it after the days of darkness, some cloud cover and a decent rain would be pretty welcome right now. We rounded a corner, the ground so dry that every step seemed to kick up a small storm of dust, and Theras and I stumbled to a stop at the same time, causing the lines behind us to crash into one another in confusion.

What the fuck was *that*?

There were deep, curved grooves in the ground like nothing I'd ever seen before. The mark they'd left in the dirt was like a footprint, or perhaps some kind of fossil? It looked as though two *giant* snakes had been lying here, close but not intertwined, but there was no path leading to or from them, no evidence they'd slithered away.

Also, snakes didn't grow this large, I was certain of it. Not even in Asia, where I was pretty sure some super fuck-off serpents lived.

Whatever it was, it was making Theras nervous.

"Ekhidna," he muttered. "Khimaira. Typhoeus. Hydra."

Hydra. That one I'd heard of, which meant he was probably listing other terrifying, very much mythological beasts. Or maybe they weren't as mythological as I liked to think. Nothing made sense anymore.

'*Let's go,*' I signed, before gesturing at my eyes and then our surroundings and the sky, telling them to look out. No more language lessons for us—not when there was some kind of monster on the loose.

I was a vegetarian, but I was hungry enough to consider eating at least a little bit of monster. And the Spartoi had no such qualms about eating meat.

Where are you, Grace? Are you safe? Are Riot and Dare taking care

46

of you?

I'll be there soon, I promised, swearing it on all the stars in the sky, and to Nyx herself. If I had to beg for Riot's forgiveness, I would. I'd prove to Grace that I was sorry, that I'd never meant to hurt him, and that I'd do anything to make up for it.

Once, I'd thought I could stay away, that maybe she'd be better off without me, and I could keep her safe from a distance. Fight her battles for her, so she didn't have to. But with a monster on the loose? No. No, more than ever, I needed to get back to her side.

Grace was my treasure, and I was her shield. Nothing would get through me if it meant keeping her safe. I just had to find her.

RIOT

CHAPTER 7

"What is this place?" I asked Arete, stepping out of the realm of the gods into what must be hell on earth.

"Poveglia," Arete replied, looking around with a resigned face. Or maybe she was just tired—I wasn't sure how much power or energy, whatever it was, she'd drawn from my blood, but it appeared as though traveling through dimensions had taken it out of her. "This entire island is a shrine to unfulfilled potential. Or perhaps a grave where it goes to die."

"Lots of losers like me on here?" I asked uneasily. The building we were standing in front of was right on the water's edge, and even the scaffolding holding up the red brick, Mediterranean-style structure looked to be decades abandoned. Even with just the moon above illuminating the place, I could see that it was thick with brown rust.

"It is long-since abandoned," Arete said solemnly. "This was a plague island, where the dead and dying were dumped and burned. In more recent centuries, it was home to an asylum." She gestured at the derelict structure we were standing in front of. "Those who died here did so... unpleasantly.

Their souls were never properly laid to rest. Even Thanatos has abandoned this island, leaving the dead in charge."

Holy shit, I was going to wet my pants and I didn't feel one ounce of shame about it.

"You brought me to a *haunted island*? At *night*? What the actual fuck? No. Hell no. Take me back. I don't fuck with ghosts."

"I can't." Arete grimaced. "Or I won't, rather. This is the Fates' favorite haunt when they're in the upperworld. Excuse the pun."

"I most certainly do *not* excuse the pun. Get me the fuck off the haunted island. Are there ghosts in the water? I can swim."

"Well, fishermen do avoid these waters..."

Great. In the moonlight, without any electricity to light up homes at night, it was hard to tell how far off the coast we were. I squinted into the darkness, wondering if that was in fact a land mass nearby. It didn't look far, but jumping into potentially ghost-filled waters blind seemed like it would be a bad life choice under the best of circumstances.

"Of course, there is no guarantee the Moirai will make themselves visible to you, as we discussed. The Fates are fickle."

I shot Arete a filthy look that she chose to ignore. "Discussed" was a polite way of her saying she kidnapped me into the realm of the gods and lectured me for who knows how long because I *accidentally* bled all over her temple and gave her a temporary power-up.

I could forgive Wild for losing control and giving into his bloodlust—Bullet's departure from this world was hard on all of us, but on him and Grace especially. I could not forgive him for making me bleed enough to wake up the psycho agathos who'd decided I had something to prove. He better let me get in a free hit for the indignation of this experience alone.

"I just want to get back to Grace, that's all I care about," I muttered, stalking along the front of the building, waiting for a ghost to pop out and shout boo in my face. "Don't forget your side of the bargain."

"I can't believe I'm being lectured on integrity by a daimon," Arete grumbled, before disappearing into the aether without so much as a goodbye. She'd warned me she would, that the Fates wouldn't reveal themselves if she was around, but it was still unnerving as hell to see her leave. What if she couldn't come back? The agathos spirits had already pooled all their remaining resources once to send Hygeia to Dare's aid, it had cost them so greatly that Sophia had barely been able to speak since. Not without a blood offering, and only at the Ephesus ruins where they resided.

Arete hadn't mentioned where Poveglia was, but knowing my luck, it was hundreds of miles away from Ephesus. If she didn't have enough juice to come back, there was a good chance I was stuck here.

This whole thing was a fool's errand. Arete had told me herself that no one had ever trapped the Fates. If they didn't want to talk to you, they wouldn't, and they didn't want to talk to anyone.

So why the fuck would they talk to *me*? Grace would have been interesting enough to get them to show their faces, but she wasn't here and I'd sacrifice both testicles to keep her away from this hellhole. Bullet would have known what to do, but he was gone, and even if he wasn't...

I didn't think *I* had whatever it took, whatever X-factor was needed, to pull this off, but I wouldn't have asked Bullet to go in my place either. He'd been through enough. With Nyx popping into his head whenever he fell asleep, and a direct line to the Fates through his cards, Bullet had experienced enough exposure to immortals to last a lifetime.

I pushed open the ancient wooden door slowly, half expecting it to fall off its rusted hinges and wincing at the loud creak. *It probably doesn't matter. If this place is inhabited by literal ghosts and immortals, they probably don't need the creaking door to know you're here.*

This was fucking awful. Not because it was derelict—the fact that nature had pervaded the building, growing through cracks in the walls like it was reclaiming the land was pretty awesome. Or it would have been if all the plants hadn't died in the great freeze. I could imagine the vines and branches that were now dead and decaying lush with green leaves, disguising the mold-covered walls and old graffiti.

No, it was the remnants of the human stuff that was depressing. The stacks of rusted single beds, the chilling institutional feel of the place. There was a restlessness in the air that gave me the distinct impression I wasn't alone, but the energy wasn't hostile.

Not yet, at least.

As I picked through the debris, the remnants of lives that definitely hadn't been well-lived, the weirdest sensation came over me. Not from the hidden paranormal activity, but from *within* me.

I was crying, I realized suddenly.

I was not a crier, and I definitely didn't cry for random people who'd died well before I was even born. Grace might have—she had empathy, which was not something that daimons were programmed with. It was just this place...

It was really awful.

"Fuck!" I gasped, stumbling back and landing on my ass on the cracked tile floor as some kind of apparition materialized in front of me. She *looked* like a young, totally alive human woman, and for a moment I thought she was, in spite of the way she'd meandered out of thin air. Aside from the fact that her clothes were odd and old-fashioned—a frilly-looking shift that fell just below her knees, no shoes, and a grandma-bun in her hair—there was an odd dullness to her skin that no regular human had. A gray lifelessness, like the light inside them had been extinguished. I was frozen in place as she walked toward me, crouching down at my side with the thin white fabric floating around her.

This was how I died. Or how I got possessed.

She reached out, making the gesture of wiping my tear-stained cheek with her thumb, but there was no sensation accompanying it. Her smile was sad, resigned as she pulled her hand back, folding them in her lap and watching me.

"Can you talk?" I asked, my voice wavering.

She gave me an apologetic look, which I took to mean 'no', but there was a confusion on her face that made me wonder if she'd actually understood my question.

"Do you speak English?"

She shook her head, standing and gesturing for me to follow. For lack of a better idea, I did, finding myself standing in front of a sign I could barely make out in the dim moonlight.

"*Reparto Psichiatria*. Italian?" I hedged.

My new ghost friend nodded. My human mom had been a little Italian, several generations removed from the homeland, but she'd taught me a few words. Ironically, considering she'd been impregnated by a daimon and birthed a daimon spawn, she was also a Catholic. Not a very diligent one, but a believer nonetheless. The Lord's Prayer was one of the first things she'd taught me.

Then again, was it that ironic? She hadn't known what we were, we had no way of telling her.

"*Cielo*," I said, the word sounding strange and foreign on my tongue. *Heaven*. That one I remembered clearly, being fascinated by the concept.

"You." I pointed at her. "Go. *Cielo*." I did a wavy motion like a spirit floating up to the sky. The underworld was under the world, but I definitely didn't have the vocabulary to explain that and she'd probably assume I was speaking of Hell if I tried.

She gestured around us before locking her fingers together like a gate. As if to demonstrate, she headed for the edge of the island, attempting to step over the ledge into the water but stopping as though she'd hit an invisible wall.

Arete was so full of shit, I could totally swim out of here if I wanted to.

If I wasn't now feeling this weird, foreign sad emotion for the island of ghosts.

"I have to talk to three goddesses," I said, miming speaking before holding up three fingers. "Er, *tre. Dio*." That definitely wasn't right—it was a singular, masculine god, but I remembered the word from Mom's prayers and hopefully she got the gist. "Help me talk to them. And I will help you, all of you—" I pointed at her and then gestured around at where I knew other spirits were hiding, before motioning up to the sky again, "—*Cielo*."

She stared at me blankly and I cursed silently under my breath that I hadn't paid more attention to what my mother had taught me, or made any effort to learn some Italian on my own.

Suddenly, she was gone.

Fuck.

I'd blown it. That had been the only idea I had, and I'd fucked it up.

Sighing heavily, I made my way back inside the building, trying not to panic. Maybe I could pray to the Fates, leave them some kind of offering that would entice them out? Except the only thing I had on me was my now-empty lighter, the one I'd taken after my mom died that I carried more for comfort than practicality. It was sentimental, and immortals were assholes who liked to see us suffer, so maybe it would work. Maybe giving up something that I didn't want to part with would be enough to pique their curiosity.

I found myself standing in what I was pretty sure was a chapel, a bunch of broken, discarded pews stacked up in a pile. It seemed like as good a place as any to make an offering in, and I reluctantly pulled the lighter out of my pocket, running my thumb over the engraved dragon carved into the metal.

Before I could figure out how to sacrifice an empty lighter, my ghost buddy appeared again, scaring the shit out of me. She was followed by roughly a million other ghosts—maybe that was a slight exaggeration, but really, only slight—all crowding around me in the rotting Chapel of Sadness.

Ghost Lady nodded at me, gesturing at her ghost crew.

"You'll help me if I help all of you," I translated, gesturing at the assortment of specters then at the sky again. I really hoped I wasn't fucking them over—I'd seen the underworld for myself; I knew it was better than this place. At the same time, I was guessing that the bodies of these souls hadn't been properly laid to rest, and I wasn't sure what that meant for them. Surely, they'd suffered enough? Surely, freaky King Hades could cut them a break?

An old dead dude with a gnarly scar and an empty eye socket materialized right in front of my face, leaning in with a menacing scowl that needed no translation. There was a reason this island was deserted. If I failed to deliver, I was going to end up as one of these lost souls while my flesh rotted in the abandoned asylum.

"Message received," I croaked, holding up my hands in what I hoped was a pacifying gesture. I had no intention of trying to screw them over, but I was banking on Thanatos' ego and I hoped I hadn't overestimated it.

But first, we had to capture the Fates.

GRACE

CHAPTER 8

I woke up with heavy, scratchy eyes, the morning sun filtering in through the window already, even though it felt as though I'd just laid my head on the pillow. I supposed I could have closed the curtains, but both Dare and I had been hesitant to. After what had felt like forever without sunlight, we both wanted to absorb every second of it we could.

"You're awake," Dare mumbled, sleeping face down on the pillow, his arm thrown across my middle.

"I am, good morning." I rubbed gentle circles into his forearm with my thumb, liking that he always kept hold of me in sleep as well as when we were awake, even if it did make it harder for me to escape. We'd been here three nights due to a combination of getting the others settled somewhere they could camp out for the time being, and my reluctance to leave when Riot and Wild were still missing.

I'd prayed. I'd yelled. I'd begged for some kind of deity to respond to me, to just let me know that they were safe, but I'd been met with silence.

I *wanted* to return to the pit; I needed to enter it and follow the path the Fates had laid out for me, to face the monster if that's what it took, but...

What if I never came out of that hole?

Was it too much to ask, that I get to say goodbye first? To see Riot and Wild with my own eyes, and know that they were safe before I left? Given how much was at stake, it was a selfish, immature desire, but I'd already lost Bullet, perhaps forever. The grief was raw and painful, and it was hard to accept that I might have to take on more of it soon. To somehow convince Dare to stay behind, and to perhaps never see Riot or Wild again.

We may not have a bond connecting us, but I knew they needed me, at least a little. At least right now. Wild had completely fallen apart after Thanatos had taken Bullet away, and I just wanted to *hug* him, to just be and exist in our grief together.

Dare was procrastinating here, waiting for Wild and Riot to return too, but he mostly just didn't want me to jump in the pit alone. If getting the others settled here and scavenging what food we could meant delaying me, Dare was more than happy to take the lead on it.

Except we were running out of food to scavenge. There were thirteen of us here, plus Milos, and what looked like had once been a bountiful vegetable garden in Eirene's backyard was just a desolate wasteland.

"Well, today is a new day that brings with it almost no hope. What do you want to do?" Dare turned his head to the side, looking up at me where I leaned against the headboard. His black hair stuck up in every direction, and I leaned over to push it out of his eyes, smiling in spite of myself at his nonchalant assessment of our dire situation. No one could roll with the punches quite like Dare could.

"I don't think we can put off the inevitable any longer," I said quietly. "It feels like a betrayal to leave when Riot and Wild are still missing, but we have to go back to the pit. If not to enter it," I tacked on hurriedly before

Dare could argue. "Then at least to check on it. And to enter the ruins. If Sophia won't answer my prayers from here, then maybe she needs another blood sacrifice to do it."

I still wasn't entirely sure how it worked, but something about pressing my blood to the base of Sophia's statue had brought her to life, at least temporarily.

Dare groaned. "Or I could tie you to the bed and you stay in the nice, safe-ish house forever. Away from the giant fire-breathing monster."

There was no point arguing with him over this. I'd already accepted that I was going to have to go against Dare's wishes to enter Tartarus, as well-meaning as they were. While I couldn't lie, cheat or steal, I could keep an open mind and look for an opportunity to present itself. That was the only thing I could do.

"We don't know the monster is still there," I pointed out. "No one has seen it, and there's been someone stationed to watch duty all the time."

"It could turn invisible for all we know," Dare countered, snuggling in a little closer to my side. "We don't exactly know the parameters of what we're working with here."

The thought had never occurred to me, but of course, he was right. We had no idea what the pit monster could do—if it could camouflage itself, or shrink down to the size of a fly, or shapeshift. Wasn't shape-shifting a common ability among the gods? I distinctly recalled stories of Zeus disguising himself in various animal forms.

"That being said," Dare continued with a resigned sigh. "Asking Sophia for answers is a good idea since she's now decided not to talk to us anymore. Plus, we're running out of food. I don't suppose you would be content to stay here under a ten-person guard while I go out and see what I can... find?"

That pause was definitely code for 'steal'.

"Absolutely not, I'm coming with you. We need my blood for the temple."

Milos stood up from her spot on the floor where she'd curled up for the night, guarding our bed, and made a show of stretching and yawning loudly. She stuck close to my side, no matter how much Foster tried to convince her to get attached to him instead. I couldn't say I minded it, but I worried about what would happen to Milos when we inevitably had to leave here. Whether she'd *want* to leave the only home she'd ever known, what would happen to her if the pit was a one-way journey for me, and if it wasn't, could we properly care for her?

We couldn't even care for ourselves right now.

Dare groaned, clearly hating every second of this. "Come on then, let's get ready. Milos, we're going on an adventure."

"Thank you. You're arguing less than I thought you would."

Dare shot me a wry smile, all deliciously rumpled from sleep. I wished we could stay in this quiet, peaceful bubble, just a little longer. "Just know that I'm arguing on the inside. I'm lost, and I don't know what the right course of action is, so my brain defaults to 'wrap Grace in cotton wool and keep her safe that way'. I know that's not realistic, or even what you want."

I nodded, giving his arm a grateful squeeze. To be an agathos or a daimon was to be ruled by instincts, often ones we didn't want. It meant a lot that Dare was even trying to fight them.

The others were lounging around the living room when we got down there—half of them awake, half asleep. If I ignored absolutely all of the circumstances, there was a nice, sort of slumber-party feel to us all being here together. We'd stayed up late the past couple of nights talking—they talked, mostly Vasileios, while Dare and I listened—and we were always lining up to take turns bathing or using the rudimentary plumbing system we'd gotten going. The darkness may have lifted, but it looked as though the sudden disappearance of utilities was permanent.

One day, when I wasn't grieving so many other more painful losses, I'd mourn running water.

I looked around the room, memorizing the faces of the strange crew of people we'd assembled here, knowing I'd miss each one of them. They weren't all here, of course. Many had stayed behind at the villa, holding that as a base for us to return to if we needed it. I hoped they were happy and comfortable, or as much as they could be given the circumstances.

There was a sharp tightening in my throat as I looked around the room. Yet another set of goodbyes I'd have to make, another group of people to miss, but knowing them had been worth it.

"Stop that," Estrella said flatly, making me startle. She was draped lazily over Foster's lap in one corner of the couch, totally comfortable in a teeny tank top and panties in front of everyone. I wished I had just a little of her self-confidence.

"Stop what?"

"That face. You are doing the self-sacrificing face."

I did my best to school my features into something less... self-sacrificing. Whatever that looked like.

"You're going to the pit?" Foster guessed, resting his chin on Estrella's shoulder.

"We're going to find food," Dare corrected. "And answers."

"And going to the pit," Vasileios said around a yawn, tangled in so many naked limbs that didn't belong to him that I could barely see him underneath. He'd solemnly sworn to me yesterday that he dedicated every one of his sexual liaisons to Dionysus in the hopes the gods were being strengthened by it, which was very thoughtful and productive of him.

"I need to go look, at least," I agreed, already shoving my feet into the boots Eirene had given me, a pang of grief hitting me square in the chest as I did. Dare made a grumbling sound of disagreement, even as he laced his own shoes and roughly yanked on his dirt-covered coat. "The pit is what we've been waiting for. *The path.*"

"Is it, though?" Foster asked hesitantly. "I just feel like if Gaia had wanted you to get to Tartarus safely, she could have made you a nice spiral staircase out of dirt, carved into the earth. Perhaps the pit is just a test. Perhaps she wants you to beg for some kind of shortcut or a ride down to the bottom or something so you don't, you know..."

"Crack like an egg all over the bowels of hell," Estrella deadpanned.

"Aren't you two cute, finishing each other's sentences?" Dare snarked, shooting her a filthy look as he wrapped an arm around my shoulders and led me toward the front door. "There's no risk of that happening. Grace isn't going to dive head first into the pit."

"Wait, we're coming with you," Estrella replied, jumping up and snagging her clothes. Foster stood, grabbing his stuff at the same time while Vasileios began wriggling his way out of the human puppy pile he was in. "You might need backup."

Well, that was a nice gesture, even if Estrella's words had given me visions of my head cracking like an eggshell while my brain leaked all over a dark rocky floor like a pink yolk.

As if I wasn't struggling enough to sleep already, now I had that nightmare in my repertoire. And no dream guardian to save me from it, as he'd saved me my entire life.

The five of us set off together—six, including Milos, who walked reluctantly at Foster's side with much encouragement from all of us to put her there. Occasionally, she'd herd us off the main road, taking us on a more circular route to the ruins than we'd ever been before.

"Good girl," Foster murmured, scratching her behind the ears as she fell into step next to him again. I could have sworn she gave him an exasperated look before nuzzling into his hand ever so slightly.

"We really need some weapons," Vasileios said, more to himself than anything. "We have some knives, but nothing long-range."

"Do you foresee us needing them?" I asked uneasily. All things considered, we'd gotten by pretty well without weapons so far.

"I do." Vasileios was more solemn than I'd ever seen him. "I'm no Keres, I can't taste violence on the wind the way they can, but... " He hesitated, frowning in concentration.

"But?" I prompted.

"But if I was a Keres, I would be tasting violence right now. There's a restlessness in the air... Can't you feel it?"

"Of course, there's a restlessness in the air," Dare scoffed. "People are hungry, and food is scarce. There's no faster way to full-blown mutiny than starvation."

I need to get into that pit. I wasn't sure liberating the Olympians would fix all of our problems, but between the twelve of them, there was a god for almost everything. Surely, at least one of them could grow food? Demeter, perhaps, goddess of agriculture? I said a few silent prayers to each of them, just in case.

"Stay here, okay?" Foster instructed Milos. She gave him a far too intelligent, unimpressed look before parking her butt on the ground, and acquiescing to Foster's pats of approval.

The steady hum of voices reached us as we drew nearer to the ruins, and Dare's hand was like a vice around mine, his discomfort at approaching a crowd clear. I draped my shawl over my head with one hand before wrapping it around the lower half of my face while Dare did the same. Frankly, it was necessary. The ground was dead and dry, the breeze from the nearby coast kicking up an incessant stream of dust.

Death. We were surrounded by death as far as the eye could see. None of this was recovering without divine intervention from *someone*.

"She could fix all of this," Dare mumbled, vocalizing the thought I hadn't spoken. "Gaia. If she wanted to."

I glanced down at my feet, a cloud of dust rising with each heavy clomp of my slightly-too-big boots. We were probably lucky that opening the ground and swallowing us whole wasn't Gaia's style. She preferred to hide behind the plausible deniability of natural disasters, or send her minions out to do her dirty work for her. Perhaps because of that lingering desire to be loved? It made sense that she wouldn't openly put her name on all of her atrocities if so. It only made me despise her more—she could at least have the courage to own what kind of monster she was. For all the things she'd said about my mother, Faith had followed closely in her goddess' footsteps. She was also great at pretending to be above the terrible things she did.

"Don't let go of my hand, Grace," Dare said quietly, squeezing my fingers. "We're about to see a lot of down-on-their-luck people, and you can't afford to let any of those agathos abilities slip. Our situation is too precarious for bad luck."

Already, I wanted to argue with him, my instincts balking at the idea of letting anyone suffer intentionally. Dare just held on tighter, content to be the bad guy if it meant keeping us both safe.

"We'll go ahead, scope things out," Foster volunteered, walking hand-in-hand with Estrella, Vasileios on his other side.

"Be careful," I whispered, panic spiking in my throat, remembering leaving Riot and Wild behind. Maybe I would have a complex about goodbyes for the rest of my life.

I'd gotten the sense that there were people around, but as Dare and I got closer, it became clear just how much of a hub of activity the surrounding edge of the pit had become. Where had all these people come from? This hadn't exactly been a bustling metropolis. Then again, it had been a few days and a sudden, giant pit was the kind of news that would travel.

Dare dragged us behind a pile of broken stone, the ruins of other ruins, and we did our best to stay out of sight while we took in the scene in front of us.

There was no giant snake monster, for one. The sky was a brilliant blue, no evidence that it had ever been filled with fire or dark for days.

Perhaps more surprisingly, the pit was a hub of activity.

"What the fuck," Dare whispered, summing up my thoughts perfectly. "What... what are they doing?"

I cleared my throat. "I think they're worshipping. They're treating it as a shrine."

"Well, that seems like an epically bad idea," he muttered. "That's basically a giant 'eat me' sign for Tartarus monsters, isn't it?"

"Maybe that's who they're worshipping. Maybe it's a nice monster," I replied hesitantly, knowing Dare disagreed. "We don't know that it has bad intentions. It could have turned that fire on us at any point, but it didn't. It blasted it at the sky. Why would it have done that if it wanted to eat us?"

"Why do lions toy with their prey?" Dare asked. "Because it's fun for them. Because they can. I'm just saying, if I'm a big fuck-off flying snake monster thing, I'm taking my time with my meals. Why not? Who's going to stop me?"

It was an annoyingly valid point.

"Let's try to get a little closer," Dare suggested, still holding onto my hand, muting the worst of my instincts to bestow luck on every human I could see. "If anyone has seen a giant monster with snakes for legs, they'll be talking about it."

Well, that was true, but there was a very good chance they wouldn't be talking about it in English. Even from a distance, I could hear a medley of different languages being spoken in hushed, reverent tones. And yet, there was an almost party-like atmosphere at the same time.

"This is wild," Dare mumbled, gripping my hand tightly as he wound past a group dancing silently in a circle. There was a glazed, faraway look to their eyes that made me think they weren't entirely sober. "Then again, the sun disappeared for days, and there's no food, why not party like we just survived Y2K-on-steroids?"

That was true. Even now the planet felt like it was on the verge of dying a permanent death. Who knew how long it would take for plants to grow again, for there to be enough food to sustain those who'd managed to survive?

"Hey," I whispered, pulling Dare to a stop. "That's one of the agathos who was staying in the ruins. I saw her by the pit before the monster came out."

She was sitting around a small campfire that someone had built, surrounded by a group of humans. Like many of the others, she'd wrapped fabric around her nose and mouth, but I recognized her because of the startling amount of pink in her opal agathos eyes.

"...it wasn't a *god* that came flying out of the pit," the agathos said, immediately capturing the group's attention. "I would know. I am an agathos."

"Like Grace the Agathos?" one of the humans gasped.

I froze, and Dare immediately moved closer, blocking me completely from their view. That agathos knew I was here, or at least nearby. She'd seen me, kneeled to me.

"Yes, like Grace. You've heard of her?" she asked in a thick accent. If pressed, it was unlikely that she'd be able to lie, but she didn't seem like she was rushing to disclose that she'd seen me at least.

"I saw her videos on the internet. Where she grew the army? Did you see that? Can you do that?"

"No," she laughed, a throaty sound. "Grace is unique, most of us are not so interesting."

"How do you know it wasn't a god?" someone else asked.

"I can't be certain," she admitted. "But I think it was one of Anesidora's—Gaia, as you call her—one of her children. Some of them were rather…" the agathos trailed off, seemingly struggling with finding the right word to describe such a creature.

"Monstrous?" the man she was talking to suggested.

"I suppose, yes."

"Gaia's monster baby," Dare grumbled, his voice low enough that only I could hear him. "Of course. Why not? You know it's definitely not secretly a good guy monster now, right?"

I could acknowledge that all signs were pointing in that direction but my stubbornly hopeful heart wouldn't give up. "Maybe he doesn't like his mom," I whispered back. "I don't like my mom."

Dare twisted to look at me, most of his face hidden by the shawl, though I could see the wry twist of his lips. "That's quite the insult coming from you, bravo."

I smiled down at the ground, my cheeks heating up.

"The others are calling us over," Dare said, guiding us away from the fire. It was a shame—I wanted to hear more of what the woman had to say, but I didn't want us to be separated from the others any longer than we had to either.

While the mood was strangely cheerful, for the most part, it felt precarious too. Yes, these people were happy to be alive, but they wanted to *stay* that way, and doing so might require making some difficult choices.

"...I still think we should throw someone in," someone mumbled to their companion as we went past. "If the beast god was happy with our sacrifices, then food would grow again. We need to offer *more*."

My blood ran cold. I had to get down there before they started throwing others down instead.

"Did you hear that?" I whispered to Dare. He grunted, pulling me behind the broken pile of rocks as Vasileios, Foster, and Estrella grew closer.

"Dare, they want to throw someone in as a *sacrifice*." I swallowed thickly, movement at the edge of the pit catching my eye. Someone had made a makeshift monster shrine out of rocks and sticks and broken pieces of stone, with ripped pieces of fabric to represent the beast's matted hair and serpent legs. Dare and I paused to watch as someone approached with some kind of bundle wrapped in paper, setting it down reverently at the base of the shrine, before dropping to their knees in front of the pit and holding a second package up in their palms toward the sky.

They mumbled something too low for us to hear before parting their hands and letting the package fall into the depths of the pit. Dare and I both stood still, listening, but there was no *thud*, no indication that it reached the floor.

Nerves churned in my stomach. How deep was it exactly?

It was my pathway to Tartarus. I *had* to go, before someone was tossed down there in my place. Everything the goddesses had put the world through—not just us, but everyone—had led to this. People had *died* for this.

Fear wasn't a good enough excuse. Not when there was this much at stake. I took a steadying breath, gripping the edges of my shawl, ready to take a running jump to my destiny, come what may. I had no idea how I'd liberate the gods once I got to Tartarus, but I had to believe I'd at least get there.

"There's that self-sacrificing face," Dare murmured, his fingers brushing up my spine. The sadness in his voice had me turning, but before I could, his fingers were on my neck, and the world faded into nothingness.

CHAPTER 9

"What the fuck?!" Vasileios hissed, glaring at me in righteous outrage as I used my scarf to bind Grace's wrists.

"Don't leave her tied up," I instructed him, swallowing past the million razors of pain in my throat as I carefully transferred her unconscious form into his arms. "I just need to get to the pit. She'll wake up any moment now. I can't let her do it, I can't."

Vasileios' expression softened, all three of Grace's friends huddling protectively around her body.

"You're going to go?" Foster confirmed, glancing warily at the giant hole in the earth. Although offerings were being thrown into it, *people* very notably weren't. In fact, a few humans looked as though they were acting as guards, warning away anyone that got too close to the edge, though I wasn't sure whose benefit it was meant to be for.

"I don't know..." Vasileios said. "I don't want Grace to go down there either, but the prophecy was for her. What if it doesn't work? You might break it somehow."

"You can't break a prophecy," I scoffed, sounding more certain than I felt. "Bullet always talked about fate like a long, meandering road, not a fixed destination. Grace will still be the one to fulfill the prophecy somehow, I'm just going to do this part for her. If it's a test... Well, Gaia can do her test on me."

I blew out a long, unsteady breath. "Just... Could you tell her I'm sorry? And that I love her more than anything?"

"Of course," Foster agreed readily.

Grace stirred slightly, and the desire to snatch her back into my arms warred with the need to keep her safe.

"This isn't goodbye," I told her quietly as I backed away, not entirely sure if she understood what I was saying or not. "I'm not saying goodbye to you because this isn't goodbye. This is see you soon, okay? Just in a little while. I love you. I'll see you in a little while." I let out a shaky breath. "I'll be back in time to make you smile. I won't let Bullet down either."

"Dare?" Grace mumbled, eyes blinking open.

I was already running.

We could argue all day long about whether or not it was a trick, whether or not Gaia was just taunting us by having our goal so close and yet still so far, or if she was just doing this to further turn the humans against us. At the end of the day, there'd be no resolution until someone made the journey to find out.

It couldn't be Grace. I loved her too much to let her put herself at risk.

Besides, it was my turn. I'd been here the least amount of time, and I'd always felt like the others had done more, given more, sacrificed more than I had.

It was my turn to take the leap.

I jumped over people sitting on the ground, shoving through the crowds, ignoring the shouts at my back. Only one person could enter that path to Tartarus, and it was going to be me.

THE SPIRIT OF DREAMS

CHAPTER 10

Why would anyone build a castle and not put any furniture inside it? I wondered, wandering through cavernous stone halls, looking for the exit. Or the entry. Or just a bench to sit down on for a bit and rest my not-quite-solid legs. I wasn't even entirely sure how I'd gotten here.

My brain was an assortment of thoughts that didn't seem to fit together properly. A puzzle with only half the pieces. I *knew* what a puzzle was, but I had no recollection of ever doing one. I knew about the concept of time and that it didn't seem to be moving the same way here, but I didn't know *how* I knew that. Had I learned it once? Had someone told me? People had parents—that much I was confident about—but who were my parents? Were they missing me?

Maybe coming here was a mistake. I was confused all the time. I wanted to go back to the warm, hazy place with the laughing baby. Instead, I was in this strange, empty stone castle. Where was everyone? Why was I alone? What exactly had I agreed to with that Persephone lady? She'd seemed so nice when I was talking to her, telling me about the people I loved. I hoped it wasn't a trick.

Eventually, I noticed a heavy wooden door with a sliver of brighter light underneath it, that fortunately was easier to open than it looked since I wasn't entirely sure I had muscles. Or maybe I did have muscles? I wasn't a *ghost* per se, but I wasn't not a ghost either.

It was deeply unsettling.

The door led out onto a stone balcony, and I walked to the railing to take in the view. Why was the sky purple? *That* was odd. Or was it normal and my freshly emptied brain had gotten confused? It was bizarre, not knowing what was real and what wasn't. What I was like before, if I'd been happy, where I'd come from.

It kind of made me want to cry. I decided not to think about it anymore.

Wherever I was, it looked to be an island. Across the strait was a harsh, jagged mountain range in the distance, standing in contrast to the lush greenery and swaying trees immediately around the empty castle. It looked a lot less inviting on the other side of the water.

"Hello."

I jumped at the voice, spinning around to find an intimidating woman standing a few feet away, observing me with interest. She had dark brown skin and even more ink than me, lines of what looked like writing trailing over every inch of her that I could see in her black Grecian-style dress, even her face. Silver piercings filled the gaps between tattoos, and her dark hair was done in tight twists, pulled up high on her head.

Had I met her before? I didn't think so.

Was she my love, Grace? Persephone hadn't given me a description to work from, but I didn't *think* so. There was something sort of inhuman about the woman in front of me, and there wasn't a shred of kindness in her eyes.

I knew nothing of my Grace, but I didn't think I could fall in love

71

with someone who wasn't kind. Could I?

Wait, maybe *this* was Persephone? Were goddesses meant to be scary?

"Oh dear," she murmured. "The lights are on, but nobody's home."

"Excuse me?"

"You're excused. You don't remember, do you? No, of course not. You probably don't even remember *yourself*, poor bastard."

I didn't think I liked this lady.

"I am Hecate." She stared at me for a long moment, as though waiting for some sign of recognition, before sighing dramatically. "Goddess of magic, witchcraft, the night, moon, ghosts, and necromancy."

"Oh, okay. I'm the Spirit of Dreams."

She blinked slowly. "That's what you're going by these days?"

"It's the only name I know."

"I see. Well, it will do for now, I suppose. Going by a title always confers a little more authority, doesn't it? I prefer the souls in my part of the underworld refer to me as Goddess of Ghosts, just so they remember their place."

"Right." I nodded as though I knew what she was talking about. "That makes sense. Is this your house?"

She snorted. "No. My house has furniture." With a lazy wave, a wooden chair appeared behind each of us, Hecate's larger and grander than mine. She was still staring unnervingly at me, like she had no idea what to make of me. "Sit."

I dropped into the seat, not wanting to argue with a goddess. Especially this one. Necromancy? Ghosts? I wasn't about to play around with those.

"Do you know about the man and the woman I loved?" I asked,

greedy for any kind of information about them. Any scrap of *something* about who I was and who I'd cared about. "I'm here to help them."

"I know plenty, but I'm not going to tell you." *Pop* went the little bubble of hope that had been building in my chest. "I'm going to tell you about your friend."

"Okay," I said eagerly. A *friend*. That was better than nothing.

"He is a young man who you've known most of your life. Grace is your soul bond, and his too."

"And I don't love him?" I clarified, because that seemed like an important thing to know.

"Not in a romantic sense, but you love and care for him deeply. You would do anything to see him safe and well." Hecate leaned forward, wrapping a hand around my wrist and lifting it before tracing the lines of ink on my skin. "He gave you these."

Oh. Well, that was nice of him. I hadn't had much of a chance to examine them, but the mysterious images that decorated my skin were one of the only clues I had about myself and my life before.

I liked this guy.

"What is his name?"

"Dare."

"Dare," I repeated slowly. "That's an interesting name. Isn't it?"

She smirked at me, releasing my arm. "Just assume going forward that you all have strange names. You're all daimons—except for Grace. The names are some kind of daimon tradition, I believe."

"And Grace is a..." I trailed off, trying to remember what Persephone had called her.

"An agathos. A personification of something good—luck, in her case. Though Sophia called her an *agathodaimon*, and perhaps that is a better term. A reminder of the connection, the balance, between both sides."

Grace the *Agathos*. Right. But what did a "personification of something good" actually mean in a practical sense? Was she a goddess too? Did "balance" mean that daimons were bad?

Hecate looked lost in thought for a moment, and I tried to decide if it was disrespectful to remind her what we'd been talking about. Sure, she was a goddess, but I was the Spirit of Dreams and that sounded kind of important too. Where did I sit in the hierarchy, exactly?

"So... about Dare."

Hecate returned her full attention to me, eyebrows slightly raised. Okay, maybe I wasn't interrupting-goddesses-level of important. Good to know for next time.

"Yes. Good friend of yours. Such a good friend, in fact, that he vowed in front of the gods to save you if you ended up in the underworld." She gestured around. "Obviously, he hasn't gotten that far yet."

He'd vowed to save... me? He sounded like a *really* good friend. Did I have a lot of friends like that in my life before? The more I learned about it, the more eager I was to get back there. Friends? Lovers? It sounded even better than the happy place with the baby.

"I don't want him to come here and save me," I said eventually. "Even though I want to go back to wherever it was I came from, this isn't a safe place for the living, I know that much."

"You're right, it's not," Hecate agreed. "But anyway, none of that matters. He's going to die soon."

I reared back, gripping the arms of the seat. "What do you mean? How? Why?"

"Does it matter?" Hecate asked, disinterested. "The question is not how he dies, but if you can save him. Do you even want to?"

"Of course I want to. He vowed to save me, right?"

"That is correct."

"Well, then, I'm vowing to save him." I stood, shoving the heavy wooden chair back with a loud scrape of the stone. Maybe I was being rash, but it strongly *felt* like the right thing to do.

"Your memories will never return, you know—not if you want to live. You could ask a deity to restore them, but emptying your head of the visions you've been bombarded with your entire life is the only thing keeping you somewhat alive."

"What has that got to do with anything?"

"You don't *know* Dare," Hecate pointed out mildly. "Not anymore. His death doesn't need to be your problem."

"You said he was my friend."

"Indeed."

"And Grace's soul bond."

"Yes."

"And she loves him too?"

Hecate looked surprised by my question. "Does that make a difference?"

"If I loved her, I'd do anything to spare her pain, wouldn't I?" That sounded right, at least. I was already here, parted from her. If it had hurt her for me to leave, and I hoped it hadn't, then the least I could do was prevent her suffering again.

"Well, alright. Don't get huffy at me, I was just checking." Hecate stood, smoothing down her toga thing before gesturing at me to follow her back into the palace. "You *might* die forever if you do this. I should probably mention that."

I stumbled slightly before righting myself. "But if I don't, it's certain death for him?"

"The Fates' shears are poised over his mortal thread."

I decided in that moment that I didn't like gods and goddesses very much. I knew nothing about anything, but I was already confident I had more empathy in my pinkie finger than a deity had in their entire body.

"Then I'll take the risk."

Hecate led me back through the empty rooms and corridors, walking with enough confidence that I guessed she knew where she was going. We didn't encounter anyone else on the way, and whatever this place was, it didn't seem like the kind of spot anyone was meant to spend a lot of time in. Hecate hummed to herself as she guided me down the front steps, directly onto grass as soft as silk under my feet.

"We're going to the coast. Come."

She turned right, and I sighed internally at the expansive view of the scary mountains on the other side of the channel. Of course, that was where we were going.

"Where am I now?" I asked, jogging to keep up.

"These are the Isles of the Blessed, and it's little more than a waiting room. There is a mirror island to this one in the upperworld—the veil separating the two is thin here. From this island, one can figure out their way back to the land of the living, if they're smart enough. From the underworld proper, it's not so simple."

"Can I get back to this island from the mainland? If I succeed in saving Dare?"

Hecate glanced back at me. "If you were anyone else, I'd say no, but you are unusual, the Spirit of Dreams."

Okay. That sounded... positive?

She gestured to a small wooden row boat. "Get in. It will take you to the mainland."

"Will you come with me?"

She snorted. "No. I have my own means of traversing the underworld. The boat will take you across, then you will need to walk through the mountains."

"And go where?" I gripped the edge of the boat tightly, clambering awkwardly into it. κτῆμα ἐς ἀεί. *Huh, I wonder what that means.* Almost immediately, the boat moved with a lurch, heading into the center of the channel while Hecate stood watching impassively from the shore. "Wait! Where am I going?!"

"If you don't figure it out, you're not worthy of saving him!" she called back.

Great. Just fucking great.

The boat sped across the channel at an alarming rate, coming to a stop with a crunch on the rocky shore at the base of the mountains.

The flimsy toga thing I was wearing felt extra pointless, but I also didn't feel like I was going to die of exposure either. Perhaps a perk of this not-quite-dead, not-quite-alive state I was in.

There was only one path in front of me, a steep walkway cut into the stone of the mountain. My not-ghost feet slipped on the smooth surface, and I lurched forward, grabbing the jagged boulders that lined the way, digging my fingertips into the rock to keep myself upright. I waited for the pain, but there was none. Just a sort of phantom sensation that let me know

I was in fact holding onto something.

I wanted to slow down to gauge where exactly I was and where I was heading, but there was this strange pressure in my chest, building, building, building.

Is this... fear?

Yes, fear. That sounded right. I was afraid—not for me, but for my friend. The friend I didn't remember, who'd made some kind of vow in front of the gods to save me. Whoever he was, wherever he was, I was going to save *him*. I was going to keep him safe for his love, my love, our Grace.

That felt right. Like the correct order of things, in a way I didn't really understand.

So instead of slowing down, I sprinted. The more momentum I gained, the more I realized that I wasn't being constrained to what I was pretty confident were normal, human running speeds. At some points, I was a decent leap away from full-blown flight.

Woah. Badass.

Take that, Persephone. I didn't even need real Spirit of Dream wings. I could fly on my feet.

Not that it was the priority right now, but it felt pretty cool to be so free. At some point, I realized I was heading down rather than up, and slowed my feet until I was just sliding down the slope. Vaguely, I was aware of eyes peeking out of crevices, and a general aura of Not Being Alone, but I was moving fast enough that I didn't think anyone would catch me.

Besides, I wasn't entirely alive. Surely that had to make me slightly more indestructible than the average person.

Now where?

To the left were more mountains, and to the right were more

mountains, but with what looked like flat plains beneath them. Neither particularly called to me and since Hecate had given me basically no instructions, I guessed that following my gut was my best option.

And my gut said straight ahead. I couldn't quite make out what it was, but something over there was glowing a fiery orange, illuminating that entire spot on the horizon. Honestly, it had a sort of evil vibe, but maybe that was just how things looked down here.

I jogged until my super speedy not-ghost feet kicked in again, and then I sprinted. There was a section of huge, craggy rocks in the way in an oddly circular shape, and I skirted around them in search of the giant glowing thing... and realized that I was running toward *fire*. Which seemed... bad? Yes, bad. Don't run into fire, that was the reigning school of thought. Except fire was meant to be hot, which would be a pretty great warning sign to stay away, and this wasn't. It was nice, but more like the memory of heat than actual heat.

Where were all the people? I mean, dead, obviously, since this was the underworld. But Hecate had mentioned souls, and I wasn't seeing any. Did they live somewhere else? This place was pretty expansive. Or maybe they were just avoiding me. Maybe in the underworld, it wasn't cool to only be partially dead.

Once I'd fully rounded the rocks and was standing in front of the fire, I realized that the two were connected. The flames were a river, and they poured over a sudden drop into a terrifying black pit, surrounded on all the other edges by high sharp rocks. Perhaps to stop anyone from accidentally wandering in and dropping into... wherever it went. Nowhere good, I was pretty sure.

The sky above the pit looked kind of weird too. There were thick clouds moving almost constantly, but above it, the sky looked off. Too light and too dark at once.

The flame river next to me started to jump, spitting enough sparks in my direction that I took a few healthy steps back in case I wasn't as invincible as I thought I was. Maybe the fire river was telling me to back off? Totally reasonable, except I didn't have any better ideas of where to go. Back to the mountains? Before I could decide, the flames began shifting into a distinct *shape*, and I paused to watch, mesmerized.

It looked kind of... human? Like a human made of fire?

The empty hole in my brain gave me nothing, but gut instinct decreed that humans were not usually made of fire.

"I am Phlegethon," a voice boomed out, seemingly coming from his chest since his fiery lips were pressed shut. "And you are the Spirit of Dreams."

"Yup. That's what people call me," I replied in a daze.

Why was I talking to fire? Did people usually talk to fire?

No, right?

Phlegethon stared at me in silence for a moment, save for the sounds of his crackling flames.

"I am not a person."

Nope, he definitely wasn't.

"Right. You're a... god?"

"I am Phlegethon." He stared at me for a long moment, waiting for some sign of recognition I was guessing. "I am this river, and I am the god of this river."

"And what is this place?" I asked, glancing at the pit in the hopes of distracting him from my faux pas.

"This is where Hades feeds his unworthy subjects to sate Tartarus' appetite." Now it was my turn to stare in confusion. "Hades, King of the

Underworld. Tartarus, king of his realm even further in the depths, prison to the worst kind of creatures."

"Liberate the treasure held in the deep,

Where no sweet-smelling smoke or prayer can reach..."

Why did I get the feeling that this pit was the 'deep' Persephone was talking about?

"Things have been falling into it for days," Phlegethon continued, glancing distastefully at the sky above the pit where the denser purplish clouds were. "Hades has attempted to cover it, but there is a hole beyond those clouds. A yawning great chasm formed in the upperworld, courtesy of Gaia herself."

"Wait," I said slowly, frustration building behind my eyes that I didn't understand. That there were pieces of my mind missing that I *knew* would have helped me. "There's a hole behind those clouds that leads all the way up to the upperworld? Where the humans live? The alive humans?"

Phlegethon nodded once. My gaze tracked down to the ground, to the pit. "And that hole goes all the way down? Through the underworld and down to the... what did you call it?"

"Tartarus," Phlegethon replied, unimpressed. "Yes, that is what I'm saying. Why do you think you're here? Someone must go," Phlegethon continued. "Someone who received the prophecy goes down there to fulfill the impossible task. Of course, Gaia hopes your mortal *Prophêtis* in her fragile mortal body, or one of her soul bonds, will throw themselves in there and die in the process."

Dare. Dare was going to jump into that death trap in Grace's place.

I didn't have a physical body. The jump wouldn't kill me.

There was no hesitation. I leaped onto the nearest steep, jagged

81

rock on the edge of the pit, attempting to clamber up the smooth surface.

"No need for that," Phlegethon said in a bored voice. "I can make it so that my flames don't burn you. I don't much care either way, but your bonded's fourth is on his way—"

"Take me there," I demanded, falling off the rock and running for the flames.

I don't know what I'm doing, Dare, but I'm doing it for all of us.

GRACE

CHAPTER 11

"I said I was sorry, Grace. Are you still mad?" Estrella asked, towing me back toward Eirene's house, using the scarf binding my wrists as a leash.

"Stupid question," Vasileios muttered at the same time I replied, "Furious."

Foster gave me an apologetic look, the boys boxing me in on each side while Estrella walked ahead, tugging me along like a rowboat. The journey was taking at least twice as long because I'd fought them the whole way. Milos had rejoined us at some point, and part of the reason I'd *stopped* fighting so hard was because it was obviously distressing her.

That didn't mean I wasn't filled with rage though.

Did their actions come from good intentions? I supposed so. Dare was trying to protect me, to fight my battles in my place. Foster had been the most vocally opposed to dragging me away, and I wondered if it was because he was an agathos and he knew there was no avoiding sacrifice. Then again, Estrella and Vasileios' daimonic nature was probably driving their actions too—they cared for me in their own ways, and that manifested in this possessive urge to hide me away.

But I was still absolutely *furious* with them. I was a grown woman, this was *my* prophecy to fulfill, *my* destiny. None of them got to cosset me away, even if they meant well. Except I was struggling to be wholly angry at Dare because my worry for him eclipsed it.

"Grace," Vasileios sighed sympathetically, sensing the direction my thoughts had gone in as my shoulders slumped forward. I was so *tired* all the time. Physically, yes, but the emotional drain was relentless.

"What if Dare—" I choked on the last word, unable to articulate it, barely able to think it. Had I lost Dare as well? I didn't understand it. Bullet had always talked about my future like the others were in it, and here I was, completely alone. I didn't even know where Riot and Wild were.

"He's going to be okay," Estrella said with fierce conviction, inadvertently yanking my arms a little harder. "You're important, you know. You have important allies. They'll keep Dare safe, just like they'll be keeping Riot and Wild safe."

"Just like they kept Bullet safe?" I rasped, forcing myself to speak his name aloud even though it hurt. What if I didn't? What if I failed to keep his memory alive, and everyone forgot about him? No. No matter how much it hurt, I couldn't let that happen.

"You said Thanatos himself showed up to take Bullet somewhere for safekeeping," Estrella pointed out. "They don't do that for just anyone, you know."

Right. She was right.

I swallowed thickly, hating the way they were all looking at me. As though my breakdown was inevitable. It probably was, but I still hated that everyone else knew it.

I'd never felt this alone before, which was strange because I'd always *been* alone when I was growing up. Back then, I hadn't realized what it was like to be loved though, not really. Having loved and *lost* was infinitely more painful, even though I wouldn't trade it for anything.

"You have to let me go," I all but pleaded. "This isn't right. I shouldn't be here, I'm meant to be in the pit. Dare is meant to be safe."

"He will be safe," Estrella replied stubbornly.

"Maybe the original agathos will appear and help him," Foster suggested weakly. "Like Sophia helped you already."

"With a blood sacrifice from me! At least take me back to the ruins, to the temple—" There was a noise overhead like a roll of thunder but a thousand times louder, cutting off my words. The ground below us shook, knocking us all to our knees.

"What the..." Estrella whispered as it faded, the long end of the scarf lying loose on the ground where she'd dropped it.

I didn't give myself a chance to think, I just got to my feet and ran, sprinting back toward the direction of the pit with my wrists still bound.

Whatever that noise was, it wasn't good. What if the pit was throwing Dare out somehow? He was never meant to go in there. It was meant to be me.

"Grace!" Vasileios yelled from behind me, footsteps thudding against the earth as he tried to catch up.

"I'm sorry!" I shouted back, sprinting away. And I was sorry. I appreciated how much they cared for me, and I didn't want to leave this way, especially since I wasn't sure I'd ever see them again. But getting to Dare was more important. Gaia had said only one person could enter the pit, and I was still holding out hope that it could be me, that he hadn't jumped yet.

I stumbled as the rumbling roar built up again, but managed to keep my footing this time. What *was* that? It was like thunder, but I'd never experienced thunder so deafening it made the ground quake.

Was it Gaia? Earthquakes were very much her style, except this didn't feel quite like an earthquake. It was coming from above.

Out of nowhere, dense gray cloud cover formed overhead and a bolt of fear ran down my spine. This was not how weather worked. Whatever was happening, it was divine intervention.

Fat, heavy raindrops fell from the sky, slowly at first before growing into a deluge. The once bone-dry ground was rapidly turning to sludge beneath my feet, and my pace slowed in spite of myself, my ill-fitting boots becoming even more of a liability in the mud.

Come on, come on, come on.

Milos barked, easily catching up to me on four legs, sounding frantic.

"Go back!" I gasped, struggling for air. "Go back, Milos. Go back to the others. Take them back to the house, can you do that for me?"

Milos hesitated for a moment before sprinting back. *Please get them back safely*, I thought as the sky rumbled again. I looked up in dread to find thick black wings flapping on the horizon, the monster from the pit approaching rapidly. I slid to a stop, clumsily yanking and twisting the now-sodden scarf until it was loose enough to get my wrists free.

"Go!" I shouted at Vasileios, realizing that he was still attempting to follow me, slipping in the mud. Milos had his sleeve between her teeth, attempting to tow him away. "Go back! Go to the house and protect the others!"

"*Please*," I added desperately, seeing the indecision on his face. If I'd learned one thing from the past few months, it was that divine beings were drawn to me. So long as they left, they'd be safe. Vasileios glanced up at the monster before returning his gaze to me, nodding once. Perhaps it was self-preservation, or perhaps his selfish daimonic tendencies kicking in, but whatever it was, I was grateful for it.

I drew myself up to my full height as the beast circled overhead, shielding my eyes from the rain with my forearm as I lifted my face to the sky. Maybe I was reading into things, but I thought I saw *restlessness* in the way that the creature was moving, flying back and forth right above me as though it was pacing in frustration. Frustration, but not anger.

Was I imagining things? Reading a kindness and compassion into the creature that wasn't really there? Was it really just a creature of pure evil?

Was *he* a creature of pure evil, I corrected mentally, glancing away. From this angle, I was getting quite the eyeful.

Maybe it was foolish, but I had this sudden, almost matriarchal urge to put him in his place. To box his ears and knock some sense into him, which was incredibly unlike me, and delusional to boot.

"Hey!" I shouted, my soaked clothes clinging to my skin. "What do you want?!"

It wasn't the most eloquent question, but ultimately that was what I needed to know, and it gave the others time to put some distance between themselves and the monster.

The beast released a stream of fire into the air that almost immediately turned into steam as thick as fog before dissipating into nothingness. He flung his head the other way, throwing another heap of flames at nothing, followed by a roar.

I'd never had a pet before—my mother would have fainted if I'd so much as suggested the concept—but my neighbors growing up had a cat called Tiffany, who was the moodiest little madam I'd ever seen. Any time she didn't get her way, she'd lash out and hiss and march off in a sulk, and that was exactly how the monster looked now.

It would be nothing for him to direct that fiery breath down and barbeque me on the spot. But if he wanted to hurt me, he'd had plenty of chances.

The monster huffed out more steam before diving straight down, pulling up at the last moment to land heavily on his serpent legs, just a few feet in front of me, staring me down. My neck ached from craning my head to look at his face. From this close, his overwhelming size became even clearer. He must have been fifty feet tall, at least.

I'd never felt so mortal.

"What do you want?" I repeated, taking a shaky step toward him. "I can see you're angry. Maybe we can help each other."

He huffed again, stamping his foot on the ground like a petulant child.

"Well, that doesn't really accomplish anything, does it?" I said, more curtly than I probably should have. "I think you can understand me, so you're going to have to find a way to reply somehow."

He stared at me flatly, a little puff of steam coming out of his nostrils before he slowly nodded once.

Yes. He bobbed his giant humanoid, yet also very monstrous, head. It had all the features of a human face—eyes, nose, mouth—but his eyes were pools of flames, his mouth was stretched wide, filled with a vicious row of fangs, and his skin was a sort of greenish color that darkened to black scales on the two serpents he had for legs.

And the giant, snake-hybrid pit monster was *nodding* at me. Surreal. And good, because maybe we could find some common ground and I could convince him to stop terrifying us all.

"Do you... do you want to hurt us?"

There was a long pause before he clumsily swung his head from side to side. No.

"Oh. Okay. That's good." I shifted my weight, slipping slightly on the wet ground. "Oh my gosh, this rain. I feel like I'm going to sink into the ground," I mumbled, to myself, thinking about Dare and the pit.

Abruptly, the rain stopped. The monster—I suddenly felt awful calling him that—blinked at me.

"Did you do that?" *A nod.* "Oh. That's really incredible."

So he had some kind of control over storms. There was only one god I knew who could do that, and he was meant to be locked in the depths of Tartarus. Still, I had to ask.

"Are you Zeus?"

If a bat-human-snake-hybrid monster could look disdainful, then that was definitely the impression I was getting from him. Not rage, not frustration, just a sort of unimpressed dismissiveness, before a single shake of his head.

"No, I didn't think so." I blew out a breath, suddenly remembering what that agathos woman had been saying around the campfire. "Are you one of Gaia's children?"

He huffed out another puff of steam before nodding his head.

"You're one of Gaia's children and you don't want to hurt us," I repeated, watching him carefully. I knew the relationships between divinities were complex—Nyx was the mother of the Fates, but they'd worked closely with Gaia in the past—but standing in front of one of Gaia's own direct descendants… It definitely had me questioning whether I was being too trusting.

He nodded, huffing once again. The puffs of smoke that came out of his nostrils were actually quite endearing.

Maybe the lack of food was affecting me more than I thought.

"What should I call you?" I asked. He didn't reply, staring blankly. "Does your name start with 'A'?"

Shake.

"B?"

Shake. We went down the alphabet, and I did my best to make it look as though I was totally fine and comfortable having this bizarre conversation with a monster while standing ankle-deep in mud. Just a normal... whatever day it was.

"T?" I asked tiredly. *Nod.* "U— Wait, T? Your name starts with T?"

Another nod. He looked quite pleased with himself.

"Well, let's just call you 'T' for now, okay? What is it that you want, T? Are you looking for something? Someone, perhaps?"

T looked at me for a long moment, before his black and red bat wings lifted, beating the air hard enough to knock me back. And then he was rising into the air, and I was more confused than ever because maybe he didn't want anything at all?

Naïve. One day I'd learn not to be so naïve.

T's enormous hand wrapped around my waist, and I screamed louder than I ever had in my life as he dragged me into the sky.

THE SPIRIT OF DREAMS

CHAPTER 12

I fell, and I fell, and I *fell*.

I fell for so long that I got bored of falling. Objectively, I was moving quickly, but it didn't feel fast because the walls were just the same unchanging smooth rock the entire way down. This was really not as fun as the fly-running I'd been doing before. I wished I was still doing that.

What would happen when I got to the bottom? Would I go splat?

Like an egg? Something in the recesses of my mind told me eggs went splat.

And if I didn't *splat*, what then? I should have asked more questions about what saving Dare entailed if only to make sure I was doing it right.

Eventually, the landscape changed, just a little and in the worst possible way.

It was getting darker. Not from below, but from *above*. As though the pit was closing over top of me, shutting me in forever. Except it wasn't all the way dark. What did that mean? I hoped it meant that the entrance in the human realm that Dare was going to use had closed and that he was safely ensconced in the land of the living. Yes, that would be ideal. That was what I wanted for the friend I didn't remember.

It was a good final thought to hold onto before I splattered like an egg, I decided. I didn't have any happy memories to hold onto, but I could still think happy *thoughts*.

Somehow, without being able to see anything, I got the impression that the ground was drawing nearer. Like the way I'd felt the memory of heat on my body by the fire river, I felt the memory of icy cold now. The air had changed somehow, though I struggled to put my finger on exactly what it was that was different. This had to be Tartarus.

I let out a muffled yelp of surprise as I was snatched out of thin air by some invisible force, and I got the impression of being sniffed at for a moment before being deposited roughly on the ground with a grunt of disapproval.

"What are you? You are not dead. What am I meant to do with you? I knew the underworld was busy, but I did not expect Hades to start throwing undead into the pit. What are you being punished for?"

"Are you... Tartarus?" I asked the empty air, looking around for some indication of where the voice had come from.

There was a long pause. "Obviously."

"Right. Okay. I'm not being punished. I jumped in the pit voluntarily."

"Ach. I am sending you back to Hades. You are strange, I don't want you in my realm."

"No, no, wait. Can't I look around, at least? This is the famous *Tartarus*, it's not every day that a mortal gets to visit here. Can I just hang around for a few minutes?"

Was Tartarus famous? I assumed so, based on the way Phlegethon had talked about it. I really should have asked more questions.

"It *is* a very impressive realm," the invisible god mused to himself. "And I have never sent anyone back before. Perhaps I will show it to you, and then you can return to Hades and tell him the ways in which my realm is superior. It would do him well to remember that I am far older and more impressive than he is."

"Um, yeah. For sure. I'll definitely tell him how much cooler this place is."

Phlegethon had mentioned Hades was the King of the Underworld and Tartarus was the king down here, and apparently, there was a sense of competition there. I could work with that.

Some unseen force hit me behind the knees, and I fell backward but instead of landing on my ass on the ground, I was being lifted into the air, sitting on some kind of floating platform.

"I will carry you. You are small and weak."

Nope, not a platform. I was definitely sitting on a god's hand. This guy must be bigger than Hecate because there was no way I would have fit in her totally average-sized hand.

Note to self: gods come in different shapes and sizes.

"It's quite hard to see," I hedged, squinting into the darkness. "I'm guessing my eyesight isn't as good as yours."

He let out a long suffering sigh, and suddenly the space around us was illuminated by bluish *things* in the rocky cavern overhead. Moving bluish things. Worms, perhaps?

"They're pretty," I murmured, staring up at them. They were writhing around the ceiling, coiling into shapes among themselves in a way that seemed intentional—like a form of communication.

"Yes," Tartarus grunted. "They are magnificent, but Erebus is the god of darkness, and he dwells in this realm. For his comfort, they usually extinguish their natural glow."

I nodded in the general direction of where I thought Tartarus was, but he was still invisible, even with the light. Maybe that was just how he looked all the time? Or maybe he preferred the anonymity? It seemed rude to ask him to reveal himself either way.

Another note to self: there is an Erebus, god of darkness.

There probably weren't that many gods, right? Ten seemed like a nice, round number. I'd already encountered Persephone, Hecate, and Tartarus, and heard of Hades and Erebus. Plus, there was Phlegethon, whatever he was. Surely, that must be about half.

"Did you know there was a pit open from the human realm all the way here?" I asked.

"You can't have come through that, or you'd have a real body. You're a soul, but not." My in-between state was clearly bothering him, which was fair enough. It was bothering me too. "And of course I know about it. My son used it to go to the upperworld."

"Oh. Just for a visit?"

There was a long moment of silence before Tartarus spoke again. "You don't know much about gods, do you?"

"I don't think so. I'm the Spirit of Dreams, or I was. Something happened to my brain to save me. Well, maybe save me. It's still up in the air."

Tartarus hummed. "Curious. Do you have a name, the Spirit of Dreams?"

That was a really great question. "No, I don't think so. Or not one

94

that anyone has told me."

"Then I shall call you Oneiroi."

"Why?"

He harrumphed. "That is what a Spirit of Dreams is, the kind of daimon you are. And if you are an Oneiroi, then you must visit your spiritual mother while you are in this realm. I will take you to her."

Huh. I had a spiritual mother? That sounded cool. I swayed back and forth with every step Tartarus took, making his way through the cavernous tunnel to wherever it was he was taking me.

"As for my son, no. I doubt I will ever see him again." There was a sadness in his voice that I recognized, that called to my own. Although I couldn't remember the ones I'd loved, I was familiar with the sense of loss, the gaping wound in my chest that I doubted would ever heal. "Typhoeus has been either used or imprisoned his entire life. He wants to be free. He will never return here voluntarily."

"That's good... right? That he's free now. Even though you'll miss him. There's a lot of things I don't know, but I'm pretty sure freedom is better than imprisonment."

"He's *not* free," Tartarus corrected sharply. "He only *thinks* he is free. Typhoeus is a monster, he will be hunted to the death, and his blood will be on my hands for not finding a way to make him happy here."

The biting edge to his voice had softened into sadness by the time he finished speaking, and while I was several leagues out of my depth, I really wanted to reassure this guy. After all, despair was one of the few emotions I'd become acquainted with recently, and honestly, *no one* deserved to feel that way.

"Far be it from me to argue, since you're an all-knowing god and all, but it sounds like it would have been pretty hard to make him happy if he never wanted to be here in the first place, you know? What exactly could you have done?" I shrugged. "I'm never going to be happy in the underworld, no matter how nice and peaceful that empty island I was on is. It isn't where I want to be."

"An island, hm? Now your strange in-between life makes more sense. You traveled here from the Isles of the Blessed. What a strange mortal you are to leave such a paradise and come here. Perhaps your spiritual mother can elaborate on why that is."

A woman, a goddess, stepped forward, veiled from head-to-toe in black fabric, with a silver crown over top that glinted in the blue light from above.

Huh. Suddenly I was glad Tartarus was invisible. It made him much less intimidating to talk to.

"Do you remember me, the Spirit of Dreams?" she asked, her voice smooth and yet a little haunting.

"Um, no. I'm sorry."

"Don't be sorry. It is a good thing you don't remember me, a miracle even. Perhaps there is hope for you yet. I am Nyx."

"Why is he here?" Tartarus asked her, his tone far grumpier than it had been with me.

"You know why."

"You said it would be a woman."

"I underestimated my Spirit of Dreams," Nyx replied affectionately. "Why not him? The prophecy was delivered to both of them. Why should he not snatch that thread of fate before it could touch the one he loved? There is a tragic sort of romance in there. Perhaps one that feels familiar to you, Tartarus."

Tartarus made a rumbling growl noise that had me feeling the teensiest bit insecure about sitting in the palm of his hand.

"I only agreed to *listen* to what the girl had to say, nothing else. And this is not the girl. I did not agree to this."

"Maybe I can help a little with that. You see, Dare—another one of my love's soul bonds who is apparently a friend of mine—was planning on coming here, but Hecate told me he was going to *die* if he did, and while I can't remember him at all, I obviously couldn't let that happen. I don't know him or Grace or anything that is going on up there, but maybe Dare was trying to take Grace's place to spare her the same way I took his place to spare him? And maybe that's how love works?"

There was a sudden swooping sensation, and I realized I was heading for the ground, but Tartarus seemed to be heading down with me. Was he... sitting on the ground? The way I was sitting on his hand? It was very unsettling not knowing what he looked like.

"You want to save loved ones you don't even remember?"

"It sounds weird when you say it like that," I agreed. "The thing is, Dare promised to save me if I ended up in the underworld, and that doesn't seem like the kind of promise you'd make for just anyone, you know? That doesn't seem like the kind of promise you'd make for just anyone, you know? That sounds like a good friend who really had my back, and I definitely don't want a guy like that to die. Besides, I'm a bit dead already, so it really makes more sense for me to jump into the mystery pit, like, on a logistical level."

"Do you actually know *why* you're here?" Nyx asked slowly. "What you're meant to be doing?"

"Well... Okay, no. Not exactly. But I'll do whatever it takes to protect the people I don't remember caring about."

It was very unnerving being the focus of such intense attention by two very much not-human beings. Their stares felt weighty, and while I'd come down here just to help my forgotten friend, it was all starting to feel a lot *bigger* than that.

"What if they are not who you think they are?" Tartarus asked quietly. "Perhaps you do this for them, and go back to them in triumph, only to discover that it was your sacrifices that had made you useful to begin with, not you."

Nyx was silent, and a calm sense of purpose came over me. I didn't know why exactly I was here, but I was guessing it had something to do with this. This conversation, this moment, this shared fear.

What if my friends and my loves forgot about me the way I forgot about them? Worse, what if they *didn't*, and by disappearing from their lives, I'd caused them some kind of pain? In coming here, I'd accepted the risk that I may never return to them, that I may get stuck in the underworld forever. That decision might hurt those I'd once cared about, or maybe they'd be relieved that *they* didn't have to come down here and they'd never think of me again? My brain kept flip-flopping between terrible outcomes, trying to figure out which one was the worst option.

"I'm very worried about that, actually. How did you know?"

"We're talking about you," Tartarus replied sharply. *Right, right, got it.* Sore spot. I blew out a long breath, trying to focus on the positive.

"Well... I figure I'd rather assume the best intentions and be wrong than assume the worst intentions and be wrong. And if I'm super lucky and find my way back to them someday, and it turns out they're total assholes, I'll still have made it back. I can start over."

"And if you don't?"

I shrugged. "I don't remember my life before anyway."

"Perhaps it is good you are here. You, with your empty mind and strange hopefulness. You are unburdened by the realities of your situation because you are too uninformed to understand it."

"Um... Yeah. I guess so," I agreed hesitantly, trying to decide if he was insulting me or not. Nyx was just quietly watching, saying nothing, so maybe she agreed that it was a good thing that my head was so empty. *Cool, cool, cool.*

"We are going for a walk," Tartarus announced. I grabbed onto his palm, steadying myself as best I could as he rose. "To the very depths of my realm where no mortal has visited before. Nyx will not be joining us."

"As you wish," she murmured, stepping away. "You have already accomplished more than you know, the Spirit of Dreams. Sometimes, just making the decision is half the battle."

"Okay." I really wished someone would just sit me down and explain what the fuck was going on. "See you later, I guess."

She laughed lightly. "I certainly hope not."

RIOT

CHAPTER 13

Souls were bossy.

It was a weird realization to have because they were dead and all—some of them had a kind of Renaissance vibe that made me wonder just how long it had been since Thanatos had paid this place a visit—but their deadness didn't stop them from having strong opinions.

They couldn't speak to me, but they could obviously speak to each other. And they argued. Like, a lot. There was lots of silent shouting and gesticulations going on while I sat on the ground and watched. Ultimately, I didn't even need to hear them to know what the plan was going to be.

This was a place of death, and I wasn't dead. There was no question that they were going to use me as Fate Bait. Not when I had all that fresh aliveness going for me.

I wandered around while they debated, occasionally stopping to pick off the sticky cobwebs that clung to my hair and clothes. What the fuck kind of spiders lived here? Giant ghost ones with toxic glue webs? Probably.

Imagine being able to visit anywhere on earth and picking this place.

The Fates must be creepy as fuck if this was the kind of place they visited to chill, and it didn't bode well for me at all.

"It'd be cool if you guys could make, like, a human-ghost spiderweb," I said out loud, ninety-nine percent sure I was just talking to myself, but finding the oppressive silence more than a little suffocating. I linked my fingers together miming a net and squished it down on an imaginary opponent, complete with sound effects.

Shit was dire, I really needed some regular mortal companions to converse with. Arete had been bossy, garbage company but the ghosts were worse. I missed my Gracie. Dare better be guarding her with his fucking life. If she had so much as a chipped nail, I was going to go full Wild on him.

As the souls debated, the air began to change, so slowly at first it took me a moment to notice. The second I did, so did they, disappearing into nothingness and leaving me standing in the dank, dark building alone. Alone except for the thousands of ghosts, and the three frightening deities who were undoubtedly around here somewhere, lurking in the darkness.

They smelled weird.

Somehow, that was the first thing I noticed. The building had already smelled like death and decay, but the arrival of the Fates had added an extra layer to it. Like suddenly the place had devolved to a new level of grim. While it didn't look any different, I got the distinct impression that they were here in the room with me, as though I was being examined like a bug under a microscope.

Damn it. I really wished I'd had more time with the ghosts to come up with a game plan. Then again, the Fates were all-seeing, right? They'd probably known what I was going to do before I did. Why hadn't that occurred to me earlier? I was so screwed.

In a sudden flash of silvery light, the souls appeared, moving like one enormous monolith, converging on the center of the room. They crawled on top of each other, and my heart beat out of my fucking chest as manic ghost faces peered down on me, the souls linking their phantom limbs together to create a webbed dome of dead people right above our heads. Holy fuck, they'd actually taken me up on my ghost human spiderweb idea?

Huh. Maybe Arete was right. Maybe I was a secret genius full of untapped potential. Couldn't the Fates just plow right through the ghost web if they wanted to, though?

The Fates blinked into sight as though they'd been startled out of invisibility, and a few of the souls, including my lady ghost friend, physically attached themselves to the goddesses, hanging off their backs like spider monkeys. I had entered the Twilight zone in more ways than one.

For the love of all that was good in the world, these three were fucking terrifying. They each wore floor-length white robes with white hoods pulled up over glimmering ice-white hair, and all three of them had white gauze wrapped around the top half of their face, hiding their eyes and top of their noses. I squinted at the material, struck by the strange way it sank where I would have expected it to rise.

Did they... Did they not have eyeballs?

They weren't hunched with age, and their hands didn't look any older than mine, but they had deep wrinkles on their faces. It was an altogether disturbing combination, and they were only distinguishable from each because of the implements they had hanging off the silver chain belts they wore around their waists. Arete had given me a rundown, and I did my best to identify them while the souls got themselves into place. I assumed Clotho was the one with the spindle. Another, Lachesis, had no instrument, but Arete said she measured the thread between her hands. The last one, with the scissors, must be Atropos. "The Inflexible", Arete had called her, and I could see that just from the lower half of her face. On closer inspection, unlike her sisters, Atropos' mouth was set in a grim line, the frown lines hinting that might be her default expression. She was the first to speak, and it sounded like her vocal cords had been doused in rust.

"How intriguing. We cannot disrespect the dead by physically moving through this barrier, and we cannot flash away with these unmoored souls attached to us, trapped as they are in this godless in-between. I think we are *caught*, sisters."

"Indeed, we are caught." Lachesis' voice and mannerisms were more serene, and I was pretty sure I liked her more. "By a common daimon of middling talent, the most wholly mediocre of the Prophêtis' soul bonds. How curious."

What the fuck.

How *rude*.

"Yeah, well, I did trap you, talentless commoner or otherwise," I snapped, standing up straight and trying to look less mediocre. "And you're stuck here until you answer my questions."

"I do hope you didn't promise too much," Clotho replied, idly twisting the spindle with her fingers. "They will not be kind to you if you cannot deliver."

"You sound very certain of that." Thanatos better live up to expectations, or I was fucked.

"Oh yes."

Lachesis suddenly plucked at the air as though she was catching a fly between two fingers. I startled as a gray thread materialized, as thin as a spider web. I couldn't see the beginning or end, just the part she was holding, head cocked to the side at an unnatural angle.

She didn't act like she had no eyeballs. I guessed they had some other way of seeing things.

"You are rather interesting, considering how mediocre you are," Lachesis observed.

"You really aren't doing great things for my ego," I muttered. *Don't fuck around, Riot. You don't want to hang out here any longer than you have to.* "I'm here to find out how to restore the soul bonds."

"Ach," Atropos hissed. "Centuries of work, undone in one tantrum. We are not restoring anything. Show him," she insisted, nudging Lachesis with her elbow.

I don't know how one gave the stink eye when they didn't have eyes, but Lachesis managed it. With practiced ease, she began pinching the air between her fingers as though she was catching tiny specks of dust, drawing more and more threads out until there was an entire web separating me from the sisters. Clotho never stopped twirling the spindle between her fingers, and I felt vaguely nauseous as Atropos snipped away at some threads, leaving space for Lachesis to reveal more.

I was watching people die right in front of my eyes in the most abstract of ways.

"Do you see these loose threads?" Lachesis asked, holding one up for me to see. It was so thin, I could barely make it out—far thinner than the threads of life. "These were bonds—this was once tied to its match. Now it hangs loose, the lovers' knot undone by Gaia's malice."

"And you won't... tie it back up again?" I asked, floundering slightly at how to describe it. It hadn't seemed like a knot when I visualized the bond, it was smooth and seamless in my head.

"That part is easy," Clotho explained, still spinning, spinning, spinning. "It is the *who* that is time-consuming. We spent so long assigning souls as matches, maintaining Gaia's tradition when she handed the fate of the

104

agathos to us. Too much was undone for us to possibly redo."

Okay. Okay, that wasn't what I wanted to hear, but it also wasn't necessarily *bad*.

For me, at least.

"Could we fix it ourselves?" I pressed. "Tie the threads back together on our own, to whoever we choose?"

Atropos leaned forward, and I could have sworn that behind the bandage, she narrowed her non-existent eyes at me. "Do you think you are better qualified to choose who should be bonded than we are?"

"I mean, no offense, but yeah, I think I'm better qualified to choose who I should be bonded to than you are. That every individual person *should* get to choose who they tie their life to."

I thought of Grace's parents—of the dad who'd helped me into the agathos temple when they'd snatched Grace away, and helped us escape when I'd gotten her out. How could he possibly be a perfect match for Grace's wretched mother? The other dad, the one who'd come to Grace's apartment and found me there, now *those two* seemed made for each other. Chance wasn't like them, though.

Atropos sniffed, unimpressed, but Clotho looked thoughtful. "It would save us a job. In fact, any mortal would be able to form a bond—agathos, daimon, or human—if we passed the gift on to them. They wouldn't know their soul's perfect counterpart—or *counterparts*, as it were—"

"—but how *fun*," Lachesis interrupted, sounding gleeful. Atropos moodily snipped at a few more threads. "We do so love when some plucky mortal twists their thread in an unexpected direction. Imagine the possibilities if they could set their own bonds—irrevocably tying themselves to the most unsuitable of partners in a fit of short-sighted lust. We shall never be bored again," she declared triumphantly.

On the one hand, this was what I wanted. What I'd come here for. On the other, these three were bad vibes, and it sort of felt as though I was the one who'd been caught in a trap.

"Not that anyone asked me," Atropos said bitterly because she was obviously the grumpy, morose one out of their trio. The Riot of the group, so to speak. "But mortals find a way to abuse every small piece of power we've ever given them. Do we really need to give them yet another thing? They'll use it as some kind of entrapment to bind unwilling lovers to them, I guarantee it."

Such little faith. Also a very valid consideration.

Lachesis waved away her concern. "The bond already can only be formed if both parties are willing."

"It will be weaponized," Atropos insisted. "Those with material wealth will use it as an incentive. Soul bonds will be *purchased*."

"Ach, you are so pessimistic." Lachesis huffed in irritation. "So we add a few extra steps to make the process more complex, more intimate."

"Like what?" I asked hopefully. This sounded good. *Possible*. All I wanted was Grace back, our bond strong and brilliant and permanent. I'd never ask the gods for another thing if I could have that.

"Hush," Atropos said, glaring at me. "We are discussing things far beyond your intellect. You could not even *begin* to understand the complexities of souls and the way they connect."

She was probably right, but she was also an asshole.

Clotho kept spinning, quiet and thoughtful, even as both of her sisters turned their full attention to her, waiting for her to speak. "I will side with Lachesis in this instance."

Atropos aggressively clipped a thread, and I winced in sympathy. Did it hurt more to die when she was so rough with the scissors?

"*Fine*. Don't complain to me when it all goes poorly," Atropos grumbled. She hung the scissors off the belt at her waist, and Clotho did the same with her spindle. The three of them began twisting their hands through the air in movements that were synchronized but not quite the same.

More threads appeared in what I'd thought were gaps, the entire web illuminating gold in flashes so bright and sudden, I had to close my eyes before my head exploded.

But still, it was happening. *Something* was happening. Mr. Mediocrity might have actually come through—maybe I could go back to Grace with my head held high and beg her to be my bonded again. *Hold on, Gracie. I'll be there as soon as I can.*

"Get comfortable, Moros," Atropos called. "This will take a while."

GAIA

CHAPTER 14

I waited.

Soon, any moment now, Tartarus would throw the Oneiroi out of his realm. He'd been an unexpected development—a tidy workaround for the Prophêtis so that neither she nor her very much *alive* soul bonds had to risk their mortal bodies to jump into the pit.

Perhaps I should have seen it coming. Then again, self-sacrifice was a very odd concept to me. Something wholly mortal and separate from my life. Why would the Oneiroi throw himself into Tartarus when he still inhabited the space between life and death? He'd thrown himself *intentionally* onto the wrong side of the veil.

Maybe he was an idiot?

As I recalled, Oneiroi didn't *tend* to be idiots, but there were always exceptions. Undoubtedly, if he *was* an exception, it made sense that the Fates would have paired him with their favored little Prophêtis.

The ground rolled restlessly in irritation as I waited. Why hadn't

Tartarus thrown him out yet? I'd already demonstrated how easily it could be done. The respectful thing to do would be for him to follow my lead, and my irritation grew at my fourth consort the longer he took to act.

I supposed I had never loved Tartarus, certainly not in the way I loved Ouranos, but his lack of immediate cooperation was displeasing to me nonetheless. I had charged him with keeping both our son and the Olympians safely tucked away in his realm, and he'd already failed on one count.

I had only let him off easily for Typhoeus' escape because it suited my needs. Wherever my son went, mortals scattered. Oh, they'd leave him quaint little offerings in the hopes of appeasing him, but they were undoubtedly terrified and wished to avoid his wrath at all costs. As an additional bonus, he'd snatched up little Grace and was dragging her around the Mediterranean, preventing her from being able to fulfill the prophecy herself.

It was all very entertaining, and really, the *least* Typhoeus could do. I had given him life, after all. And eventually, Tartarus would do his duty, because his loyalty was to me and me alone. In the meantime, perhaps I would bestow some favor on the *mortals* who had shown me loyalty.

Everywhere agathos lived, at least a few of them had congregated in support of me, and were making their way to known sacred locations, intending to hold those spaces in my honor. I'd been content to watch and do nothing—why should I help them after their centuries of lazy worship?— but now I found myself willing to intervene. After all, the Prophêtis had a soul bond wandering around with a toy army of blood and dragon teeth; why shouldn't those gathering under my metaphorical banner be better equipped?

Besides, why not put the Prophêtis' pretty little army to the test? It would give me something to amuse myself with while Tartarus took his time doing whatever he was doing with the Oneiroi.

A sizable group of agathos—and some human followers—were already approaching the Spartoi, and I sprouted a row of olive trees in their path, directing them to where they would encounter the Keres and his forces. For now, I would provide them with enough food to survive, and perhaps some good quality rocks for throwing since they weren't outfitted with swords and shields and armor as the Spartoi were. Yes, that was enough to be going on.

It hadn't escaped my knowledge that this strange collection had probably been my least favorite subsect of the agathos population. Those who'd twisted my doctrine into something that suited their own interests so entirely that I scarcely recognized it with their enormous vehicles and concrete-covered towns. I disliked them, and yet they fought for my cause, advocates for maintaining the world as it was. Let them demonstrate their loyalty. Let them make amends for their past behavior.

I wasn't going to go silently into obscurity, without so much as a final battle to my name. Until Tartarus fulfilled his duties to me as his beloved and consort, I would take down as many traitors as I could, and remind humanity just why I was a goddess worth worshipping.

WILD

CHAPTER 15

We all came to a stop as one, without instruction, without intention.

We stilled because the earth had stilled. The wind died, the waves flattened, and the already limited sounds of life on this ravaged planet went silent.

It wasn't peaceful. It was eerie and unsettling.

The taste of impending battle grew sharper, the phantom scent of blood in the air more potent. Whatever this stillness was, it wasn't a sign of peace but the uneasy quiet before a war. The night before battle, when the soldiers were restless, filled with a fear they disguised with overconfident bluster because they didn't want to believe—couldn't let themselves believe—that they would become a casualty of combat.

The metallic tang of blood filled my lungs and coated my tongue, a sensory memory of violence, calling to me like a siren song. *Soon.* If soldiers of Gaia were coming to meet us on the battlefield, then I was going to unleash every drop of Keres rage I possessed on them and I wouldn't regret it for an instant. I welcomed it.

The breeze picked up again, lazily winding its way around us like a caress. The ocean moved, waves lapping at the shore as though someone had hit the unpause button. The Spartoi moved restlessly around me, and Theras and I exchanged a knowing look.

Something had changed. In a split second of perfect quiet, something was different. An image of the Fates as giant spiders came into my mind, weaving new threads as chess pieces moved across the board, changing the game in real-time.

But *what* was the change?

Had Grace been successful?

That thought was bittersweet. The idea of her traveling to Tartarus alone...

Fuck. I wanted her to succeed; I wanted a safe, peaceful world with food to eat so that she would be happy and never have to worry about anything again. I just didn't want Grace to be the one who had to do it. My throat ached with the need to scream at the injustice of it all.

She's okay. Grace will be fine. Bullet saw a bright future ahead of her.

Somehow that future never seemed even remotely within reach.

I looked back at the Spartoi, finding them anxiously glancing skyward. With a sigh that I almost managed to hide, I gestured to Theras to let them go ahead and pray. For the Spartoi, who seemed to have vague memories of an ancient time, praying to the gods was their version of self-care. They weren't just making offerings and expressing gratitude, they were making sense of the world. It didn't hurt me to pause for a moment to let them do what they needed to do, even if in my experience, deities were selfish assholes.

I flopped down to the ground while they went about their worship, pulling out a few nuts from my satchel to stave off the worst of my hunger. One of the farms we'd passed must have once produced almonds, and while

112

the trees had died off in the darkness, we'd found stores that had been miraculously untouched by scavengers. The owners hadn't been so lucky and their bodies were well atrophied by the time we'd arrived; but we'd made sure to give them proper burial rites after clearing out the entirety of their food supplies.

The Spartoi were all distracted with their worship, which gave me a moment of silence.

I hated moments of silence.

When we were marching—toward what I hoped was the direction of Ephesus and Grace—or when we were sitting around a fire, teaching each other ways of communicating despite our language barrier, or when I was so exhausted that I fell down, asleep, on the hard ground of wherever we were staying, I didn't have time to think.

But in moments like this, when I still had enough energy to carry on, and the Spartoi were distracted, and it was just me and my head...

That was when the walls pressed in. When oxygen felt hard to come by, and grief tightened its grip around my throat.

"I wish we had more time. There are so many things I'd do differently. I knew this moment was coming, and I still let fear rule my actions. I should have made the most of the time we had..."

Bullet's last words to me had haunted me from the moment I'd shaken off the bloodlust. Not just because I missed him—which I did, terribly—but because I felt the crush of time just as keenly now. For whatever reason, the gods had given me more time, even though Bullet was the one who deserved it. And what was I doing with it? Was I making the most of it? Each day felt painfully long and like it passed all too quickly at once.

If these were my last days on this earth, I hadn't made the most of them. Far from Grace, separated from Riot and Dare, I just felt... lost.

"Stratēgós?" Theras hedged, gently breaking me out of my melancholy thoughts. I looked around, finding my handful of almonds gone and the Spartoi rising to their feet, dusting off their legs where they'd been kneeling in the dirt.

I nodded once, securing my bag back in place and heading to the front as the men fell into formation easily behind me and Theras.

Between my inability to speak or to understand anything but a few words of basic Ancient Greek, even after spending time on the road together, I struggled to ascertain exactly what the Spartoi *were*. They had the same physical needs as mortals, but they weren't human, daimon, or agathos. They had a sixth sense for battle, but didn't appear to crave it to the point of self-destruction the way Keres daimons did. They could move as a group and understand formations with almost no direction, but didn't seem *lost* without it, necessarily.

I had no idea what it meant for them if they were ever free, if the battles were over and they had nothing left to do. Would they sink back into the ground? Or would they have to find some kind of normalcy here in the upperworld?

We continued our march south, having moved back to the coastline after raiding farms further inland for food and shelter. Aside from the rising and setting sun giving us a sense of direction, the only thing I knew about where Grace was, was that it was near the coast. It wasn't much to go on, but it was something.

The sky rumbled overhead, a shadow spreading over us as we headed south past a sandy beach with the broken remnants of lounge chairs and umbrellas marring the landscape.

What the fuck is that? I thought, pausing to squint up at the sky.

There was... something flying over us. I had no idea what that something was, but it was not of this world, that was for fucking sure.

"Typhoeus!" someone shouted from the ranks. What the fuck was a Typhoeus? It had enormous black bat wings and what appeared to be two giant snakes for legs, and was absolutely terrifying. And as it flew closer, I realized that it was carrying something in its greenish-leathery hands.

No. No, it couldn't be.

Please not her.

"Prophêtis," Theras confirmed quietly, standing at my right. He was shaking slightly, and I'd never seen him look anything less than stoic and completely put together. "Grace."

I mouthed her name, reaching for the sky, helpless to do anything as she flew overhead. Grace was looking down—undoubtedly noticing the sea of plumed helmets—and I silently prayed to every deity there was that she'd see me. That she'd know I was here, and that I was coming for her.

My throat burned in violent protest as I attempted to scream her name, wishing I could speak, wishing I could *fly* so I could somehow get up there and steal her away. Stab that fucking beast in the eye and take my girl back. What was he going to do with her? She wasn't in Tartarus, but she was being carted around by what looked like a monster from the bowels of that prison, and only the very worst of the worst were sent there.

Had she attempted to enter Tartarus? Had that creature brought her back?

I took off at a run, the Spartoi falling into line behind me as we sprinted in the direction that the beast was flying. Had Grace seen me? Did she know I was following her? That I'd follow her anywhere?

My heart hurt to think of her up there, afraid and alone. Grace was tougher than she looked, full of more inner fire and compassion than anyone I'd ever met, but she wasn't meant to be by herself. Grace came alive around people. She was so full of love and light that it spilled out of her. I had to get to her.

"Wild!" Theras called, pointing at something falling from the sky up in the beast's wake, so tiny I wouldn't have seen it if it hadn't been catching the sunlight as it fell. It landed on the ground a few hundred feet away, and I picked up the pace, sprinting toward whatever it was.

I was breathing hard as I searched, unsure what I was looking for exactly but hoping it was some kind of sign. A glint of gold in the light caught my eye, and I fell to my knees in the dirt, picking up Grace's opal ring with shaky fingers. I knew it was some kind of symbolic agathos thing, probably some sort of puritanical bullshit that she didn't believe anymore, but I'd never seen her take it off.

Grace had seen me, she had to have. This was her way of letting me know, of offering me some kind of reassurance. She shouldn't be reassuring me. I should be reassuring *her*.

I gripped the ring tightly in my fist, the metal prongs that held the stone digging into my palm. I was going to find her and slip this back onto her finger in person. *I'm coming for you, Grace. I'll slay the monster and save the girl, and spend the rest of my life trying to be the man you deserve.*

THE SPIRIT OF DREAMS

CHAPTER 16

Tartarus set me down at the mouth of a well-lit cave, the entrance to it very much human-sized. Not... however big he was.

"You're not coming with me?" I asked, slightly forlorn.

He hesitated for a moment. "No."

"Oh. That's a shame. I like you, Tartarus. I think if my friends back in the upperworld were anything like you, I must have had quite a happy life."

I was being honest, and I thought that telling Tartarus the truth about how great I thought he was would make him feel better since he seemed pretty down about his son, but it seemed that I shocked him into silence instead. Maybe I was meant to be more formal with him? Say something more respectful and profound?

"I appreciate that, tiny Oneiroi. You and your blustering ignorance have made a profound impact on the way I think about mortals' lives. You are not as insignificant as I supposed you were."

O...kay? I couldn't tell if everyone I'd met was kind of rude, or if that was just my confusion about the world talking.

"There are some gods here for you to meet. I want you to speak to them."

"Okay. About anything in particular?"

"The things you talked about with me. Life. Love. Humanity."

"Just talk to them?" There was a test in here somewhere, but I didn't understand the parameters. Probably because I was swanning around blind and stupid, and apparently that was an advantage.

Tartarus hummed. "Nyx spoke to you of choice. Well, I have a choice of my own to make. A love of my own to consider. A son I can no longer protect."

"And these gods... they can help?"

"Perhaps. Or perhaps they will hinder. The decision is in your hands."

That seemed very serious. Like the kind of thing someone with more knowledge of the situation should be entrusted with.

Tartarus gently pushed me forward, a ripple of strange pressure passing over my skin as he guided me through the mouth of the cave. Was it some kind of invisible wall? I turned around, trying to stick my hand back through and finding it solid though I couldn't see anything blocking the way.

Okay. Okay, not great.

Hopefully, he'd come back and let me out. We were friends, right?

I wandered through the short tunnel into a large but comfortable cavern. It was filled with fancy carved furniture made of both wood and marble, with tapestries, rugs, and blankets covering most of the hard surfaces, giving the place an oddly cozy feel, despite its cave basement location.

"Well, aren't you a little treat," a feminine voice purred, making me jump. Somehow, a woman—a goddess—had snuck up behind me, and she was leaning down to speak in my ear, twisting my hair around her finger before trailing it down the side of my neck in a way that felt vaguely threatening.

I didn't like her touching me, I decided. Somewhere out there, there were people who loved me, and it felt wrong to have someone else touching me like this.

"Has Tartarus finally sent us some entertainment?" she asked, her voice a low rasp in my ear.

"I don't think so, sorry. I'm just here to talk."

Her hand froze in place for a moment before she withdrew completely, stalking around to face me and looking me up and down.

I swallowed thickly, beyond intimidated by the goddess' appearance. She had curly dark red hair that fell past her waist, and the most perfectly symmetrical face, with full lips and bright golden eyes. Her body was draped in almost completely sheer purple fabric, showcasing generous curves, and I focused my gaze somewhere over her left shoulder, suddenly feeling very guilty for even noticing them.

"No need to be shy, halfling. It's only natural that you look—I am the Goddess of Beauty, you can't help being drawn to my... charms."

"Um, that's okay. I don't think I'm a halfling, I'm the Spirit of Dreams."

"You're half dead, half alive," she clarified, narrowing her golden eyes at me. Oh dear, this was not off to a good start, I didn't think. She seemed annoyed.

"Aphrodite, this is the *prophecy*," another goddess said quietly, appearing at the far end of the room. She had more of an air of authority than the one I'd been speaking to—partly because of her stiff, white drapey dress and the impressive cloak of peacock feathers that trailed on the floor behind her, secured with a gold broach at her collarbone. Her hair and eyes were dark, a gold not-quite-crown sitting atop her head.

I stood up a little straighter, feeling as though I was under scrutiny as she approached, looking me up and down.

"I wouldn't get your hopes up, Hera," Aphrodite replied, staring at me. "Surely, this rather unimpressive creature isn't the hero that was promised. His arms are like olive branches."

Was that rude? I was pretty sure it was rude.

Rudeness, everywhere. Maybe it was a god thing.

"I think the prophecy was for my soul bond. Her name is Grace, and we love each other. But I don't want her to get hurt, and my friend Dare—also her soul bond—probably doesn't want that either, so I'm here."

"Prophecies are foretold, yes," a golden-haired man drawled, flopping dramatically down onto a sofa in the corner. "But above all else, they are delivered. If the prophecy was delivered to you, then it is yours. If it was delivered to many of you, and you acted on it first, then it is yours. You certainly got here first."

He picked up a stringed instrument, plucking idly at it while watching me from his spot at the furthest end of the room. Whoever this god was, he was deceptively pretty—with shoulder-length blonde curls and delicate features—but even from here, I could spot a hint of callousness in his eyes and smile. *Humanity*, Tartarus had said. I wasn't sold so far.

"That's Apollo," Aphrodite said, leaning in close to inspect me again. It was deeply uncomfortable. "He knows all about prophecy."

"Oh. Well, I know nothing about any of that." I thought about asking them to elaborate, but I didn't want to let my new friend down. *Life. Love. Humanity. That's what he'd said.*

"Don't you?" I hadn't seen many people in my life—that I could remember at least—but the man who approached me was by far the most beautiful, with dark hair, a sharp jaw, and full pouting lips. "Are you lying to us? I recognize your voice, Oneiroi. I am Dionysus. I've heard your prayers. I make it a point to remember those who host orgies in my name, you know."

I blinked at him, his words taking a moment to register. "I hosted a what? No, that doesn't sound right. I'm in love, you see. With two people. So I don't think I'd have done anything like that."

The god hummed, circling me with his head tilted to one side. "There's no question it was you, but something has been done to you, hasn't it? Your mind isn't what it was. Do you remember who I am? Who any of us are?"

"You're gods. Tartarus told me." It came out a smidge more defensive than I'd intended.

"And who are *you*?" Dionysus pressed. "Do you know?"

"I'm the Spirit of Dreams. I'm an Oneiroi. I'm a daimon. I'm beloved of Grace."

Aphrodite sighed, all but swooning onto a long wooden couch, draped with blankets. "Oh, how sweet."

"How tragic, more like," Dionysus muttered, taking a swig of something from a golden goblet.

"He is rather old for an Oneiroi." A *mountain* of a god strolled up to me, the others parting for him like water. He made the high ceiling of this strange cavern-palace seem low. His skin was golden, but everything else was silver—from his long curled hair, to his thick beard, to his eyes. While he didn't *need* the symbol to convey authority, he wore a crown of leaves on top of his head. "Someone has extended his life by removing his memories. How interesting."

"Is it?" I asked, staring up at him. If I were checking for signs of humanity, I'd say that was a negative strike, wasn't it? There was no compassion there, no empathy. He looked at me as though I was a bug under a microscope, and I decided I didn't like that feeling much.

I couldn't let Tartarus down by choosing wrong. Tartarus seemed like he'd suffered enough, I didn't want to add to that.

The god stared back for a long moment, his face unreadable before his beard twitched. "Ah, I see. All this time we expected a Prophêtis, a confident young woman with the ear of the gods, finding her way past Tartarus through violence or cunning to liberate us, golden armor gleaming in the firelight—"

"With a sword," another god piped up, head-to-toe in golden armor of his own and a wistful look in his eye. "A sword with a name, as all the best swords have."

The enormous silver god cut him an irritated look. "Yes, perhaps that is what we expected, but that isn't you."

Well, no. In every possible way, that wasn't me.

"Instead what we have is Tartarus' conscience. Come, sit. It is a heavy burden of duty for any mortal to carry."

"Would it be rude of me to ask your name?" I said hesitantly, taking the seat he gestured to because he didn't seem like the kind of guy I'd win an argument with on my best day.

"I am Zeus, Father of Gods and Men, god of the sky, weather, kings and fate, known also as the Cloud-Gatherer. Come now, halfling, the Spirit of Dreams. Ask your questions. Tell us of your humanity, and we will tell you of your history."

GRACE

CHAPTER 17

I'd seen Wild.

For one brief, beautiful moment, I'd seen him. He was alive. He was safe, and reunited with the Spartoi. I had no idea how he'd gotten here—I wasn't even entirely sure where *here* was, but I'd been watching the ground, trying desperately to remember the route we'd taken so I could find my way back again, and T had covered a *lot* of ground. More than Wild could have realistically covered on foot, which meant there was some kind of divine force at work here.

The wind had stolen my voice every time I'd tried to scream for him, and as much as I pleaded with T to land, to turn around, he wouldn't.

I had to admit, all things considered, T was quite gentle. It wasn't as though he couldn't crush me—he was entirely capable of it. That he was choosing to gently cradle me in his terrifying large hands meant that he very intentionally didn't want to hurt me.

I was clinging to that sliver of hope with everything I had.

"Please don't fly us over the ocean," I whispered as the bright blue

Mediterranean Sea crashed against the shore below us. I wasn't sure I'd ever get back again if he flew me to a different country.

Fortunately, T banked left suddenly, landing with surprising gentleness on what appeared to be a castle. It was definitely an old structure made of stone, and it had an incredible view over a small seaside town and a quiet harbor.

"What is this place?"

I don't know why I insisted on speaking to him when he never replied. Maybe it was just for my own peace of mind.

T shuffled around, serpent legs slithering over the stone. The rest of the castle, the rest of the town was coated in a fine layer of dust from the dry earth that spread over everything every time the wind changed. Not this spot, though. And T wasn't looking around as though this was unfamiliar territory.

He'd been here before.

I wouldn't say he seemed *at home*, per se, but he certainly seemed more comfortable here than I'd seen him anywhere else. I glanced down, trying to see the town below, to deduce if there was a single person around, and seeing no one. Maybe that was why he was comfortable here.

"T," I said gently, trembling like a leaf, still surveying the town. "Why are we here?"

I waited for his huff of annoyance, but he surprised me by pinching the top of my skull with enormous fingers and lifting my head, forcing me to look out at the gold-streaked horizon.

"You want me to watch the sunset?" I hedged, the words sounding entirely ridiculous as I voiced them. I glanced up in time to see T nod, this time accompanied by an affirmative grunt. "Oh. Well, okay then. We can watch the sunset."

I had some very real, urgent issues that needed addressing, but they could wait until the sun had gone down.

The sky slowly turned golden orange, reflecting off the surface of the water and bathing the houses below us in warm light. With only the sound of the waves gently lapping at the shore, I could admit that it was surprisingly peaceful, and my nerves settled enough that I at least stopped trembling.

After so long in darkness, there was nothing more startlingly beautiful than the light. Suddenly I wondered if T and I had that in common.

"You were in Tartarus," I stated quietly. *Grunt.* "And it's dark there?" *Grunt again.*

Maybe the most straightforward answer was the right one.

"It is beautiful," I murmured, not entirely sure if he wanted me to speak or not. "We had no sun here for just a few days—Nyx cast a veil of darkness across the earth. I didn't appreciate the sun enough until it was gone. We should all take some time to watch the sunset."

T grunted again but was otherwise silent, and I didn't say anything else until the golden light had disappeared completely beyond the horizon, the darkness closing in.

Now what?

"Where are all the people?" I asked, climbing out of T's relaxed grip to stand at the edge of the balcony, staring out over the silent houses. He came to stand next to me, legs slithering over the stone, and I could have sworn he looked slightly sheepish. "Did they run away?"

He nodded.

"Did you breathe fire? It's quite intimidating when you do that, you know."

T puffed an irritable cloud of smoke out, refusing to look at me.

I rubbed my ring finger with my thumb, the spot where I usually wore my agathos opal feeling strangely empty. I hoped Wild had found it. That he'd known I'd seen him and that I wanted to go to him but hadn't been able to. I worried about all of my soul bonds but perhaps Wild the most. He internalized his guilt, carrying the heavy burden of it around with him wherever he went, and I knew he'd struggle with the fact that he'd lost control and succumbed to bloodlust the last time I'd seen him. That he'd *hurt* Riot, even after Riot had volunteered to fight him.

It hadn't escaped my notice that Riot wasn't with Wild, and it was only the fact that there were clearly some immortal forces at play that eased my mind. Wild was a soldier at heart, and the Spartoi were his people. It made sense that whatever god or goddess had intervened had taken him there, but it wouldn't have made sense for Riot.

He had to be somewhere else. I refused to believe any other outcome was possible. Riot had been given a task of his own, and that was the only thing keeping him away from me. He was safe, and he was busy, and he would be back the very first moment that he possibly could be.

"You can't keep me here, you know," I pointed out after the silence had extended. Not that T could talk, but he made plenty of noise when he wanted to—huffing and grunting mostly. "I can't stay. I have an important job to do. I have to go to Tartarus."

At that, T stomped his foot so hard the stones vibrated beneath me, shaking his enormous head back and forth.

"You don't want me to go?"

Another vicious shake of his head. I was doing my best not to think of just how terrifying Tartarus would be, but T had come from there and knew just how awful it was. It wasn't a great show of confidence.

126

T shuffled forward, gesturing out at the world below as if to say, 'look at it'. I could admit, somehow, things looked less dire than they had just a few hours ago. I'd wondered if it was just because we were in the air and high above the worst of the devastation, but there had been a strange moment while we were flying. It was almost as though time itself stopped for a second, the world freezing mid-spin. It was strange and surreal, and even T had noticed it because his grip on me had tightened ever so slightly.

Maybe... Maybe Dare had been successful?

Could it be? Could he have been the one to fulfill the prophecy?

If so, was he safely back in the upperworld?

I waited, hopeful, but no explosion of deities rained down from the sky. *Disappointing.*

My head was swimming, probably from a mixture of adrenaline, hunger, and thirst. Maybe a little exhaustion, too. It was all catching up with me.

"I at least need to go back to Ephesus," I amended, thinking out loud. "One of my soul bonds jumped into the pit you came out of in my place, and I need to check that he's okay. I had a job to do. That pit was for me."

T side-eyed me with such impressive apathy that I knew without a doubt he understood me just fine. He just didn't care about my problems, and I sort of got that too—I probably seemed very small and silly and mortal to him.

"Are you lonely?" I asked quietly. Thunderclouds gathered almost instantly overhead, centered almost perfectly on where we were standing. I gave T my most unimpressed face, though I was fighting the absurd urge to laugh. "There's no need for that."

He grunted, and the clouds dissipated as though they'd never been. Neat trick.

"I didn't mean it in a bad way. It's okay if you're lonely. It's not really okay that you kidnapped me because you wanted company," I added, surveying the abandoned town below with new eyes. "But that's my theory on why you did it. Everyone else runs away from you."

There was no huffing or grunting this time, just a heavy enough silence to make me think I was on the right track.

"Were you lonely in Tartarus?" T glanced at me, inclining his head ever-so-slightly, and I nodded slowly in understanding. He must have been there for thousands of years in who knows what kind of conditions. He just wanted to be *free*.

Maybe I was naïve—almost certainly, in fact—but I understood that urge.

I knew what it was to want freedom more than anything, to feel suffocated by your surroundings, to just want to *be*, with no judgment. I'd probably experienced less than a fraction of what T had, but I got the general idea of it. Every part of living in agathos society had felt like a cage where the walls pressed in a little closer each day.

Maybe it was that shared experience, the small sliver of imprisonment I'd felt in comparison to what living in Tartarus must have been like, that made me suited to this. To this creature, this conversation, this moment.

I understood what it was to be lonely. I remembered perfectly feeling like the world was full of people and not a single one of them wanted *me*, connected with *me*, understood *me*. It was a fate I wouldn't even wish on Gaia, and I certainly wasn't going to let T live that way.

"Maybe I can speak for you," I volunteered. "I guess that's what I am, isn't it? A Prophêtis. A mouthpiece for the divine. I want to convince everyone that they don't have to be afraid of you, that your intentions are good, but I think you might need to prove that to the world first."

Resting my arms on the stone ledge of the balcony, I leaned forward to inspect the strange, still silence of the world below. I'd been so excited to see Wild, that it was only now that I truly registered what he and the Spartoi had been doing.

They'd been *marching*. Marching in neat, orderly formation. Like soldiers.

Like they were going to war.

Were they going to war?

My empty stomach roiled uneasily. Of course they were. It wasn't as though Gaia's followers were going to give up. I needed to get back to the pit.

"Fight for us," I whispered to T. "Fight with us. When your mother sends her disasters, and her minions, and whatever else she sends. When she emerges herself to try and stop change in its tracks once and for all, fight on our side."

T wrapped a snake leg around my waist, yanking me off my feet, and I shrieked in terror at the sudden movement, the sound bouncing off the stones. *Oh gods, this is it. He's going to kill me for asking him to fight against Gaia. What was I thinking?*

The thick flesh of his leg caught me before my head could smack onto the ground, and then I was coiled up, almost protectively, in serpent limbs. I held my breath, waiting for him to crush me to death like a boa constrictor. Except he didn't. The deathly squeeze never came.

After a long, tense moment, T bent himself sideways to peer down at me, a giant hand lowering gently and brushing over my eyes as though he was closing them.

"Do you... Are you trying to put me to sleep?" I asked, dumbfounded. "Like a child?"

There was that indignant expression again, but he continued to brush his hand over my eyelids, forcing me to close them on instinct.

"This is ridiculous," I muttered, my fear disappearing as I tried to squirm free. "I'm not going to sleep here. You have to take me back to Ephesus, T."

I thought of Dare and the pit, and wondered if he was in Tartarus right now, or if the earth itself had rejected him because the prophecy hadn't been his, it was mine.

"I want to help you, but I can't stay. You have to take me back."

If Wild and the Spartoi were readying themselves to fight, then I was going to prepare myself for battle too. A battle of wills, of prophecies, of power.

You may not be willing to give up, Gaia, but neither am I.

CHAPTER 18

I fell, and fell, and fell. I fell for so long that my mind began to wander, my guilt at rendering Grace unconscious even for a moment making my stomach churn. I really hoped she could forgive me for being such a piece of shit, but ultimately I couldn't find it in myself to regret it even if she didn't.

Saving her from the terror of this fall and everything that followed it was more important than anything else.

Was that...

Was that the bottom?

It wasn't what I was expecting. I'd assumed Tartarus was pitch black, but I was definitely heading for a bright red glowing light. A light that reminded me uncomfortably of fire.

Was I falling into fire?

Fuck.

I flailed in the air—panic getting the better of me for a moment even though I knew there was nothing I could do. Above me, a darkness seemed to be spreading, and I could only assume that the pit was filling in with earth, the pathway now blocked off since I'd jumped.

This is fine, I told myself. It was probably some kind of test of Gaia's, just like I'd told Grace. And that I was falling face-first into it instead of her was a good thing, so there was no need to be *fucking terrified* now.

Except there was because yes, actually, I was heading right for a waterfall made of fire that was spilling over into yet *another* pit, and no matter how much I kicked and struggled, I didn't think I was going to clear the magma.

Of all the ways to go, burning alive was probably the least appealing for me.

Suddenly, the fire river morphed into the shape of a giant man, and I let out a terrified scream as its arms reached for me before I could drop into the second pit, snatching me out of the air and tossing me roughly toward the riverbank.

Everything hurt. I ached as though I'd body slammed a slab of solid rock, and I struggled to make my brain focus on *why* every bone in my body felt broken.

This was like Plane Crash Two: Electric Boogaloo. I couldn't catch a fucking break. Was it too much to ask that I *not* be regularly tossed around like a rag doll and put through a metaphorical blender? I just wanted a rest. A good night's sleep, and maybe a giant mushroom burger.

"Do you live, Philotes?" a rumbling masculine voice asked.

I froze at the realization I wasn't alone before attempting to speak, but only a pained sound came out. It wasn't *that* long ago that I'd been healed from my last set of near-fatal wounds. And not long before that,

I'd recovered the old-fashioned way on Rogue's couch after receiving the beating of my life.

I was getting kind of sick of being on death's door.

"Yes, you must live. Your mortal body remains intact, your soul housed within," the voice mused. *Cool, cool.* Good news. It was great to hear my soul hadn't up and left my body yet. I wriggled my fingers and toes—glad to find they still had movement—before analyzing my other aches and pains. My body felt like one big bruise, but hopefully that was the worst of it.

Though now that I was taking stock of my limbs, I noticed the weirdest sensation around one of my ankles. It was weirdly *hot*.

My head spun, vague memories of a fire giant morphing out of a river of flames and batting me away from the second pit before I could make it through, swatting me down like a fly.

"Where am I?" I slurred, spitting out a mouthful of dirt and attempting to push myself up into a sitting position. I gave up after a few attempts, lying on my stomach on the ground. Soon. I'd get up soon.

"You are in the underworld, of course. The path to Tartarus has closed, it was only available to one."

"Yeah, *me*. I was meant to be the one." Fighting through the pain, I struggled upright, that warm sensation still tight around my ankle. As soon I managed to sit, facing the river with my palms splayed on the ground to support my weight, I realized it was a thin line of fire, anchoring me in place. "Why... why am I tethered to the fire river?"

"My name is *Phlegethon*," the fire giant shot back in annoyance, though he was more regular-sized now. He was sort of moving back and forth, like the fire-person version of pacing, except he had no legs. His humanoid upper body morphed into flames from the waist-down, connecting seamlessly with the fiery river. Oh, he was the river. The river

133

was a... god?

How hard had I hit my head exactly?

"You are tethered to me because you need a guide in the underworld or your soul will leave you and be lost forever. You are mortal, with your breathing lungs and your beating heart. This place is not meant for you."

"Right. I hadn't exactly planned on stopping here. I was trying to get to Tartarus." I glanced to my left, where the river ended in the giant pit. That was where I needed to go, and definitely wasn't closed. I looked up at the purplish sky overhead, finding nothing to indicate there had ever been a hole there.

"You are too late. Someone has already gone in your place." Phlegethon looked oddly pleased with himself, considering his facial expressions were almost impossible to read.

No. No, that wasn't possible. Unless someone jumped in before I got there? There had been a few minutes between when I'd rendered Grace unconscious and the moment I jumped in. Perhaps someone had been falling ahead of me? Though it would likely be a human and no use to our cause at all. Fuck.

The rope of living flame around my leg began dragging me into the river, and I did my best to scramble backward with my weak limbs.

"Relax, I won't burn you," Phlegethon scoffed, sounding annoyed. "I'm going to be your chaperone for the time being. You will travel on my flames until we reach Akeron's waters. Then he can carry you to Styx, and then through the Stygian Marshlands to the palace. Yes, that will work. Surely, your soul can't wander on the short walk from the marshlands to the palace..."

"I really don't think my soul will get lost at all," I objected, being hauled into the flames completely. They didn't burn, but they sort of tickled at my skin, and I had no idea how I was floating when I was pretty sure fire wasn't buoyant. "And I don't need to go to the palace, I need to go to Tartarus—"

"Someone has already gone in your place," Phlegethon reiterated sounding annoyed. "You are tiresome. Would you let the Oneiroi's sacrifice be in vain?"

I froze, vaguely aware that the underworld was passing me by as Phlegethon ferried me in the opposite direction of the pit. "The Oneiroi?"

It couldn't be him. There must be thousands of Oneiroi in the underworld—Bullet was the only one of his kind who wasn't dead.

"Yes, *The* Oneiroi. Your Oneiroi."

"That's impossible."

Phlegethon made a strange noise that sounded sort of like a laugh. "He was half dead already, what is so impossible about it?"

"But Thanatos said he'd tell us if Bullet went to the underworld," I replied slowly, wading through the sludge in my brain to find a coherent thought.

"If I were being charitable, I would point out that Thanatos is one of the busiest of all the gods. People die awfully frequently, you know. If I were being uncharitable, I would call you foolish to trust his word. This is the same god that stole your fellow consort's voice, is it not?"

Fuck.

"And Bullet went to Tartarus?" Dread trickled down my spine. No. No, this wasn't how it was meant to be. Bullet had suffered enough.

"Yes, as I have already said. In your place. If he returns, he will undoubtedly be welcomed into Hades' halls as a hero, which is why you should make for the palace. Do you understand now? Do I need to explain

135

it to you again?"

What a dick.

"No, no, I got it," I grumbled. We traveled in silence for a long while, and I wished I could at least take in the view, but the flames either side of me were too high to see anything, so I just stared up at the purple sky overhead, wondering if Bullet was okay. Of all of us, he knew the most about the gods. He'd been studying them his entire life, and he was used to conversing with deities.

Maybe...

Maybe this was a good thing? Or was that just my selfishness talking?

Suddenly, the flames morphed into water, and I gasped at the shock of the cold on my skin.

"A live one! What have you brought me, Phlegethon?" "Akeron, this Philotes daimon must make it unharmed to Hades' palace. See that he gets there." Phlegethon could not have sounded less interested, rushing away in a sudden burst of flames back in the direction we'd come.

Okay, see you later then, I guess.

"He is tempestuous, that one," Akeron told me, as though he was bestowing a great secret on me. I looked around, but Akeron was ushering me along the river, and apparently had no interest in showing his face. While I didn't think we were moving as quickly as I had been with Phlegethon, water sprayed up on either side of me, blocking my view. "I won't terrify you by tarrying, on these shores are The Restless Dead, those whose souls had no payment for Charon. It is very crowded right now, and not a pleasant sight."

I swallowed thickly, suddenly glad for the wall of water.

"Any news from the upperworld?" Akeron asked cheerfully. "Last I heard, the battle lines are being drawn up, the stubborn agathos who fight in Gaia's name getting ready to take their final stand."

"What?" I asked, alarmed. I guessed, on reflection, it wasn't that shocking. It wasn't like Gaia had given us any indication before now that she was going to just give up.

"You're not surprised, surely?" Akeron asked. "Agathos are hardly beings that do well with societal change. It was always going to come to this."

"Isn't there like... an agathos of compassion or something? Empathy?" I mumbled. Why'd everything have to be so *difficult*?

"No," Akeron scoffed. "There are agathos of peace, good order, victory, obedience. There are the Philophrosyne, agathos of kindliness, but they encourage individual acts of kindness and charity. The agathos were not put on earth to make humans good, they were put there to make them manageable."

That was a grim assessment.

"Grace, *my* agathos, is an agathos of luck. That doesn't seem like a make-people-manageable kind of trait."

"No one can be manageable unless they have some kind of hope to cling onto. The very human belief that no matter how dire things are, there's always the possibility that they'll improve, is essential for a peaceful, cooperative society. There's no incentive for those at the very bottom to participate within it otherwise."

That was a chilling thought.

It also made a lot harder to see the agathos as the enemy—even the real asshole ones who'd beaten the crap out of me before I'd left for Greece. I wasn't going to chalk up their behavior entirely to instinct and let them off the hook—I had daimon instincts and I fought against them when it was the right thing to do. But it did shine a more sympathetic light on them, I supposed.

"We are approaching the Port of Charon, which separates my waters from the Styx's. You have a choice to make, Philotes."

"What's that?" I asked uneasily.

"Well, since we are already going past, I can drop you on the living side of the Styx for you to make your way back to the safety of the upperworld. Where you belong, seeing as you're not dead and all."

"Without Bullet," I stated flatly.

"Without the Oneiroi, yes, as he is no longer in this realm."

"But he'll come back," I said slowly. "He *will* come back. Bullet would do anything to get back to us."

"There are no guarantees that he will return from Tartarus. Even if he does, he may not be the same Oneiroi you remember," Akeron said cryptically.

"Well, I'll take the chance and wait," I replied stubbornly. "I made him a promise. A deal. I told him I'd bring him back, and I won't let him down."

"Even knowing he could find happiness in the underworld? It's really rather lovely—Queen Persephone has filled it with flowers, and there are plenty of interesting souls to talk to. The ones who haven't drugged themselves on the waters of the Lethe to forget their mortal lives, that is."

"He won't be happy. Not without Grace, not without Wild. Not without me and Riot. We're Bullet's *family*. We'd never leave him behind."

As I spoke the words aloud, there was a weird sense of certainty that they applied to me too. I knew—without a doubt—that Grace was furious with me for knocking her out, though I was sure the others had immediately let her go. But I also knew that she'd come for me if I needed saving, that any of them would.

Bond or no bond, it was always going to be us against the world.

As much as I hated to be away from Grace even longer, I knew she'd be grateful in the long run. Grace would never be truly happy without Bullet.

GRACE

CHAPTER 19

I woke up with a splutter, coughing as water filled my mouth and soaked my face. No matter how much I turned my head away, throwing my arms up to protect myself, the water was incessant.

But then again, it was quite refreshing, actually. And I hadn't realized how thirsty I was until I started gulping down the cool liquid. Just before I drank enough to feel like I might be sick, the water vanished. I blinked through wet eyelashes, seeing a miniature rain cloud right over my face disappearing before my eyes, replaced by T's intense gaze.

He looked... worried.

"Thanks for the water," I rasped, my throat feeling like sandpaper. It had been dark when I closed my eyes, and it was dark now, but I got the sort of alarming feeling that I might have slept the whole day away. Or maybe I'd fallen unconscious for a bit? I was groggy and disoriented in a way that I wouldn't usually be after a few hours' sleep.

And I was *so* hungry.

My eyes were drifting shut despite my best efforts to keep them open, exhaustion and hunger weighing down heavily on me. There was a strange, almost ticklish sensation against my mouth, and I attempted to bat it away, forcing my eyes open.

And finding myself staring into the eyes of a very unhappy lizard. I screamed before I could stop myself, and T shoved his hand forward with alarming speed, attempting to drop the still very much alive, wriggling lizard in my open mouth.

I slammed my jaw shut, pressing both hands over my lips for extra protection, and shook my head wildly at him.

"No!" I yelled, voice muffled by hands. "Are you trying to *feed* me that?"

T nodded, frowning as he attempted to push the lizard at me again.

"No. No, I don't eat lizards. Especially not live lizards."

T scoffed like that was the most ridiculous thing he'd ever heard before opening his enormous fang-filled mouth and dropping the squirming lizard directly down his throat. I gagged behind my hands before I could stop myself, and T gave me an impressively judgmental side-eye for it.

I *was* starving, so I supposed I could see why he thought I was being ridiculous. Still. There had to be a line in the sand somewhere, and *live* lizards were it.

With an impatient huff, T had me scooped up in his hands as he launched himself into the sky before diving down to the coast. I clung onto his enormous thumb, worried he was going to dump me in the ocean to fend for myself, and glad when he coasted to a gentle landing on the rocks. He set me down on a rock next to him, crouching on a boulder like an oversized bird as he stared down into the water. Was he looking for fish? Fish would be infinitely preferable to lizard.

"I'm not running away, I'm just going to wash a bit," I told him, unlacing my boots and setting them aside before slipping off the rock into the water, fully clothed. I'd probably regret it later, but my clothes were so covered in a thick layer of dust and grime that I needed to wash them, no matter how cold I'd be afterward.

I maintained my grip on the rocks as I dunked my head under the water, coming up with a gasp and using my free hand to scrub at the bits of exposed skin I could reach. T watched me impassively, before grabbing my boots with one hand and the back of my shirt with the other and launching into the sky with me dangling like a wet cat in his grip.

"Hey! What are you doing?!"

He deposited me down with surprising gentleness on a dry area of dirt, making quick work of gathering up rocks and sticks, easily snapping whole branches off dead trees. I wrapped my arms around my waist, shivering so hard that my teeth chattered, but within seconds T had built a rock circle with a small pyre of kindling, and was gently blowing a stream of fire into the middle.

Oh.

That was really thoughtful actually.

"Thank you," I murmured, standing as close as I could without catching alight.

He grunted, looking at me and holding up his palm in the very universal gesture of *stay*, that only made me feel a little bit like a pet, and then he was gone again, taking off into the sky.

Leaving me alone.

Perhaps I should have tried to run, but I wasn't sure there was any point. I wasn't strong enough or fast enough to get away right now, and I had no idea where I was.

And when T returned with two fish, eating one raw and throwing one on the fire for me, I was pretty confident I'd made the right call.

I'd find my way back to my loves, back to where I was meant to be, but I had a strong feeling that T wasn't a diversion in my journey, but a necessary part of it.

We took off again a few hours after we'd eaten at T's insistence, and I tried to decide whether itchy, salt-encrusted clothes were better than grimy, dirt-covered clothes until a startling sight below drew my attention.

"By the gods," I whispered, tightly clutched in T's hand as he flew inland from the coast. From what I thought was the north, marched Wild and the Spartoi. There were so few of them, and despite the gleam of the Spartoi's armor in the moonlight and the rigid, uniform lines they marched in, they still looked slightly *bedraggled*.

The opposing group—the opposing *army*—marching from the south in loose, unstructured lines definitely had the numbers. And *food*. They were following a trail of fruit trees, which seemed to be disappearing behind them as the army passed.

Stupid, wretched Gaia.

Both sides were converging. This was the beginning of a battle. Wild was going to war.

"T," I gasped, squirming in his grip. "You have to let me go. I have to get down there. They're going to fight!"

I felt, rather than heard, the irritable huff he let out, a gust of hot breath ruffling my hair. It was dark, and he was taking care to be quiet, so I wasn't sure that anyone below had seen us. It helped that T had conjured a fierce wind that was keeping the soldiers' attention restricted to their immediate surroundings and the opposing force in front of them.

Surely, they wouldn't fight now? No, it didn't look like it. It seemed as though they were slowing down, each settling in a few miles apart. Camping for the night, perhaps? That would make more sense than attempting to fight on unfamiliar terrain in the darkness. If I had figured that out, then Wild and the Spartoi definitely would have, they were far more strategic than I was.

T seemed to be circling, giving me a chance to observe what was happening below. I couldn't tell whether it was an act of kindness or if he was torturing me.

"Wild!" I shouted, cupping my mouth and projecting my voice as loud as I could. The wind immediately picked up, carrying the sound away, and I twisted to glare at T. "Why am I here, T? Just let me go, *please*. You don't have to land down there if you're worried they'll hurt you." Which was a very valid concern. "Just drop me somewhere nearby and I'll walk. I have to get to Wild, he needs me."

T swooped away from the makeshift battlefield, slowing down slightly as we lost altitude. Hope spiked in my chest. Maybe he was going to put me down? Let me go? I didn't hate T—in spite of the kidnapping, he'd done his best to take care of me and he just seemed so lonely. But I had things to do; I had to find my soul bonds, my loves, and I had to fulfill the prophecy. As much as I wanted to be T's friend, to show him what a friend could be, I couldn't stay here.

That spike of hope shriveled up and died in my chest as instead of landing on the ground, T banked right, landing on the roof of a tall, cube-shaped building at least three stories high.

"Seriously?" I muttered under my breath, cursing my luck. There were no other buildings around here. The battlefield they'd chosen seemed to be miles of flat plains, though it was hard to tell for sure in the darkness. T could have landed anywhere else and I'd have been on the ground.

144

Unsurprisingly, he didn't seem keen to let me go once he'd landed. He slithered around the roof, still clutching me in his hand like a toy he didn't want to let go of, inspecting his surroundings. The roof was a flat square with a chain link fence around all sides, presumably as a safety measure. There was internal access via a door in one corner to whatever the building below was, but T happily parked his butt right in front of it, blocking off the only obvious exit. Or at least the only *safe* one.

"You're being really mean, did you know that?" I wriggled free of T's fingers the moment I could, sprinting for the chain link fence and squinting out into the darkness. We were probably only half a mile at most away, and if I looked hard enough, I swore I could make out shapes moving in the darkness. "I'm not a *pet*. You can't just keep me here."

T slumped back in the corner he'd chosen, completely concealing the rooftop door from view, an almost petulant look on his face as he tucked his serpent legs beneath him. I turned my back on him, annoyed, and hoisted myself up the fence, arm muscles shaking with exertion as I did so.

The fish, sleep and gallons of fresh rainwater had helped, but I was still weak and my body let me know about it with every shake and tremble. How was Wild marching into battle right now? I was sure he'd found more food sources than me, given that I was being flown around everywhere, but he also required a lot more food than me to function.

With a resigned sigh, I half fell, half climbed back down to the roof, leaning my forehead against the fence for a moment while I caught my breath. The thick wire dug uncomfortably into my skin, distracting me from the simmering burn in my muscles. There was no point even trying to get away tonight. At first light, I'd assess my options and go from there.

As if to reiterate my point, a sudden, entirely unnatural gust of wind blasted me back from the fence, all but shoving me backward across the roof until I was within reaching distance of T's legs. One of them wound around my middle, yanking me back into the strange little nest he kept making for me.

Like a pet.

I did my best to swat his oversized hand away when he started stroking over my eyelids again, encouraging me to go to sleep.

"Can't you at least send them some rain? Some fresh water to drink?" I pressed. "Those people down there are my friends. One of them is a man I love. If you want *us* to be friends, then you can't let *my* friends suffer."

T huffed impatiently, but as I watched, rain clouds formed over the Spartoi army.

"Thank you," I murmured, hoping I was helping and not hindering. "I'm going to be on that battlefield. And you, T, are going to help me."

I woke up to the clang of metal against metal and the sound of shouting in the distance. I scrunched my eyes shut, fear and grief hitting me in an overwhelming wave. This was inevitable, I always knew it had been, but I still wished that it wasn't.

T made a strange rumbling sound of reassurance, patting my head while his legs unwound, more out of pent-up frustration than to intentionally release me from his grip, I thought. I wriggled free, standing on shaky legs. The sun was only just beginning to rise, bathing the world reddish-gold. From the edge of the roof, I watched as the two sides clashed, only able to tell which was which from the shining armor and weapons of the Spartoi. Where was Wild? Was he okay? Had they given him a weapon?

We'd come a long way from the first time we'd met in person. When he'd been the one on the roof, armed with throwing knives that he'd hurled with perfect accuracy at the agathos trying to kidnap me. Then again, there was a very good chance he was fighting agathos, and I'd ended up kidnapped yet again, just by a different captor, so perhaps we hadn't come so far after all.

"What if your mother appears?" I asked T, stalking back across the roof and stopping in front of him with my hands on my hips. He was curled up like an oversized cat, butt still firmly planted in front of the door. "Those are probably agathos down there, and the agathos are her army, whether she wants them or not. Will you fight for her if she asks you to?"

This time, when T opened his eyes, it was to give me an indignant stare. He huffed out a puff of smoke before lifting his giant head, shaking it once. He clambered onto his strange legs, slithering forward while hunching to keep a low profile, and I briefly got my hopes up that we were going to go down there and intervene. Instead, T cocked his head, and the entire battlefield was hidden from view under thick, charcoal-colored clouds, occasionally lit up by flashes of lightning running through them.

If I was being charitable, I'd say that he was trying to limit the extent of the damage both sides could do by raining them out, but it was more likely that he thought I wouldn't pay them any attention if I couldn't *see* them.

Not likely. I was getting to that battlefield if it was the last thing I did.

MERCY

CHAPTER 20

I disentangled myself from a sniping, bitter conversation between two of the human families staying in the camp, waving over Brio to intervene with his Harmonia gifts. It wasn't sustainable—every agathos gift required a sacrifice, and Brio maintaining harmony among other relationships created discord in his own with us, which was especially frustrating since all of us outcasts lived together at The Lodge. It wasn't fair to keep relying on him so heavily, especially when the in-fighting had been so relentless. We were all exhausted.

Brio gave me a nod of acknowledgment as he waded into the fray, and instead of returning to The Lodge to grab the linen that needed washing, I made my way down to the river without any laundry to catch my breath.

The very air itself felt different, and with it had come a fresh wave of restlessness. The constant buzz of agitation had built to a roar of frustration, and I had no idea why. *Why* the winds of change had blown in this angrier, more violent direction. What did it mean?

Hadn't we gone through enough?

"How are you doing?" Chance asked, coming to stand next to me as I looked out over the river.

"I'm tired," I admitted, staring down at the still surface and trying to compose myself.

"I'm not surprised. You're so busy all the time." He laughed humorlessly. "You left our place a teenage girl, and now you're a grown woman with more responsibility than any one person should carry."

"I found a gray hair the other day," I whispered, entirely appalled about it. I'd plucked it out and hadn't admitted it out loud to anyone. "I'm *eighteen*. That should be impossible, right?"

I glanced up in time to see Chance's lips twitch. "Not impossible, no."

Then again, there was a strong possibility I was middle-aged now, or at least my version of it. Using my gift to heal others came at a cost to my own health, and from the whispers surrounding me in Auburn after my emergence, Hygeia weren't known to make it to old age.

"There's something in the air," Chance said, frowning at the still surface of the river. "Something I can't quite put my finger on."

"People are angrier," I pointed out.

"Edgier, certainly," Chance agreed. "Even the humans can feel that we're on the precipice of *something*."

"Something to do with Grace?"

Chance smiled sadly. "Almost certainly."

Grace was the elephant in the room that none of us had really addressed in the time that Chance, Creed, and the boys had been here. Leon and Tobin had come close a couple of times before backing off, which was probably a lingering side-effect of their mom's brainwashing. I doubted they'd have been allowed to talk about their sister at all at home after Grace left Auburn with Riot. Maybe even before then.

As for my uncles, I figured they didn't like to talk about her for the same reason I didn't—guilt. Except we were never going to move forward, never going to heal, if we let that wound fester.

"I regret what happened that day in Milton every waking moment," I said, staring down, unable to meet Chance's eye. "Grace's soul bond, Bullet, called me and told me to follow the Basilinna's orders because the half-baked alternative I was trying to come up with on my own would have resulted in far worse outcomes. But it never should have gotten to that point. I should have run away, should have confided in Dice, bonded with him even. I wish I had even a tenth of the backbone Grace has. The ability to stand up to *everyone* and tell them that they were wrong and I didn't care about their opinions anyway."

"Well, Grace wasn't so confident at eighteen," Chance replied wryly. "Unfortunately, it took a few more years of mistreatment by her family and community for her to get to the point where she could tell us all where to go."

"Do you... Do you regret it? I know you weren't necessarily in a position to stop it—"

"I regret it every day," he interjected. "So does Creed. Don't grant us any leniency, Mercy. We were adults. Grace was a child. We could have— *should* have—done more to protect her. Should have left with her, bond or no bond. If I ever get the honor of seeing my daughter again, I'll tell her the same thing. No excuses, no begging for forgiveness—that's Grace's to offer, if and when she sees fit."

I nodded in agreement, finding myself quite liking that concept. I'd apologize, and offer her an explanation if she wanted one, though after her bonded got shot because of my actions, I wasn't sure she would. But I wasn't going to push. Ultimately, our lives had gone in such drastically different directions, I'd probably have to accept that our relationship was never going to be the same even if I hadn't screwed everything up.

"What about Earnest and Valor?" I asked curiously. They'd made enough throwaway comments out of earshot of the boys for me to understand exactly how they felt about Aunt Faith, but I was less certain where he stood on her other bonded.

Chance snorted. "Valor is Faith's mirror, her counterpart in every way. If I'm lucky, I'll never see him again. Earnest is more complicated. Sometimes, I think he could have been a good, kind, empathetic parent if only the Fates had given him a different soul bond. He's too much of an idealist, idolizing the bond at the expense of everything else. Even his children."

I could see that. It wasn't uncommon either, plenty of agathos were like that. Or they had been, before all the bonds were broken.

"Grace will forgive you," I told Chance confidently. "She's very forgiving, and her relationship with you in particular really comforted her when things were hard at home. She'll—"

A commotion at the gate cut me off, and we both turned back to investigate, though we were too far away here to see anything.

"More new arrivals, I'm guessing." I massaged my temples, the constant hum of anxiety around supply levels and housing all of the people who had come to us looking for help moving back to the forefront of my mind. To be an agathos was to want to help, and for the most part, I hadn't minded that instinct recently. Not when so many people needed us. But without adequate resources to support them all, and fights breaking out over every scrap of food or drop of clean drinking water, sometimes it felt as though we were doing more harm than good.

"I'll gather whoever I can, send more prayers to Demeter for food," Chance offered, mouth set in a grim line. He and Creed had taken the lead on making prayers and offerings to the gods, and while I hadn't been super confident that it was doing anything, it had helped give people purpose so I hadn't objected.

"That sounds great."

"Chance!" Harbor yelled, jogging down toward us, eyes wild. "She's here. Faith is here. I'm not letting her in, you're going to have to confront her at the gate."

"She's here?" Chance looked stricken, though we'd always known this was a possibility.

"Creed is already on the way to meet her," Harbor added. That got Chance moving. I followed behind, torn between never wanting to see Aunt Faith again and wanting to support Chance and Creed. And maybe being just a smidge nosy.

Harbor grabbed my hand, linking our fingers together and giving me a slightly impatient look. He didn't want me to go, but he wouldn't stop me either.

Chance sprinted through the gate that Sterling was guarding, and Harbor pulled me aside before I could follow, guiding me around to a small gap in the fence hidden on this side by the makeshift watchtower he and the guys had erected.

I went to slip between the watchtower and the fence, nearly crushing Leon and Tobin in the process. They both looked up at me with matching expressions of guilt that made me feel like I was probably meant to be the responsible adult in this situation, but instead I gestured for them to scooch over a bit so I could see through the gap over their heads.

Through the small sliver where the fence joined, I could see Aunt Faith and Valor, standing side by side, looking very much worse for wear. I'd never seen either of them look less than perfectly put together, but both of them were in torn, dirty travel clothes, matted hair coated with dust.

152

Where was Earnest? Valor was Faith's first bonded, the one she'd always blatantly favored, but Earnest was always more likely to side with the two of them than with Chance or Creed.

"You need to leave," Creed said roughly, standing shoulder-to-shoulder with Chance.

"I'm not leaving without my *sons*," Aunt Faith hissed, looking slightly crazed. "I have lost *everything*—even Earnest foolishly walked away from me. My sons belong to me."

Leon pressed his back against my leg, and I rested a hand on his shoulder, giving it a quick squeeze. *No way, kiddo. They're not taking you.*

"That daughter *you* wanted so badly cost me everything. My reputation, my community, my home, one of the bonded I actually cared about—"

Harbor sucked in a horrified breath next to me at her cruel words, and I was right there with him. How had Gaia—or whoever chose the soul bonds—gotten this group so wrong? I thought of my own parents, and while I'd always assumed they were the average level of agathos happy, on reflection there were some cracks in their relationship that they hadn't been quite able to cover up.

Was it because they were incompatible? Or was it just the pressure of trying to *seem* perfectly compatible at all times? It wasn't a way of life that allowed for natural and healthy disagreements between partners.

"The boys are safe and happy here," Creed said firmly. Leon slipped his hand into my free one, holding on tight. "They are staying here. What you have lost is immaterial."

"They are *my* sons. I will have them," Faith hissed, as Valor took a menacing step forward. Not that he could do anything—agathos couldn't physically attack each other. Or at least they hadn't been able to before...

"Do you think we'd have taken them away from their mother if we weren't sure they were better off without you? We're only doing now what we should have done for Grace," Chance clipped.

"On that, we can agree. You'd have saved me some headaches if the two of you had left earlier and taken that failure of a child with you. Leon and Tobin are mine."

Leon clung to my hand so hard that my fingers were aching. "I don't want to go. Mercy, I don't want to leave here. Please don't let her take us."

"I won't," I promised, meaning it. In the unlikely event that Chance and Creed caved to Aunt Faith's demands, she'd have to get through me first to get to the boys. Through most of the camp too, probably. Leon and Tobin deserved better than the lives Grace and I had lived, and I was going to make sure they got it.

"Harbor," I murmured, glancing uneasily down at them. Maybe I was the responsible adult here after all. Harbor nodded once in understanding, and I squatted down, giving each of the boys a hug in turn. "Go inside, okay? This is some heavy grown-up stuff that you don't need to hear. Just know that you're not leaving, no matter what."

Leon looked ready to argue but Tobin's quiet sniffling tears had him nodding in agreement. He was a good big brother, who'd seen too much and taken on too much for an eight-year-old kid.

Harbor led them away as the voices on the other side of the fence grew louder. Creed had always been the mildest, and the fact that he was standing up for himself was only making Faith angrier.

"I will have them, and I will keep them. There are no more soul bonds; the boys will stay with me *forever*," Faith hissed, the vehemence in her voice sending a shiver of fear down my spine. "I will find a community of agathos who understand what I have suffered, I will tell *my sons* every day how blessed they are to be raised by the good and true agathos, and they will be grateful for me. I will tell them that you two stole them away from me like the traitorous thieves you are, that their famous sister abandoned them, and they will thank me for saving them from all of you. Not even death itself will stop me—"

The very air around us changed, shimmering somehow. The wind picked up, and Sterling scrambled off the watchtower seat, coming to peer through the gap in the fence beside me.

And then a man appeared.

I had no idea who *he* was, but he was definitely not mortal. He had an air of power and authority to him that no mere mortal possessed. While he had the hair and beard of the traditional Greek gods, he was wearing a sparkling multicolored jumpsuit and seventies-style silver platform boots. It took my eyes a moment to adjust, trying to take in this brilliant, terrifying riot of color in front of me.

"What the..." Sterling whispered, trembling like a leaf.

"You rang?" the god drawled, adjusting the long, flared sleeves of his jumpsuit as though he was fiddling with some cufflinks.

Chance and Creed both dropped to one knee, bowing their heads in supplication, and Sterling and I followed suit from our hidden spot because that seemed like a good course of action. Whoever this guy was, I did *not* want to piss him off.

Fortunately, we could still see through the crack from down here.

"*Death itself,*" the god repeated as Faith continued to stare at him, dumbstruck. "Here I am. Thanatos, God of Death. No, no, don't clap, it's fine," he sighed into the silence.

"Have you come to take me to the underworld?" Faith asked, voice trembling.

Thanatos snorted. "No. I can't see what the Fates have in store for you, or how long your thread is, but I certainly hope you have plenty of time left here to suffer. Don't worry—I'll be putting in a good word with Hades to banish you straight to Tartarus. We can't have the mother of *The Prophêtis* strutting around the place, taking credit for her daughter's success."

I silently climbed back onto my feet, peering through the fence while Faith gaped like a fish at the God of Death. It was sort of... poetic. Satisfying. Something very un-agathos to be thinking, undoubtedly.

"Anyway, we have that little challenge of yours to address. You see, I take it rather personally when someone spouts "death itself can't make me do this!" I know it's something of a personality flaw, but I have a very demanding job, and we all have to get our kicks where we can. My kicks, so to speak, come in the form of divine karma."

Wow, the God of Death was absolutely terrifying. Not in an ominous, blatantly intimidating kind of way like I expected. More in a slightly unstable, never-know-what-he'll-do-next kind of way.

It was definitely worse.

"You said "death itself won't stop you" from making all your ludicrous claims—that the only decent parents your sons have are traitorous thieves, that their famous sister abandoned them, that you are the "good and true" agathos—I tell you, that one made me giggle. It's fascinating to me that you can say all these things with your inability to lie. A real case study in how deep delusions can run. Someone should put you in a lab and devote research to this." Thanatos held up his wrist as though he was looking at a watch, except he wasn't wearing one. "Anyway, I'm in a bit of a rush—incessant piles of dead people to get to and all that—so speak now, or forever hold your silence."

Aunt Faith didn't speak. I knew why—she was confused by all the information Thanatos had quick-fire thrown at her, and that must have been by design since he only gave her half a second before he spoke again.

"Forever hold your silence it is."

The grin on his face was the most terrifying thing I'd ever seen.

"You know, I know a guy who was also cursed to hold his silence, same as you. Well, technically *I* cursed him. And I can't lift a curse, but I *can* change it, so I think I might tie this one to your life," Thanatos mused. "For as long as *you* live... Yes, that works. A little treat for him. Not that he'll be grateful, they never are. Ah well, it can be my act of charity for this century— don't say I never do anything nice. Actually, don't say anything at all."

He laughed at his own strange joke, and with a twirl of his fingers, he was gone, leaving Aunt Faith on the ground, clutching her throat with both hands.

Screaming.

Silently.

By the gods, he'd taken her voice.

WILD

CHAPTER 21

These fucking agathos were relentless.

I hesitated to call them an army, they weren't that organized, but they were determined. They came at us in waves, shouting that Gaia herself had sent them to rid the earth of our presence, armed with garden implements and kitchen utensils. The projectiles they kept throwing were proving the most problematic. A well-placed hit from a rock at high speed was a very effective method of taking down an opponent.

There were no loose rocks handy for *us* to use.

For whatever reason, Gaia was holding back, not getting fully involved. But she did seem to be supplying the army fighting in her name with some basic resources. If I wasn't mistaken, there were fruit trees behind their ranks, and they certainly appeared to be less hungry than we were.

Ariston growled, both of us throwing up shields at the same time as another wave of rocks hurtled toward us. One of the Spartoi on the back line had given me their armor since I was at the front, and I cursed myself internally for not practicing with it earlier.

"Assholes," Ariston muttered, a word he'd probably picked up from one of the daimons when we were staying in the villa.

Assholes, indeed.

There were definitely humans mixed in amongst their side, and while I thought they were idiots, I sort of got it. They didn't have the knowledge we had—even the agathos hadn't seen and experienced the things I'd seen that made me feel somewhat confident that the world wasn't actually ending right this second. From the outside looking in... it didn't look so promising.

We were a moving target, the easiest direction to point all that fear and anger at.

I didn't care. I was stressed as fuck and couldn't find Grace and longed for Bullet. Let 'em fight if they wanted to fight. I could use the stress relief.

Annoyed at the seemingly endless supply of rocks they had, I waved to get Theras' attention further along the line. We needed to split some of our group off to try to double around the back of the agathos forces. We were outnumbered but not out-skilled. If we could hem them in and knock them out of commission one by one from the outside in, they didn't stand a chance, but we couldn't send too large a group, or we'd be seen.

If only I had an armed cavalry waiting in the wings. Or at least some catapults. Bows and arrows. *Something* other than spears, short swords, and shields that required us to fight at short range.

We had to get ahead of our mortal opponents before the immortal ones came out to play.

The logical part of my brain, the part that knew Grace would be scared and hurting, wanted Gaia to concede. To decide that we'd suffered enough and begin healing the earth so we could find some sense of peace again.

But I was still a Keres, and the Keres in me craved blood and destruction. The Keres in me said *let Gaia send her armies so we could bury them back in her earth.*

Theras was watching me sign, mouthing to himself in his language as he translated the words. It was because he was paying such diligent attention, because he'd lowered his shield to reply, that he didn't see the jagged rock coming right for his head.

"MOVE!" I shouted, eyes wide in alarm as it arced toward his temple. Theras startled, stumbling backward in time for the rock to miss him by an inch, landing with a *thud* in the ground just behind where he'd been standing.

Fuck my life. That had been far too close.

"Wild," Ariston rasped, standing the closest to me. "You *speak*."

I— What?

My hand clasped my throat, shock briefly immobilizing me.

"*Speak*," Ariston urged, closing the gap between us and resting a hand on my shoulder, giving me a small shake.

"Speak," I repeated slowly. The burning agony in my throat never came. The word was raspy and uncertain, but it was audible to me, to Ariston, to the soldiers around us who were staring at me in amazement. "*Speak*. I can speak."

One of the soldiers next to me fell to his knees, reaching his hands up to the sky and praying fervently in ancient Greek. For once, I was tempted to join him.

Except we had a battle to win, and the gods could have prevented all of this already if they wanted to, so I wasn't about to start relying on them now.

"Go around them!" I shouted to Theras, motioning with my hand what I wanted him to do—a combination of gestures and sign language—since his English and my Ancient Greek were both limited. "We'll launch an all-out charge, take a few men and circle them in. I'll send more to support you when they're distracted."

While the flat plain we were fighting on didn't make for easy sneaking, we were fighting amongst some kind of ruins. If Theras was able to hide soldiers among the crumbling structures of whatever this place was, we might stand a chance.

I was filled with a hunger to fight that I'd never experienced before, not to this extent. I shoved my sword into the sky and roared a battle cry that echoed all around me, the Spartoi banging the hilts of their weapons on their shields, creating a clattering din that had the agathos army shrinking back in alarm.

We moved as one, a wave of bronze and scarlet fury heading toward them, but the earth rumbled in protest, disintegrating before our very eyes.

"Stop!" I yelled, Ariston relaying the charge in their native tongue. One of the Spartoi slid forward, his brothers yanking him back from the ditch Gaia was creating in real time around her army, securing them safely on the other side of a river of dirt where their projectiles gave them an advantage. The circular patch of earth they were standing on rumbled before rising up, creating a plateau that made them even less accessible.

"For fuck's sake," I muttered. "Shields up! Move back, out of range!"

The rocks were already raining down on us, landing with ringing thumps against our shields. I dragged the men on my left and right towards me, urging them to overlap their shields with mine. I dropped into a crouch, knowing the second row would get the hint to bend and interlock their shields over us. The third row would remain standing tall with the bottom of their shields covering the second row. The protective, tortoise-like formation was instinctive—it covered all of us so long as we worked together, and that came naturally. Theras began calling the steps, the others falling into a chant with them so that we moved backward in time as one armored shell getting out of range.

How the hell were we supposed to take on an army when the very earth itself was bending and shifting to their needs? It was impossible. We needed divine assistance of our own, but I wasn't exactly in the right headspace to stop and make offerings to fickle deities, begging for help.

Divine assholes. No, if they weren't going to come to our aid in our obvious time of need, I wasn't going to use my newly recovered voice to bow and scrape for their attention.

Gaia may have given her army the defensive advantage, but she'd also constrained them to one small location—for now, at least. I could work with that.

"Have someone start a fire," I instructed Ariston, thinking of the pile of javelins we'd made with branches found along the way, whittled into shape. "They have vegetation on their little island. Let's see if we can set it ablaze."

GRACE

CHAPTER 22

Was that *fire*? Somehow, fire was flying through the air, hurtling toward Gaia's army. And they were definitely her army, because I'd seen the ground rise beneath them for myself, a ditch forming the moment the Spartoi had charged against them.

T didn't stop me as I took another run at climbing the fence to get a better view. Perhaps he thought, once the battle picked up intensity as it had, that there was no risk of me wanting to go down there. It had only made me more determined. I mumbled a steady litany of prayers to warrior gods under my breath, begging for assistance, but there had to be more I could do.

I balanced carefully on the top of the chain link fence, ignoring T's quiet huff behind me. The building itself was a modern design, with enormous steel beams arranged vertically around the whole thing in some kind of architectural effect. Climbing down the fence slowly, I stood in the small gap between the top of the row of beams with the fence at my back, peering down at the intimidating drop. There must have been some kind of underground parking lot, and I inched to my right, away from the downward-sloping concrete driveway, so if I jumped, I would at least land on softer dirt.

If I landed.

It hadn't escaped my notice that T was no longer lounging comfortably in front of the interior door but up on his serpent legs, slithering back and forth across the rooftop, his eyes never leaving my back. The chances of me jumping, surviving, and running the mile or so to the battlefield were slim.

I'd been willing to jump in the pit, though, hadn't I? There'd been so much at stake that I hadn't let physical fear enter the equation. There was plenty at stake now, and I just had to channel that same energy.

I wasn't going to give up. I *couldn't* give up. I was so close to Wild I could almost feel his solid muscles beneath my fingertips, see those intense dark red eyes staring down at me, looking impassive to others but filled with an affection that only those who knew him well could discern.

He needed me, and I needed him, and I was going to make it happen. But it wouldn't be through brute strength—which I had none of anyway, even if I hadn't been taking on a giant winged beast.

I was the Prophêtis. I was going to talk my way out of this somehow.

Maybe it wasn't a god of war I needed. Perhaps logic was the way out of this.

"Sophia," I said quietly under my breath. "I could really use your wisdom right now."

I had hoped to hear a soft voice in my ear, but to my surprise, a figure stepped out of thin air on the ledge next to me, and I nearly fell off the building, grasping clumsily at the fence to steady myself.

"Grace," she said softly, a kind smile on her face.

"Sophia?" I asked hesitantly. While she looked different from the sculpture, which I supposed had been a human interpretation of her appearance, the voice was familiar. How was she here? Had she scrounged up some power the way Hygeia had when Dare had needed her?

"In the flesh, as it were."

She held up an arm, examining it with mild interest. The *real* Sophia was more buxom than the statue had portrayed, with a rounder face and wide, guileless eyes. I wasn't fooled though—there was a steely core beneath that affable exterior.

"How are you here?"

Perhaps I should have been more deferential, but I was starving and confused, and a little bit concerned that I was hallucinating this whole thing.

Sophia clasped her hands in front of her, looking at me for a long moment. "Gaia's hold on the lesser deities is slipping. Between the very generous offerings of the agathos staying at Ephesus—nowhere near as potent as you or your daimons' blood, but good enough—and our gaoler being distracted... Well, I won't be able to stay for long, but I'm here now and I'll stay with you as long as I can. You have been very calm and very brave in extraordinary circumstances, Grace. You should be proud of how you have conducted yourself."

"Thank you," I whispered, fighting back the unexpected urge to cry. I was so dehydrated, I was surprised I had enough liquid in me to produce tears. I'd been floundering and struggling and questioning every decision I'd made this entire time, and it was so *nice* to hear some reassurance that I wasn't screwing everything up. "Can you give me any news from Ephesus? Is Dare okay? Did he make it to Tartarus?"

Sophia was silent for a long moment, and I held my breath waiting for her response.

"Your Philotes is fine," she said carefully. "But no, he did not make it to Tartarus."

"Oh." I rubbed hard at the empty space in my chest where the bond was meant to be. "But he's okay, that's the most important thing. I just need to get back to Ephesus, to the pit—"

"The pit is closed," Sophia interrupted. "It was only meant for one."

"Closed," I repeated numbly. "But Dare didn't make it to Tartarus."

We'd failed.

We'd *failed*.

"Your focus needs to be here, Grace," Sophia chided, gesturing vaguely at the battlefield. "The earth rumbles, its displeasure clear. The agathos army are drawn here, and wherever else Gaia wants them, through a trail of fresh food and water—both are strong motivators. And the scorpions are coming, at the very least. Perhaps others. Win the battle, Grace, then turn your attention to the war."

"Right." I blew out a steadying breath. "You're right, of course. This is the most pressing concern."

Even if I wanted to, even if the pit was still open, I doubted I'd have been able to leave Wild on the frontline of a battle when push came to shove, but I was definitely feeling pulled in multiple different directions.

"What about Riot?" I asked, my voice trembling. "I didn't see him down there when we flew overhead."

"Arete had a job for him. She will bring him here when his job is complete. They will all find their way here."

"What kind of job?" I wrapped my arms around my waist, feeling incredibly helpless. Was he okay? Was he stressed? Riot didn't necessarily *care* for responsibility...

"I'm sure he'll tell you himself." Sophia glanced at the massive beast observing our interaction closely. "An interesting choice of travel companion you have here. Hello, Typhoeus."

"Oh! Is that your name? Typhoeus?" He nodded once, but looked genuinely disgruntled about it. "Do you prefer when I call you 'T'?"

Another nod, slightly less irate. *Okay, T it is.*

"You're being kind of rude, you know," I scolded him gently, pushing his face back as he pressed it harder against the fence. "Sophia and I are just talking. You don't need to physically butt your head in."

T pushed back a little harder, and I gave him my best school teacher face until he flopped onto his back with a huff, wriggling until he was lying alongside the fence, eavesdropping in a slightly less confrontational manner.

"A *Prophêtis*, indeed," Sophia murmured, her gaze turning pitying. "This is a new world, Grace. A new series of challenges to navigate, a new set of rules to establish. You may fantasize about a quiet life after this battle is over and you are reunited with your soul bonds, but I would caution you against such dreams. The work of rebuilding is only just beginning."

I nodded, resigned. She wasn't telling me anything I hadn't already worked out for myself. Those peaceful visions Bullet had shown me of my future in the dreamscape wouldn't be our norm if they came to pass, but our reprieve. That didn't bother me so much, though. As long as we were together. I just needed them back.

All of them.

"You summoned me for my wisdom, and here it is: everything you need for success is here. There is no secret weapon, no ancient sword that ensures victory, no magical amulet that will grant you the power to overcome your enemy. You have your voice, your conviction, an army, and an aggrieved immortal already at your disposal. Use them."

T was still watching and listening, but he hadn't reacted at all to Sophia's "aggrieved immortal" comment, so perhaps she wasn't talking about him. Either that, or he didn't see himself that way.

"Even with the path closed?"

Sophia smiled grimly. "You would have leaped willingly to your death, Prophêtis. Be glad your Philotes stopped you from making such a foolhardy decision without losing his own life in the process."

Her words stunned me into silence. Evidently, I still hadn't learned not to be a silly, trusting fool, even after all this time. Hadn't Dare warned me? He'd known, and I'd been idiotically optimistic.

"Peace, Grace. That you and your daimons provide each other with balance is a strength, not a weakness. They temper your optimism, and you temper their pessimism. Their love for you has bolstered your confidence, but I am glad to see that your ego has not grown so large that you believe yourself to be infallible. I have often theorized to myself that the prophecy— at least in part—fell on your shoulders because your cripplingly low self-worth meant you would never abuse the authority you were given."

T snorted louder than I'd ever heard him.

"Thank... you?" Even T looked embarrassed that I'd thanked her for that. It hadn't exactly been a glowing endorsement, but she wasn't exactly wrong either. The Grace who'd hidden away in the lonely sanctuary of her apartment in Milton, away from the judgmental agathos of Auburn where she'd never fit in, that Grace *did* have cripplingly low self-esteem.

I wasn't *that* Grace anymore.

I almost laughed at the idea of being afraid to go to the bastion of snobby privilege that was Auburn. After the things I'd seen and experienced, I couldn't help but think of that community as petty and insignificant. Toy tyrants with plastic thrones, so absorbed in themselves that they didn't even realize how ridiculous they looked to the outside world.

"Of course, you're not the same young agathos you were when you started out on this journey," Sophia continued, her thoughts mirroring my own. "You've grown. Changed. Developed a little backbone, and you'll need it. For eons, Gaia has been a dictator—mostly a benevolent one, though, in recent times, we have seen how dangerous she can be when she is not feeling so benevolent. The Olympians are a tangled mess of strong wills and dissident opinions, but they are balanced in their power, in the way that all things must be."

"You still think we'll be successful? Even with the pit closed?" I asked hopefully.

"I'm sure of it." Sophia opened her hand, showing me a handful of orange dirt she'd somehow gathered. "Someday soon, this soil will be fertile once more. The land will be lush and green, and filled with all manner of creatures. It will not be a world of steel buildings and endless paved roads. It will not be a world you, or any of the generations currently living, recognize. But it will be *good*. It will bring more good to more people from all walks of life, and I believe that is the reassurance you sought when you requested my presence, but my time is running out."

She dusted off her hands, surveying the battlefield in the distance.

"You are scared. I suggest you follow your beloved Oneiroi's advice."

Do what scares you.

Sophia disappeared, and I blew out a long breath, turning to look at a wary Typhoeus. Monster, son of Gaia, and unlikely ally. Perhaps even a friend.

He was still staring at me through the fence, eyes full of challenge, but something more too. Resignation, perhaps. Loneliness, too. That much was familiar to me.

"Help me help you, T."

He huffed, and in that small, dismissive sound, I heard his silent question. *What exactly is it you think you can do?*

"I'm very important, I'll have you know," I told him sternly, impressed I could get the words out without my brain flagging them as a lie. "I'm the Prophêtis."

He all but rolled his eyes, ignoring me. At first, I'd assumed me being the Prophêtis was *why* T had kidnapped me, but now I wondered if it was just because I was the only mortal who had spoken to him.

The earth rumbled in the distance, and we both snapped to attention, watching as the horizon itself seemed to shift. The coastline, I was sure of it. T had flown us in from that direction.

I could have sworn the ground was *growling*; it was the strangest noise I'd ever heard, and the fence shook where I clung desperately to it.

Gaia was ready to intervene.

The battleground was suddenly crawling with a mass of black shapes that I immediately recognized as the oversized scorpions we'd faced in Athens. As frightening as that was, it was nothing to whatever was happening on the horizon. Whatever was *growing* on the horizon.

By the gods... It was a *volcano*. It had to be. A steep blackened cone had risen from the ocean, dominating the skyline. Smoke poured out of the opening in the top, and whether there was an explosion coming or something worse, I wasn't about to sit on the sidelines while Wild was directly in the line of fire.

"Fight with me," I told T. "Stand by my side. Ally with us. Show everyone that you have values and principles, that you are a being as worthy of freedom as any other."

T stood, peering over the fence at me curiously. Perhaps a little nervously.

"You want friends, this is how you earn them. Every soldier on that battlefield will want to be your friend if you fight in their ranks."

I was taking a gamble, and perhaps it was a foolish one, but underneath all that dismissive irritation, T was at least a little fond of me, or he wouldn't have tried so hard to keep me alive. I stepped up onto the row of beams, legs shaking as I turned to face him.

T growled in warning.

I ignored him, taking a deep, steadying breath.

T growled more aggressively, but there was still an edge of impatience to it. He didn't really believe I'd follow through, and he was huffing like I was massively inconveniencing him by making baseless threats.

There was nothing baseless about them, though. I'd come too far to cower away in fear now, watching the conflict unfold from my safe perch in the clouds, away from it all.

I'd spent my entire life watching on the sidelines. I'd managed to convince my parents to let me escape to Milton, just to really cement my place on the outside looking in. I'd lost count of the number of times I'd bitten my tongue, and stood aside when I knew what I was seeing was wrong. Ever the dutiful agathos, the dutiful employee, the dutiful daughter.

Not anymore.

The calm sense of otherness that lived within me—not my darkness, though I'd always thought of it that way—spread through my body, warming my limbs. It had never been darkness, it had been strength. It had been *potential*, if only I was brave enough to reach for it.

I looked T in the eye, giving him a soft smile as that feeling of rightness settled in my gut. "If you drag me back here, I'll only leave again. I'll never stop trying to get away. Not when there are people I care about on that field who need my help."

And with that, I threw myself backward, free-falling into the air.

The mere seconds I fell felt like the longest of my life, then T was there, snatching me out of the air with such a ferocious growl that sparks flew out of his nose.

He was livid, but to my relief, he headed for the battlefield, adjusting his grip until I was held in a somewhat dignified position in his hands, my long, tangled hair flying through the wind behind me.

T looped around the enemy forces, blowing out a stream of fire that made my skin uncomfortably hot, encircling them in flames for a brief moment before the soil itself seemed to rise and swallow it. It had effectively destabilized the mostly agathos army though, and T left them scrambling as he flew down to where the Spartoi had retreated, setting me down carefully before turning to face the plateau, standing guard.

Wild lowered his shield, staring at me with a mixture of awe and disbelief as I crossed the distance between us, the rest of our surroundings fading away for a brief moment.

He was here. *Safe.* And I was going to hold onto him and never let him go.

GRACE

CHAPTER 23

"Grace," Wild rasped as I picked up my pace.

I'd been halfway to running toward him, to throwing myself in his arms, but hearing my name on his lips for the first time in real life, outside of the dreamscape, brought me to my knees.

"Fuck, Grace," Wild said, panicking slightly as he closed the distance between us, dropping his weapons and sinking to the ground on his knees along with me. "I'm so sorry. I'm so fucking sorry."

I was crying so hard that I couldn't speak—big, ugly, gasping sobs for air. Why was he so far away? Why was he apologizing? I just wanted him to wrap me in his giant arms and tell me it was okay, to *hear* reassurance in his beautiful, deep voice.

"I'm so sorry, I'm so sorry," he chanted under his breath, reaching for me but still not touching me.

"Stop saying sorry!" I sobbed, grabbing at his bronze breast plate and trying to yank him forward, but he was as solid as a mountain. I ended up pulling myself forward until I was clambering onto his lap.

"Do you forgive me?" Wild asked, banding his arms around my back and burying his head in my shoulder, finally holding me like he was supposed to, with the annoying addition of the solid armor between us.

"For what? Wild, I love you. I missed you so much. You just disappeared." I gulped down some air, my voice verging on a full-blown wail.

"I hurt Riot. I thought you'd hate me."

I grabbed his head, forcing it back so I could look into his eyes. The Spartoi surged forward around us, creating a protective wall of muscle at our backs.

"Riot is fine." I swallowed thickly. "I don't know where he is. I don't know where anyone is, but they're... well, Sophia said they're safe. I'm not mad at you, Wild. I'm just so happy to see you. To *hear* you. How? How is that possible?"

"I don't know." Wild scanned my eyes, the intensity of his gaze sending a shiver down my spine. "Given that it's Thanatos, it's probably a trick, but I'll take what I can get."

"Your voice is so nice," I whispered, running my hands over his cheeks, the thick beard covering his jaw, down to his chest, over the cool, smooth armor. Taking stock of him, making sure he was okay. "I know we're in the middle of a battlefield where a million things could kill us, but can I kiss you yet?"

Wild made a pained sound, as though he was wounded that I even had to ask, before wrapping an enormous hand around the back of my neck and dragging me into him. We met in a desperate clash of lips, teeth, and tongue, a ragged, needy edge to our messy movements. I'd run the gamut of emotions since he'd disappeared—worrying for him, missing him, loving him, occasionally being angry at him for losing his temper, chased quickly by guilt because I knew to be a Keres was to be cursed with bloodlust.

Our movements slowed into a kiss less rushed, more finessed, ruined slightly by the salt of my tears on our lips.

"Tell me how to make you stop crying," Wild whispered against my mouth. "I need to make it stop. I'll do anything to see you smile again."

"These are happy tears," I promised him. "I'm working my way up to a smile."

I had so many questions, so many things I wanted to say, but the din of the battle, the crunch of the Spartoi's spears into the backs of the scorpions that occasionally got past T's literal line of fire drowned me out. It wasn't the time.

Wild looked over my shoulder at the fight, his hands tightening around my waist, clearly torn.

"Go," I told him seriously, cupping his cheeks and planting a firm kiss against his lips before we both climbed to our feet. "I'll be here."

"*Here* isn't safe for you—"

"Nowhere is safe." I straightened my spine. "And we don't have the luxury of wasting manpower by letting anyone sit on the sidelines. Think you can bring me some scorpion corpses?"

Wild startled. "Um, okay. Here, take this. It's not much, but it's some defense."

I nodded once, my hand wrapping around the handle of the heavy knife Wild unclipped from his belt before I took a step back. "Let's get to work. We've got a battle to win."

Wild growled once, pulling me in for a hard kiss, his eyes searching mine. "You're damn fucking right we're going to win. Then I'm going to greet you properly, and show you exactly how much I missed you."

"I can't wait," I whispered, walking backward a few steps, hating to let him out of my sight but needing to. Just for a moment, at least. We all had a job to do.

The Spartoi parted for me as I made my way to the very back of the ranks, then back a little further still, not wanting to get in their way. The fight continued while I gathered up all the branches and broken bits of spears I could, building the base of a fire in a ring of stones.

I paused, looking at it. *No, two.* I needed two fires. With a resigned sigh, I began the process all over again a few feet away until I had two piles of sticks, encircled by rocks, ready to ignite.

I couldn't fight the way the Spartoi and Wild could, but I had weapons of my own.

"T!" I yelled, somehow knowing he'd be able to hear me over the crash of weapons even if no mortal would ever be able to. "I need fire!"

There was a pause, and then the Spartoi were shouting as T rose into the air, looping around the back of the army just long enough to blow a stream of fire onto my pile of wood, and I used a stick as a torch to light the second one.

The mass of scorpion carcasses was steadily growing nearby as Wild sent them back down the lines, and I grabbed the first one, careful not to get anywhere near the stinger. They were heavier than I expected, and it took all of my meager strength to drag them along the ground to the fire, before dumping them next to the flames.

I remembered, what felt like a million years ago now, Bullet telling me that the meat of sacrifices used to be consumed by the people, with the inedible parts burned in offering. It was that tradition that had led to me being smeared in sheep blood in the basement of the agathos temple—a long-lost relic of the tradition of sacrifice.

How edible were giant scorpions?

I guess we'd find out.

I kicked the scorpion over to reveal the soft belly and, feeling more squeamish than I ever had in my life, sliced the tail about halfway down, taking off the stinger and hopefully the source of venom.

Pausing for a moment to gag into my elbow, I straightened, setting the knife aside and lifted the scorpion, holding it as far away from my body as possible, before tossing it onto the flames.

While it crackled away—possibly the most disgusting sound I'd ever heard—I headed over to the pile and began the process all over again, slicing off the tail and dragging it to my makeshift kitchen-cum-sacrificial-altar, ready for cooking once the first one was done.

Now, how was I going to get it out of the fire? I mused, staring at the scorpion which looked... cooked? I wasn't exactly sure what I was looking for, but surely it had been on there long enough to kill any bacteria at the very least. One of the Spartoi from the back ranks jogged over, gesturing at himself, and holding up his spear before pointing at the flames.

"Oh! Yes please, if you don't mind."

He made quick work of dragging it off the fire, picking up the knife and holding it over the flame for a moment before expertly butchering it to pull the fleshy meat out of the claws and remaining tail.

"Here we go," I muttered, pulling the overly long sleeves of my jacket down and scooping the still hot scraps of scorpion shell into my arms.

What next?

"I just... Could you pay close attention to the ritual, Amazing Grace? Just in case you ever need to do it on your own."

I scrunched my eyes shut at the memory of Bullet's smiling face tinged with resignation. He'd known, and I'd argued.

"I won't need to, but I'll pay attention because you asked me to."

It felt so foolish in hindsight, but at least I'd been sensible enough to listen to his instructions, even when I thought I wouldn't need them. Even when I was naïve enough to believe that nothing in this world or any other could have separated us.

Blowing out a shaky breath, I tossed the broken bits of shell onto the second fire and lowered my hands toward the ground, spreading my arms wide and keeping my palms up, the way Bullet had done that day.

"Usually, I would lift my hands to the sky for an Olympian, but as we know they're in Tartarus, I'm going to keep them lowered towards the ground like I would for an underworld deity."

Sinking into that feeling of *other*, of a world bigger than myself and gods who listened, I spoke. "I make this offering to you, Athena, Goddess of War, that it might strengthen you in preparation for your return, and grant us the wisdom and cunning we need to win this fight with as few casualties as possible on both sides."

The Spartoi had bowed his head during my offering, but raised it the moment I was done to pass me a handful of white meat.

"It's just like lobster," I chanted quietly under my breath, accepting half of it with a grateful smile because I was *starving* and indicating that he should have the rest. "Just like lobster. Claws, tail, all the same. They're just lobsters of the earth. This is fine."

I nibbled on a small bit of the meat, glad that it was at least fairly bland in flavor. And it was a good source of protein, right? Right. Eating for fuel.

Hopefully, Wild would be able to have some. Daimons were vegetarians because Nyx favored animals, but the scorpions were Gaia's hell bugs so I was hoping the rules didn't apply. In the brief time I'd spent with

178

him, even beneath the Spartoi armor he was wearing, it was clear from his face that Wild hadn't been getting enough food.

The moment I'd eaten, I got myself back into position, repeating the process but this time offering my prayers to Ares, requesting his guidance in battle, then used another scorpion carcass to request Zeus' guidance and leadership.

The battle raged on, and the Spartoi took turns falling back from the ranks to rest for a moment, eat some meat, and drink from water bottles they'd left back here. They must have been collecting up bits and pieces as they'd traveled because there were some metal pots too. I contemplated asking T to fill them with rain water, but he seemed pretty busy pelting the plateau with a very concentrated storm, forcing Gaia and the agathos to hole up in a more defensive structure, rock walls bursting out of the ground to protect them. The sun was setting now, and in the low light, the action on both sides was dying down.

"There are no more scorpions," Wild announced, appearing through the back ranks, covered in dirt and dried blood, but looking oddly invigorated. "It might just be a pause for the night—the way battles were fought in the old days—or perhaps Gaia realized you were using her weapons as tools to bolster her enemy. Both the divine and the mortal ones."

He grinned, a more carefree expression than I'd ever seen on his face, and it took my breath away. "You're quite the strategist, my darling Grace."

"I'm going to swoon if you keep that up," I laughed. And I wasn't exaggerating—I was so tired that I was swaying on my feet already. "Want some scorpion meat?"

Wild grimaced. "Not particularly, but an army can't run on an empty stomach and beggars can't be choosers. Thank you for feeding us, Grace. You've been incredible today."

I beamed at the compliment, handing him some freshly cooked scorpion while he conversed with Theras about keeping the bonfires going for the night so most of the army could stay here and be comfortable, but they'd take turns to go somewhere else for proper rest, though I couldn't figure out where they meant. Considering how stilted the conversations had been between us and the Spartoi when I'd last seen them, it was *amazing* to see how well they were communicating using a combination of English, Ancient Greek, and ASL.

"Come on," Wild said to me, handing his spear and shield to one of the Spartoi hanging back, but sheathing the sword at his hip. "We scouted a place nearby to stay. We'll sleep there tonight, and the Spartoi will take it in shifts to get a couple of hours rest. They don't sleep as much as we do."

Impressed at what a well-oiled machine they were, I let Wild take my hand and guide me away from the field the battle had taken place on. Past the stone ruins of whatever this place had once been. I hoped nothing historically significant had been destroyed in the line of fire, but I was almost certain it would have been.

A few Spartoi fell into step behind us, watching our back, and I looked at T over my shoulder where he was resting before the front line. He tilted his head, giving me the barest hint of a nod that seemed to say *it's okay. I'll keep watch*. Or maybe I was just seeing what I wanted to see.

I was surprised to see that we were heading back toward the cube-shaped building I'd been camped out on with T the night before, though instead of heading right toward it, we veered left into what appeared to have once been a campsite.

"Were you here last night?" I asked. "I was so close, up there on that roof."

I pointed out the building as we passed it. Wild shook his head.

"We stayed on the battlefield. I sent Lycus to scout for somewhere we could use as a base during the fight today. Gaia won't be creating a comfortable resting spot for us for the night," he added wryly.

I was so distracted by the low rumble of his voice that I barely registered what he'd said. I'd heard Wild speak in the dreamscape, but it wasn't quite the same. The dreamscape smoothed over rough edges, made everything seem a little bit prettier and glowier and *nicer* than it was in reality. I'd take the natural roughness of his real voice over the glossy dreamscape version any day.

"Wild, how did you get here? We're so far from Ephesus." I swallowed thickly. "From Dare…"

"Thanatos brought me here to the Spartoi. Where is Dare? How did you get separated? Where is Riot?"

I blew out an unsteady breath, squeezing Wild's hand with one of my own, and periodically running my free hand over every inch of him I could reach. He'd never been the most tactile of my bonded, but he was doing the same to me, both of us reassuring each other that we were here. As we walked, I told him about everything that had happened since the bloodlust hit after Thanatos collected Bullet. I told him about the pit, which he'd apparently never seen, about Typhoeus' emergence, Dare knocking me out so he could go to the pit in my place—that didn't go down particularly well—T snatching me away and the things we'd seen, all of it.

"And you haven't seen Dare since?" Wild asked, frowning. "I'd like to think he's not the kind of guy to abandon you all alone, but I didn't expect him to knock you out and restrain you either…"

I gave him an affronted look. "I don't doubt Dare, just like I never doubted you." Wild looked appropriately shamefaced at that. "All I know from Sophia is that Dare is fine, but he didn't make it to Tartarus. T snatched me up right after he left, and while we've flown around the coast a lot, I don't *think* we've gotten close to Ephesus." I sighed heavily.

"You're right; I shouldn't be so hard on him," Wild murmured. "There is a visceral wrongness to the idea of any of us incapacitating you, but I'm not sure I wouldn't have done the exact same thing in his shoes. There's no fucking way I'd have let you dive into the mystery pit."

"You would have been right not to," I said, relaying the rest of Sophia's words to him. "She said he's okay and that he would make his way here, and while I miss him so much, part of me just wants him to stay safely at Eirene's house with the others rather than put himself at any more risk."

"There's nowhere we wouldn't follow you, Grace. I have no doubt he's on his way. We're here."

Wild exchanged a few words—a combination of spoken and signed—with one of the Spartoi before leading me to a small cabin.

"There's a stream we've been collecting water from and boiling to drink. They're going to heat some so we can wash," Wild volunteered. They'd really developed their own unique way of communicating because I hadn't gathered that from their brief conversation at all.

"Are we getting special treatment?" I asked.

Wild gave me a wry smile. "Most definitely. But you are their Prophêtis, and they want to see you cared for."

"And you're their General, aren't you? You fought hard beside them today. They'll want to see you cared for too," I pointed out. Wild shrugged, always surprisingly shy when it came to anything resembling a compliment. "I wonder what happened to the people who lived here. Someone must have stayed on-site to run this place, right?"

"They probably ran when they realized there were armies approaching. Lycus said there were no corpses in any of the buildings. Or I think that's what he said."

Wild led me into a basic, clean room with a double bed in the center and a twin bed pressed up against the wall. It was all decorated in dated shades of pale yellow and light turquoise, but the bedding looked clean and undisturbed. In the week of darkness and the fallout that followed, it appeared this place had been unoccupied.

At the back of the cabin was a small tile bathroom. Optimistically, I turned the tap on, but only a drop of water came out.

"They're boiling more water for us to drink," Wild said apologetically, leaning against the door frame.

"I'm grateful for it," I replied hurriedly. "I just miss, you know, plumbing. Electricity. Internet." I thought about it for a moment, remembering sitting on those castle ruins with T and watching the sunset without distractions. "Actually, I haven't missed internet access as much as I thought I would."

Wild hummed in agreement, holding out his arms for me to step into. I practically threw myself against him, resting my head against his breastplate and gripping him tightly around the waist. *How did I get this thing off? I wanted to feel his skin on mine.*

"What about you?" I mumbled against his armor, feeling around for the whatever was holding this thing on his body. "You must be missing technology. You relied on it so much to keep in touch with your Keres daimons in Milton, and with Onyx..."

Wild hummed as my fingers found latches down the sides of the armor. "I'm probably not as worried about them as you'd think. They're Keres daimons—I worried about them more in times of peace. We're built for this violence, this chaos."

I held him a little tighter and snuggled in a little closer, my eyes shooting open when I realized the hard thing nudging my ribs *wasn't* his sword.

"Ignore it," he murmured, sounding amused. "Like I said, I'm built for this. Fucking and fighting go hand-in-hand."

"Did you have that *while* you were on the battlefield?" I asked, baffled. That seemed like a massive liability.

Wild snorted. "No. The bloodlust is waning for the night, leaving some regular lust in its place."

We broke apart at the knock on the door, the Spartoi coming in with an enormous steaming basin of water that two of them heaved between them into the bathroom while one of the other Spartoi set down a smaller jug of cooling water on the nightstand before they all excused themselves. I felt embarrassingly pampered.

Wild dug around in the bathroom while I hovered, coming up with some wrapped bars of generic-looking hotel soap and washcloths, and I nearly cried with gratitude.

With zero hesitancy, Wild stripped undid the latches on the sides and at his shoulders, slipping out of the bronze armor and the worn clothes underneath that I recognized from Eirene's house. I pulled off my own filthy clothes, setting them aside with the intention of scrubbing them all in the bath water and hoping they dried overnight.

"Before I forget," Wild said, catching my hand. I looked down in surprise as he slid my opal ring back onto my ring finger. "Thank you for letting me borrow it, for letting me know you saw me." He swallowed thickly. "That you were alive."

I nodded, blinking away my own tears. No, we weren't doing that right now. This was a quiet moment of peace—maybe even a little happiness, despite all the worry pressing down on us—and I didn't want to waste it.

Reading the expression on my face, Wild quirked a small half smile and pressed a light kiss to my forehead.

"Come here." He pulled me into the shower stall with the basin sitting on the side, so the water we used had somewhere to drain. Wild dunked a washcloth in the warm water, handing it to me, and my lip trembled just enough to catch his attention.

"I'm sorry," I whispered. "It's just been so long since I had a decent wash. I'm still itching from dunking myself in salt water which was my last attempt at getting clean. Or at least, not smelling so awful."

Wild laughed, working the bar of soap into a lather and handing it to me. If I thought his half smile had me weak in the knees, his laugh nearly reduced me to a puddle on the floor.

How was this moment real? In the midst of all the awful, this sweet moment of bathing each other in a cramped shower stall, the biting chill setting into my damp skin, felt like paradise.

Wild wasn't shy about staring at me as I *thoroughly* washed every inch of my body, and I discreetly watched him in return. In the time we'd been separated, both of our bodies looked slightly different, and I imagined it was as strange for him to see as it was for me. Wild had always been buff and *huge*, but now he was leaner, his muscles more defined after the almost constant exercise and not enough food. I knew I was thinner—the clothes I'd left Eirene's house in were hanging off my body, and my ribs and hip bones were showing through my skin.

I didn't need the bond to know that Wild was just as worried about me as I was worried about him.

"It's okay," I murmured, encouraging him to crouch down so I could wash his hair, wishing I had something better for his curls than bar soap. "All this chaos will pass soon. I have to believe that. We'll find some new kind of normal, and we're going to be okay."

"You still can't lie?" Wild verified, kneeling in front of me, putting

185

him perfectly eye level with my breasts. His hands came to rest on my waist, thumbs brushing over my lower ribs.

"Still no lies," I promised, doing my best to scrub the dust out of his hair and using a cup next to the sink to scoop some water from the basin to rinse it. I'd almost forgotten how much taller than me Wild was.

After I was done, Wild stood, encouraging me to turn around so he could return the favor. I winced as his fingers hit one tangle after another. It was heavy, too. Matted, full of dirt, and a hindrance to deal with.

"Chop it," I whispered. Wild stilled. "With your blade. Please, Wild. It's so uncomfortable."

"You're sure?"

I nodded stiffly, doing my best to repress my shivers as he fetched the knife-like weapon he'd been wearing earlier. Maybe it was vain to be sad, but I'd always had long, glossy hair and it was one of my favorite things about my appearance.

Wild was efficient and careful, gathering my hair into a bushy ponytail before slicing it in one fell swoop at the base of my neck. The heaviness disappeared instantly, and even though I missed the security blanket, the relief on my scalp more than made up for it.

He threw the hair in the trash can under the sink before returning to washing what was left, gently detangling the chin-length strands. I tilted my head back as he rinsed out the soap before grabbing my shoulders and encouraging me to turn to face him.

"Beautiful," he assured me, twisting my hair around his fingers and brushing my jaw in the process. I rested my palms on his chest, pressing my body against his for warmth.

We were both still avoiding the elephant in the room, the grief neither of us wanted to process. But holding each other like this, no clothes between us, washed clean of the days of dirt that had been coating our skin... We were naked and exposed in more ways than one.

"I miss him so much," I breathed, managing a weak smile. "I know you do too."

Wild's jaw tightened, his fingers flexing where he cupped my face. "It's... it's hard to think about Bullet. Not because of the bloodlust; I don't think I'm going to lose control." He swallowed hard. "I'm fighting more than enough each day to keep the violent urges under control. It's just... fuck, it's just hard."

"I know." I went up on my tiptoes to press my forehead against his, and Wild's arms shifted to my waist, easily lifting me off the ground, so our faces were level. "But we can think about the happy things too. I need to think about the happy things. I need to remember those positive moments because I'm worried I'll *forget*—"

My voice cracked on the word, and I cleared my throat, not wanting to cry anymore. "What do you think Bullet would say if he were here right now?"

Wild's lips twitched. He leaned back slightly, dropping his gaze to my breasts. "With both of us here naked? I'm not sure he'd say anything. He'd be blushing so bright he'd light up this whole room."

I laughed, the sound echoing around the walls. "You're probably right. He was more shy when you were there, you know. Maybe because he and I both had no idea what we were doing."

Wild hummed, one hand drifting down to my butt, kneading my flesh. "You know what you're doing now. That last night at Eirene's with all of us..."

My face heated, core clenching at the memory of all of us together.

"We're going to be together again someday," Wild murmured,

biting my shoulder gently before soothing the sting with his tongue. "All of us. Riot and Dare will come back." Another bite, another soothing kiss. "I'll give Thanatos my voice willingly if he'll bring Bullet back. Whatever it takes, I'll get him back. We'll all be together again."

"I believe you," I replied breathily, tipping my head back to give Wild access to my neck. He encouraged me to wrap my legs around his waist, and I sucked in a quiet breath at the sudden pressure on my clit.

"And the world will be at peace," Wild continued, vocalizing all my fantasies. "And the five of us... We're all going to live somewhere so fucking private we never have to speak to anyone except each other."

My laugh turned into a gasp as he rolled his hips gently.

"And you, my darling Grace..."

"Mm, and me?" I prompted, tightening my grip and trying to ride him as best I could with my too-weak thigh muscles.

"You will be so tangled up in at least one of your soul bonds at a time that you won't know where one ends, and you begin. You won't need clothes ever again."

Wild held me steady, pausing so I could grab a towel and carrying me back into the bedroom. It took no time at all for him to set me down and dry me off before quickly drying himself, and guiding me onto my back on the bed. He parted my knees with no hesitation, making space to lie between my legs, covering my body with his and keeping me warm.

"I'll be cold if I don't ever wear clothes again," I pointed out, arching into his touch as Wild trailed his lips down my body, pausing to drag his teeth over my nipple before settling between my legs. He didn't give me a chance to be shy, encouraging me to put my ankles on his shoulders and parting me with his thumbs, swiping a hard lick up to my clit.

"We'll keep you warm. Fuck, I've missed the taste of you," Wild

188

growled against my skin before resuming his *feast*. There was a desperation to his movements that had never been there before, and I was right there with him. I needed this, needed this physical connection with him, the reminder that he was healthy and here and real.

"Come here," I encouraged, reaching for him. "I need you. I just... I just need you."

"You have me," Wild assured me, crawling over my body, his cock brushing my clit. "You always have me."

He didn't tease me, bracing his weight on one arm, grabbing his shaft, lining up with my entrance, and pushing forward slowly. I sucked in a breath at the stretch I hadn't been quite ready for but craved nonetheless, my back arching into his touch.

"I love you, my darling Grace," Wild murmured, rocking his hips gently, giving me time to adjust. "I always have, I always will. I think I fell in love with you just watching you from afar through the cameras, even if I wasn't ready to admit it to myself. The way you were so out of your element in Milton and yet so brave. So determined."

"Don't make me cry," I ordered, wrapping my legs around his back.

Wild laughed silently, burying his head in my neck. "Can I make you scream instead?"

"It's probably inadvisable," I whispered, not protesting when he hooked his forearms behind my knees, bending me in half. Each thrust hit that much deeper, and a strangled cry escaped me despite my best intentions to stay quiet.

"That's it," Wild encouraged roughly, his rasping grunts of pleasure like music to my ears. "Relax for me."

"Harder," I whispered, taking us both by surprise. But Wild was wound up from the battle, primed to *fuck*, not to make love, and I wanted to meet his needs the same way he always met mine.

I still felt shy *asking* for what I wanted, but there was no doubt that I knew exactly what that was. No. I knew exactly what I needed to feel good.

Wild didn't argue, the bed creaked and bumped against the wall as he powered into me the way he'd been craving. I sucked in a surprised breath when he snatched up my wrist, sucking my fingers into his mouth before encouraging me to slide my hand between our bodies. Forgetting my inhibitions, I circled my clit just the way I liked it, finding release in an embarrassingly short time. Wild groaned as I clenched around him, his movements growing jerky before he pulled out completely and flipped me onto my front.

Half boneless, my upper body lay on the mattress, and I pushed my hips into the air, making a muffled sound of impatience at how long he was taking.

"This view," Wild growled, squeezing my cheeks roughly. "Fuck, Grace. One day when I have time, I'm going to worship this ass properly." Once upon a time, I'd have been mortified by the idea, but remembering how good it felt when Riot had been teasing me there...

"Okay," I agreed breathily.

With a frustrated groan—perhaps that he didn't have the time now—Wild grabbed me by the hips, *yanking* me back on his cock. I pressed my mouth against my forearm to stifle the sounds I was making, rocking back against him but mostly letting Wild set the pace, as he did in every aspect of life.

It wasn't long until I was tightening around him again, pleasure rippling out to every inch of my body. Wild followed a moment later, with another delicious groan of pleasure. I'd never get used to *hearing* him. It wasn't the same as feeling him through the bond, but it was definitely its own kind of miracle.

Wild held me close, rolling us until we were on our sides, his cock softening inside me. After we'd caught our breath, he got up, insisting I stay still while he cleaned us both up before climbing under the blankets. I draped myself half over his chest and thigh, wanting to be as close to him as possible for as long as possible.

"The bond didn't come back," Wild murmured, sounding half-asleep already. He was probably exhausted.

"No," I agreed quietly, a twinge of disappointment hitting me square in the chest.

"You don't sound surprised. Did you and Dare already test this? For science?" he teased sleepily.

"We did," I laughed quietly. "I knew not to get my hopes up this time."

Wild hummed before falling silent for so long that I assumed he'd gone to sleep.

"I miss it, but it doesn't change anything, Grace. The bond didn't make me love you, and it's not going to take my love away."

Wild woke me before dawn, his armor clinking lightly as he did his best to dress quietly. He'd lit a candle to see by, and I took a moment to admire him in the flickering low light.

"You can stay here," Wild murmured as I sat up. "Theodoros, one of the Spartoi, will stay outside the room and watch over you."

"Oh no, I don't want to split your resources just so that I can sleep a little later." I was already pushing off the blankets. "I want to help, wherever I can. Besides, I have offerings to make."

Hopefully Gaia would send something else I could use if the scorpions were no more.

191

Wild nodded in approval, handing me a stack of fabric. "Theodoros found some clothes that look to be close to your size. They're clean, at least."

I barely restrained myself from squealing, grabbing a pair of cotton pants that were so small I couldn't do up the top button, a slightly-too-large t-shirt, and a scratchy brown knitted sweater that I had to roll up a few times at the sleeves.

I didn't care. They were clean, and it was the most comfortable I'd been in days. I even had woolen socks that were long enough to cover my ankles where the too-short pants finished and were thick enough to fill out the ill-fitting boots. Since the darkness had lifted, the weather had warmed significantly, but it was still approaching winter and there was a definite chill in the air.

"The short hair is a lot easier to manage," I said, running my fingers through it as I came to stand by Wild, kitted out in his full armor and cutting quite the dashing, albeit slightly intimidating figure.

The corners of his lips tipped up. "It suits you. Though I'd find you beautiful no matter what."

We made our way out just as the sun was rising, the air smelling deceptively fresh and pretty while we headed for the battlefield. T flew over head, looping back and dropping low enough in the sky to cuff the short ends of my hair with a snakey leg, before swooping away with a huff.

Wild looked down at me with his eyebrows raised. "Have you got an admirer, darling?"

I laughed, shaking my head. "No. I'm his friend. He needs one."

I leaned up to kiss Wild's cheek, and he turned to catch my lips in a chaste kiss. It wasn't nearly enough, but neither of us pressed for a heavier goodbye as we made our way back along the empty road to the battlefield. Anything more would have been an admission that today carried real risk, and neither of us wanted that. No, we were going to head out there as though this was any normal day, and we'd see each other later because no other alternative was acceptable.

"Stay safe for me," Wild instructed as we arrived among the Spartoi. "Stay back. Don't do anything rash."

"I could say the same to you," I pointed out. The sun was rising higher. The wall of stone that had hidden the agathos army seemed to have shifted and changed, allowing for some offensive attack through gaps in the rock. The Spartoi were already falling into formation, but I couldn't see how they could penetrate the fortress Gaia had built for her army. Was there any point trying?

The volcano that appeared out of the ground yesterday directly blocked the horizon, and the sky had turned an ominous shade of blood red. Part of me wanted to ask Wild to turn around, to march the Spartoi away from what seemed like impossible odds. But it would just put this fight off for another day, wouldn't it?

T flew into action while I deliberated, sending a black cloud of rain and lightning right over the plateau, forcing Gaia to close in the open ceiling of the rock structure to shield the army from above.

Wild grimaced, grabbing me and pressing a hard kiss to my lips. "I love you, my Prophêtis. See you at sunset."

"I love you," I whispered at his back as he walked away, the Spartoi parting respectfully for him to make his way to the front line.

The agathos attempted to hurl a wave of stones down, but T directed gale force winds that flung their own stones right back at them. The rain was coming down in a sheet at the cave's mouth, turning the ground beneath them to sludge. A flash of lightning struck at the already weakened plateau, a targeted attack on the structural integrity. Gaia was a formidable foe, but

T was her son, and it was clear that he knew what he was doing.

Had he just been warming up yesterday?

I strayed a little further back from the field, but not too far, to gather more branches to throw on the low-burning fire, watching T work out of the corner of my eye. He *had* just been warming up yesterday, I decided. Or holding back, at the very least. Possibly, he was feeling a little more fired up this morning since the Spartoi hadn't run from him in terror overnight.

As he fought, the volcano began to spit and rumble, the faint trickle of white smoke that had been drifting out of it thickening and growing into a dense, black plume. Immediately, there were Spartoi surrounding me, holding their shields up so I could only see through a small sliver where they overlapped. They were moving forward to rejoin the broken formation, carrying me along on the tide with them as they moved.

Shouldn't we run? I thought vaguely. After all, swords and shields wouldn't protect us from magma. Then again, with the speed that it moved, maybe we were too late to run anyway. Maybe Wild and the Spartoi were assuming that Gaia wouldn't risk her own army by sending lava this way.

I wasn't quite so confident.

Before I could vocalize my thoughts that maybe retreat was the best option, a deafening screech filled our ears, sending all of us ducking for cover. The motion caused the shields to lower, just in time to see something enormous and red, with fiery wings fly out of the volcano, shooting into the sky with another shriek of displeasure.

T wasn't the only monster in the skies anymore.

"*Drakon*," one of the men next to me whispered. I didn't need a translator for that. *Dragon*. Gaia had sent a dragon.

CHAPTER 24

The glowing web faded into nothingness, leaving the three sisters standing in front of me. I climbed to my feet, having all but collapsed from exhaustion at some point while they worked. I may have even fallen asleep, it had all been a blur of staring souls, mumbling creepy goddesses, and the incessantly flickering web of mortality.

Ten out of ten would not recommend.

"It is done," Clotho murmured.

I looked at her, searching inside myself for any sign of change. The hollowness in my chest felt as cold and empty as ever.

"Is it?"

"Don't you question us, *boy*," Atropos hissed. "We have given you the means, you will need to do the work for yourself. Perhaps your agathos won't even want you anymore."

Fucking *ouch*.

"Then I wish her all the luck in the world getting rid of me because

I'm not going willingly. Tell me how to bond with her again, and these kind souls here will be happy to release you."

Atropos looked ready to argue, but Clotho beat her to it. I barely dared to breathe as she spoke, absorbing every word of her instructions. I couldn't mess this up. I *wouldn't*. Not when I'd come this far.

"Can we leave now?" Atropos asked the moment her sister finished speaking. "We are very busy, you know. You've taken up enough of our time."

"And we have given you what you came here for," Clotho added, more serene than her sister.

Lachesis suddenly plucked at the air as though she was catching a fly between two fingers. I startled as a gray thread materialized, as thin as a spider web. She held it up, all three of them leaning in to observe it as the thread morphed from a burnished gray to a brilliant silver.

"Whose thread is that?" I rasped, watching in wonder. That had to be someone special. Someone like my Gracie.

"Yours."

"*Mine*? Why is it silver?"

"A perk of being what you are, I suppose," Atropos grumbled. "Apparently, holding us against our will so we could restore your precious soul bonds is an act of heroism."

"You didn't actually restore them," I pointed out, a weird bubble of what might have been happiness expanding in my chest. No, that wasn't right.

Pride?

Was I proud of myself? I was pretty sure I'd never been proud of myself in my life.

Heroism? That was quite the word to be tossed around in relation

196

to me, of all people.

"Ingrate," Atropos hissed. "Let us be, Moros. We all have more important places to be; you wouldn't want the scales of fate to tip against your love's favor, would you?"

She certainly knew how to hit where it hurt with the threats.

"Release them," I instructed the souls, gesturing at the Fates. The ghosts moved instantly, some of them vanishing, others hanging around, but all disconnecting from the web they'd created to pin the sisters in place.

I did my best to ignore the spike of panic in my gut about what I had to do next. *Just a few more steps, and then you can get back to Grace. Don't fumble the ball this late in the game, Riot.*

Clotho stilled, turning that unseeing gaze on me. "We have a palace in the underworld. When your time comes, many years from now, when you are hunched and gray and a life well-lived shows in the lines of your face, you are welcome to visit us there, Moros."

"Um, thanks," I replied, silently vowing to never take her up on that offer because the Fates were fucking terrifying.

"If you make it there, of course," Atropos said wryly. "Since you still have an island of trapped souls to deal with first. Perhaps we will see you here the next time we visit Poveglia. As dead and hopeless as the rest of these poor mortals."

And with that, the three sisters disappeared, leaving me in a room full of expectant ghosts.

Okay. Cool. No pressure.

Except quite a lot of pressure, actually, because they were already pressing in, impatient. And I couldn't blame them for that because I'd barely spent any time on this island, and I was very much in a hurry to leave.

My ghost lady friend stared at me with wide, hopeful eyes, moving directly in front of me in a gesture that may have been friendly, designed to keep the others from getting any closer.

"This island is a fucking dump," I told her flatly, clenching my hands into fists at my sides to stop them from shaking. "It's a stain on the reputation of the underworld. They should be *ashamed* that they have left so many souls here to rot. Specifically, the God of Death himself should be ashamed that he hasn't been fulfilling his duties. That he's created a wasteland of forgotten souls so extensive that not even *Death himself* could clean it up—"

"I will kill you," Thanatos announced, stepping out of nothing and storming toward me, his purple leather pants squeaking with each step, unbuttoned paisley shirt flapping in the breeze. "I won't be drawn into this. I'm not even a little bit tempted."

"Liar," I snorted.

"I'm not. You are not putting this much work on me. Do you know how many souls are here?"

"Well, maybe you should have kept on top of it over the centuries," I retorted, leaning in and barely resisting the impulse to poke him in the chest. I was dehydrated, starving, and tired. Fuck this shit, I didn't have time for a god's tantrum. "Not even you, Thanatos, God of Death, could transport all of these souls to the underworld."

"I can do *anything*," he snarled, a slightly feral look in his eyes that reminded me he'd thoroughly kicked Wild's ass once, and I knew for a fact I was weaker than Wild.

"No, you can't. If you could take these souls to the underworld, you'd have done it already," I replied dismissively, pretending I wasn't three seconds away from passing out. "You're just scared of this place, scared of the Fates. As though they're frightening or something—I'm a mediocre Moros, and I faced them just fine."

I rolled my neck, trying to loosen up my muscles after sitting on the broken tile floor for however long it had taken the Fates to do their thing. Time was an abstract concept at this point.

"I fucking hate you," Thanatos clipped, pointing a finger at me. "I fucking hate that Keres and I hate the two spare daimons whose names I refuse to learn. You're lucky that I'm so intrigued by your agathos—what kind of sweet, innocent Eutychia would tie herself to useless shitbags like you? She should be on her knees, praying in gratitude that the bonds were broken and she was released from her ties to you four stains on society, but no, she actually seemed quite disappointed. Fascinating."

I would greatly prefer Thanatos *not* be intrigued by Grace, but my life couldn't be that easy.

"Death *himself* can clean this wasteland up just fine. I'm not afraid of the Fates." He linked his fingers, stretching his arms in front of him and cracking his neck. "Now, move. Unless you want to find your soul in the underworld too—I don't plan on being careful."

Lunatic.

I half ran, half stumbled out of the chapel, running through a corridor of anxious, excited souls and heading for the exit. If I had to swim off this island, I'd swim. Whatever it took. Though I was pretty sure I wasn't within swimming distance of Grace, which was a massive issue, but not one I was able to address at this exact moment.

The second I was outside, I sucked down a lungful of clean air, tipping my head up to feel the warm sun on my face. Maybe it was what I'd just accomplished with the Fates, maybe it was the lack of souls pressing directly down on top of me, or maybe it was something else, but the world felt different somehow. Brighter. More hopeful.

It was probably just the hunger talking.

Arete appeared before me, looking far more impressed with me than she had the last time she'd seen me.

"Well, look at you," she crooned, crossing her arms and looking me up and down. "You have that glow of fulfilled potential. As well as a little something extra."

"Cool," I replied, glancing over my shoulder. I didn't want to be rude, but I was in a real hurry to get the fuck out of here. "Can you give me a lift back to my girl now? I have a bond to restore."

"You are a *hero*, and the best you can respond with is 'cool'?" Arete looked faintly appalled, which was much more familiar territory.

"A *hero*? That can't be right." I thought back to that silvery thread that represented my life. I thought Atropos had meant 'act of heroism' in a metaphorical sense. "No, that's not me. That's Grace's whole thing. Bringing in the Second Age of Heroes or whatever."

"Or whatever," Arete muttered to herself. "*Heroes*, plural. The receiver of the prophecy, who saw it through to completion, was never going to be the only one. That's how plurals work."

"Yes, thank you for the English lesson; very helpful," I grumbled, my face heating slightly with a mixture of embarrassment and something more self-conscious. "Can we go now?"

There was a weird, shrieking sound from inside the building that I really didn't want to examine too closely. Since I hadn't been able to hear the souls, I could only assume it was Thanatos having his version of a dead ferry party, and I wanted nothing to do with it.

Arete cut an annoyed sidelong look at the building, pursing her lips

200

in disapproval. "Yes, let's. I suppose, in a world of change, it's nice to see that some things never do. Thanatos is... exactly who he has always been."

And with that, she grabbed me roughly by the arm and stepped into nothingness. For a moment, there was only golden light and a peach-colored sky.

It was a split second of perfect peace before she abruptly released me, and I stumbled onto a battlefield, right behind an army.

"Riot!"

My arms came out automatically, catching Grace around the middle as she broke through a group of soldiers—Spartoi—and threw herself at me, knocking me a step backward.

There was a shriek from above us, and I dragged Grace to the ground instinctively, sheltering her as best I could as an enormous red-winged *beast* flew overhead.

And then crashed headlong into *another* enormous black-winged beast.

What the fuck was going on? I'd walked out of a horror movie and into some kind of epic fantasy where apparently *dragons* were flying around.

Or at least one of them was a dragon. The other one was... Honestly, I had no idea. Humanoid-ish, but with giant bat wings and snake legs.

I clutched Grace a little tighter to my chest, looking around, trying to figure out where exactly I was and what was happening. Why was Grace here? Who was this fight between?

"Riot, you're here," Grace sobbed. I wrapped a hand around the back of her head, vaguely registering her hair was shorter than before.

"I'm here. Are you okay, Gracie? What's going on? Where are we?"

The snake monster unleashed a wave of fire that the dragon seemed to bat away with apparently flame-proof wings. Maybe... maybe wings made of fire?

"I'm okay," Grace breathed, trembling as she watched the monsters above us do battle. "A little terrified for T, but I'm safe. Gaia's army of agathos is over there, on the fortification she made for them. Wild is leading the Spartoi, trying to penetrate the fortress now there's no more scorpions, but there isn't much they can do. Where have you been? Are you okay? Riot, I missed you so much—"

Her voice broke on a sob, and my limbs shook with relief and love and gratitude that Grace was here and she was safe—against all odds—and that she hadn't forgotten about me. I couldn't even process the rundown she'd given me of the battle. All of that had been going on while I'd been holed up for who knew how long on Poveglia?

I pressed a hard kiss to her temple, followed by three more. "I missed you more than you can believe, Gracie. Fucking hell, I've been so worried. Wild is here too?"

She nodded against my chest. "Dare is okay, but not here. Sophia said he's on his way."

She didn't volunteer any information about Bullet, and I didn't ask. Not yet.

"You need to sit, you're shaking," Grace said, sniffling. "Here, by the fire. The Spartoi are going to fuss at me being away from the shields, but if you collapse in the formation, you'll get trampled. Besides, T won't let the dragon get close."

"Who is T?" I asked, letting Grace lead me to the fire and dropping on the ground while she threw some branches on to keep it burning. After a minute, she appeared with a bottle of water and a handful of almonds in hand, looking apologetic.

"I'm sorry. There was scorpion meat, but I guess they ate the last of it overnight. It probably wouldn't store well. Though I'm guessing you'd prefer the almonds?"

"Almonds are good," I assured her, taking a swig of water before belatedly realizing I should probably sip it, given how dehydrated I was. "Honestly, I'd eat the scorpions whole—bulletproof casing and everything—at this point, I'm starving."

"Slowly," Grace cautioned, sinking down to the ground on her knees next to me and looking worried. Maybe it made me a total bastard, but there was a part of me that liked when Grace directed her worried-face at me. Maybe because I hadn't been on the receiving end of a lot of genuine concern in my life. "Where have you been? Sophia said that Arete had some kind of mission for you."

I snorted in spite of the dire circumstances. "I guess it was a mission, though it felt more like being kidnapped by a statue because I happened to be bleeding out at her feet and that's her version of a superfood."

Grace looked horrified and I hurried to explain despite how much I wanted to stuff my face full of almonds. "After my, er, altercation with Wild, I was bleeding a bit and Arete's statue sucked up all the blood the way Sophia's did for yours. And then she decided I was the one to go and visit the Fates and figure out the whole soul bond issue—"

"*What*?" Grace asked, eyes wide. There was a crash overhead, the two beasts flying into one another before bursting apart in a swirl of fire. I couldn't decide which one had caused it—both of them seemed impervious to flames. "Come on, T," Grace muttered, glaring daggers at the dragon.

"You never told me who T is," I murmured, shoving an almond in my mouth and setting the water down so I could wrap an arm around her waist. "And why you think we're even remotely safe sitting out in the open like this."

"Oh, T is Typhoeus. He's Gaia's son, but he's on our side." She pointed him out, the humanoid-type one with snake legs and black wings.

Who was apparently on our side.

"He's just lonely," Grace added, as though that was an entirely logical explanation. "The dragon flew out of the volcano that sprouted out of nowhere." She tipped her chin toward the towering, black volcano on the horizon and my head spun slightly. "T is fierce though. He can conjure storms and breathe fire. I have full confidence in him."

I panic ate some almonds and held Grace a little closer. I hadn't even *kissed* her yet, but I felt filthy and disgusting, and we were sitting courtside on a battlefield with a couple of not-so-mythical beasts fighting above us. It wasn't exactly the romantic reunion I'd envisioned.

But it didn't matter. Grace was here and healthy, and there'd be time to kiss her breathless later.

"Are they brothers, do you think?" I asked, wincing as the dragon flew at T, clawed feet first, catching him in the chest. T let out a roar, accompanied by a stream of fire, but managed to shake the dragon off, flying at him with his fist cocked.

"Brothers?" Grace repeated, frowning.

"Presumably Gaia sent the dragon, right? And you said T was Gaia's son, and he's, you know... Kind of beastly looking. No offense. And so is the dragon, so..."

"How did I not realize that?" Grace's hand clamped down on my thigh, I grimaced slightly, realizing how disgusting my clothes were.

One of the Spartoi stumbled toward us, breaking through the

formation, face bleeding.

"Shoot." Grace jumped up, digging through the ragtag bundle of supplies they had and pulling out some water and a rag. "What happened?"

The Spartoi sheepishly mimed a rock flying from the plateau and hitting him in the face. He stumbled slightly, eyes moving in and out of focus, obviously hurting more than he wanted to let on.

"Sit," Grace ordered, fussing over the soldier while she cleaned up his face, gesturing at him to take off his helmet.

I finished my water and almonds, climbing heavily to my feet and stretching. Already the lines of soldiers were looking kind of messy, and I didn't know shit about fighting rank and file, but I was pretty sure maintaining numbers was an important element.

"Hey, give me your weapons," I told the Spartoi. "I'm gonna sub in."

Grace gave me a look that was somewhat akin to horrified, and I did my best not to be offended about it.

"Riot, you're exhausted—"

"I'll sleep after. Come here, give me a hug, Gracie."

She wrapped her arms around my waist, clinging to me for a long moment before reaching up to kiss my jaw. "Come back to me soon, okay?"

I heaved a sigh, propped up by adrenaline alone, and donned the Spartoi's armor. "This is our last goodbye, Gracie. I'm not doing it anymore. After this battle is over, I'm going to handcuff us together if I have to, but I'm not letting you go."

CHAPTER 25

This was so fucked.

We were so fucked.

Gaia must have grown a catapult out of the ground, because the rocks were coming harder and faster, and reaching further back into the ranks. Through the whispers from the back line, I'd heard that Riot had arrived, but in the chaos, I hadn't had a chance to see him yet.

And T was flagging.

He'd already been throwing everything at the fortress before the dragon had shown up, and he'd stayed up all night to watch over our soldiers.

Grace had good instincts. T was a solid ally, and I had to find a way to assist him.

"We need to help him!" I shouted to Ariston, gesturing up at T then lifting my spear. "Maybe we can hit the dragon the next time he swoops low. I think we need to aim for the throat, the skin there looks thinner."

We both raised our shields, the ring of the rocks denting the shield almost deafening when we were holding them so close to our heads.

Ariston was trying to communicate something with me, but it took a moment for my ears to stop ringing enough to understand him. Now that I was looking, I realized how *unsettled* he seemed to be. Glancing back, *all* of the Spartoi looked slightly unsettled. They were staunchly fighting the agathos, but studiously avoiding the battle happening overhead.

They hadn't responded to T that way.

"Drakon," Ariston said, staring at the shrieking dragon that was attacking T right above us. "Drakon *Kolkhikos*."

"You know him?" I asked, signing one-handed while I spoke.

Ariston looked apologetic. He pointed at the dragon before opening his mouth and pointing at his teeth, then his chest, before miming scattering seeds on the ground.

"Men sown from the teeth of dragons." That's what Bullet had said. The dragons teeth that Persephone had given Grace when we were in the underworld.

Teeth from *that* dragon.

"I can't catch a fucking break," I muttered, scooping a rock off the ground that the agathos had thrown and biffing it back before raising my shield again. They were just an annoyance for now. The dragon was the priority.

"Is that... your father? Can you not fight it?"

Ariston shook his head apologetically, though his nose wrinkled slightly at the word father. There was a good chance he hadn't understood me, though.

"Will it attack you?" I shouted over the din, gesturing at the dragon and then at the Spartoi.

Ariston shook his head again, but he didn't look as confident in that as I would like. Glancing up at the dragon, it *did* look more hesitant to unleash a full attack when T was driving it directly over our army. Perhaps he knew that, which was why T was so happy to risk crushing us all if either fell from the sky.

We all ducked as T took a fierce blow that knocked him down a few feet. He unleashed a stream of fire, forcing the dragon to duck to the side, but since the dragon appeared to be flame-proof, it didn't make much difference. From what I could tell, it couldn't breathe fire the way Typhoeus could, but the edges of its wings were edged with flames which it was using as a weapon by trying to sideswipe T.

Okay. Make a plan. What was the next logical step? Weak spot around the throat, wings were lethal, Spartoi were potentially safe—

With a roar of pain, T finally went down, slamming wings first into the base of the plateau. Time stood still as the tower, already weakened by T's incessant rain and lightning, teetered. Rock and dirt fell away, showering down on him as T slid down into the ditch.

Grace screamed from somewhere behind me, and the base of the plateau cracked, the whole thing tilting hard to the right, sending the structure Gaia had created on top sliding off—complete with the agathos in it. The dragon dived hard toward the base, and for a brief, hopeful moment, I thought he was going to try to save the mortals falling to certain death, trapped within the rock shield that had become a prison. No, a *tomb*.

But he didn't. The dragon was aiming for T.

I hefted my spear into the air, surprising both the beast and myself when it embedded in his tail. Shit. *I didn't think this through.*

There was no doubt in his gaze that I was responsible. He was clearly aware that the Spartoi weren't able to harm him and despite the armor, I apparently wasn't passing as one of them.

The stone structure fell with a deafening crash, but I couldn't let myself think about that. Couldn't let myself analyze the cost of war, and whether it was right for those agathos to pay it when they'd been drawn in by the temptation of food and trapped up there with no way of leaving.

I grabbed Ariston's spear, aiming at the dragon's left eye this time, though it bounced off his face as he spun away. He was creeping closer on all four giant lizard legs, flaming wings outstretched either side of him, clearly debating how best to get me alone to fry me with his appendages.

"Sorry," I mumbled, discarding my shield and grabbing Ariston by the back of his body armor, and marching him forward, unsheathing my sword from my hip at the same time. I wasn't proud of using one of my fellow soldiers as a human shield, but I wasn't going to let him get hurt, either.

Ariston didn't struggle, but he was dragging his feet, leaning as far back from the dragon as possible. The dragon lifted itself to its full height, wings beginning to beat the air, readying itself for takeoff where it would regain the airborne advantage.

But the distraction had been just long enough for T to rouse himself, and he slid up the wall of the ditch with impressive speed and silence before launching himself onto the dragon's back, flattening him to the ground. The dragon bent its wings back, pressing the flames against T's skin, and I didn't allow myself time to hesitate.

I shoved Ariston aside, grabbing his sword, so I had one in each hand, and charged. The dragon thrashed, and T's roars of pain were morphing into something a little more weak and reedy. If T *could* die, then this would be the moment it happened.

The dragon spotted me approaching, and I darted out of the way as it made a snap for me with a mouthful of vicious teeth. Calling on all of my experience in the ring, I forced my feet to move rather than to plant firmly in place, dancing in close before shifting away again, taunting the dragon with my proximity while he alternated his attention between me and T.

There were shouts behind me, though I couldn't tell if they were encouragement or discouragement, nearly drowned out by the agonizing sounds of human suffering where the structure had collapsed. Something arose in me that wasn't quite bloodlust, but it was similar enough. It was rage and frustration, horror and disbelief.

And unlike with the bloodlust, where I ran from the sensation until it caught up and smothered me, I leaned into the feeling. And when T dragged himself higher up the dragon, grabbing his face and digging his thumbs into the beast's eyeballs, I seized the opening.

I ran forward on steady feet, raising the blades above my head and plunging them into either side of the dragon's throat. It let out a piercing howl, the movement of its vocal cords making it even harder to push the blades all the way to their hilts, twisting and digging into the thick, armor-like flesh.

"I'm sorry," I grunted, silently saying a prayer that this dragon could in fact be killed, and that if it was, Thanatos would take care with its soul. He had been a weapon, and now he was dying for it.

My arm muscles strained and burned as I twisted the blades again, black blood spurting out of the wounds and hitting my face, my helmet, my breastplate.

And finally, *finally*, the dragon fell still.

THE SPIRIT OF DREAMS

CHAPTER 26

Gods liked to hear themselves talk, I decided. I wasn't complaining necessarily, because hearing about the world and the primordial gods who'd come from Chaos, about the Titans who'd risen to prominence through violence, and then the Olympians who'd taken their place—also through violence, it was a theme—was fascinating. And in some ways, I saw hints of what I thought it was that Tartarus was looking for.

They spoke about their lives before with longing, and they spoke of Gaia's victory that sent them here to this prison with a sense of calm, rather than a cold, vicious need for revenge.

And I knew nothing about anything, but that seemed good, didn't it? The problem was that I didn't *know*. All I knew about the upperworld—the ones who'd be most impacted by this decision—was the snippets I'd heard from the various underworld deities I'd spoken to. The only *concrete* memory I had of the upperworld was the sunshine on my face, the sound of rustling trees, and the baby laughing.

In my head, it was perfect the way it was. Why mess with perfection?

"Halfling," a low voice growled, making me jump. Aphrodite shot an impatient look at the god who'd interrupted her story, but the ire melted out of her expression after a moment.

"My husband," she explained. "Hephaestus."

"Oh." The god narrowed his eyes at me, and I guessed I didn't school my surprise fast enough. It was just that Aphrodite was so beautiful, and Hephaestus was... more rugged. He was bulkier than most of the other gods, though not as tall as Zeus. While a couple of them had beards and long hair, none were as wild as Hephaestus'. In his toga-like outfit, it was clear to see that hair extended over his entire upper body.

"Come," he commanded. "They all talk too much. Let me show you more of what has been our home these past millennia."

"Oh, okay." I stood, staying a step behind as he limped out of the lounge room full of couches, heading down a stone corridor before taking a sharp left and heading down a narrow, winding staircase.

"You looked as though you needed a break. They will talk and talk and tell you nothing," Hephaestus grumbled. "They all like to hear the sounds of their own voices, and all believe they have something of value to add. Something that *must* be heard. However, in the time we've been trapped here, we have learned to listen to one another much better. We collaborate better."

The spiral staircase ended, and I heard the roar of flames before I saw the enormous fire. It was some kind of forge, I guessed. The walls were lined with weapons and helmets and armor, each one entirely unique and some quite odd.

"I have a limited amount of material to work with, so most of what you see has been melted down and made anew many times over. For centuries, I had no space to myself, but once it became clear to the others that I was struggling without somewhere quiet to go, they decided to create this area exclusively for my use."

That was nice of them. Collaborative. Kind.

Hephaestus picked up an axe, spinning it easily in his hand before mounting it back on the wall again.

"My wife and I used to have... a contentious relationship. She loves Ares, always has. Ares loves her back."

"And now?"

Hephaestus' smile was vaguely menacing, but I was pretty sure that was just how his face looked. "Now, Ares has learned to share."

Huh. I mean, no judgment here. Apparently, I'd had a boyfriend and a girlfriend once.

For a long while, we sat in silence. Or rather, I sat in silence while Hephaestus pottered around his workshop. I hadn't realized I'd needed a break from the information overload until I had one, and now my brain was trying to process everything I'd seen and learned and heard, basically from the moment I'd materialized in that empty stone palace.

"What would you do in my shoes?" I asked, staring into the flames of the forge.

"You're in an unfortunate position," Hephaestus said quietly, metal clinking against metal in the background. "If you don't remember the time before, then how are you supposed to decide if we are a better choice?"

"There was a baby." Hephaestus was silent, his movements stopping, and I took that as an invitation to continue. "Wherever I was, I could hear a baby. And the baby cried sometimes but mostly laughed a lot. And it was really nice."

Hephaestus sighed heavily. "I miss watching mortal lives. The way they take pleasure in the small things that we can never appreciate—a hot meal on a cold day, a warm bath after a hard day's work. A good *fuck* with an enthusiastic partner." He paused for a moment. "I suppose I can appreciate that last one."

I laughed before I could help myself, catching his beard twitch out of the corner of my eye.

"There is no perfect answer, halfling. You can only do the best with what you have. Are you ready to go back in? If we're truly lucky, Ares will regale us with a long detailed description of his exploits during the Trojan War." Hephaestus smirked. "But my wife has ways of making him quiet if you get bored."

There was a sort of strange muscle memory in my face, and I was pretty sure that if I was in my regular body, I'd be blushing.

The moment we were back, the regal, important-looking goddess—Hera—gestured for me to join her on a long seat. I made myself as small as possible as I sat down, feeling as though I was breaking some invisible protocol. She was the *Queen* of the Gods. Then again, I was important at this moment, wasn't I? I was the deciding factor here.

I'd just act important and hope for the best.

"There are many things we'd all like to tell you," Hera began. "I have been sitting here, thinking of the things I myself wanted to say while you visited Hephaestus' forge. We have only had each other's company for so long, and perhaps we are a little *enthusiastic* in regaling you with our stories, but I'd like to ask you to listen to just one more. I don't tell you this to sway you, Conscience of Tartarus, but to help you understand why I believe Tartarus *needs* a conscience. *Why* he is conflicted."

Considering how enthusiastic they'd all been to talk before, the other eleven gods had gone eerily silent.

"Okay," I replied slowly, hoping I wasn't betraying Tartarus by agreeing.

"We have already told you that we are here because of Gaia's hunger for power; well, you should know that Gaia is Tartarus' great love. There was a time in which he'd do anything she demanded of him without question. He gave her the son she asked for, knowing the child would be used as a weapon before being hidden away and ignored. He imprisoned us here, despite his personal concerns about leaving the running of the upperworld to Gaia alone, because she demanded it of him. And though she's never offered him a scrap of affection in return, he has always lived in hope that if he does everything she asks of him, she'll finally, *finally* love him."

This was a really sad story.

"We are immortal beings," Aphrodite added, perching on the edge of a stool in front of the couch. "However long we've been trapped here—we lived even longer on Olympus, even longer in power. I tell you this so you understand we cannot see and interpret time the way mortals can. Usually, for immortal beings, to wait is nothing, and Tartarus is older than all the gods you see here—"

"—but even he cannot wait forever," Hera continued. There was a hint of genuine sadness in her eyes, of compassion and sorrow, that spoke louder than any of her words ever could. "Tartarus is the only one who can free us, but to do so would be in direct opposition to Gaia's wishes, and he has *never* gone against her wishes before."

"What's to stop Gaia throwing you back in here again if Tartarus frees you? Just his will?" I asked, trying to understand it.

"Don't underestimate his will," Zeus warned. "Or us."

"We are stronger than we have been in so long," Dionysus added. "Because of you and the others inspired by your worship. Here—*where no prayers or sweet-smelling smoke can reach*—we are rather restricted. We can hear hints of prayers, but the power that worship and offerings give us cannot penetrate this clever cell Tartarus made for us. It is building, though, collecting on the outside, waiting for us to be free and claim it. For a few blissful days, the sounds of worship were so loud through the pit Gaia opened." He closed his eyes, a languid smile spreading across his face. "So loud, I can taste the power of them on my tongue."

"We have been thoroughly humbled by mortals," Zeus said wryly. "It is abundantly clear that we needed them more than they needed us."

"We are gods. We have roles. We need *purpose*. We need prayers, we need to be *needed*. Crave it," Dionysus sighed, still looking sort of blissed out, lounging in a chair.

Humanity. I was supposed to be looking for humanity.

But I wasn't going to find it, not entirely. With no memory of my previous life and only vague ideas of what I *thought* humans were supposed to be, I could understand that gods would never see the world or its inhabitants the same way we did.

"So all of this comes down to Tartarus?" I confirmed.

"I can say with certainty Gaia will not think Tartarus is capable of going against her. She will have full confidence in her control of him," Hera said slowly. "But no. All of this comes down to you."

I didn't like any of this. Tartarus was a good dude, he deserved better than that. He deserved love, or at the very least not to be treated like *that*.

"Their son is in the upperworld now," I said absently, thinking of how great Tartarus was and how much he obviously cared for his son. His son's *happiness*.

All twelve deities froze, turning to stare at me in an eerily coordinated action.

"Typhoeus is free?" someone asked. "And the upperworld still stands?"

"He is a giant of storms who can breathe fire," Hera said with more urgency. "This is not the kind of creature mortals can overcome alone. He brought us here. He is a formidable enemy."

"Only because we were already weakened," Ares added, somewhat petulantly.

Typhoeus has been either used or imprisoned his entire life. He wants to be free.

"Maybe he just wants what you want. Maybe he's been just as imprisoned here as you have."

Zeus looked at me thoughtfully. "Perhaps it is a rather un-divine thing to admit, but none of us can pretend to know what the world is like now, what mortals are like now, what Typhoeus is like now. Freedom for us would be like being reborn anew."

Stronger. That was what Dionysus said. They'd grown stronger from worship because of some trend that I'd perhaps been part of. They hadn't come out and explicitly said it, but they'd hinted at it enough for me to work out that *without* worship, they'd grown weaker.

They weren't infallible.

There was a way to curtail them if they acted against humanity's best interests, and they could do an immense amount of good if they were truly there to help.

Without any memories of the time before, the choice seemed obvious. I just had to hope that I was making the right one.

I stood, and walked across the room, past the Olympians to the entrance of the cavern. I couldn't see Tartarus, but I knew he was there.

Watching. Waiting.

"Can I come out? Talk to you?" I asked, pressing against the invisible shield in the doorway.

Tartarus was silent for a long moment. "What is your decision, the Spirit of Dreams?"

Okay, no small talk, I guess.

"I don't want to decide. I want you to decide." I sighed, leaning against the wall with my shoulder. "I want you to decide that you're worth more than what you've been accepting. You're not table scraps, you're the whole feast, and you deserve someone who recognizes that."

I nodded to myself, that sounded right.

"If someone treated Typhoeus that way, would you call it love and tell him to accept it?" I pressed.

"She already treats him the same way, under the guise of motherly love." He was silent for a long moment. "And it has never been okay."

"Then make your decision, Tartarus," I encouraged gently.

He let out a low growl, though it was more exasperated than anything. "Zeus, a word."

I flattened myself against the wall, the corridor feeling very narrow with a giant god's body in it.

"I want to strike a deal," Tartarus said coolly.

"You want this cell occupied in our place," Zeus replied easily. "We don't need to strike a deal for that, we are perfectly in accord."

"The deal is for you, not me," Tartarus growled. "You will bring Gaia here where she will reside in this cell. And if The Twelve ever forget that their loyalty is to humanity, that you are obligated to help and guide them, then you will join her here, one by one. You will agree to this deal, and I will release you."

Tartarus was a total badass.

"We are not beholden to you," Zeus replied, chest heaving as he blew out an aggrieved breath.

I felt Tartarus move forward, even if I couldn't see him. "Yes, little Olympian, you are. Accept your place, or stay in this prison for all of eternity. I don't care either way."

I really hoped Tartarus would at least get *me* out if these guys decided to stay here. We were friends, right? Friends didn't leave each other in prison cells.

Zeus continued to breathe heavily for a long moment, hands flexing at his sides before he finally made a furious noise of assent.

"Fine. *Fine.* The threat is irrelevant. We won't forget our obligations. We never did."

The force field keeping us in the cavern suddenly vanished. A pressure that had been so constant that I didn't realize how suffocating it was lifted, and I scrunched my eyes shut as Zeus began to glow like he was housing the sun itself within his body.

"Time for you to go," one of them said, their heavy hands landing on my shoulders and pushing me out of the cavern. "You are alive enough that seeing a god in their true form would kill you. We are not in control of ourselves right now—it's been so long since we've been able to access our divine forms that it's impossible to rein in."

Hermes, I recognized his voice. He groaned as though he was experiencing something intensely pleasurable and it gave me all the uncomfy feels.

"Where are we going? Where's Tartarus?"

"*You* are going back to the underworld. Tartarus has gone back to his hidey-hole." Hermes sighed blissfully again, tightening his grip on my shoulders and steering me forward so I couldn't see him. "I'm a little out of practice with my wings, so don't panic if we flop around a bit in midair. Promise I won't drop you."

That was very unreassuring.

"Can't I go back to the upperworld? I want to see if the people who loved me still remember me."

Hermes froze for a moment, his grip on my shoulders keeping me in place.

"Wow, that may be the saddest thing I've ever heard."

"So, you will take me back?" I asked hopefully. His hands felt like they were growing, encompassing more of my shoulders. The rock cavern around us was glowing slightly too, and I guessed he was illuminating the place.

"Patience, little halfling. As I said, we're not fully in control of our divine forms right now. I won't make the best second first impression with mortals if I show up and kill them all with my blinding greatness. Give me a minute."

"That doesn't sound ideal," I agreed, stumbling over the rocky path a little as we approached the bottom of the pit.

"Besides, you wouldn't want to miss your party. Be a good boy and don't eat or drink anything, or you'll be stuck in the underworld forever," he said in a sing-song voice.

What a strange fellow.

"What party?"

Hermes suddenly leaped into the air, hooking an arm around my middle and dragging me up with him as though I weighed nothing. We flew through the tunnels Tartarus had carried me through at least a hundred times faster than the pace I'd run through the underworld at. The fiery flames of the Phlegethon poured through the pit on every side, but Hermes flew directly up the middle, avoiding the magma. What felt like an eternity later—but still faster than it had taken me to get down to Tartarus—we emerged in the underworld, flying above the pit.

I was so disoriented from the speed at which we'd moved, it took my brain a minute to catch up.

"I'll deposit you at the palace. I'm assuming Hades and Persephone are able to hold their forms, so you should be safe there. Actually, Persephone will probably want me to take her straight to her mother after all this time," Hermes mused. "It won't be much of a celebration if Hades is in charge of it, I'm afraid—unless he has *drastically* changed in the time we've been imprisoned. You deserve better than what you'll get, probably."

"A celebration? Are we celebrating you?"

Hermes chuckled. "We're celebrating you."

I wasn't sure I'd done anything worthy of celebration. I'd just been in the right place at the right time, and I'd made a decision that I could only *hope* was the right one.

"You did it, the Spirit of Dreams," Hermes replied, slightly more somber now. "You liberated the Olympians. This is your hero's welcome."

GRACE

CHAPTER 27

The Spartoi—usually so deferential and respectful when it came to me—were in too much of an uproar to notice me fighting my way through their messy ranks, Riot at my side, to get to Wild.

I'd only caught glimpses of the action through the wall of bodies, and Riot trying to hold me back, but I knew Wild had struck the fatal blow.

I was proud and a little shaky in equal measure.

"Are they happy?" Riot shouted over the din. "I can't tell."

"Me neither," I admitted, slightly uneasy. The Spartoi had seemed very hesitant to attack the dragon. On reflection, they seemed to find it hard to even *look* at the dragon. They weren't swarming Wild, though. Just slamming their weapons on their shields and stomping their feet on the ground so hard that the earth vibrated beneath us.

They were bolstered by the fight, I guessed. It was the violence that was spurring them on, not Wild's victory necessarily.

Riot and I broke through the first rank, and I froze at seeing the fallen agathos structure up close, the giant slabs of rock smashed into a thousand pieces in the ditch, disguising the carnage underneath.

Why hadn't she saved them?

Wild limped forward, pulling me into his embrace. My cheek was immediately wet and sticky from the thick blood that had spurted onto his breastplate, but I didn't care. He was here. He was whole. He'd slayed the dragon and lived to tell the tale.

I burst into tears.

"I'm sorry!" I gasped. "I don't know why I'm crying. Yes, I do. You were amazing, but I was so scared. And all those people. Those people!" I sucked down a desperate lungful of oxygen. "T! T, are you okay?"

T had rolled off the dead, no-longer-flaming dragon. He was on his back, his greenish skin tinged black where the dragon's wings had burned him. He tilted his head to meet my eye, giving me an affirmative grunt. I doubted anyone else could tell, but there was a soft, faint gratitude in his gaze that I'd asked, and I made a note to make sure he felt valued and appreciated going forward.

"You're okay?" Wild rasped, wavering slightly on his feet.

Riot made a strangled sound, diving forward to drag Wild's arm over his shoulders to keep him upright. "You can talk?"

I slipped under Wild's arm on the other side, wrapping my arms around his middle. "I didn't tell you that?"

Wild was staring at Riot uncertainly, but Riot gave him a lazy grin that immediately had the tension in Wild's body easing.

"It's water under the bridge. We all lose control sometimes."

"Don't let me off the hook so easily," Wild replied hoarsely. "There was no excuse. You could hold this over my head for the rest of our lives, if you liked."

Riot flashed him a grin. "Maybe I will."

Wild's answering half smile was weak, fading to a somber expression as he took in the destruction that had once been the agathos army.

"We need to search for survivors," he said grimly, wincing as he attempted to straighten and step away from Riot and me.

"No." I stopped him with a firm hand against his chest, though it wasn't *that* firm. On any normal day, Wild could overpower me with his pinkie finger. "You just slayed a *dragon*, Wild. You're exhausted, and you're more hindrance than help to them in this state."

The barest flicker of a smile crossed Wild's face. "Are you giving me orders, my darling?"

My face flushed. "Maybe I am. Theras, could you..." I gestured at the wreckage, my throat complaining painfully as I mimed digging and pulling out survivors.

Theras didn't seem entirely convinced, but he called instructions to the Spartoi anyway, gesturing for them to follow him. Two Spartoi lay lifeless on the ground where their fellow soldiers had dragged them so their bodies would be safe from the fighting, ready for their burial rites.

There had been so much violence, so much death. How much had the agathos who'd been trapped on the plateau even wanted to be there? Maybe they'd begun their march in service of Gaia's honor, but she'd bribed them with food—a powerful motivator for starving people. They had been battling on the plains, and Gaia had raised them up, isolated them, trapped them in a stone cave.

For what?

What was the *point*?

I'd prayed, and I'd offered, and I'd prayed some more. I'd used my voice like Sophia had instructed me—though I was beginning to think she was wrong because she'd also told me Dare was on his way here, and he still hadn't appeared. I'd done what I was supposed to do, and yet here we were. Not *losing*, but certainly not winning. In a field of death and despair, there were no victors.

So why do this? What was all of this for?

What was the *point*?

I thought back to the times Gaia had answered me—the community center confrontation, the moment of quiet outside Zeus' temple in Athens—they'd all been times when I'd appealed to her ego. And as much as I didn't *want* to now, as much as it pricked at my pride to be even a little bit civilized to this monster after she'd let those agathos who fought in her name fall to their deaths, this was my role. I understood that now.

It wasn't just that I had some strange affinity to deities, that they heard me when I spoke; it was that I reached out to immortals even when they didn't deserve it. When no agathos spoke to Nyx, I'd bridged the gap. When I'd found out my soul bonds were daimons, I'd fallen for them anyway. I hadn't shied away from T when everyone else had. So often, I'd questioned myself, my usefulness, and wondered what my strengths were, but maybe it was this simple.

"Gracie," Riot said uneasily. "What is that face? What are you planning?"

I almost smiled, remembering Estrella talking about my *self-sacrifice face.*

"Just a conversation," I assured him, stepping out from underneath Wild's arm and taking a few steps backward before falling to my knees and slamming my hands down in the dirt.

"Gracie—"

"Face us," I demanded, not giving him and Wild a chance to object. "Gaia, face us. You wanted this fight. You equipped your army. You led them here. Come here and face the aftermath of this battle; see the bodies of the agathos who died in *your* name. Tell me you're satisfied with what you've done."

All eyes were on me as I stared down at the dirt, I could feel it, but I didn't look up. Not until the air around me shimmered and changed. *Then* I looked up, hastily climbing to my feet. Wild snatched my hand, pulling me into him, and T pushed himself to a sitting position, breathing heavily.

The Spartoi had frozen in place, and for a brief moment, it seemed as though all the oxygen was sucked out of the atmosphere. I couldn't breathe, couldn't speak, couldn't *scream*. But then it all came back in a rush, in a wave of golden light. I scrunched my eyes shut, throwing my arm over my face to shield myself against the blinding brilliance for a second before forcing myself to look, not wanting to miss a moment of whatever was happening.

They descended on chariots.

Six golden chariots the size of buses, pulled by white, winged horses, two riders standing on the back of each.

The Spartoi rushed forward, standing at our backs, careful to keep me front and center. Out of the corner of my eye, I noticed that they dropped to the ground, bending a knee and bowing their heads in reverence.

I straightened my spine, standing a little taller, while Wild and Riot shifted around to keep me in the middle, not bothering to bow either.

I wanted to decide for myself whether they were worthy of bowing to.

Despite the heavy *thud* of the chariots hitting the earth, the ground didn't shake. Almost as though Gaia herself was holding her breath, deciding what to do with this turn of events.

How were they here? Dare hadn't been able to get to Tartarus. The pit had closed up. Had there been another way in?

Then again, I supposed it didn't matter. Not really. However, the prophecy had been fulfilled, it was done now, and this was the moment we'd been waiting for. The culmination of all of our efforts. It was all for these golden, ethereal creatures who we had to hope would act in our best interests.

I didn't need an explanation of who was who. The many depictions of the gods that had survived since antiquity had done them plenty of justice. As the silver-bearded, enormous man stepped off the first chariot, a regal, slightly haughty goddess at his side, her palm resting on his forearm, I didn't wonder which deities they were. This was clearly Zeus and Hera, and the others behind them were just as clear—the lovely, bored Aphrodite, the stern, attentive Athena, the imposing, tempestuous Poseidon... They were all here.

They stepped off the chariots, and the winged horses took off into the air, leaving the twelve deities standing imperiously before us. The moment their feet hit the ground, another wave of dusky golden light washed over the earth.

And then the scent of *grass* filled my nose. Grass and *flowers*. The wind picked up, carrying the salt of the sea with it. In the distance, I could have sworn I heard the buzz of insects, and was that... birdsong? Or was I dreaming? The world had been so dead and silent for what felt like so long that I wondered if I was hallucinating.

For the briefest moment, I just let myself enjoy it. Let myself enjoy the beautiful, perfect peace of a lush and vibrant earth. The world the way it was meant to be.

By the time I opened my eyes, the golden color had faded, leaving behind verdant green surroundings beneath a brilliant dusky sky. The muddy battlefield was now a soft grassy plain with patches of brilliant wildflowers, though the jagged rocks, deep ditch, and remnants of the plateau were still standing.

My cheeks were wet with tears before I even realized I was crying.

Zeus, King of the Gods, surveyed his surroundings with interest before looking past me.

"Typhoeus," he called, inclining his head in greeting. "It's been a long time. You're looking well."

T huffed in annoyance, slithering closer until he was a looming presence at my back, casting a shadow over me, Riot, and Wild. Zeus turned his attention to me, his beard twitching slightly.

"Prophêtis. I have heard so much about you. I look forward to speaking to you more, but there is something I believe you'd like us to take care of here first, hm? Of course, that is the priority."

Hera nodded encouragingly at Zeus' side while he turned his impassive gaze down to the ground. "Come now, Mother Gaia," Zeus called, not bothering to raise his voice. "We have much to catch up on. Won't you visit with us?"

Silence.

"You were about to," he added, sounding bored. "At the Prophêtis' request. As you should, of course. She is our go-between, speaking for the gods to mortals, and for mortals to the gods. The very least we can do is respond to her call."

Riot pressed up against my shoulder, his hand finding mine, while Wild stiffened, a sword in his hand once again.

228

More silence. A silence that dragged on for a painfully long time before the volcano rumbled ominously. We all turned to face it, my hands trembling as Gaia climbed out of the crater, not much smaller than the volcano itself. Somehow, her footsteps were light as she crossed the *miles* between us in three steps, shrinking down to a slightly larger-than-human-sized form in line with the other gods.

As we'd seen her in the Realm of the Gods, she was not particularly *human* looking. Her skin was like bark, and in place of hair were thick, leafy vines that sprouted from the top of her head and twisted around her body like a living, moving garment.

"Grandson," Gaia said cordially. "Welcome back."

"Indeed, it has been eons." Zeus tilted his head to the side. "At your insistence."

Riot was squeezing my fingers to the point of pain, his panic at how this was going to play out clear. I was strangely *not* worried, though. Maybe that was just hope speaking. Hope that we could finally find some sense of *peace* after all the suffering we'd experienced.

"I won't apologize," Gaia said, somewhat petulantly. "The mortals had grown tired of The Twelve. Their meager worship did not sustain you. It was nothing for Typhoeus to drag you to Tartarus."

She glared at T with blatant hatred and betrayal in her eyes. Had the dragon been a response to T fighting on our side?

"It was nothing for Typhoeus to drag us to Tartarus *after* we'd already successfully fought off a horde of your *Gigantes,*" Ares growled, everything about his body language ready to attack. He had a surprisingly angelic face, with soft blonde curls just visible beneath a shining golden helmet, but his expression was fierce and unyielding. "Don't pretend you didn't wage a full-scale war on Olympus to get what you wanted."

"A war you wouldn't have lost if you hadn't been so weak."

"Come now," Zeus said cajolingly. "We can let bygones be bygones. Our strength grows by the minute—more so now the plants grow again, and mortals seek someone to pin their gratitude on. Thanks to the Prophêtis, word of our names, our roles, has never been more widespread."

"Let bygones be—"

"Of course, you will need to spend a small period of rest and relaxation in Tartarus to cool off." Zeus observed the broken rock pile at the base of the plateau with disinterest.

Gaia scoffed. "I don't know how you got out, what was going through Tartarus' head, or what trick you played on him, but he would never entrap me. I am his beloved."

There was a burst of outraged flame over my head that had Riot, Wild, and me ducking for cover. T obviously did not agree with that assessment. Gaia spared him a scathing look but didn't attempt to speak to him or defend herself in any way.

"Then what harm is it?" Zeus pressed, shrugging his shoulders. "If you are so confident of his obsequiousness—"

"His *love*."

"Of course, of course. His *love*. Go and visit, say hello. If he lets you walk free as you're so confident he will, then your reign in the upperworld continues—how can we possibly defeat you?"

I held my breath, waiting to see if Gaia would walk into this neat little trap. But she had been wooed by appeals to her ego before, and I got the feeling that this was her biggest one. Tartarus. Her own personal prison guard.

Was I meant to get involved here? On the one hand, I was the

Prophêtis. On the other, a wise person knew when to keep their mouth shut, and this seemed like one of those times.

"*Fine,*" she hissed. "I will return here shortly, wearing Tartarus' ring as a symbol of his devotion, and you will bow to me and admit my preeminence. You will *yield* to me, and you will never challenge me again."

"We have a deal, Mother Gaia," Zeus replied serenely, inclining his head respectfully.

Gaia didn't break eye contact as her root-like feet sunk into the ground, followed by the rest of her body, staring at the King of the Gods until her eyes disappeared into the dirt.

DARE

CHAPTER 28

I followed the Styx's instructions to the letter, staring determinedly at the palace as I approached through the marshlands, rounding the building to get to the front steps. *Don't take your eyes off it for a moment,* the Styx had whispered. *Or your soul will wander.*

My legs wobbled slightly beneath me as I climbed the steps, the gnawing hunger in my stomach growing to an acute pain while I'd been down here. In some ways, it felt like no time had passed at all while I'd been traveling on the rivers, but my body begged to disagree.

As I made my way up the final steps and passed through the white columns to the interior, I stumbled into the middle of a party that I definitely wasn't invited to.

I'd crashed plenty of parties in my time, usually with Riot along for the ride, but being glared at or gasped at in horror by a bunch of what were clearly dead people was definitely a new experience. There was definitely no sneaking in, no discreetly trying to figure out where Bullet was and subtly getting his attention.

"Alive! It's alive!" one of the souls gasped, pointing at me in disgust. Rude. They were the ones who were unsettling to look at. While they were all human enough—and came in all different shapes and shades and sizes—they had this uncanny valley-look to them that clearly separated them from the living. It wasn't just that they were all dressed in the same plain black toga thing, either. It was that there was something intangible *missing* about them.

Considering how unsettlingly odd the souls were, the palace itself was remarkably ordinary, in a grand, divine power sort of way. Maybe it was because I'd been expecting some gothic nightmare with chandeliers made of human skulls, but the white marble palace, tinged a faint shade of violet from the purple sky, seemed pretty tame. Boring, even.

"Get away," another soul hissed, leaping back at my approach.

"You're the talking dead guy, I don't know why you sound so grossed out," I mumbled, weirdly offended that everyone was jumping away from me like I smelled bad. *Was Ma here?* I couldn't imagine her partying at the palace; she'd probably find the whole thing gauche and beneath her, but I hoped she was nonetheless. It'd be nice to encounter a dead person who was actually happy to see me.

A veritable sea of souls parted down the center of the grand hall, revealing two thrones on a dais at the front of the room. There was an onyx throne on one side, while the other was made of interlinked vines, with dark red flowers growing along the back of it. That throne was empty.

Hades' was not.

He didn't speak, though, just sat slumped and bored-looking, watching as I made my way toward him. *Limped* my way toward him, rather.

Before I could get to the front of the room, to plead my case to the King of the Underworld, a group of tittering souls to the left of the dais scattered, and I froze.

There he was.

I thought I'd be hunting forever to find Bullet, but he was standing right in front of me, observing his surroundings with that air of curiosity that was so typical of Bullet, but it *wasn't* typical Bullet at the same time. There was none of the amusement he usually carried around with him, no mischievous grin, no twinkling eyes... It was *him*, but it wasn't.

Was I too late?

"Bullet?" I called hesitantly, taking a step towards him.

He blinked at me in surprise, but not recognition. My heart sank into the depths of the underworld.

"Bullet?" he repeated, frowning slightly to himself. "Bullet, Bullet, Bullet..."

He rolled the name around his mouth like he was trying it out for the first time, and he looked at me like I was an interesting stranger. Somehow, in all the scenarios I'd envisioned, *this* hadn't been one of them.

"You don't remember me," I rasped, vaguely aware that every soul and deity in the room had fallen silent and was watching us with rapt attention. "You don't remember *you*."

Bullet grimaced. "Not exactly, no. Apparently, losing my memories is what's keeping me, you know, functional. Alive-ish. Not alive like you though." He gave me an appraising look that I had no idea what to make of. "Are you the man I love?"

I nearly choked on my own spit. "I mean, as friends, yeah, for sure. We definitely love each other as friends."

"Oh! We're friends. Are you Dare?"

"Yeah. Yeah, I'm Dare," I replied quietly, my voice catching slightly. That was a good sign, right? Maybe he remembered *some* things? "Do you remember Grace?"

Please say yes. Please say yes.

"Grace the Agathos. Grace, who loves me." It was an assertion that was confident and empty all at once. Someone had told him that, and he remembered the words.

He didn't remember her.

"I wouldn't say that I *remember* her, necessarily," Bullet continued, his bravado faltering slightly. I roughly wiped away the wetness on my cheek, wondering when it had gotten there. "But I wish I did."

He sighed wistfully, shoving his hand back through his hair. He wasn't dull like the other souls, but he didn't look entirely whole either. What did that mean? How was I meant to get him out of here when he didn't appear to have an actual body?

"I'm going to get you out of here," I promised. "I made a deal with you that I would. I'm going to bring you home to the upperworld, and you're going to see her again. Wild, too. He's the man you love. And Riot, your friend. We're all going to be together again."

Not that I knew where any of them were, but once I had Bullet, I was one step closer to reuniting our little group.

"What did you call me before?" he asked. "Bullet? Everyone here calls me Oneiroi, or the Spirit of Dreams."

"That may be *what* you are, but *who* you are is Bullet." I thought about telling him he'd earned his nickname from being shot in a drive-by and wearing the gold bullet on a chain around his neck after he'd had it surgically removed, but that seemed like a lot to dump on a guy who didn't know his own name. "You're a friend, a soul bond, a lover, you're... so much more than just the *Spirit of Dreams*, okay?"

Bullet nodded, thoughtful. "It's kind of a weird name, but that's good to know. It makes me feel more human, I think, to have a name."

"Hold on," Hades cut in, looking affronted. "He can't leave. This is *his* party. I don't want to have a party."

"Why are you having a party in the underworld?" I muttered to Bullet.

"Well," Bullet began, leaning in conspiratorially. "They say I'm a *hero*. I'm a little fuzzy on the details, but apparently, if you're a hero, you get a party."

I blinked at him, and he blinked right back at me.

"You're a hero?"

"So they say." Bullet shrugged. "I don't really *feel* particularly heroic. Should I feel a certain way? Powerful or something?"

"Wait, Bullet, did you... Did you go to Tartarus?"

"Oh yes. Hecate said that *you* were going to go in Grace's place, but you're all-the-way alive, and so going to Tartarus might not have been the best idea for you if you wanted to, you know, stay alive. And since I'm sort of half-alive at best, and you're my friend, I went instead. It was quite interesting, actually. I met all kinds of people. Well, gods. Some of them I liked more than others. Tartarus was my favorite."

I wasn't about to be all-the-way alive if he kept talking. I was going to keel over from a heart attack right here in the middle of the underworld.

"The Olympians... are free?"

I turned to Hades for confirmation, and he huffed in annoyance. "Where do you think my wife is? Apparently, seeing her mother again after all these centuries was *urgent*."

That sounded totally reasonable to me, but he seemed incredibly put out by it.

"Then, Bullet, you did it. You brought forth the Second Age of Heroes. You liberated the gods, the treasure in the deep. *You* fulfilled the prophecy."

"Mostly. Slow on the uptake, aren't you?" Hades cut in drily. Asshole.

"Surely, that means he's free to leave. He's a *hero*," I said, spinning to face the God of the Underworld.

"And there's a nice little spot in the Elysian Fields with his name on it," Hades replied. "Heroes are very comfortable in the underworld, there's no *need* for them to leave. And perhaps I quite like housing the one who fulfilled the prophecy in my realm, away from my siblings as they all come back into their power."

"You want him for leverage."

"I don't like that," Bullet mumbled, stepping a little closer to my side. "I don't want to be leverage."

Back when we'd been kids, Bullet got picked on occasionally by assholes like Viper, who thought less of him and his abilities. Riot and I would always defend him, but Bullet had been plenty able to hold his own when the occasion called for it. He'd pop into someone's dreams and leave scars so deep on their psyche that they never fully recovered from them.

That was the Bullet I knew, the Bullet who could defend himself just fine when he chose to. That wasn't this Bullet, though, not yet, at least. He *needed* me, *needed* us, in a way that he never had before. We'd always relied on his knowledge and abilities, and now it was time to repay the favor.

"Name your price, King of the Underworld," I said evenly, inclining my head respectfully as I did so. "This is the final resting place of us all. You will have Bullet's soul for eternity, eventually. Why the rush? Why can't he grow old with those he loves first?"

Hades just watched, mildly curious. "He doesn't remember those who he loves."

"He didn't remember me, and yet he jumped into a pit to Tartarus to save me just because Hecate *told* him I was his friend." I swallowed thickly. "His head may not remember us, but his heart will find its way back where it belongs. When he gets to the upperworld and sees Grace and Wild, *feels* the love they have for him, feels how much Riot and I care for him..." I trailed off, emotion clogging my throat, making it hard to speak.

"I'll fall in love all over again," Bullet finished confidently, enough that I managed a weak smile because *that* was the Bullet I recognized. His love for Grace had been overwhelming and obsessive before he'd even met her, purely through the dreamscape. Apparently, that was a core part of his personality that not even the loss of his memories could shake. Bullet *wanted* to be in love. Craved it, chased after it, threw himself entirely into the feeling no matter how vulnerable it made him.

He was kind of a miracle.

Hades waved someone over, some kind of immortal assistant, I was guessing, murmuring something quietly in his ear while watching us carefully.

"You certainly have my curiosity, Philotes. However, humor me for a moment. I have a little test of sorts for you. Won't be long."

He turned away, dismissing us to speak to someone else and leaving Bullet and me in relative privacy for a moment.

"I can't believe you came down here for me," Bullet murmured in amazement, staring at me wide-eyed. "You must be a really good friend."

"Not to everyone," I replied wryly. "I definitely don't dive into the underworld for just anyone—you're special."

Bullet beamed at me, his smile the same as before and yet different. A little more guileless, a little less jaded. He was more like an enthusiastic golden retriever than a sly fox, like his old self had been, but maybe he'd get that sense of cunning back when he lived in the upperworld for a while. Or maybe he wouldn't. Maybe this dazzling enthusiasm was who he was now, and we'd all adapt to it.

After everything we'd been through, maybe we *needed* that dazzling enthusiasm.

"How is Grace?" he asked, cocking his head to the side. "Can you tell me about her? And Wild? And Riot?"

I grimaced. "I haven't seen Wild and Riot since you... Since your memories disappeared." That seemed like the politest way of saying 'since you sort of died'. "Wild didn't take it well, and he's a Keres daimon, so when they get mad, they get lost in a violent bloodlust. Riot challenged him, encouraged Wild to take it out on him, and told me to get Grace somewhere safe."

"And they just disappeared? How long has it been? Isn't Grace sad?"

"Yeah," I rasped, nodding my head. "She's really sad. I have no idea how long it's been now." Time had been a fairly abstract concept before I'd attempted to leap into the pit. Now that I was here, I had no clue how much time had passed in the upperworld.

Bullet looked at me warily. "I don't know, Dare. I'm not sure you should have come here to get me. That means Grace is all alone."

"I left her with friends," I replied uneasily. "Friends who care about her, and will protect her with their lives. And soon, she'll have half her soul bonds back soon, and we'll track down Riot and Wild, and we'll all be together again."

And hopefully she'd forgive me for leaving her in the first place.

"Just one thing first," Hades called, the crowd parting as a soul approached. My stomach dropped through my feet, probably sinking all the way to Tartarus.

"Ma?" My voice cracked on the word. I took a step back toward

Bullet, away from the grayish soul of my mother. What the fuck was this?

"Son," she said with a sad half-smile, a more affectionate look than I'd ever seen on her face in life. "How far you've come, my boy. I hear of your exploits, and I am continuously amazed that you are my child."

She looked to Hades, raising an unimpressed eyebrow. "This all seems very unnecessary. I have no desire to return to the upperworld."

"You're spoiling it," Hades sighed. "You're supposed to make it hard for him to choose."

"Choose?" I repeated.

"Yes, choose. The mother who was bloodily murdered in the middle of her kitchen, who gave you life, who *remembers* you, or the friend who doesn't." Hades tilted his head thoughtfully. "You should know that if you pick your friend, your mother will be fed to the Phlegethon whose flames will consume her soul, permanently erasing her from this realm or any other."

"*Why*?" I choked out. "Why are you doing this? Is this just entertainment for you?"

Hades waved lazily around the throne room. "You are asking for quite the gift, Philotes. The Oneiroi was already in the Isles of the Blessed. He could have found his own way back to the upperworld, if he'd chosen to. No gift from the gods comes without sacrifice; you should know this by now."

I did know that. And I hated it, and resented it, but I also understood it. Balance had to be maintained in all things. This wasn't the first sacrifice I'd had to make, and it wouldn't be the last.

"You should save her," Bullet whispered, pressing his shoulder against mine, though I could barely feel it. "I knew when I left the Isles of the Blessed that I might not be able to return. And I'll be okay here. It seems quite nice, you know. And there's this flowery place I get to go because I'm a hero. I'll get to see you guys one day when you all come to the underworld.

When you're old."

"*No*," I bit out, hands balling into fists at my side. "I'm not leaving here without you."

Because Bullet was mine and Riot's friend and one of the loves of Grace's life and she needed him by her side, and Wild would never be okay unless I brought him home. Plus, I needed some kind of apology gift after knocking Grace out to beat her to the pit, and there was nothing she wanted more than getting Bullet back.

"But he's right," Bullet insisted, more resigned than I'd ever heard him in life. "You seem like a great friend, but I don't remember you. Any of you. And I never will if I want to live, Hecate told me that."

Fuck me, I thought being beaten up by the agathos had hurt. I thought the plane crash had hurt. Nothing hurt more than hearing those words come out of Bullet's mouth.

"Then we'll make new memories. Even better ones—"

"But your mom—"

"Will walk into Phlegethon's flames with my head held high," Ma cut in, and it made me a total bastard because I knew she'd say that. I knew she'd volunteer, because she had far more empathy and compassion than any daimon of her generation ought to have had.

"I'm sorry, Ma," I whispered, guilt burning a hole in my gut.

She scoffed, throwing her hair back imperiously. Just as regal and impatient in death as she had been in life. "It isn't even a question. It is not my child's place to make sacrifices for me."

"Make your choice, Philotes," Hades drawled, as though there weren't eternal souls hanging in the balance. Fuck this guy.

"Take him home, Dare," Ma said softly. "Go and live, live every single day, whatever new challenges it brings. You are strong enough to face them."

I nodded weakly. "I'll never forget you, never stop being grateful to you. Your memory will live on through me."

Even if her immortal soul wouldn't.

"Bullet," I rasped, turning to face Hades. "I choose Bullet. I want Bullet to return to the upperworld, to his body, safe and whole."

One of Hades' minions rushed to his side, and the King of the Underworld inclined his head to listen, looking at me impassively before eventually nodding once.

"I find myself moved by your theatrics, Philotes. I have decided not to sacrifice your mother's soul."

I blew out a shaky breath of relief, and Ma's rigid posture relaxed slightly.

"Oh, that's great news!" Bullet whispered excitedly, ghost shoulder bumping against mine again.

"Instead, I'll throw your father's soul into the Phlegethon," Hades finished, watching me for a reaction.

Bullet sighed quietly next to me, audibly disappointed and I couldn't help but snort. "Sure, throw him in. We don't even know the guy. Right, Ma?"

"Well, technically I do, but I thought I'd better keep it to myself since you were always so sensitive for a Philotes daimon. You might find the idea that you were conceived while he was cheating on his pregnant wife... distasteful."

I blinked at her. "Yeah, for sure throw that guy in the flames."

Hades gestured at the door. "Done. Find your own way out. Don't let go of his hand, Oneiroi. The underworld is not meant for mortals. For this part, at least, he needs you more than you need him."

That's it? That was all the instruction we got?

Ma gave me a wan smile. "This is how it goes when you bargain with gods, a lesson I'm sure you'll learn quickly."

She crossed the small space between us, and while Hades huffed impatiently, it seemed as though he was going to give us a moment to say goodbye.

"Don't screw up, okay?" Ma asked solemnly.

I laughed unexpectedly. "That sounds more like the mother I know. I was worried the underworld had made you soft."

"Perhaps a little. I am very lazy here, you know. I spend most of my time gossiping."

"That's good. That sounds nice, actually. You deserve a break, Ma. You worked hard."

"I did, didn't I?" She gave me a small half-smile. "I'll see you again someday, when you are old and tired and ready for your rest in the underworld. Until then, you have a job to do. Go. Beg Charon for passage to the upperworld if you have to, or see if you can convince Thanatos to take you back."

"Love you, Ma. I'll see you in a few years. Don't cause too much trouble down here in the meantime."

She didn't say it back, but she never had, so I wasn't surprised. For a daimon of her generation, she was unusual—a more engaged parent than most and slightly more empathetic, but *love* was still a concept she struggled with. But that was okay. I'd always had enough love in me for the both of us.

"Come on, Bullet. Let's find a way out of here. It's time to get you home." I reached for his hand, and he set his light, not-quite-solid palm on mine. "Don't let go, I don't want to get stuck down here."

"You trust me to keep you safe?" Bullet asked, bewildered and awestruck in equal measure. Like I was giving him a gift so overwhelmingly generous that he didn't know how to respond.

"Yeah, man, I do. With or without your memories, there are very few people I trust more in this world or any other to have my back than you. And when we get back to the upperworld, it's going to be my turn to have *your* back while we figure out how to get to the others. Deal?"

Bullet blew out a shaky breath, though the movement seemed more driven by muscle memory than an actual need to breathe.

"Deal."

RIOT
CHAPTER 29

The wait was terrifying. How long did it take to get to Tartarus anyway? Ares had been strutting around, as confident as can be, observing the Spartoi like they were his own personal army and proclaiming loudly that there was no way Tartarus would let Gaia go free.

But he'd also been turning a plastic water bottle over in his hands for the past five minutes, scrunching it loudly in his fist, and staring like it was the most interesting thing he'd ever seen. Basically, his judgment was questionable at best.

"You should rest," Grace murmured, resting a palm on my back. "You and Wild both. You're exhausted."

"You know I can't sit this out, Gracie," I said grimly, looking at the pile of bodies laying on the grass. Grace had been diligently preparing them for the pyre the gods had built, working alongside Persephone, who had suddenly appeared from the underworld to reunite with her mother. "Maybe it's not very daimonic of me, but I want to give these agathos their due. The way they died..."

I swallowed thickly, and Grace pressed into my side, trembling despite her best attempts to keep it together.

"I saw Atropos cut threads of life right in front of me." I shook my head slightly, remembering the horrible creak of the plateau cracking and collapsing; the sounds of the screams and the crash of the rocks would haunt me for the rest of my days. "I just keep envisioning taking those shears to a giant swathe of web, slicing away at those lives in one fell swoop."

"I've been praying for their souls in the underworld. For them to find peace," Grace said quietly. "It should have never happened. There was no need for it to be like this."

Suddenly, Hermes appeared, winged sandals fluttering as he landed lightly in the center of the field. We were all silent—Olympians and mortals alike—as we watched him hold up a glinting silver ring the size of a dinner plate in the air above his head. He had the ring.

Not Gaia.

She hadn't returned, and Tartarus hadn't given her the ring.

Could it really be—

"Nenikēkamen!" the Spartoi shouted among themselves, jumping on each other and clapping one another on the back.

Grace was gripping my arm tightly, and Wild jogged over from the wreckage to join us, covered in blood and dirt.

"Tartarus is upholding his end of the bargain," Hermes announced. "Not that I could hear him over Gaia's outraged shouting. It'll take a few centuries for her to cool off."

Zeus grinned, clapping Hermes on the shoulder before nodding at the ring. "You should probably return that to Tartarus right away. Let's not get back on his bad side so quickly."

Hermes grinned, shooting off into the air again. I wasn't even sure how he was traveling between realms—as I watched, he sort of flew into nothingness and disappeared. God stuff, I guessed.

"Unfortunately, now is not the time to celebrate," Zeus sighed, looking around the battlefield. "But someday. Someday, Prophêtis, you will spend your nights going from celebration to celebration, and we will join you because you join *us*—gods and mortals. Until the world is comfortable with us once again, you are our link."

Grace managed an impressively calm smile, though I was pretty sure she was ready to faint on the inside based on how shaky her hand was.

The Spartoi broke apart, shaking off their cheerfulness to get back to the business of clearing the dead. Persephone walked past them, wandering over to the dragon's corpse and yanking his giant mouth open to peer inside.

"What... what is she doing?" I whispered.

"Harvesting Spartoi, I imagine," Wild said drily, startling me and Grace. "The Spartoi couldn't attack him because they're harvested from his teeth."

"Sown men," Grace said, eyes lighting up in understanding. "Bullet told us that."

I glanced nervously at Wild, waiting to see if the mention of Bullet was going to set him off on another round of bloodlust, but Wild just managed a sad half-smile, staring while Persephone started hacking out teeth. Thank the gods for that. I didn't have anything in the tank to fight with right now.

We spent hours giving rites to the dead, burning their bodies on the multiple pyres set up on the battlefield. The base of them was made of perfectly stacked stones—courtesy of Hephaestus—with wood stacked neatly on top. I assumed that the stones would stay, and I liked the idea that there would be some kind of monument here. Some physical reminder of the lives that had been lost in the chaos, for a cause that was long since lost.

There was also a brand new volcano, of course, and the remnants of the raised plateau, surrounded by the ditch. But those were reminders of Gaia's wrath, not tributes to the fallen.

Grace, Wild, and I stood side-by-side in front of the flames, watching in silence. The Olympians had trickled away, one at a time, off to begin the daunting task of rebuilding, going to wherever their skills were needed most. And maybe to do a victory lap too, and collect more of those sweet, sweet worship points for the power boost.

"It is time for me to leave," Athena said, startling us. We hadn't spoken to her yet—of all the deities, she may have been the least approachable. "But I wished to congratulate you, heroes. Yes, all of you," she said, raising an eyebrow ever-so-slightly at Wild. "Surely, you assumed that slaying a dragon would elevate your status. And you, Prophêtis, making a deal with a monster and throwing yourself off a building to push him into joining your cause. You were the first, you know. *You* brought forth the Second Age of Heroes."

"You threw yourself off a building?" I hissed. Grace glanced at me out of the corner of her eye, blushing a fierce shade of red. Oh, we were having words about *that* later. By the look on Wild's face, he was thinking the same thing.

Athena looked around, beyond the pyre. "It was no accident that you all ended up at this site. These lands are where the last great battle between mortals took place before our fall. For ten years, they fought. And we on Olympus were divided, supporting different sides, torn apart by our own petty squabbles."

Athena turned her penetrating gaze on Grace. "Eutychia is not a particularly appealing gift for agathos, no?"

Grace grimaced slightly in the firelight. "It's not considered one of the more desirable lines, no."

"You would never have been what you have become without it," Athena replied, her voice giving nothing away. "Long before all of this began, before you called to the Goddess of Night for help, you were already accustomed to reaching out to those who were overlooked. There is nothing *grand* about bestowing a little luck on someone to make sure they have a bed for the night or enough money to pay for their groceries, not in the way that the agathos perceive grandness. It is not the solemn dispensing of wisdom or the self-sacrifice of good health, nor does it bring with it the savior element of providing safety. But never doubt that you wouldn't be *this* Grace, had you never been *that* Grace. I'd like to think that over the centuries, we Olympians have turned our past experiences into our strengths too. I suppose time will tell."

And with that rather ominous proclamation, she whistled for her chariot and disappeared into the night.

BULLET

CHAPTER 30

It was a lot slower traversing the underworld with Dare than it had been alone. There was no running so fast I was flying, that was for sure. On the plus side, we didn't have to navigate any crowds because all the souls leaped out of Dare's way like he smelled bad. And yet...

"I'm going to miss this place," I sighed.

Dare startled, gripping my hand a little tighter as though I was going to just ditch him here.

"Why?"

"Oh. Well, because this is basically all I know?" I tilted my head to the side, thinking about it. "Yeah, that's why. I'm sure the upperworld is nice, and I'm excited to meet the people there I've heard so much about, but it's all brand new to me."

"Shit, I'm sorry, Bullet. I wasn't thinking." Dare sounded genuinely upset, which was both distressing and reassuring. I didn't want to make him sad, but I'd really thrown all my eggs in this guy's basket, and it was comforting that he seemed to genuinely care about me and my feelings.

He'd been willing to sacrifice his mom's soul to get me back to the upperworld. It didn't get much more caring than that, right?

"You don't have to worry, okay? I'm going to be there every step of the way. And once we get there, once Grace and Wild see you..." he trailed off with a light laugh. "They're not going to let you out of their sight. You're going to be so fucking happy, okay? We're going to make sure of it."

"Okay. I believe you." Dare was quiet, and I glanced back at him over my shoulder, finding him frowning. "What?"

"Don't be this trusting with anyone outside our group," he grumbled.

"Got it," I agreed with a nod. I'd already been questioning if I was too trusting after the encounter with the Olympians, so it was good to have some reassurance that I did, in fact, have no idea what I was doing.

Dare was silent and wary as we passed the Phlegethon and the pit to Tartarus, clutching my hand even tighter though I didn't really have enough sensation in my phantom limbs to appreciate it. In the dregs of my mind—the remainders of memories I'd once had, I decided—I understood that the upperworld didn't look like the underworld.

"Have you been here before?" I asked absently, watching the foothills of the mountain come into view and worrying exactly how we were going to cross them. They'd be physically challenging for someone with a proper body, and Dare was already kind of beaten up and struggling for breath.

"To the underworld?" Dare laughed. "Uh, no. Not before this trip. Though I guess it isn't that weird of a question—you've been here before. With Grace, Wild, and Riot."

I had?

"Did I meet Hades? Hecate?" I was getting a headache, and I didn't even really have a head. The memories that I'd lost were just a big black hole that gave me nothing, no matter how much I poked and prodded and hoped for even a *hint* that would help me understand.

"Yeah, man. You've met them before," Dare said quietly, giving my hand a supportive squeeze. He was a good friend already.

"Boo." Hecate dropped out of the sky like a stone, landing with a thud on the path and grinning at us. Dare startled so hard he almost dropped my hand, clinging on to me at the last minute. "Well, haven't you been a busy boy, the Spirit of Dreams?"

I glanced up, seeing a black chariot pulled by black horses swooping around overhead as though they were waiting for her.

"I guess so. Do horses usually fly?"

"No," Dare replied before Hecate could. "But I'm not sure that's the most pressing concern we have right now."

"Relax, Philotes." Hecate let out a full-on cackle that only had Dare shrinking back further, yanking me along with him. "You didn't wonder why it was me who came to see you on the Isles of the Blessed rather than the king or queen?" she asked, directing her attention to me.

"I honestly never thought about it."

"Right, right," she sighed. "Well, I am the goddess of ghosts and necromancy. You, in your halfling in-between state, fall under my purview. Lucky me. Anyway, since you are heroes, I have decided to help you. It is very good for my reputation, you see. They will recount tales of your heroic journey for the rest of time, and they will say, 'and Hecate! She was there; she guided the two young heroes on their journey out of the underworld.'"

"I'm not a hero," Dare replied cautiously. "I'm also not saying no to help getting out of here."

"Well, that's true enough. You're not *yet*. Then again, Orpheus gets to live in the Elysian Fields, and he didn't even *succeed* in bringing his charge home from the underworld." She frowned. "Though you're not really doing the hard work, are you? The Spirit of Dreams is leading *you*."

Dare huffed impatiently. "Just to be clear, I really don't care about the whole hero thing. I just want to get out of here."

Hecate pursed her lips, staring at him. "Well, I suppose it wouldn't be good for the Oneiroi's hero story if he left you here, so you'll have to come along." She whistled sharply, and the horses above us dove toward the ground at an alarming rate, coming to a stop at the last minute, the chariot bouncing along the ground.

"Hop on then," she said impatiently, gesturing at the chariot. "And hold onto that Philotes, for gods' sake. You'll be all a tizzy if you drop him, I can tell."

Dare didn't seem that jazzed about mounting the flying chariot, but he wasn't about to let me go either. He grumbled under his breath as we climbed aboard, each using our free hand to grip the edge of the chariot. There was no back to it, no gate, and when it took off into the sky, I really thought that this was the end for real. That we were going to tip backward off the edge and fall into the Phlegethon, and that would be that.

"Fuck this," Dare chanted quietly, his knuckles white where his hand held onto the lip of the chariot. "Fuck this, fuck this, fuck this."

"Not far now," I assured him, raising my voice so he could hear me over the rushing wind.

"Do you know where we're going?"

"I think so?"

"That's not as reassuring as you think it is," Dare shouted back.

The chariot arced over the top of the jagged mountain ranges, revealing the dark water of the strait that separated the mainland from the

Isles of the Blessed. The strange, empty stone castle stood at the top of the island, the rest of the small patch of land covered in lush vegetation.

I expected the horses to swoop downwards, depositing us on the patch of grass outside the castle.

They didn't.

They swooped *up*.

Dare cursed, scrambling up and dipping his knees so he could hook his forearm over the front of the chariot. We were almost parallel to the ground, and I copied his position even though I felt lighter and not as prone to flying off as he appeared to be.

"What is happening?!" Dare yelled, the horses climbing at a rapid pace toward the purple sky. The wind bore down on us, and Dare had to bow his head, but I could keep my eyes trained upward. I saw the shimmery patch of sky we were aiming for. It was a tiny, rippling square, and it already looked like it was on the move, shifting about the sky. The horses followed it, turning at an angle I wouldn't have thought possible for horses to turn out, but they were flying, so what did I know?

"I think we're going to fly through the sky," I called out, realizing I hadn't answered Dare's question, and he was still huddling from the wind.

"We're going to what—" Dare began, but his words were cut off as the chariot plunged headlong into the glimmering patch of sky.

The upperworld came into focus slowly, one hazy detail at a time.

I could hear wind. There was sun on my face, and it was warm. Borderline uncomfortable, actually. *Sunlight.*

There was that lingering sense of *knowing*, that familiarity that made me confident that I knew what it was, but I hadn't been prepared for the way it *felt*. I groaned out loud at the delicious sensation on my skin. *Oh yeah, it was definitely a good call not to stay in the underworld.* Was the sun always so hot?

I licked my lips—I had lips!—and tasted salt.

Also, I was very hungry.

Definite ups and downs to having a corporeal body.

"Bullet? Are you alive or not?" a feminine voice said hesitantly, poking me in the shoulder. The baby babbled, and I cracked an eye open to finally put faces to the sounds I'd been hearing before I'd gone to the underworld.

It took a moment for my eyes to adjust, as though they'd forgotten how to function properly. The first thing I noticed was *blue*. Whatever this structure was, it had no roof. Three sides looked to be stone walls, though it was hard to see the material underneath with such thick vines growing up the sides. To my right were two rows of columns, densely packed so that I could only catch a glimpse of the greenery beyond.

A rather disinterested-looking woman peered down at me with red and purple eyes and a fat, gurgling baby on one hip. She pulled her sheet of silvery blonde hair to the side, nose ring glinting in the sunlight. The baby was reaching for me, and though my arms felt heavy and weak all at once, I instinctively reached back.

"Oh, thank the gods." The woman deposited the baby on my chest, and I wheezed at the sudden weight, holding the kid steady, so she didn't fall off since whatever I was lying on was quite high off the ground and uncomfortably hard at my back.

Was it... an altar?

The word rattled around in my head, though I didn't know how I knew it.

"I have done a *relentless* amount of childcare while you've been napping," the woman groused, loudly setting a ceramic jug and cup down on a nearby table and pouring some water. "Don't get me wrong, shit was very dire in Milton, and my house was starting to collapse around me, so your god friend swooping in and bringing us here was a good thing. I might go so far as to say I'm grateful, even." She sounded not-at-all grateful. "But having no help with the baby and keeping you alive has been extremely exhausting for me."

"I'm... sorry?" I hedged. I was wearing some kind of underworld-style black toga thing, and the baby grabbed my necklace, pulling on a golden bullet that I apparently wore on a chain, attempting to yank it clean off my neck. Huh. *That was an interesting choice of accessory*. Did I wear it because my name was Bullet?

"I don't know if babies should play with that," I told her seriously, my voice raspy from disuse, but her lip wobbled when I tried to take it away, and I immediately caved. "What's your name?"

The woman approached with a cup in hand, passing it to me and giving me a strange look. "That's Quinn."

"Quinn. Cute. What's your name? Where's Dare?"

Her frown grew more pronounced. "I'm Rogue," she said slowly. "Remember? You've known me almost your whole life?"

She shook her head slightly, looking annoyed. I held onto Quinn with one hand, pushing myself up with the other until I was sitting, avoiding Rogue's gaze for some reason. What was this sensation? Guilt, perhaps? I felt bad that I didn't remember her, especially when it sounded like she'd been really suffering to keep me alive.

"Here." She thrust the cup into my hand. "Drink slowly. I've been soaking a cloth in water and dripping some into your mouth a few times a day. You must be starving, though."

"Thanks. I, um, I really appreciate you doing all that for me. I'm sorry I don't remember you. Apparently, my brain was overloaded with visions or something, and my memories were sacrificed to save me. Have you seen Dare?" I repeated, realizing she'd never answered the question.

Rogue looked at me, startled, and I took a moment to sip on the cool water, nearly groaning at how good it felt on my parched throat. She gestured vaguely at the row of tightly packed together white columns, through which I could see hints of trees.

"Quinn and I are your *phylakes*," Rogue said cautiously. "Thanatos explained it when he brought us here. We're wardens, of sorts. Here to protect you and watch over you while you were vulnerable. This place, the Isles of the Blessed, isn't meant for just *anyone* to visit."

She stared out at the columns, looking slightly concerned for a moment before her face returned to its impassive expression. "I was in here, watching over you. I didn't see what it was that deposited you on the island, but suddenly your *soul* was floating through the air and slamming into your body, and Dare was shouting from the outside of some unseen barrier. He's still there, right on the edge of the cliff."

"Shit, I have to go. I can't leave him there," I said, still holding Quinn while I swung my legs over the side of the altar, feet dangling above the ground for a moment. My head was swimming slightly from the sudden movement, and I was glad when Rogue plucked Quinn out of my arms because I really didn't want to drop her.

"You're in no condition to go anywhere," Rogue pointed out flatly. "There's always fresh fruit and nuts magically appearing on that table; I think you should probably eat something first. I'll even go out and check on Dare for you."

"No, I have to get out there. We were in a rush. We have to get back to Grace."

Rogue's lips twitched as she shoved an apple into my hand. "I'm glad you haven't forgotten her. That could be awkward."

Yep. It was definitely that.

There was a shout of panic from outside. I half jumped, half fell off the altar and ran through the wall of columns, stumbling to a stop at the top of a few steps that led down to a dense forest.

"Dare!" I yelled, gaze darting through the trees, trying to figure out which direction the shout had come from. I couldn't hear anything now, just an eerie kind of silence. "Dare! Where are you?"

Rogue came to stand behind me, holding a whimpering Quinn in one arm and a freaking *sword*, loosely dangling from her other hand.

"This is not good," Rogue muttered as Quinn fell silent, emphasizing just how quiet the world around us was. "This place is always loud—the forest is full of birds and insects, and on the other side of the trees is an ocean in every direction. The waves crash against the cliffs all day and night. Something is very wrong."

There was another shout, and while I couldn't quite make out the words, this one sounded like a warning rather than a panicked surprise. Rogue shoved Quinn into my arms, the kid promptly bursting into wailing tears as her mother descended the steps, lifting the sword into a battle-ready position.

"Shouldn't you stay with Quinn—"

"I'm your *phylakes*," Rogue interjected, scanning the forest in front of her. "My job is to protect you; Thanatos made that very clear. If you didn't want to babysit, you should have chosen two fully grown protectors."

I honestly didn't know why I hadn't, that seemed much more sensible.

There was a rustling sound, barely audible beneath Quinn's tears, and Rogue adjusted her stance, tensing in readiness. *What do I do?* From what I'd seen, the inside of the building was just one room with an altar and what looked like a sort of nest in the corner where Rogue and Quinn had probably slept. If I put Quinn inside, surely she could just get back out again?

I gave her an appraising look, trying to decide if she was capable of moving on her own or not. She definitely wasn't a newborn—

"Don't let go of her," Rogue ordered, her back still to us. "Whatever happens, okay? I've got my job, you've got yours. Go grab the other sword from inside, though, just in case."

She didn't need to tell me twice. I looked around, trying to find any other weapons, but there was just the one heavy silver sword with the golden hilt that scraped painfully along the ground when I picked it up.

"No," I told Quinn firmly as she attempted to flop forward and grab it. "Definitely no swords for babies. Where's Dare? Dare needs a sword. I don't know how to use a sword. My brain has conveniently forgotten that information."

Or maybe I never had it?

I rushed back out right as the strange rustling sound grew into something far louder and more ominous. There was an almost scrabbling, scratching, clicking noise, and Quinn trembled silently in my arms.

And then we were overrun. Enormous, monstrous insects—no, scorpions—rushed out of the trees, scuttling toward the temple in a swarm.

If Rogue was afraid, she didn't show it, immediately jumping into action and stabbing indiscriminately at the approaching creatures.

"Don't put her down!" she screamed, though I didn't need the reminder this time. No way was I putting Quinn down at eye level with these things. I tightened my grip around her, using my sword-wielding hand to slice at the approaching beast. To my relief, one clean cut took off the head, and I yelled at Rogue to lop them off at the throat instead while she attempted to shake off a corpse stuck at the end of her blade.

There was a crashing noise, and I stiffened, wondering what terrible creature we were going to face next, but it was only Dare. He was armed with a branch and was beating the scorpions over the head with it as he approached, cutting down their numbers from the back of the swarm.

Fighting his way to us.

"I don't think this is killing them!" he yelled, heaving the heavy branch down on top of the scorpion closest to him. "You're going to have to follow up with the blades."

"Got it!" I called back, heading down another step and moving closer to Rogue. Her movements were sluggish, and I wondered if she was also struggling under the not-inconsiderable weight of the sword.

"We can't win this," Rogue said suddenly, her words a little slurred. "There's too many of them. They just keep coming."

We were both slicing and dicing in earnest, Quinn wailing in my ear, and I hated to admit that I thought Rogue was probably right. I'd lost count of how many I'd decapitated, and yet the flow of scorpions coming out of the forest didn't seem to be slowing down. Dare had fought his way to us, and the three of us pressed our backs together, Dare facing the building as scorpions scaled the wall from the other side, rushing down toward our little huddle in a wave.

We were going to die here, I thought helplessly. I'd clawed my way back from the brink of death, only to be immediately faced with it all over again. I'd never see Grace or Wild, never see Riot, never meet the people who'd once meant everything to me.

What cruelty was this? Where were the gods now?

I didn't stop fighting, though. I didn't let Quinn slip an inch, and I didn't break our haphazard formation. As pointless, as needlessly cruel, as it all felt, if I was going down, I was taking as many of these scorpions with me as I could.

Suddenly, black horses were descending from the sky—even larger than the ones that had dragged us out of the underworld—pulling a golden chariot with a *furious*-looking Hades on the back.

"Out!" he growled, pointing a two-pronged scepter I hadn't noticed in the underworld at the scorpions as he flew over the treetops. While I couldn't see the scepter doing anything, the scorpions were dropping dead one by one around us, and I pressed further back against Dare and Rogue, not wanting to get in the way of the invisible death blasts.

"You are not *allowed* here," Hades fumed, leaping down from the chariot in front of us and picking off the remaining scorpions individually. "This island is the domain of the *underworld*."

Oh, he was big mad.

"HERMES!" he roared at the sky, his voice so loud that it rattled the trees. "Bring me the Queen of the Underworld. Bring me my *wife*."

Dare panted while Rogue slumped to the ground, weakly tugging at Quinn. I crouched down to pass her back to her mom, noticing that Rogue really wasn't looking so good.

"Hey, are you okay?" I murmured. Why was she so gray? That didn't seem right. A thick coating of sweat covered her skin, and while she was looking at Quinn on her lap, she seemed to have trouble focusing her eyes.

261

"I think one of 'em got me," Rogue slurred, wobbling enough that I grabbed the back of Quinn's top in case Rogue lost her grip on her.

"Where?" Dare asked urgently, crouching down on Rogue's other side. She stretched out one leg, far redder and more swollen than it was meant to be.

"Hades—" I began, ready to beg and plead if I had to.

"Her thread has been cut," he replied curtly, though his expression was almost sympathetic. "Her time was already at an end, though it should not have come to pass *here*, in this *safe*, sacred place."

Seconds later, a lopsided shape appeared in the sky, and it took a moment to realize that it was *people*. Or gods, rather. Hermes was in the middle, the wings on his sandals flapping as he carried a goddess in each arm, shooting Hades a smug expression that the King of the Underworld did not return.

"Great," he mumbled. "My mother-in-law is here."

The three of them landed in front of us as one of the goddesses— the shorter, curvier one with golden hair that trailed down to the ground— immediately crossed the distance, wrapping her arms around Hades and pressing a kiss to his cheek. Persephone, I assumed.

She looked so happy that it took her a moment to absorb the carnage around us. "What happened here?! My *island*," she added, outraged.

"Yours, daughter?" Demeter asked. She'd been quiet in Tartarus, content to sit back and let the others do the talking. She was speaking to Persephone but looking at Hades with pure disdain.

"Mine," Persephone agreed. "Created with the remnants of the power I had as the Goddess of Spring when Gaia locked you all away, but tied to my power as Queen of the Underworld. It is both; it straddles the veil. It should have been free from Gaia's machinations. It is not *her* soil."

Hades looked at Dare. "There are rules around who can enter this place, as Thanatos told you. When you attempted to enter, you inadvertently weakened the barrier around it, enough for Gaia's little monstrosities to pass." Dare was stricken, staring at Rogue's injured leg in horror.

"However," Hades continued. "Without you coming to collect him, the Oneiroi would not have returned to the upperworld—the Fates themselves confirmed it. Ennui would have set in, and he would have stayed in an apathetic sort of discomfort in the underworld for all of time. A waste of potential, really, considering what they have hinted lies ahead."

Was he trying to comfort us? Because none of us looked particularly comforted.

"And that you fought your way through the remaining barrier, forged by my wife's own magic, to save those you care for... You have a stronger spine than I thought, Philotes."

"But you're saying by coming back, I've essentially traded my life for hers," I rasped. "That's what it is, isn't it? I return, Rogue..."

"Dies," Rogue finished for me, voice weak. "Rogue dies."

"It isn't a trade," Persephone corrected gently. She approached us, crouching down in front of Rogue and brushing a hand down her cheek. Maybe it was hope speaking, but Rogue's pain seemed to lessen slightly. "You are mortal. You are each only allotted so much time. But, Oizys daimon, you died an honorable death as a *phylakes*, and you will take your rest in the Elysian Fields."

"The Fates are cruel," Rogue rasped.

"They are indifferent," Demeter corrected, her voice a little less soothing than Persephone's. "For mortals are many, and you are all just tiny threads in a great and complex web to them."

"Yes, well, none of that's very comforting when you're about to leave your infant daughter behind," Dare snapped.

A single tear ran down Rogue's face as she stared at a crying, clearly exhausted Quinn.

"Riot owes me a favor." Rogue closed her eyes for a long moment, her breath sawing in and out of her lungs. "A blank check for helping Grace once. Tell him... tell him I'm calling it in. Tell him looking after Quinn, raising her, caring for her—him and Grace, and you two and Wild... That's my favor."

"It's not a favor at all," Dare said quietly. "It's an honor. But are you sure? Because we can find a way to get her back to Dice—"

"No." Rogue coughed, shaking her head hard. "No. I want her with you."

"Of course," Dare agreed. "Of course. We'll take such good care of Quinn, Rogue. She will be *so* loved."

Rogue nodded feebly, leaning forward to press a kiss to Quinn's forehead with blue lips before gesturing for Dare to take her. Another tear tracked down Rogue's cheek as Quinn bawled harder, reaching for her mom. My own cheeks were wet, though I didn't know when I'd started crying.

"I'm going to rest now," Rogue announced, swaying slightly before allowing Persephone to lay her down on the ground, her head in the goddess' lap, stroking her hair.

There was the faintest hint of a smile on Rogue's face as she drew her last breath. It wasn't loud or dramatic or violent. She was here one moment, gone the next. Her journey in this realm had ended, and we were left here to muddle through the grief, to pick up the pieces that had fallen with her departure. I didn't even know her, not anymore, and my heart still felt like it was cracking in two.

"Mamaaaaaaaaaa!" Quinn wailed. Dare scrunched his eyes shut, and I gently lifted Quinn from his arms to give him a moment, bouncing

264

her awkwardly on my hip on instinct.

"Thanatos will hold off collecting her soul for now," Persephone said kindly. "I will personally give this daimon her burial rites."

She lifted Rogue's body as though she was no heavier than Quinn, carrying her into the building where I assumed she'd be laid out on the altar.

"There is too much to be done for you to stay here and grieve," Demeter sniffed. "Your agathos is waiting for you."

My head shot up. "You've seen her?"

"I have. Now it is your turn—my son-in-law will take you to Ilion, where they are."

Hades looked very alarmed by this. "I have a realm to run. Hermes will take them."

"I require Hermes, and my daughter will be coming with us. You've had her all to yourself for centuries! Besides, the earth is in great need of our agricultural gifts at this time."

The family drama had the effect of breaking Dare out of his near-catatonic state at least. He stood slowly, gaze darting between the gods and Quinn, who was snuggling into my chest and showing signs of falling asleep.

"Come now, Hades," Hermes said, striding forward with a dazzling smile that felt totally out of place with the general mood. "We've all got a part to play. You can help us out by delivering these fine heroes to Ilion."

Hades looked ready to send Hermes back to Tartarus.

"It's not called *Ilion* anymore," Hades muttered, climbing onto his awaiting chariot and glaring at us. "Come on, then. Unless you don't want to see your agathos?"

Dare and I scrambled over—me at the front with Quinn and Dare behind me, arms caging me in while he gripped onto the chariot.

We were both as far to the side as possible, not that it made much difference. Hades was enormous.

Without any warning or command, the four steeds leaped into the air, dragging the chariot in a sweeping upward arc over the Isles of the Blessed and out to sea.

CHAPTER 31

Darkness had well and truly fallen over *Ilion*—wherever that was—by the time Hades dropped us off. And it was barely one step above *literally* dropping us; he'd basically hovered a foot off the ground so we could jump, Bullet cradling Quinn tightly to his chest, then he'd disappeared into the sky without a word.

"Dare? Bullet?"

One of the Spartoi—Theodoros, if my memory served correctly—approached, looking as though he could scarcely believe what he was seeing. He looked like he'd been in a hard fight, judging by the head-to-toe bruises. He wasn't wearing armor like the Spartoi almost always had—he'd stripped off to just the kilt-type thing they wore underneath all the bronze layers.

"Hey," I said with a weak attempt at a smile. Fuck, I was exhausted. Aching everywhere. Devastated after seeing Rogue die right in front of my eyes. Terrified for the little girl in Bullet's arms, who we'd sworn to protect. "Grace?"

"Come," he replied instantly, eyes wide as he gestured for us to follow.

"Hey, let me carry Quinn," I said, stopping Bullet with a hand on his arm. "This is about to be a lot for you. Let me look after her."

Bullet nodded mutely. Quinn was fast asleep, and I held my breath as he carefully deposited her into the cradle of my arms, hoping she didn't wake up. There was already so much going on, and she was going to be so scared.

She would grow up without Rogue but not without a family. I was going to make sure my little Quinbee had a happy life full of love, and I knew without asking that Grace would want the same thing.

I knew that. But at the same time, how the fuck were we going to get through this?

One step at a time, I reminded myself. *Just get to Grace.*

As terrifying as it was, I doubted there was much we couldn't get through together.

"Is Wild here?" I asked Theodoros. "Riot?"

He nodded once for each, and I blew out a shaky breath of relief. We were all here. We were all together. At... wherever this place was.

"Is this where we live?" Bullet asked curiously.

"No." Though we didn't *really* live anywhere, on reflection. Not yet. "This looks to be some kind of campsite, I think. I've never been here before."

Flaming torches had been lit along the paths that led to one larger central building, and what looked to be cabins behind it. A few Spartoi were hanging around outside, bathing in buckets of water. They startled in surprise when they saw us, but based on the noise, it was clear that the majority of them were inside the main building.

Theodoros led us through the open doors, and silence fell almost instantly. The tired collection of soldiers stood, inclining their heads respectfully as they parted to let us through.

"This is... I don't even know what to say," Bullet whispered, fidgeting with the toga he was wearing. *It was quite the outfit to make an entrance in,* I thought wryly.

The final Spartoi moved out of the way, revealing my girl, tucked between an exhausted-looking Wild and Riot. They were huddled together in a pile of blankets at the front of the room, Grace leaning against Wild's chest with his arms around her waist, both of her hands clutching Riot as she looked at him with eyes full of adoration, murmuring something too low for us to hear. Riot was giving her heart eyes right back, and I did my best to memorize every inch of the picture they made, so happy and content in each other.

She looked different from the last time I'd seen her, and it took me a moment to realize that she'd cut her hair.

"Is that..." Bullet trailed off, sounding suddenly unsure. Right, this was *a lot* for him.

"That's Grace in the middle," I told him. "Riot to her left, Wild to her right."

Grace's attention snapped to me, her jaw dropping open. Wild and Riot froze, all three of them cycling through too many emotions on their face to identify. I knew how they felt. I was a confusing cocktail of happiness, relief, and sadness, too.

"How..." Grace whispered, disentangling herself from the other two and standing on shaky legs. She walked toward us like she didn't believe we were really here, reaching out with trembling hands, cupping my cheek with one hand and Bullet's with another, before looking down at Quinn in confusion.

"I've got a story to tell you," I laughed weakly, trying to break some of the tension. "Uh, this is Quinn."

"Quinn," Grace repeated, nodding to herself in a slightly bemused way.

"I'm going to give you two a moment though," I added, stepping back and giving her a reassuring smile. While there was a lot for Grace to absorb, Bullet had just come back from the almost-dead, and this reunion was a long time coming.

Bullet's hand came up to cover Grace's, holding her in place as he stared at her reverently. "You're so beautiful. Even more beautiful than I imagined. I wish I could remember you."

I closed my eyes for a moment, the heartbreak on Grace's face so acute that I couldn't bring myself to see it. I'd known this was going to be hard, but fuck, it was agony. The usually stoic Wild wasn't faring much better, and Riot looked devastated.

"You don't remember me?" Grace rasped.

"Well, no. Not exactly. This is the cost of me being, you know, alive. My brain had to be emptied of all my memories and the things I'd seen."

Grace went to move back, probably worried that she was touching someone so intimately who didn't know her, but Bullet held her hand in place almost desperately, eyes wide with panic.

"I don't know you yet, but I want to. So much. Every step I took in the underworld, all of it was driven by my love for you—all of you— romantic or platonic. Just *hearing* about the love we had for each other pushed me forward, brought me here."

Grace was bawling, but so were the rest of us.

"You loved me once—" Bullet pressed, his voice cracking slightly.

"I love you still," Grace interrupted, sniffling. "Bullet, it's not even a question in my mind. When I forgot you each morning after you visited me in the dreamscape, you never stopped loving me. It's my turn to hold onto our memories, to share them with you, make new ones with you."

"Even if I'm not the same?" he whispered. "Even if I'm not the old Bullet?"

GRACE

CHAPTER 32

The agony of discovering Bullet had no memory of me was replaced by disbelief at his question. What had he been through in the time we'd been apart, when I thought he'd been sleeping?

"You're still Bullet," Dare interjected sharply. "Your memories aren't the only thing that made you *you*. Your heart hasn't changed. I've seen that for myself."

A fresh wave of tears hit me at that. They'd been together. I wasn't entirely sure how, but I was glad that neither of them had been alone.

"I want to get to know you," I told Bullet. "To hear about how you feel and what you want and what you've been through. You're still mine, though. You always have been."

Wild approached while we were talking, standing at my shoulder, but holding himself back. There was enough longing and confusion on Bullet's face as he looked between us that he must have been told something about us, but couldn't quite figure out where he fit. Where we all fit.

My resolve firmed. I wasn't going to give up on Bullet, not ever, but I didn't want to overwhelm him either. However long it took, whatever path we ended up on, whatever road to happiness Bullet found, I'd support him. If he lost his romantic love for me—a fate too painful to contemplate—then I'd accept that, and never push him for more than he wanted to offer. My love for him was unconditional, whatever the future held.

Wild pressed against my back, strong and steady, and I knew we were on the same page.

"Whatever you need, Bullet. Let me show you the patience that you always showed me."

"In the dreamscape?" Bullet asked curiously, testing out the word on his tongue.

"You visited me every night in my dreams. You created the most beautiful places for me. You made me smile every night even when my days were full of loneliness." I swallowed thickly, not wanting to cry in case it upset Bullet when he was already so clearly overwhelmed. "I can't create a dreamscape full of beautiful memories for you, but I can do it in real life. I will. *We* will." I glanced up at Wild, offering him a strained smile. He was clearly struggling to find the words, but he gave my free hand a quick squeeze of support.

"That sounds really nice," Bullet said softly. "All of us. And Quinn."

My throat was so tight, I felt like I was swallowing a knife. How had Quinn come to end up here with us? *Without* Rogue? Except I already knew the answer, and it was too agonizing to bear.

"Yes. All of us *and* Quinn. We're going to find our own happy, okay?"

"We'll find our own happy," Bullet agreed, sounding faintly awed.

"Can I hug you?" I whispered to Bullet, not wanting to rush him.

"Oh, fuck yes. Whenever you want," he assured me, yanking me forward with surprising confidence and wrapping his arms around my waist, lifting me a couple of inches off the ground. I laughed at the unexpected enthusiasm, clinging to his neck and pressing my face into his shoulder. He was still *my* Bullet, I could sense it underneath all that uncertainty, but he was changed too. The insecurity that stemmed from my forgetting his face every single night was gone. Undoubtedly, he'd have new worries—I knew I did after everything we'd experienced—and we'd have to find a way to navigate those together too.

I wasn't giving up.

"I missed you so much," I mumbled against his skin. "I don't want to let you go. But I know this is probably really confusing for you, so tell me if it's too much."

Bullet sighed, a dreamy sort of sound, squeezing me tighter. "If this is what it's like to be loved, I think I'm going to like it a lot."

I lost my battle with my tears, squeezing my eyes shut as a few stray ones escaped. Wild tentatively pressed his chest to my back, wrapping us both up in a hug, and after a moment, Riot and Dare were there, pressing in either side of our huddle. Reassuring ourselves that we were all together again. *Finally.*

With one new addition.

"Dare," Riot murmured, speaking quietly so as not to break the magic of the moment. "Where is Rogue?"

All at once, a fresh wave of grief washed over us. We knew where Rogue was. Why she wasn't here with her baby.

Wild took control, guiding us back up the steps to the little nest we'd made for ourselves while the Spartoi did their best to give us privacy. I clung onto Bullet's arm, and he didn't seem inclined to pull away as we sat down together on the blankets in a small circle, Quinn cradled gently against Dare's chest.

"Rogue said she was calling in her favor," Bullet told Riot, glancing at him uncertainly. "Before she..."

"I wasn't meant to go to the Isles of the Blessed," Dare said quietly, staring down at Quinn's face. "Not as alive as I am, in my mortal body, and not as a *phylakes*. My presence there weakened the protective shield around the island, and Gaia's leftover scorpions got in. Rogue..."

Rogue didn't make it.

"Persephone said Rogue died a hero's death, and that she'd be honored for it in the underworld," Bullet said. It was strange to see him talking about the gods with such little confidence in his words—he'd always been our main source of knowledge about them. "I know it's not much consolation."

"Oh, I don't know about that," Riot mused. "Is it awful that Rogue is gone, and Quinn is going to grow up without her mother? Fuck yeah, absolutely it is. But Rogue was never *happy* in this life, necessarily. Maybe she can find her happiness now. Or maybe I'm just being weirdly naïve."

"No, I'm not sure you are," Dare replied. "When I went to the underworld to fetch Bullet, I saw my mom. I think she found a peace in the underworld that she never found in this life. She was freed from her daimon instincts for the first time. It's been... liberating for her."

Dare looked at Bullet curiously at the same moment I did. Would Bullet still experience daimon instincts? Was he still an Oneiroi now? I supposed we'd have to wait and see if the dreamscape squirreled him away once we fell asleep.

"I can't believe you went to the underworld," Riot said, shaking his head in disbelief.

"Where were you two?" Dare asked, glancing between him and Wild.

"Thanatos showed up—" Wild began, but Dare's strangled exclamation cut him off.

"You can *speak*? What the fuck? Since when?"

"It's a recent development," Wild replied, looking slightly bashful at Bullet's enquiring expression. "I was, uh, cursed by the God of Death and couldn't speak for many years."

"Oh." Bullet blinked. "I'm sorry to hear it."

Riot snorted. "No guesses on how or why the curse has lifted?"

"Some fun trick of Thanatos', I assume," Wild replied, scowling for a moment before schooling his expression. "He hasn't told me. The last time I saw him was after Riot and I finished, er, fighting, Thanatos appeared and took me to the Spartoi."

"*Finished fighting*, hm?" Riot asked, smirking at just how much Wild had downplayed it. "I bled all over the agathos temple and woke up Arete. She took me to an island of ghosts to trap the Fates and get some answers."

Dare stared slack-jawed at Riot.

"Is that... like a normal thing to do?" Bullet whispered, leaning in so close that his lips brushed my shoulder. An entirely inappropriate shiver of desire ran down my spine. *Later. One step at a time.* "Trapping Fates and visiting ghost islands and stuff? There are some things I instinctively seem to know and other things I'm confused about, and I feel like... that's not normal."

I leaned a little harder into his side, relishing the solid feel of him against me. "That is definitely not normal. You can probably assume that nothing about our lives is normal."

"Start at the beginning," Dare commanded, staring wide-eyed at the bowl of fruit Wild handed him, freshly harvested from the trees that had sprung back to life outside, before splitting the portion between him and Bullet. "Actually, no. Bullet first. Tell us the story of how you freed the gods and became a hero."

"*You* did that?" I gasped, twisting to stare at him.

Bullet looked adorably shy. "Hecate told me about my friend, Dare, and said that he was going to jump into the pit and that he'd probably die if he did."

I spared Dare a look that promised we were not done talking about that, and he had the grace to look suitably sheepish.

"And while I didn't remember him, he sounded like he'd been a really good friend to me, and he loved Grace and she loved him, and I couldn't just let him die. And I was already sort of dead, so it really just made more sense for me to go."

"No, it's more than that," I disagreed, a sense of calmness and fulfillment washing over me. This was always the way it was meant to be, we just hadn't known it at the time. "It was fate—*your* fate. My fate. We were both given a prophecy, though, at the time, we thought it was just for me. It was always a toss-up as to which of us would fulfill it, we just didn't realize it."

"You split it," Riot pointed out. "Athena herself said Grace brought forth the Second Age of Heroes. It was for both of you." He looked at Dare, his grin briefly turning smug. "We're all heroes, by the way. You better do something cool if you want to join this club."

Dare snorted. "Obviously, me and Bullet are also heroes. Though I feel exactly the same and I'm in no rush to get to the underworld, so I don't really understand the hype, honestly."

Oh, I'd missed them so much.

We all took turns exchanging stories while the Spartoi came and went, bringing us fruit they'd harvested and bringing jugs of water to drink from the stream that had just appeared next to the campsite. There was no question of any of us going to bed—as exhausted as we were, sleep would never come.

Dare adjusted his position, discreetly stretching his back, and I held out my arms with a soft smile.

"Want a break?" The question was nervous. I didn't know how he'd feel about handing Quinn over, and I wasn't entirely sure how *I* felt about it either. There was no question that we'd honor Rogue's request, it had never occurred to me to do otherwise, but the level of responsibility was intimidating.

Dare gave me a shaky smile, moving carefully so as not to wake her, and gently depositing Quinn into my arms. I snuggled her in close, Wild taking my weight from where he sat behind me.

"She's heavier than I expected," I murmured, watching her chest rise and fall, her mouth half open, snoring lightly. It was the most precious thing I'd ever seen in my life. "How old is she?"

Riot and Dare exchanged thoughtful looks.

"About one, I guess?" Dare hedged. "It didn't come up when I was staying with them. We can always check with Dice. Whenever we see him again."

Riot frowned. "If he's still alive. Humanity has been through some *shit*, you know? I'm assuming everyone I know is dead until proven otherwise."

"That seems pessimistic," Bullet said, giving Riot a wide-eyed look.

Riot's answering smile was a little sad, but mostly teasing. "Pessimistic is very on-brand for me, B. You'll learn."

"*B*," Bullet repeated, smiling slightly to himself before gnawing on a fig.

"Well, I believe everyone is whole and healthy until proven otherwise," I said, shifting a lock of hair off Quinn's forehead with my finger. "I think I have to believe that, or I won't be able to wake up in the morning."

Wild hummed, stroking my hip. "I know you won't sleep, but I think we should move to the cabin we stayed in last night. We can set up a bed for Quinn, and I can get a break from the Spartoi, who I've spent plenty of nights lying next to, listening to their snores."

"Maybe we can heat up some water," Dare suggested around a yawn. "We're all covered in dirt and scorpion juice. We need to find some supplies for Quinn too. Diapers and stuff. Bottles? What do babies need?"

I had no idea, but I knew we'd figure it out. As challenging as life could be, there was nothing we couldn't face together.

GRACE

CHAPTER 33

It had been a quiet couple of days at the camp. As much as we knew there was work to be done, we were all in various states of injury and exhaustion, and—much to all of my soul bonds' surprise—I'd been the one to put my foot down and demand we all hide away from the world and the expectations it had of us.

There would be time for all of that later.

For now, we had to find a new rhythm. Get used to one another again, and learn how to take care of a distraught one-year-old. She'd been up most of last night screaming, and Sophia had shown up in the morning—oh so helpfully—to inform us that Quinn was teething, and none of our shushing or rocking or singing was useful in the slightest.

"Do you think she's okay?" Dare asked, glancing nervously out the window.

In her capacity as the personified spirit of wisdom, Sophia had decided we needed a break, and taken Quinn to the main camp house for dinner with the Spartoi.

"I do," I replied, surprising myself with the level of certainty I felt. "You know they all adore Quinn."

She was like the Spartoi's little mascot, and while she was still very confused and unsettled about everything, bashing their noisy armor around the floor was always guaranteed to spark a smile.

"I wonder where they'll go," Riot mused. He stretched out on the bed, folding his hands behind his head, and I sat at the end of it, tucking one leg beneath me, the other dangling off the edge. "I don't think they're cut for a 9-to-5 with a picket fence and a commute."

"Neither are we," Dare laughed. "Besides, I don't think the world is going to be exactly like that anymore. Or not for a long time at least. Humanity is in its second hunter-gatherer era."

I rolled my eyes, smiling as Dare came to sit next to me, wrapping an arm around my waist and resting his chin on my shoulder.

Wild was leaning against the wall next to the travel crib we'd found in the storage room for Quinn, observing us with a small smile on his face, while Bullet had taken the twin bed against the wall. He was observing too, a mixture of curiosity, longing, and wariness on his face.

For now, he was sleeping on that bed alone, more comfortable there while he got used to us. So far, the dreamscape hadn't called him away once, and I wasn't even a little bit sad about it. The last thing any of us wanted was for Bullet's head to be overloaded with visions again.

"I think we're a little beyond that. We still *have* all the technology that we had before, and mortals are very adaptable," I pointed out.

"If someone could get started on indoor plumbing, that'd be great," Riot sighed, tipping his head back. "Build some aqueducts or something, Roman-style."

"I'm sure that'll be a top priority," I laughed, nudging Riot's foot.

"But in the meantime, why don't you *finally* tell us what you learned from the Fates about the bonds?"

I didn't think Riot had been holding out on us to be difficult, but rather in a ham-fisted attempt at tactfulness. He didn't want Bullet to feel any kind of pressure, which was sweet, but even Bullet himself was getting frustrated at the lack of answers, and Sophia warned us she and Aphrodite were going to begin disseminating the information about how to form bonds through whispers among mortals within the next few days or so.

It was time. We couldn't put off this conversation any longer.

"I will, but I feel like it should come with a disclaimer."

"Go on then, oh wise one," Dare replied, smiling against my shoulder.

"Just because we know *how* to reestablish the bonds, doesn't mean that we have to go ahead and do it right away. The bonds are permanent, but they aren't limited in number or by time-constraints. We can all move at whatever pace we're comfortable with. That is my disclaimer," Riot finished lamely, very consciously not looking at Bullet.

"I'm pretty sure you said that for my benefit, and I appreciate you for it," Bullet replied cheerfully. *Same, same, but different.* Still merry, still brightly self-assured in his own way, but less confident when it came to things like teasing any of us or needling Riot. It was okay. It'd come in time, or it wouldn't, and I'd adore him anyway.

"You're welcome," Riot said with a smirk. "Anyway, it's not so complicated—hold hands and repeat a vow to each other as the sun sets."

"Romantic," I murmured, surprised the Fates would bother with romanticism. Especially after the way the bonds had been sealed in the past.

"Sure," Riot deadpanned. "The Fates are all about romance. They love fresh air and golden light and physical touch. Anyway, the added safeguard they built in is preexisting mutual feelings. There can be no bond until both parties reach a certain level of trust, love, and confidence—that kind of thing. If it doesn't go both ways, the bond won't take. Not like before when it was meet your soul bond, physical agony until you couldn't take it any more and boned, then you're bonded for life with no return policy. Not that I ever wanted to return you, Gracie," he added hastily. I attempted to give him a chastising look, but couldn't inject any real heat into it.

Preexisting mutual feelings. That was the way it should be, the way it should have always been, and yet I couldn't help but be nervous. What if it *didn't* take? I loved all of them more than I could comprehend, but what if it wasn't enough?

Riot was watching me closely, and Dare's arms tightened around my waist, his lips brushing lightly over my shoulder.

"We're not going to have a problem with that." Riot's voice was confident. He looked out the window, where the sky was just beginning to turn orange. "I'll show you that myself right now."

"Are you sure? I don't want to rush you—"

"I lied when I said we can *all* move at whatever pace we're comfortable with," Riot interjected. "That was just for Bullet. I want you right now, Gracie. I don't want to wait."

I pressed my lips together to stop myself from smiling. "You'd wait if I asked you to."

"He'd be a real surly prick about it, though," Dare laughed. "For what it's worth, I don't want to wait either."

I nodded, looking at Wild, a silent conversation passing between us as we'd got so in the habit of doing before his voice came back. We'd wait. As hard as it would be, we'd wait until Bullet was ready or until he decided what he wanted, even if it wasn't us.

"Alright. I'm ready," I said with a decisive nod.

Riot grinned. "We need to be outside, with the setting sun on us."

Dare half dragged me off the bed, spinning me around until we were facing each other. "Me next?" he confirmed.

I went up on my tiptoes and pressed a kiss to his lips. "It's not a question. I'm not waiting."

"What did I do to deserve you, hm?"

We left the room with Wild and Bullet walking ahead, scouting out a place for us to have our ceremony away from any prying eyes. They both seemed to actively want to be involved, which soothed some of my internal anxiety at us all moving at different paces. They certainly didn't *look* resentful.

"Here?" Bullet suggested, leading us into a small grassy patch between a copse of trees, the golden sunlight filtering through the gaps, giving it a wholly magical feel, while maintaining a good level of privacy.

Sometimes, I still felt like this wasn't real—the grass between my feet, the scent of flowers, the buzz of insects. I'd never grow tired of being outside, and I wished I'd appreciated it more before.

"It's perfect," I breathed, turning in a circle to admire it before sitting cross-legged on the ground at Riot's encouragement, laying my palms flat against his. Already, there was a tingle of magic in the air, a strange sense of fizzy lightness mixed with a feeling of weight and duty. Though that made sense, didn't it? The bubbly joy of love and the gravity of commitment, coming together as one.

"What do we do?" I asked.

"Join our hands, and repeat the three magic words to each other." Riot's lips twitched. "They definitely made it easy because Atropos thinks

I'm an idiot who can't follow instructions."

He didn't seem upset, so I chose not to renew my irritation at the Fates for the way they'd spoken to him. No, he seemed happy. Happier, maybe, than I'd ever seen him.

Riot stared into my eyes, looking so perfectly content that my simmering insecurity that this wouldn't work just melted away. He believed in us, and I was going to believe in us too. I was going to choose to believe in us.

"Pístis, elpís, agápē." He said the words clearly and calmly, and I smiled at the perfect simplicity of them. *Faith, hope, love.*

"Pístis, elpís, agápē," I repeated, a warm sense of comfort and familiarity radiating out from where our palms were connected, running up my arms and settling in the hollow place in my chest. It was like the bond we had before, but different. More intentional, more solid, and more secure.

Nothing—no force in this realm or any other—was going to tear this bond apart.

"Come here," Riot said hoarsely, pulling me into his lap and capturing my mouth in a desperate kiss. I straddled his lap, unable to get close enough as his lust mingled with mine, drawing us more tightly together. Dare chuckled quietly from somewhere behind me, and my face heated at the reminder that I had three sets of eyes on me, watching my every move.

I wasn't embarrassed—not anymore. But there'd been a chasteness to our interactions since we'd all come back together that I knew wasn't going to last much longer.

His hands slid beneath my dress, squeezing my ass, and I spread my thighs wider to accommodate him, grinding down on his lap.

"Nope," Dare announced, wrapping his arms around my chest and hauling me off a laughing Riot's lap. "Fuck that. I want my bond before the sun goes down, and Riot is greedy."

"So are you," Riot shot back, all delicious arrogance. While we hadn't been around humans yet to see if our gifts had changed at all, I was pretty confident Dare's was the same. We'd already been aroused, but Dare's desire had ramped that feeling up to eleven just by being near us. Where I'd been considering cementing the bond out here in the open before returning to our cabin to celebrate sans clothes, I was now thinking it'd be a very good idea to celebrate sans clothes right here. Necessary, even.

"Fuck," Dare groaned, spinning around to press a hard kiss to my mouth before guiding my hips down, sitting me in Riot's lap while he sat cross-legged in front of us. I blinked at him somewhat dazedly. I'd forgotten how potent arousal was when it was being shared between us this way, and I vaguely wondered how I'd coped when there had been four bonds' worth.

Hopefully, someday soon, I'd find out again.

Dare grabbed my hands, and there was no soft, staring-into-my-soul moment like the one Riot and I had just shared. Dare was practically vibrating in place, staring at me with a hungry look in his eyes that I knew was reflected in my own.

"*Pístis, elpís, agápē.*" Dare practically shouted the words, announcing them to the world, full of absolute confidence and enthusiasm.

And perhaps a touch of impatience.

"*Pístis, elpís, agápē,*" I repeated, not quite suppressing a laugh at his exuberance. I groaned at the sensation of the bond unfurling and filling me up, tying us together. I leaned forward, still sitting on Riot's lap, and all but devoured Dare's mouth, needing to get closer.

We were out of control, and I was vaguely aware of it, but I couldn't drag myself away either. There were two sets of hands moving all over my body, sliding over my thighs, the heat of their hands sinking through the thin cotton fabric. There were hands on my waist, on my breasts, massaging the flesh, pinching my nipples, stroking my throat. Clothes were removed—from me, from them—but the mechanics were a blur. I just needed to feel their skin on mine, needed to connect with them, to experience the intimacy we'd once shared before we'd been torn apart.

"Gracie," Riot groaned, lying back in the grass, leaving me straddling him, facing his feet.

Dare grinned from in front of me, half-dressed and working on removing the rest. "Go on, I know that clit is feeling needy. Your bonded is right there, waiting for you to use him to make yourself feel good."

I looked over my shoulder at Riot, whose breathing had grown ragged.

"This fucking view," he muttered, grabbing my ass and kneading the flesh. "Unreal. Make yourself feel good, Gracie. If I had some lube, we'd be working on taking you together right now."

"Well," Wild began, startling me. I hadn't forgotten that he and Bullet were there, but they *had* been very quiet. "I do have something. A gift for the heroes, Aphrodite said."

He pulled a small stoppered bottle out of his pocket, filled with a pale, golden liquid.

"Lube?" Dare asked hopefully. Wild smirked, tossing him the bottle.

"Gracie?" Riot asked, still massaging my ass cheeks. "You know we'd never push—"

"I want to," I said hurriedly. "Or at least I want to try."

I lifted myself up onto my knees, shuffling backward a bit so I could rock my clit over Riot's cock, every nerve in my body lighting up in anticipation. I didn't *need* foreplay, not really. I was ridiculously aroused already, and I had a live feed of Riot and Dare's arousal pumping into my body, coiling me tighter.

Riot was thrusting shallowly against me, and he made another delicious, masculine groaning sound as I wrapped my hand around his shaft, lifting it so I could rub the cool metal of his piercing in circles around my clit, just how I liked it.

"I don't want to come like this," I gasped, right on the edge of bliss. Moving as fast as my jelly legs would let me, I raised myself up and held Riot's cock to my entrance, sinking down on it, inch by delicious inch. This *angle*. Almost the moment I started moving, I reached my peak, relying on Dare to hold me up while Riot continued to thrust into me from below.

"Turn around for me?" Dare asked softly. "I'm going to make you feel so good."

"Oh, I know. I have full confidence in you," I slurred, lust drunk. Dare lifted me up, helping me turn around on weak legs while Riot grumbled impatiently, reaching for me instantly. I lined him up with me again, rocking my hips until I was fully settled. I braced myself with a hand on either side of his head, my breasts brushing against Riot's chest as he leaned up for a kiss.

I heard Dare unstop the bottle from behind me, and immediately a *mouthwatering* scent filled the air, which wasn't exactly what I expected from lube, but I wasn't complaining.

"I'm going to test this on me first," Dare mumbled. "This smells suspiciously good."

"Aphrodite mentioned it had some relaxing properties. To make things more comfortable," Wild offered.

I could hear Dare doing something behind me, the sound of slick movements filling the air as he tested the lube on himself, but Riot had lost his patience. He grabbed my hips roughly, bouncing me on his cock at a brutal pace while I dug my fingers into the grass, loving the way he took control.

"Slow down," Dare commanded raspily, stroking my spine. "Oh, fuck. This feels so good. Grace, you're going to feel *amazing*."

Riot grit his teeth, forcing himself to stay still while Dare began massaging the lube teasingly around my back entrance, pressing one finger past the tight ring of muscle, making me clench around Riot's cock. *Oh, this magic lube was incredible.* Dare must have been reading my reactions through the bond, because he added a second finger at the exact moment I was ready for it, dripping more lube onto my skin before adding a third finger.

"Fuck," Riot rasped, bucking up beneath me. "That is intense. Gracie, you good? You feel like you're doing good."

"I'm doing very good. I want more," I gasped, catching myself by surprise as an intense orgasm wracked my body out of nowhere. Riot and Dare held themselves admirably still as I writhed between them, letting me set the pace.

"I'm going to give you more," Dare promised, withdrawing his fingers and settling behind me, the blunt head of his cock pushing slowly forward.

"Are you relaxing?" Wild asked, crouching down close and cupping my chin, dragging my face up to look at him.

"Oh, I am very relaxed," I assured him, giving him a somewhat dopey smile. Bullet had moved closer too, his cheeks flushed red while he took in the cozy depravity unfolding in front of him.

Dare's hips pressed against my ass cheeks, his breathing hard. They gave me a moment to adjust, before they moved, synchronizing themselves perfectly. Wild kept ahold of my chin, stroking my jaw occasionally with his thumb, grounding me when the avalanche of sensation threatened to wash me away.

"You look so beautiful," Wild murmured, a litany of compliments pouring out of his mouth. I knew he was perfectly capable of filling my ears with pure filth if he was so inclined, which made the moments where he was all syrupy sweetness all the more special. "So fucking sexy like this, all relaxed and confident in your sexuality. You undo us."

"Yeah," Bullet agreed, his voice like sandpaper. "You're... you're really beautiful. That doesn't seem like a big enough word for it."

I tried to reply, but I was orgasming again, and it set both Riot and Dare off until we were one big, noisy, sticky, perfect mess.

There were still two very prominent empty spots in my chest, and there was a sense of feeling slightly lopsided, but I was still content. With everything we'd experienced, we'd find our way all the way back to each other in our time, and it would be perfect.

MERCY

CHAPTER 34

"Mercy..." Harbor warned. "You need a break."

"I'm fine," I lied, my head throbbing. I'd been using my Hygeia healing gift more frequently since the world had bloomed back to life, immortals darting through the skies and popping down to visit us like it was just an entirely normal occurrence. In this new world, filled with hope, it seemed stingy not to use my gift.

Besides, Hygeia herself had appeared once while I was washing clothes in the river with no one else around.

She hadn't *said* anything, but she also hadn't needed to. She'd just stared in judgmental silence, and that had been enough to motivate me into using my gift more proactively.

I'd kept that information to myself though. I didn't want Harbor to worry.

"Nope, I'm overruling you," he announced, wrapping an arm around my waist and leading me away from the campsite. "No one is in any mortal danger. They have some scrapes and bruises at most, nothing that requires the direct intervention of a Hygeia."

I slumped slightly against him, reveling in the feel of his strong, solid body against mine. We knew from the gods' whispers that mortals could choose bonds for themselves now—Chance and Creed had already done it, and they were so sickeningly in love that I found it hard to believe they were the same two miserable men I'd lived with for so long in Auburn.

Of course, they weren't happy and relaxed all of the time. While Tobin and Leon had settled in well to camp life, and were louder and more confident than I'd ever known them to be back home, they all still missed Grace. The immortals who passed through raved about her—in a slightly antagonizing way, I was pretty sure—and it reminded us all just how far away she was. How much she'd grown and changed since we'd last seen her.

I think we all wondered if Grace had outgrown her relationships with us, even if she was able to forgive us for the various ways we'd all let her down over the years.

"Felix wrote again this week, asking if I'd come and visit," Harbor was saying, and I forced myself to focus, not realizing I'd been tuning out. Maybe I had expended a little too much of my gift healing Margaret's migraine after all. "With the dissolution of the Basilinnas and the Elders by the original agathos, he assumed some kind of leadership position. I guess the immortals favor him? I mean, there aren't many better options in Auburn to be fair." He snorted. "He and Joy's other soul bonds have, er, bonded to each other. Like in a friendship-type way? He said they're platonic soulmates and they're raising their kids together, and none of them have any desire to meet someone romantically after Joy."

"That's sweet," I said quietly, embarrassingly conscious of Harbor's reaction.

He'd been standing next to me, as stiff as a board, when we'd heard about the new way of bonding, and he'd kept his distance for a couple of days after that. I may not know much about relationships, but I could take a hint.

He was attracted to me, but he didn't want to permanently tie his soul to mine. I didn't judge him for it—everyone here knew I'd been given a soul bond by the gods and I'd betrayed him and run away. I wasn't exactly reliable partner material.

And while I wanted Harbor to myself, I'd be lying if I said I was entirely comfortable with the idea of a bond. There was a niggling voice in the back of my mind that asked *what about Dice?* every time I considered it.

"Let's go lie down," Harbor murmured.

"Together?" I cringed at the hopefulness in my voice. Why couldn't I sound more cool and sophisticated?

He gave me one of my least favorite Harbor smiles—the one that was a little strained, a little tinged with sadness, and filled with something akin to longing, though I doubted it was actually that.

"Yeah, together. I can't... This can't be..." He made a sound of frustration, glancing up at the sky as though the gods themselves would swoop down and provide him with the words he was struggling to find. "Just let me hold you, please? Let me care for you. You're hurting from taking on everyone else's ills. Just let me look after you."

I nodded, my throat tight. It was more than I deserved after what I'd done to Dice.

And it was nowhere near enough.

BULLET

CHAPTER 35

Even with the grapevines growing over the verandah overhead, providing some shade, it was a fucking *hot* day. The skies were blue and the sun was out in full force, and while everyone claimed that it was nearly winter and *really, not that warm, Bullet,* I was sweating a little in my thin shirt and shorts while I shucked peas in the shade. A quirk of me coming back from the dead, we'd all decided. I found hot weather intolerable, could only eat meagre amounts of sweet food before I felt sick, and fell into a deep, dreamless sleep every night.

All things considered, they were very reasonable quirks and I didn't mind them at all.

"Do you still like musicals?" Orion asked me, sitting down with his own bowl of peas to shuck while I worked through mine. We'd been staying at his family's villa since returning to Greece four weeks ago on Arsène's boat—Grace, Wild, Riot, and Dare had made lots of friends on their travels apparently. We were staying with a lot of them now.

They treated me like one of their friends too, even though I didn't remember any of them. It was nice. It had made it easier to fall into some kind of rhythm here. There was room for the Spartoi, and a bunch of the other agathos and daimon friends Grace and the others had collected up in their travels, and we had our own space upstairs where we all slept chastely next to one another in a big puppy pile on the bed.

Not that the others weren't getting frisky, they were all just careful not to do it when I was around—with the exception of the incredible bonding moment between Grace, Riot, and Dare—I guessed not to pressure me.

Which was nice—really it was—but I was getting very well acquainted with my hand and it was kind of bumming me out. It wasn't as though I wasn't attracted to Grace and Wild.

I was *definitely* attracted to them.

Orion was staring at me, and I searched my brain, trying to remember if he'd asked me a question.

"Musicals, brother," he laughed. "Do you still like musicals?"

"Oh! Um, I don't know. I *think* so." I frowned. "Grace tells me that we used to be able to just *play* music whenever, you know, sung by amazing singers. Maybe I'd like the songs more if I heard those versions? Not that Grace is a *bad* singer," I added hastily.

She wasn't. She was... she was fine. And I really appreciated her trying to reacquaint me with what had once been my favorite songs.

Orion snorted. "It isn't easy being the Prophêtis. I guess Grace can't be amazing at everything, even though it seems like she is. She was sitting on the cliff ledge next to Typhoeus earlier, teaching him sign language, did you see?"

"I did." I decided I didn't like other guys talking about how amazing Grace was and telling me about her day. She was my amazing Grace. It was only okay when Riot, Wild, or Dare talked about her.

294

"Are you going to bond with someone?" I asked.

Orion choked on his saliva, and I realized that maybe it was a kind of personal question. After Riot had passed on the instructions on how to bond, those who'd already *been* bonded had quickly reestablished their connections, but new ones hadn't been forged yet. Between the original agathos and Aphrodite, news about bonds was apparently being disseminated quickly among mortals.

"I mean, I'd like to. One day. I'm glad I have the option now." He blushed looking down at the bowl of peas. "But I haven't met the right person yet. Or people. Whatever."

Milos, an unusually smart dog that some of Grace's friends had been looking after in Ephesus, flopped down under the long dining table a few feet away, also hiding from the sun. Smart girl. She'd really made herself at home here at the villa. She definitely preferred the agathos though—specifically Foster. A couple of the daimons, Vasileios and Estrella, had been trying to win her over to no avail.

After a long silence, Orion spoke again. "My parents came before you guys got here—a weak attempt to get their property back. They re-bonded with each other, and sort of said that it would be blasphemous of me to even consider a bond. That being alone was my fate."

"With all due respect, fuck that. Your parents sound like idiots."

Orion let out a startled laugh. "Yeah. Yeah, they kind of are. They've accepted Gaia's defeat, but I don't see them letting go of the old ways any time soon."

There would be plenty of agathos like that out in the world by the sounds of it, but I wasn't worried. None of us were, really.

One, they were outnumbered.

Two, Grace had never met a challenge she couldn't overcome.

Those stubborn agathos hadn't encountered my girl yet, she'd soon have them seeing the light.

"You okay?" Wild asked, coming over to join me in the shade after he'd spent the afternoon harvesting olives. The seasons were changing and going forward, apparently in the future there'd be some kind of regular growing schedule, but for now, it had just been Demeter and Persephone hard at work, forcing plants to grow so we didn't all starve.

"I'm good," I assured him, rolling my shoulders. "Hephaestus dropped by with an olive press; he was showing Dare and me how to use it for when the olives are fermented, or whatever."

It had been a month of this. The Olympians rarely left the upperworld because there was so much restoration to be done, and every community needed something, and there were still scorpions on the loose. Besides, they had to reestablish their presence among mortals, so it was a good thing that they were willing to get their hands dirty.

Wild flopped down on the ground, whipping off his shirt to cool down, and my mouth went dry as the dirt had been when I'd arrived back in this realm. He'd bulked up over the past couple of weeks, and I could have stared at his pecs and arm muscles for hours and never gotten bored.

I did my best to discreetly memorize the sight of him leaning back on his hands, head tipped up to the sky, eyes closed, for later when I was alone with my hand again.

"Don't be shy," Wild drawled, lips twitching slightly, his eyes still shut. "Look your fill, I don't mind."

"I wasn't looking," I replied instantly, face growing hot after I'd been busted checking him out. I wasn't even entirely sure why—both he and Grace had made it clear that the power was in my hands.

"Yeah, you were." Wild's voice practically dripped with arrogance, and I discreetly adjusted myself in my light linen pants that hid nothing. "And I fucking loved it. Look. Touch. Better yet, tell me you're ready for more and let me touch you."

I blew out a shaky breath, my legs trembling slightly as I lowered myself to the ground next to him. Wild had opened his eyes, watching every movement, and I felt a bit like a fluffy bunny caught in the gaze of a wolf.

And it made me super fucking aroused, so I don't know what that said about me but I wasn't going to question it too hard.

"You can touch me." I mentally patted myself on the back for sounding so cool and calm when I was all but panting on the inside.

Wild cocked an eyebrow, twisting his upper body to face me. He was that much taller, and the movement had him sort of looming over me in the best kind of way. I chanced a quick glance around, making sure we were still alone, and finding the field empty. I didn't care if Grace, Riot, or Dare approached, but I was still finding my feet around the others.

"There's no one here," Wild assured me. "Riot is giving Quinn her dinner, and Dare was on his way to wash up when I passed him on the way out here. You know what that means, though."

"Grace will come looking for us soon?" I asked hopefully, my cock growing painfully hard at the thought of her finding us tangled up together in the dirt. Maybe even joining in...

They may have been careful not to push me, but I wouldn't get that image of her bonding with Riot and Dare out of my head for as long as I lived.

Wild was holding himself back, watching me carefully, waiting for me to make the first move.

"There's no rush, Bullet," he murmured, even though he was staring at my mouth when he spoke. "We'll wait for you as long as you need us to wait—"

297

I cut him off by pressing my lips to his, following my instincts. I didn't want to wait any longer, I didn't want Grace and Wild to keep silently wondering if I actually wanted them or if I was going to change my mind and walk away.

They needed to know they were mine. It was essential.

Wild's tongue teased mine, encouraging me to open to him, and I was more than happy to let him take the lead. His hand wrapped around the back of my neck, supporting my head as he lowered me to the ground, his big body bearing down on mine without ever breaking the kiss. I grabbed his hip without a second thought, thrusting upwards, greedy for friction. *Fuck*, he was big. A noise somewhere between a groan and a gasp escaped me as Wild shifted fully over me, pinning my hips in place and grinding his cock against mine through the thin fabric of our trousers.

Wild trailed kisses down my jaw, my neck, teeth scraping at the junction of my neck and shoulder. "So fucking responsive. So *pretty* when you're losing your mind, desperate to come. Don't you agree, darling Grace?"

My eyes flew open, finding Grace standing over us with her teeth sinking into her lower lip, cheeks flushed the prettiest shade of dark pink.

"You going to roll around in the dirt with us?" he teased, flashing her a seductive smirk before making me choke on my breath with a well-timed roll of his hips.

He was really good at this.

"I don't know," Grace replied, dropping to her knees a foot away. "You two *do* make a pretty picture..."

"Bullet?" Wild prompted, nipping at my ear. "What do you want?"

"The bond," I replied instantly, startling all three of us. It was the truth though. I wanted it more than I wanted my memories, more than I wanted anything. "If you still want it," I added hurriedly.

298

"So much," Grace whispered, shuffling closer on her knees. She looked like she was about to speak, but Wild beat her to it.

"You two first."

He rolled off me, deftly slipping behind me to lean against the trunk of the tree, and encouraging me to sit back in the V of his thighs. And then encouraging me back a little more. And then *up*.

I arched my back instantly as his thick cock settled in the cleft of my ass, pleasure rocketing up my spine with each slow, subtle movement, his hands gripping my hips tightly to keep me in place.

I held out a hand, reaching for Grace, and she placed her palm in mine, willingly closing the distance between us. With surprising firmness, she cupped my jaw, kneeling next to me and leaning in to kiss me.

"Hop on, Grace," Wild encouraged, his lips moving against my shoulder.

"We might crush you," Grace laughed, but she threw her leg over my thighs the moment I pulled her forward.

"Mm, but what a way to go," Wild murmured, groaning as Grace seated herself over my cock, looking up at me coyly through her lashes. There was a hint of worry behind her eyes, and I leaned forward, kissing each eyelid, her nose, her lips.

"I came out here at sunset for a reason," I whispered. "Promise."

"I want to bond you while you're inside me," she whispered back, derailing the romantic train of thought I'd been on. *Yeah. That. Let's do that.*

"Take your panties off," Wild grunted, still doing phenomenal things to my ass with each subtle shift of his hips.

"I'm not wearing any." Wild and I both groaned as Grace laughed. "It's washing day! They're all drying—"

"We're not complaining," I assured her, sliding my hands up her

299

thighs, beneath the blue skirt she was wearing. "Help me?" I asked, wincing at the question. I *thought* I knew what she liked, but I didn't want to let her down either.

"Of course," Grace agreed easily, pulling up her dress and guiding my hand where she wanted me, showing me how to circle her clit the way she liked.

"So good," she whispered, guiding two fingers to her entrance and rocking forward to grind her clit on the heel of my hand. "Though I was already so wet, so close just from watching the two of you."

"You can come on his cock," Wild growled, the command in his voice affecting both me and Grace. One of his hands left my hip, sliding up my body to gently cup my throat, guiding my head back to his shoulder. "I want to watch," he whispered in my ear.

Grace made a soft, needy sound of agreement, reluctantly releasing my hand before deftly undoing my trousers and freeing my cock. Just the feeling of her wrapping her hand around my shaft and moving the fabric out of the way had me questioning if I was going to come on the spot.

That would be embarrassing. This was meant to be our moment.

"I don't think... Grace, I'm not sure I'm going to last," I admitted, face burning hot.

"Good, me neither," she replied breezily, half standing to climb into place and rubbing my cock once, twice, over her clit before notching me at her entrance and sinking down.

"Fuck, fuck, fuck," I whispered, my stomach contracting as I fought back my orgasm. Wild's thumb continued stroking teasing circles on my throat as Grace lowered until she was sitting on my thighs, pushing my ass further against Wild's cock. "Oh no. No, no, this is way too good. I'm going to embarrass myself. Fuck."

Grace leaned in, teasing my lower lip with her teeth, smiling against my lips.

"Bullet?" she asked, all soft seduction while her pussy strangled my cock.

"Yes?" I rasped. Grace grabbed both of my hands, holding them up and linking our fingers together.

"Pístis, elpís, agápē."

The fear I'd been harboring that the bond wouldn't take melted away into nothing. Of course, this would work. Of course, our bond would be bright and vibrant, and perfect.

"Pístis, elpís, agápē," I repeated, closing my eyes as it unfurled within me, stretching between us, tying us together. Grace's love for me—more powerful and all-consuming than I could have ever imagined—poured freely through the connection between us, mingling with her lust. It was too much in the best kind of way, and despite my best efforts, I couldn't hold off my orgasm any longer.

"That's it," Grace encouraged, not disappointed in me in the least. "Feel how much I love you. You're mine, Bullet. You always have been."

"Always," I agreed, gasping for air. "Fuck, Grace, you didn't—"

"Don't worry about that," Wild interjected, all arrogance. "I'm going to take good care of both of you."

"You always do," Grace laughed, climbing off me at Wild's encouragement.

"Don't go anywhere," he warned me, shifting me off his lap and pressing a hard kiss to my mouth, sucking on my tongue for a moment before turning his gaze to Grace. "On your back, darling. Let me clean you up."

Wait. Did he mean...?

Oh my giddy goddesses.

Yes, that was exactly what he meant.

Grace flopped back into the grass, blushing furiously as Wild threw her legs over his shoulders and flipped her skirt up to her stomach, before settling his face between her thighs and feasting.

On my cum.

I might have been redder than Grace, though according to the bond, both of us seemed to have hit a level beyond *turned on*. Grace squirmed, her embarrassment drowned out by lust as she found her release, one orgasm stretching languidly into another as Wild lavished more attention on her clit.

Hoping I wasn't being too obvious, I leaned in a little closer, memorizing what he was doing. Just in case.

"So good, so good, so good," Grace chanted, gasping for air. Wild let up his relentless ministrations, crawling over her body with a smug grin, lips shining from our shared release.

"You always taste good, darling, but *that*." He groaned, fisting his shaft before lining it up and sliding into her pussy with one smooth thrust. "Fucking delicious."

He grabbed Grace's hands, pinning them on either side of her head.

"Pístis, elpís, agápē."

She smiled beatifically up at him, legs wrapping around his waist.

"Pístis, elpís, agápē," Grace repeated as her eyes fell closed, the act of reclaiming her final bonded enough to push her over the edge again. My head spun at the sudden rush of blood back to my cock. This couldn't be healthy. I was going to die all over again, this time from being too horny.

Wild lost whatever restraint he'd been managing, hitching Grace's legs up with his forearms and fucking her into the ground. And she *loved* it. It was such a feast for the eyes, I couldn't decide where to look. My gaze darted between Grace's blissed-out face, the swell of her breasts, Wild's hungry expression, and the way his powerful thighs and butt flexed as he pumped into her.

Did I really get to call these two mine? How was I this lucky?

"Give me one more," Wild demanded, shifting his angle slightly so he was hitting Grace's clit with each thrust. Her eyes rolled back into her head, spine arching clean off the ground as she peaked, Wild's movements stuttering to a stop as he followed.

I groaned quietly, hunching forward and massaging my aching cock. Feeling Grace's lust magnified the sensations by a million, and I vaguely wondered how Riot and Dare ever got anything done.

"Happy?" Grace whispered, glancing between us. Her face shone with sweat, making her look like a glowy goddess in the last vestiges of the low, golden sunlight.

"You can feel we are," Wild rasped while I nodded, maybe a little enthusiastically.

"Wouldn't it be nice if you could feel each other?" Grace pressed, a sleepy, coy smile on her face.

"Minx." Wild propped himself up on his elbows, dropping a kiss on Grace's nose before pulling out, using his shirt to clean her up and smoothing her skirt down over her legs. "The sun has gone down. But we're not in a rush, are we?"

He was checking in on me and verifying that I was okay all at once, and I appreciated it. There was no rush, and I was glad that I had a moment to adjust to the bond with Grace for a minute. Unlike the others, it wasn't a familiar coming home sensation for me, not anymore. It was new, and incredible, and strange. And when Wild and I took that step, I knew I'd love it then too.

"Come here," Wild ordered softly, wrapping an arm around Grace's shoulder and lying back down in the grass, spreading his other arm out for me to snuggle into his other side.

The three of us lay together in perfect, contented silence, staring up at the skies as the stars emerged, watching the occasional streaks of gold of gods traversing the earth flashing through the night.

EPILOGUE 1

TWO YEARS AFTER THE RESTORATION

You're getting too big for this, I thought, staring down at where Quinn was napping in the sling, her cheek pressed to my chest, and her arms and legs sticking straight out like scarecrow limbs at her sides. At age three, naps were mostly a rare occurrence these days, but we were on the boat, Arsène ferrying us up the coast of Croatia on official Prophêtis business, and Quinn couldn't keep her eyes open with Poseidon's gentle waves rocking us day in and day out.

"Let me take her?" Dare asked, crossing the deck to where I was pacing, admiring the view of the Adriatic and the white coastline, covered in a healthy smattering of lush green vegetation. He set down two cups of watered-down wine he'd brought out for us, pressing a lingering kiss to my lips, before disentangling Quinn with ease and shifting her into his arms.

It was unfair how easy he made that look. If I so much as thought about putting her down, she'd be awake and giving me accusatory eyes before I could blink.

"Want the sling?" I offered, untying it from around my waist.

"Nah, I'll go lie down with her in the cabin." Dare grimaced. "Daimons may be immune to hangovers, but even I'm feeling a little sore after the past few days."

"I'm not surprised," I laughed. Wherever our merry band of heroes went, parties usually followed. Often because gods followed, instinctively called to worship in general, but also to wherever I was, because I'd been blessed with a voice that carried, even if it sometimes felt like a curse.

Especially last night, in Split. What had meant to be a small gathering at a fledgling temple dedicated to Artemis—a place formed specifically for women who'd been displaced during the time of change— had been hijacked by Dionysus and many gallons of wine. Artemis had followed, outraged and slightly amused, to keep an eye on him, and it had all devolved into revelry from there.

Who knew what we'd find tonight in Hvar. Or after that in Korčula. Or the night after that in Dubrovnik. *Where were we supposed to go after that?* Sophia had given us a suggested itinerary. Oh yes, Poveglia, to pay our respects—Riot had been quietly terrified about that suggestion—then north on land. Salzburg, perhaps?

It wasn't as though it was *bad* work. The advantage of being able to call upon gods when necessary was that it helped vastly in the work of rebuilding, and we'd already allayed tensions in plenty of places that had suffered and struggled by requesting divine intervention. Things were getting better. It was a *blessing* that we could provide that to people.

And yet...

"What are you thinking?" Dare asked, his curiosity prodding at my psyche through the bond as I stared out at the water.

"Do you ever miss home?"

Dare blinked in surprise, and I had to admit that I felt a little traitorous even asking the question, considering how fortunate we'd been.

"Not necessarily," Dare replied slowly. "I have everything I need right here—you, Quinbee, Riot, Wild, Bullet... There's nothing *for* me in Milton anymore. But I do get curious about how things are going back there. I wouldn't mind visiting. If you want to go home, Grace, we'll make it happen. Didn't people sail from London to New York all the time back in ye olden days? How hard can it be?"

"How hard can what be?" Riot asked, shoving his messy hair out of his eyes as he walked across the deck in bare feet, looking deliciously rumpled and sun-kissed after a mid-morning nap outside. Of all my daimon bonded, he was probably the most attached to the nocturnal schedule. It wasn't uncommon for him to fall asleep a few hours after us and catch up on sleep in the morning. It didn't matter so much now, but when Quinn had been a regular night-waker, having Riot still up to tend to her had been a life-saver.

"Sailing across the Atlantic," Dare replied as Riot came to stand behind me, wrapping his arms around my waist and resting his chin on my shoulder. "Back stateside."

I felt a flicker of surprise through the bond. "Yeah? I kind of hoped we were going back to Victoria Falls once we finished this trip, but I guess going home could be interesting. Unless we're visiting your mom, in which case, hard pass."

I shook my head instantly, horrified at the suggestion. I didn't even know where my mother and Valor had gone after their confrontation with Chance and Creed where Thanatos had snatched her voice—tying it somehow to Wild's curse. Thanatos had shared that much with us in his gloating on an impromptu visit, but he was too bad-tempered to elaborate on the specifics despite me asking very nicely. Apparently, he only gave us

307

information on *his* terms.

Chance, Creed, and Mercy had all reached out to me in turn in the months after The Twelve had returned. They'd sent letters through various original agathos—tentative at first, though my relationship with my dads had improved dramatically in the past year or so. They'd been fighting their own battles while I was growing up, and while I didn't necessarily *excuse* all that they'd let me be subjected to, I understood that the issue wasn't quite as clear-cut as I'd thought it was.

My relationship with Mercy wasn't quite as straightforward, but part of it was just life getting in the way. We both had so much going on that we were just keeping our heads above water a lot of the time.

"Definitely no visits to my mother in my future," I assured Riot. "I'd like to see Chance, Creed, my brothers, and Mercy if we can get up to Maine. Earnest is still somewhere in the south, last I heard. In that agathos temple."

He'd apparently devoted his life to helping humans and daimons impacted by the negative actions of the agathos, though I still found the concept a little difficult to believe. Hermes had taken great relish in telling us all about it.

"Do you want to visit your dad?" I asked Riot hesitantly.

"Um, hell yeah," he replied instantly, taking me by surprise.

"Because you've missed him?"

"No," he snorted. "Because I'm a big fucking deal these days and I want to rub it in his face for all the times he told me I'd never amount to anything."

"Oh."

Dare laughed. "I guarantee your old man is a local hero by now, telling everyone how important his boy is and how he always knew you had greatness in you."

"Probably," Riot huffed. "Maybe I don't want to visit him after all. I don't want to give him the satisfaction." He paused for a moment. "I'll decide when we get there. I'm sure Onyx can fill us in, give us the lay of the land."

I hummed in agreement. I'd love to see Onyx again, and all of the daimons Wild had once looked after at Underworld. I wanted to see Dice, to assure him that Quinn was safe and loved beyond measure with us, and so she could spend time with her uncle, if he was even in Milton these days. I even wanted to catch up with some of my old agathos friends, to see if they'd changed or if we could find common ground these days.

"Then let's get through this trip, and go home," Dare said, as though it were that simple. "Arsène's sailboat won't be up for the journey, but I'm sure we can track down a vessel and a crew. I'm not above throwing your name around to get results, Grace. If you want to go home, we'll go home."

"Good girl," Onyx said with a cocky smile that softened into something far sweeter than I was used to seeing on her face. She pulled me into a tight hug, careful not to jostle Quinn who was balanced on my hip. "What the fuck are you doing here?"

She glanced at Quinn as she pulled away, frowning. "Am I allowed to swear in front of the baby?"

"Technically no, but Riot does it all the time," Dare replied drily.

Onyx looked at him, a catlike grin on her face. "You owe me a tattoo."

Dare let out a surprised burst of laughter. "So I do. But I'm a little out of practice, and electricity is hard to come by. Though we could always test out the old ways, pushing the ink under your skin with a needle, one drop at a time—"

"I'm good," Onyx replied hastily. "I'll wait until we have a reliable power source again."

Wild was hanging back slightly, a sense of hesitancy coming through the bond. Probably because the building we were standing in front didn't really resemble his once magnificent club any more. By the looks of it, half of the structure had collapsed, and they'd done their best to fortify the remaining area with makeshift scaffolding at stacks of bricks.

It could have been worse. We'd gone past my old apartment building—or the remains of it, rather—and I'd thrown up at the sight. That building, and that one alone, had been completely flattened. It had been an act of spite against me that my neighbors had paid the price for.

The ruins themselves were inaccessible because of the thick sea of rose bushes that had sprouted up around the entire thing. The same roses that I'd grown in pots on my balcony all those years ago, when I'd first moved to Milton alone. I suspected it had been a gesture of kindness from Persephone, and it had quickly become something of a pilgrimage spot.

Onyx's expression was slightly sheepish as she looked past me to where Wild stood. "Sorry, bossman. We did our best to keep the place standing. It was packed to the rafters when the world went dark, and we all did our best to make it habitable while we camped out. I know it isn't what it used to be—"

"You did a better job holding it together than I could have," Wild interrupted. Onyx's jaw dropped open.

"You can *speak*? How? Since when? I swear to the gods, if you've been able to talk this whole time and were just choosing not to..."

Wild snorted. "No. Are you going to invite us in?"

"It's your building," Onyx pointed out, gesturing at the door.

"Not anymore," Wild replied easily, striding past her. "It's yours now."

Onyx looked at me in disbelief, and I gave her a reassuring nod, brushing the crumbs from the bread Quinn was munching on off my shoulder. "We discussed on the way here. We're not exactly sure where we want our home base to be, if we're even ready to choose one yet, but none of us want to be in a city."

"Everyone wants a piece of Grace," Bullet added absently, observing his surroundings curiously. "Apparently, I have a property not too far from here that's more private."

"Apparently," Onyx repeated faintly. We didn't advertise the fact that Bullet had lost his memories at his own request, so I wasn't surprised that the news hadn't traveled back here yet. While all of our friends across the sea knew, they were extremely protective of us, and would never spill our secrets. "Well, come in. How long are you staying? We've set aside a room for you. Memphis has even offered to babysit. He needs the practice, he got a little overexcited when Dionysus came to visit recently and knocked up a human."

"He's not practicing with our kid," Riot grumbled, sticking close to my back and gently tugging Quinn's baby curls.

"That's very kind of you," I said, sliding in with the diplomacy that my bonded lacked. "But we're only staying one night, unfortunately. As nice as it is to see all of you, we're called to go where we're needed, and Milton doesn't need us, not really."

It was hard to describe, the restless itchiness underneath my skin that demanded I find a community to help. It wasn't dissimilar to the agathos urge to provide assistance to mortals in need—and that certainly hadn't gone away—but this was something *more*. Bigger, grander, more urgent.

"Ah, so you're going back to Auburn then," Onyx deduced. "Then we are definitely having a bigass party tonight before we send you to the bad place. Let's get you a tequila, good girl."

"How are you feeling about this?" Bullet asked, plucking the brush out of my hands where I sat in front of the mirror and running it through my now long hair. "Nervous? I think the bond is saying nervous."

I smiled, pushing a pulse of love and gratitude for him down the bond. We were all finding our feet in this new world, but Bullet more than anyone. He tended to stick like glue to my side or Wild's at all times, relying on us to navigate social situations. It really felt like the least I could do after all the guidance he'd given me over the years, even when I hadn't been able to remember it.

"A little," I admitted. "The last time I was in the agathos temple in Auburn, they had me on an altar and Riot had to break me out. It feels odd to return to that willingly."

Bullet nodded solemnly, setting the brush aside to plait two thin braids on either side of my head, pulling them to the back and securing them with a tie. The affinity for elaborate hairstyles was a new thing—a hobby he'd picked up once he'd returned from the underworld. He found it relaxing doing mine or Quinn's hair, and we definitely weren't complaining.

"Let's just tell them to go fuck themselves and leave if we don't like it," he suggested. "They sound like assholes, and we've encountered plenty of agathos on our travels who refuse to concede they were ever wrong."

That was true. They'd become rarer as time went on, but pride was a powerful motivator.

Wild slipped into the bedroom silently, shutting the door behind him. My family home had been burned to the ground in an arson attack a few years ago, which I had some very mixed feelings about, but I wouldn't have wanted to stay there anyway. Instead, we were staying in Felix Lyon's home, since he and his family were the only agathos in Auburn I trusted. They'd given us the guest bedroom and their old nursery for Quinn to sleep in, since their kids had outgrown it.

"How's Quinny?" I asked, standing now that Bullet was done with my hair.

Wild snorted. "They have a bunch of dolls from when Liberty was a kid. Quinn is in her element. She's having a tea party with Riot."

I checked through the bond, my smile widening at the contentment tinged with exasperation Riot was feeling. When it came to any kind of pretend play, he and Wild had the least patience for it, but they always gave it a go.

"Are they all ready to leave? I just need to put my shoes on and I'm done."

Wild and Bullet exchanged a knowing look, possibly communicating through their own bond.

"Grace..." Wild warned, grabbing my hips and walking me backward until Bullet's front pressed against my back. "You're not even a little bit ready to leave. You're freaking out."

"I'm freaking out a *little*," I corrected, smoothing my palms over the front of his shirt. "I don't even know why. I've obviously faced scarier things than this."

"True," Wild agreed, running his hands over my hips, messing up the tuck of my navy shirt in my dark pants because I'd wanted to wear something as un-agathos as possible. "I felt weird walking into my old neighborhood when we were in London. There will always be a part of you that feels like the kid you once were in these situations. Just remember that you're not, that we're right here with you, and that none of their opinions of you matter—good, bad, or indifferent."

I nodded, squaring my shoulders and taking a deep, steadying breath. Their opinions didn't matter, and even if they did, I had more than enough good opinions of me in my life to balance out whatever they thought.

We all made our way to the auditorium in central Auburn opposite the town hall, Felix leading the way. The last time I'd been here was for his bonded's funeral, not long after I met Riot. It felt like a million years ago now.

The outside of the building had sustained some damage—the white stone facade wasn't quite as pristine as it once had been—mostly from attacks by daimons before the darkness had fallen. But the inside was exactly as bright and gleaming as I remembered it, and just as clinical. The coffered ceilings, carpet, walls and rows of pews were all the same spotless shade of white, and only the gold chandeliers and pale gold curtains added any semblance of warmth.

I wondered if any of the gods had visited this place before immediately dismissing the thought. This was not the kind of place that gods liked to spend time in.

"This place gives me the creeps," Bullet muttered, his fingers tangling with mine. "Let's not stay long."

"Definitely not," I murmured. Felix shot me a wry smile over his shoulder, and I guessed I wasn't as quiet as I thought I'd been.

At his insistence, we were led past the packed pews of agathos to the stage at the front of the room, Dare hanging off to the side with Quinn. It was a strange feeling, recognizing so many of the faces and yet feeling so incredibly separate from them. I had relatives in this room—aunts and uncles, grandparents, even—but they'd given up on me long before I'd moved away to Milton, and I wasn't much interested in hearing what they had to say to me now.

Felix cleared his throat. "We are fortunate to have one of our own here today. Grace Bellamy, Grace the Prophêtis. Her presence here is an honor we don't deserve. Grace, will you share your story with us today?"

I'd planned on giving them a pretty speech about the nature of power, a lecture disguised as unspecific philosophical rhetoric, in the hopes that they'd learn something valuable from it. I was *going* to muse over the question of whether power corrupts or whether it merely reveals what was there all along, hoping it would provoke some soul searching and self-reflection.

But I didn't do any of those things.

Instead, I stood at the front of the stage and did exactly as Felix asked. I told them my story—the raw, unvarnished version that didn't shy away from all the ways that living here had chipped away at my happiness and self-worth. Nor did I shy away from my achievements since, because leaving Auburn had been the best thing I'd ever done, and I wanted them to know that.

It was a little more petty than I'd intended it to be, but as I finished speaking and the entire room sat staring at me in slightly uncomfortable silence, I found that I actually felt *much* better. I'd been carrying around this resentment that I'd harbored for these people and this community for *years*.

And now I could let it go.

"Thank you so much, Grace," Felix said, beaming at me. He'd already told us that nothing brought him more joy than antagonizing the agathos who'd clung so desperately on to the old ways, to the detriment of everyone and everything else. "That was inspiring indeed. Shall we move to the foyer for food and refreshments?"

Riot groaned. "Do we have to?"

"It would make them very uncomfortable, having to make small talk after their flaws have been so thoroughly dissected in a way that no one can dispute," Felix pointed out cheerfully.

Riot pursed his lips. "I mean, I could eat."

A quiet laugh escaped me before I could stop it, drawing some discomfited looks from the agathos in the front row of pews, waiting for their turn to exit the auditorium.

We made our way into the foyer, bypassing the small groups of agathos huddling together to help ourselves to some cheese and bread. No sooner had I started eating than someone was rushing toward me, a startling break in the stilted near-silence of the room.

"Grace!" Verity Mae rushed across the room, tears spilling over before she'd even gotten to me, a little dark-haired girl slightly younger than Quinn balanced on her hip. "Oh my goodness, it's so good to see you."

"Is it?" I asked before I could help myself, but she was already pulling me into a tight, one-armed hug and I don't think she heard me.

"You're so amazing, Grace! You're the Prophêtis! You've been, like, saving the world." She pulled back, one arm still wrapped around my neck, eyes shining with tears. "I'm so honored to know you. And I'm so, so *sorry*."

"You don't need to—"

"No, I do. I do. When I found out that Pax was one of the agathos who went after you and your soul bond, that he was rampaging through Milton with a baseball bat, going through your apartment..." She looked ill. "We had a huge fight. I actually went into labor right after."

"Verity Mae, I'm so sorry..."

She swallowed thickly, shaking her head. "After the bonds broke, I told him I didn't want to be with him anymore. I think he lives in Charleston these days, I'm not sure. It doesn't matter. He wasn't interested in keeping in touch with us."

Verity Mae bumped her hip, managing a wavering smile at the toddler happily munching on a piece of bread and getting soggy crumbs all over her mom's top. "This is Felicity Grace, by the way. I wanted to add your name because you're the bravest agathos I know."

"*All good*?" Riot mouthed, appearing over her shoulder, probably concerned at the level of emotion I was feeling, especially when they were all on edge being here.

I nodded before returning my attention to Verity Mae. "You're so lovely, thank you. I was nervous coming back here today, and it means so much to hear those words."

I pulled her in, giving her another quick hug.

"I'm going to go now."

Verity Mae gave me a sad smile. "I wish you'd stay, but I can't say I would if I was you. You were always too good for this place, you know. How differently it all would have played out if we'd had an nth of your compassion."

The six of us walked from the auditorium, a feeling of contentment rippling back and forth through the bonds like water. I didn't regret coming here, it gave me the closure I needed to move on. We had a whole life, a whole world ahead of us. Now, I could look back on my past without wondering, without discontent.

This place, this terrible place that had caused me so much misery for so many years, had been a stepping stone to get to where I was now. If I hadn't been driven out of Auburn, I'd have never had the courage to build a life in Milton, I'd have never found my bonded, never known what it was to love and be loved by them. The world would have continued in its state of increasing decay, and I'd have never met Quinn. It was a fate too awful to contemplate, and for that, I was grateful for the painful parts of my past. My present wouldn't have been so perfect without them.

T landed gracefully in front of us, carrying a full-sized boat in his arms and setting down on the street, blocking the entire thing. He'd attempted to pluck us out of the water and fly us back to Europe multiple times on our Atlantic journey, so it wasn't altogether surprising, but this time I didn't tell him off.

He crossed his arms over his chest, the vessel leaning sideways against his body, waiting for me to grumble, while Bullet and Dare laughed, inspecting the bottom of the boat for damage.

"We're going to Maine," I told T sternly. "You can give us a lift, but you can't take us back to the Mediterranean. Not yet, at least."

"*Fine*," he signed, as petulant as ever, ushering us toward the boat so he could carefully pick us up one at a time and set us on the deck like we were little dolls for him to play with.

Quinn shrieked in delight as she went soaring through the air in Wild's arms, attempting to scramble up T's hand. If I thought he was gentle with me, it was nothing compared to how careful he was with Quinn. I was pretty sure it was the only reason he hung around these days, since he'd have more to do staying in the Spartoi camp. They were nominally an enforcement squad of sorts, but mostly they just trained others and learned for themselves how to live in this new society.

"Just to Maine," I reminded T. He all but rolled his eyes at me, and we got into position, clinging on to the railing as he scooped the entire vessel up, cradling it to his chest and launching us into the sky.

EPILOGUE 2

FIVE YEARS AFTER THE RESTORATION

"Fuck!" Bullet cursed, as I tightened my grip on his cock, his legs thrown back as I fucked him hard and fast on the bed we'd all waken up together on this morning. We had a busy day ahead, we couldn't afford to take our time.

Not that I was going to last very long.

I loved fucking him when he was on his back like this, loved seeing every blissed out expression cross his face as I milked his cock and spilled his cum all over his belly while I filled his ass.

"Quiet," I warned. "You look so fucking pretty like this, but maybe I should flip you over so you can bite the pillow."

Bullet let out a muffled whine at the idea of changing positions now when he was so close to the edge.

A sudden surge of lust hit both of us as Grace walked into the room, hair and skin damp from using the rainwater shower in the sheltered outdoor area next to the bedroom.

"I already got myself off once in the shower just feeling you two through the bond and now I'm ready to go all over again," she complained breathily, staring at us entranced. It was fucking intoxicating the way she looked at us, and my balls drew up almost painfully with the need to come.

"Come sit on my face, I'll take care of you," Bullet gasped, the fucking liar. His multitasking skills were abysmal when he was this close.

I saw the flash of mischief on Grace's face as she dropped the towel and climbed on the bed. Instead of sitting over his face like he'd requested, she laid over him, tongue darting out to swipe the precum beading at the tip of his cock.

"You want to swallow his cum, darling?" I asked, moving my hand so she could wrap hers around the base of his cock, and shifting her hair out of her face.

Bullet groaned, bucking up as much as he could while I had his ass impaled on my dick. Grace nodded, a satisfied smile on her face. "We really need to get going soon. The least I can do is help reduce the cleanup."

Bullet swatted her on the ass, managing a raspy laugh. "Minx."

She made good on her word, swallowing Bullet's cock and sucking hard, tipping him over the edge almost immediately.

"Show me," I demanded, but she was already moving, knowing what I wanted. She sat up, resting her sweet cunt on Bullet's chest and opening her mouth for me to see the evidence. "Beautiful. Swallow for me, darling."

She didn't hesitate, opening her mouth again with a confident wink to show me it was gone. I grabbed the back of her neck, yanking her up to me for a filthy kiss as I found my own release, my thrusts stuttering to a stop while I attempted to catch my breath. Nothing on earth wore me out the way these two did, in the best possible way.

"Shower. Get dressed," Grace ordered, smiling against my lips. "We've got to leave soon."

"To be continued," Bullet groaned as I pulled out. "I'm going to fucking devour you for dessert, Amazing Grace."

I could get used to this, I thought, admiring the remote Uluwatu beach we were lounging on after a long morning building a series of homes with assistance from a proud, diligent Hephaestus and a bored-but-useful Ares. I *wouldn't* get used to this because it was just a short break, but a much-needed one.

Bullet was stretched out next to me, hands folded behind his head and eyes closed, and I took a moment to admire the ink on his chest. The image of the bronze shield in the likeness of the one I'd carried in the Battle of Ilion was in pride of place—Dare's first piece since he'd gotten access to a tattoo machine and one of the portable solar power generators that were now commonplace in the parts of the world that got a lot of sunshine. We'd all got the same tattoo eventually—a tribute and a reminder of the moment the world changed.

"You're staring," Bullet murmured, his eyes still closed, lips twitching.

"You're very easy to stare at." That was an understatement, and through the bond, we both knew it. Maybe I'd spend some time staring at him later on, tied to the bed for the edging of his fucking life while Grace rode his face. And then his cock. Or both of our cocks, that was always fun—

"Can you not?" Riot laughed, throwing a shell at my back. "You two get horny, then Grace gets horny, then me and Dare get horny, and we don't have time to fuck it out of our system right now. *And* you stole Grace after her shower this morning, and Dare and I have *plans.*"

That was true, and I didn't regret it at all.

"Besides," Wild continued. "Foster and Estrella are coming down for lunch."

"Fine, fine," I sighed, reminding myself that I liked Foster and Estrella and seeing them wouldn't be entirely unpleasant. They were ambassadors of sorts, a showcase of an unfated bonded agathos and daimon relationship. Sophia and Arete often sent them to work with particularly obstinate agathos communities, though they were fewer and farther between these days.

It was hard to cling to the conviction that the old ways were right when life was now so much better for so many more people. Yes, everything moved at a slower pace and things weren't always easy, but there was a sense of community and connectedness among mortals again that we'd once lost.

Grace's amusement trickled through the bond—she'd been so relaxed, I half wondered if she'd fallen asleep, stretched out on a towel with her shins in the soft white sand, wearing her skimpiest bikini, possibly just to torture us.

"You need lotion, Grace," I rasped, making a mental note to tamp down my lust. Later. When Grace's long brown legs and pert ass cheeks were thoroughly protected and cared for. That was my role, after all. I was her defender.

"Any excuse," Bullet teased.

"Avoiding sunburn is a reasonable excuse." I squeezed a dollop of the organic, lightly scented sun lotion into my palms, rubbing them together before massaging it into the backs of Grace's thighs, my fingertips brushing the curve of her ass. Grace squirmed, legs parting for me ever-so-slightly.

I glanced back at the house we were staying at. Dare had taken Quinn back to change into her swimsuit, but they'd be back at any moment and I'd have to start behaving myself.

Grace let out a breathy sigh, and Riot chuckled as he stalked past, heading for the water. "Careful, Gracie. This is a public beach."

"Pft, no one is stumbling across us here, it's too hard to access," Bullet said around a yawn. "I should probably get up and make some bread before Foster and Estrella show up."

"I'll help you," Grace promised. "Let's wait until Quinn has a little swim first."

Bullet hummed in agreement. Maybe it was just part of being six, but Quinn was at an age where if we didn't all watch her do whatever The Thing was, then The Thing hadn't happened and must be repeated. None of us were complaining—she was a great kid and we were honored that Rogue had entrusted us with her care, and we always made sure to tell Quinn about her mom and kept Rogue's memory alive.

Like we'd summoned her, Quinn came barreling out of the house, sprinting toward the ocean with roughly zero caution, Dare hot on her heels while Riot stood in the waves up to his knees, ready to run defense if she aimed for open sea. We traveled by boat enough that she was well aware of how dangerous the water could be, but she also thought she was invincible, so we could never get complacent. Hopefully, Poseidon and his nymphs would do us a solid and throw her back on land if she ever got past us.

"Come here, hellion," Riot said drily, catching her around the waist and throwing her over his shoulder to march her back to the shallows. Quinn giggled and shrieked, a sheet of straight blonde hair just like Rogue's hanging over her face.

"I'm sure she's great, but nothing puts me off parenthood more than children," Estrella said by way of greeting, approaching from the rocky path that led to the beach hand-in-hand with an apologetic-looking Foster.

"She means children are high energy and it looks like a lot of work," he said hurriedly.

"I mean I don't like kids," Estrella replied flatly, raising an amused eyebrow at him. "Except Quinn. She's okay."

I snorted at the ringing endorsement while Grace climbed to her feet, pulling Estrella into a hug.

"You guys are early," Grace accused, no ire in her voice. "We were going to have lunch ready for you."

"We'll help, you all work too hard," Estrella replied, flipping her hand dismissively. "Come, show us this house you're staying at. The Prophêtis always gets the nicest accommodation."

Eventually, all of us ended up back at the house, sharing an enormous platter of brightly colored fresh fruit, fried banana, flat bread, and a couple of bottles of wine on the covered deck, the ocean gently lapping at the beach directly below us. I stretched an arm over the back of Bullet's chair while Grace lounged in Riot's lap, her legs extended over Bullet's thighs, Quinn alternating between climbing up to perch on Grace's stomach like a queen on a throne or trying to drag Dare back down to the beach for another swim.

Foster and Estrella regaled us with stories from their journey on land from Europe through Asia, guided by Sophia and Arete, and we updated them on friends like Orion and Ovie and the Spartoi who we'd seen recently.

And as Nyx's night fell, I couldn't imagine a life more perfect than this.

THANK YOU

489,807 words later, the State of Grace series is finished!

If you're still here and you've been with these characters on their often painful journey to happily ever after, I can't thank you enough. It's a commitment to read five books in one series, and I really appreciate you for taking a chance on Grace, Riot, Bullet, Wild and Dare.

I have to say a huge thank you to my editing team on this one—Kari for alpha reading, Steph from Rawls Reads Edits for dev editing, and Lorie Collins for proofreading. They are all so wonderful, and I really hope they don't all block me and never speak to me again after the chaos that was the final week of edits.

Thank you also to all of my amazing friends and fellow authors, who put up with me stressing and panicking in their DMs for the past month or so. You guys are the best.

So, what's next for this world?

I do have plans for a series for Mercy, taking place in this new ancient-slash-urban-fantasy setting. There is currently no preorder or release date set, but keep an eye on the Facebook group, Instagram (@coletterhodes_ author) or my newsletter for the latest info.

If you'd like to read Hades and Persephone's love story (as in the characters who appeared in these books), Dead of Spring is out now: coletterhodes. com/deadofspring

Thank you again, reader. None of this happens without you.

Colette x

GLOSSARY

TYPES OF AGATHOS MENTIONED:

Arete = Virtue
Eusebia = Piety
Eutychia = Good Luck
Hygeia = Good Health
Sophia = Wisdom
Sophrosyne = Self-Control
Soteria = Safety

TYPES OF DAIMONS MENTIONED:

Apate = Deceit
Ate = Delusion
Dolos = Trickery
Geras = Old Age
Keres = Violent Death
Moros = Doom
Oizys = Misery
Oneiroi = Dreams
Philotes = Sex, Affection

ABOUT THE AUTHOR

Colette Rhodes is a paranormal romance author from New Zealand. She loves to write about love in all its forms, and adores imperfect heroes and heroines who find perfection in each other. You'll often find her trying to justify her degree by including ancient history and mythological influences in her work.

If she's not writing, then you're almost certain to find her reading—ideally with a cup of tea in hand and a scented candle burning to match the mood.

Keep up with Colette here:

coletterhodes.com

@coletterhodes_author

ALSO BY COLETTE RHODES

STATE OF GRACE:

Run Riot

Silver Bullet

Wild Game

Dare Not

Saving Grace

SHADES OF SIN:

(MF monster romance)

Luxuria

Superbia

Gula

THREE BEARS DUET:

Gilded Mess

Golden Chaos

LITTLE RED DUET:

Scarlet Disaster

Seeing Red

KNOTTY BY NATURE:

(RH omegaverse with T.S. Snow)

Allure Part 1

Allure Part 2

EMPATH FOUND:

The Terrible Gift

The Unwanted Challenge

The Reluctant Keeper

DEADLY DRAGONS:

The (Not) Cursed Dragon

The (Not) Satisfied Dragon

STANDALONE:

Dead of Spring (MF - Hades & Persephone retelling)

Blood Nor Money (RH - vampires)

Fire & Gasoline (MF - wolf shifter fated mates)